STRAIGHT OUTTA DEADWOOD

BAEN BOOKS edited by DAVID BOOP

Straight Outta Tombstone
Straight Outta Deadwood
Straight Outta Dodge City (forthcoming)

To purchase Baen Book titles in e-book format,
visit www.baen.com

STRAIGHT OUTTA DEADWOOD

Edited By
DAVID BOOP

Straight Outta Deadwood copyright © 2019 by David Boop

Additional Copyright information:
Foreword copyright © 2019 by David Boop; "Cookie" copyright © 2019 by Shane Lacy Hensley; "A Talk with My Mother" copyright © 2019 by Charlaine Harris Inc.; "The Greatest Horse Thief in History" copyright © 2019 by D.J. Butler; "The Doctor and the Spectre" copyright © 2019 by Mike Resnick; "Doth Make Thee Mad" copyright © 2019 by Obsidian Tiger Inc.; "Sunlight and Silver" copyright © 2019 by Jeffrey J. Mariotte; "Pinkerton's Prey" copyright © 2019 by Frog and Esther Jones; "The Relay Station at Wrigley's Pass" copyright © 2019 by Derrick Ferguson; "Not Fade Away" copyright © 2019 by Cliff Winnig; "The Spinners" copyright © 2019 by Jennifer Campbell-Hicks; "The Stoker and the Plague Doctor" copyright © 2019 by Alex Acks; "Bigger than Life" copyright © 2019 by Steve Rasnic Tem; "Dreamcatcher" copyright © 2019 by Marsheila Rockwell; "El Jefe de la Comancheria" copyright © 2019 by Mario Acevedo; "The Petrified Man" copyright © 2019 by Betsy Dornbusch; "Stands Twice and the Magpie Man" copyright © 2019 by Stephen Graham Jones; "Blood Lust and Gold Dust" copyright © 2019 by Travis Heermann.

A Baen Books Original

Baen Publishing Enterprises
P.O. Box 1403
Riverdale, NY 10471
www.baen.com

ISBN: 978-1-4814-8432-9

Cover art by Dominic Harman

First printing, October 2019

Distributed by Simon & Schuster
1230 Avenue of the Americas
New York, NY 10020

Library of Congress Cataloging-in-Publication Data

Names: Boop, David, editor.
Title: Straight outta Deadwood / edited by David Boop.
Description: Riverdale, NY : Baen, [2019] | "A Baen Books original." |
Identifiers: LCCN 2019026260 | ISBN 9781481484329 (trade paperback)
Subjects: LCSH: Western stories. | Frontier and pioneer life—West
   (U.S.)—Fiction. | Short stories, American—21st century.
Classification: LCC PS648.W4 S763 2019 | DDC 813/.087408—dc23
LC record available at https://lccn.loc.gov/2019026260

Pages by Joy Freeman (www.pagesbyjoy.com)
Printed in the United States of America
10   9   8   7   6   5   4   3   2   1

Dedicated to
Dylan Boop:
My amazing son, who has overcome
much, especially his writer-father.
Know that I'm more proud of you than
any word I've written, or book I've edited.

CONTENTS

FOREWORD
HISTORY'S MYSTERIES

David Boop

September 11, 2018

History has a funny way of changing on us.

Events our grandparents experienced, which had been imparted to our parents, are now taught in our children's history classes. I remember a time when the majority of my classmates were able to hold up their hands when asked if they had a family member who fought in World War II, Korea or Vietnam. How many of today's young adults even remember Desert Storm? My son was a two-year-old when 9/11 happened. What will the next generation be taught about the causes and aftereffects of that era of history? More to the point...how *accurately* will the history be taught?

I remember distinctly my first college-level American history class. My professor was a southern gentleman from the "Great and Sovereign State of North Carolina." He said his style of teaching tended to upset some of his students, as he would explain history from both points of view, not just the "winners." I found this fascinating right up to the moment we hit the American Revolution.

"What do you mean the Founding Fathers weren't best friends? What do you mean they hated each other, backstabbed one another, and even tried to kill each other?"

I still possessed an elementary school, idealized version of the Founding Fathers being of one mind—united to stop oppression by the British rule and shape our great country. I had no concept of agendas, betrayal, political parties, and how our country nearly fell apart in those first years after the war.

That's when history woke up in me. I came to recognize that my elementary and high school views of major events were no better than a Hollywood treatment of the topic. It only hit the highlights. Everyone is perfect. And the good guys always win. This is not how history played out, *and* it's certainly not what happened in the era we call the Old West.

The Old West is one of the tricky times in history to write because it has become romanticized. We're over a hundred years from what is classically referred to as the end of that era, 1910. (I've heard some historians go as late as the early twenties. As a recent researcher into my own family history, that's still quite a few generations back.) Most peoples' understanding about westward expansion is from movies like *Far and Away*, and television shows like *Little House on the Prairie*. There are so few people left to hand down those stories to their families that were handed down to them. For many modern audiences, a "Cowboy" is someone who "Bebops" in a spaceship with a corgi.

So, short of taking college history courses, how does one remove the glamorized picture of the Old West without diving down the rabbit hole into research hell? What responsibility do we as writers and editors have to explain the struggle between Manifest Destiny and Native American rights? Or do readers even need to know the rail baron wars were mostly fought by mercenaries, such as Bat Masterson, Wyatt Earp and Doc Holliday (portrayed as heroes in most movies)? And what about the influx of elves, aliens, vampires, and wizards into a recently re-United States of America?

Okay, that last part might fall under an inaccurate teaching of history. We certainly don't have any "proof" of these fantastical elements in the past. However, it makes for a better story than great-grandpa's tale of when he went fishing one day and pulled up a mermaid, who he threw back because he was already in love with your great-grandmother (like we'd believe that). The combination of weird and west is exciting to explore, but it also carries a chance to view history in a new way.

My directive to all the authors in these anthologies were to give me the Old West the way it *really* was, where applicable. I wanted the history within to be accurate, the voices authentic.

They will attest that I called them on anything I had doubts on, and they, in turn, backed their assertions with facts. They did an excellent job, in my humble opinion.

But I also asked them to give me, and you the readers, the world we wished to see: dragons flying overhead, or the ability to drink with dwarves, or hear how grandpappy fought off zombies in Deadwood. Fear of the unknown should play big, because that is a reality to the era. I wanted triumphs (or failures) over adversity, which forms the basis of every tall tale, and these authors rose to the occasion. Not every story has a happy ending, but they are real to the stories—the true stories—that inspired them.

For those of you who read *Straight Outta Tombstone*, this second anthology is my *Empire Strikes Back*. It's darker, and includes a couple pieces that left me shaken afterward. I challenge you to read all the stories and let them infuse you with the images, smells (and, in some cases, the tastes) of the West. Don't worry if you get scared easily, though. I have broken the narrative up with humor, victories over evil, and gunfights.

Lots of gunfights.

Which, if you've studied the Old West, did not happen as often, or in the way that's been portrayed in the aforementioned popular media.

But then, it wouldn't be a weird *western* anthology without them, would it?

STRAIGHT OUTTA DEADWOOD

COOKIE
A Deadlands™ Story

Shane Lacy Hensley

It was an event of momentous proportions. Some of the greatest legends of the West had gathered together in Deadwood for a single purpose. Cookie didn't know what that purpose was. He was just the cook. Hence the name. But he was sure it was important.

He'd heard something about a "Twilight Protocol," something that brought Texas Rangers, Union agents, and independent lawmen alike to the city, but he didn't know much more than that. It must have been important to bring them through the fickle Sioux Nations though. Especially after the recent troubles.

But then, there were always troubles out here.

Despite all the talk of a ceasefire, the North was still at war with the South, Deseret was its own nation in what was once Utah territory, California had split not only into the Maze after the devastating Great Quake of '68, but also into North and South territories as the nation's wounds continued to keep it apart.

All that was fine by Cookie. Armies had to eat, and someone had to cook all that food.

He wasn't a great cook, but he was resourceful. He could feed a company with a few pounds of turnips, chewy meat scraps, and moldy bread. He'd done it, in fact. More than once.

He'd cooked and served chow for over twenty years. From the battlefields of the East to the new ones out West. He'd served the rail bosses and enforcers at the Battle of the Cauldron of the

Great Rail Wars and even made it to Alaska once—though that adventure had cost him a toe.

Today, Cookie had plenty of ingredients. The Earp boys had brought him an elk and Ranger Hank Ketchum had dragged in an antelope. Bat Masterson had come to town with a brace of conies, and "Bad Luck" Betty McGrew drove a wagon full of potatoes, carrots, and onions in from Rapid City. The always smiling Bass Reeves somehow found enough apples and molasses to make pies.

It would be a feast fit for a . . . well, maybe not a king . . . but certainly fine fare for these august personalities.

Cookie sharpened his cleaver one last time and got to work carving.

"Where you goin', little missy?" The tall stranger sat atop a white horse. It wasn't symbolism. It was almost exactly as it appeared. His name was Jasper Stone, and he served Death itself.

The girl scratched at her head. Flakes fell from her long, tangled black hair. She'd clearly been wandering the area around the Black Hills for days. She stopped, somewhat dazed, and looked up at the Servitor of Death. He was terrifying to behold—gaunt, white skin stretched taut by undeath, a rictus smile upon a face that wasn't built for anything but cruelty, and dead but somehow sharp eyes. He wore a ragged brown coat and a ratty top hat with a bloody feather in it—recently taken from a Sioux brave who dared cross Stone's path.

But Millicent wasn't afraid. She had her own secret.

She looked up at the man on the horse with glazed eyes and rubbed down her dirty gown more out of habit than any effort to clean up or impress.

"I'm lookin' for people," she said, her voice dry and almost as raspy as Stone's.

Stone looked about. "Your people?"

"Just . . . people," she replied.

"You need water, little one." Stone looked on the back of his horse to a collection of packs and other items that weren't his. One was a canteen. He plucked it off and handed it down to the girl. He smelled her secret. Death did not speak directly to Stone, but he could sense when someone—or some *thing*—had common cause with his master's aim to bring about a literal Hell on Earth.

Millicent took the canteen. Though it was covered in dirt

and maybe a little caked blood, she didn't seem to mind. She slurped it down and gazed out through the woods and over the prairie. Toward Deadwood.

"Yup. That way, little one. Go there and do what you do. It will save me some effort." Stone looked out toward the distant speck that was Deadwood himself. "Not that I mind. But let's see what happens. A little mayhem is right up my alley."

The papers were there to cover the event, despite it being at least nominally secret.

Reporters from the *Black Hills Weekly* and even the *Chicago Tribune* were on hand, probably following the gunslingers or the increasingly famous Bass Reeves. Cookie was especially impressed to see the famous Lacy O'Malley of the *Tombstone Epitaph* in his trademark white suit and hat. Everyone knew O'Malley, but none of the big gunslingers, agents, or Rangers seemed to care for him much. That was fine by Cookie. It meant he might get a little of the renowned newsman's time.

"Evenin', Mr. O'Malley! Will you be joinin' us for the dinner?" Cookie said a bit too enthusiastically. He tried to cover his eagerness by hacking at the elk's loins again, then busily and pointlessly stirring the hot water he'd set to boiling.

Lacy O'Malley was a blonde-haired Irishman in his early forties going on untold eons. He'd seen things few others would believe in their wildest nightmares, and it showed in his tired but sparkling blue eyes.

He looked Cookie over. Every chef in the West was called "Cookie" it seemed. This one seemed no more special than any other. He was tubby with a dirty white shirt covered in blood and grease. His red face was topped by an equally red, bald pate...the former courtesy of the hot cook stove and the latter from the deceptively bright South Dakota sun. It was August, after all. Come winter, it would be just as red and cold as Hell.

"Yes. Yes, I will," Lacy nodded as if he were considering it. Truth be told, traveling so far from his home in Tombstone, Arizona, funds were always short. If he could get in on this big feast for free, he wouldn't complain.

"Say, Cookie, do you know..." he paused, remembering his manners. Or at least what passed close enough to get him what he wanted. "Is that your real name, Cookie?"

The chef grinned sheepishly. "Nah. It's Milton. But no one calls me that. Cookie's fine."

Lacy nodded, his look of concern quickly changing to a friendly smile wide as the Great Plains. "Say, Cookie. What's all the hubbub for? Any idea? That's quite the gathering, isn't it?"

Cookie nodded, eyes wide. "Most famous table I've ever set. Some law dogs from Kansas City. Bass Reeves. 'Liver Eatin'' Johnson. The Earps. Masterson. Those dime novel folks...Lynch, 'Bad Luck' Betty, Van Helter. You read those dime novels, Mr. O'Malley?"

Lacy's grin turned slightly sardonic. "I sure have." Memories of the trio's adventures ran through his head. The dime novels made them sound heroic and romantic, but Lacy remembered the gore and the death and the abject terror of learning just what kinds of things lurked in the dark corners of the Earth. "I've...read a few."

Lacy changed the subject. "So what have you heard? About the gathering, I mean."

"Not much. The US agents hired me from Denver. I was workin' at this place called the Buckhorn, and I guess they liked something they ate. Said they needed a cook for a big important meal. Pay was good and I like to get around, so here I am." O'Malley seemed to be losing interest. Cookie struggled to think of something that might keep him around a little longer. "Oh! I saw some of the Sioux puttin' in totems around the town. Some kinda protective boundary, I reckon. The agent who hired me, Mr. Jones...though I don't think that's his real name...said somethin' about 'stayin' within the totems.' I don't really understand all the politics here, but there's a whole bunch o' Sioux livin' in town now. A few are joinin' us for dinner, I hear."

Lacy looked up Broadway and across Gold Street. He could see Sitting Bull and some of his people camped out there. He'd talk to them next. "Anything else?"

Cookie thought for a moment. Remembered something. "Oh, I did hear Wyatt...that's one of the Earps...say something about a 'Twilight Protocol' when he was talkin' to that Ranger from Texas. Ketchum, I think is his name. That mean anything to you, Mr. O'Malley?"

Lacy nodded. He knew exactly what it meant. The protocol was a truce between the North and South, who'd been engaged in a long cold war with occasional hot flashes since 1860. It was now August 1881. The public thought the hostilities had died down, but Lacy and a few others knew that was only because the two governments had finally caught on to something far more dangerous...an event they called the Reckoning. Lacy believed the Reckoners were the Four Horsemen of the Apocalypse... like right out of the Bible. They'd brought magic and monsters back into the world and some said even changed history. A shaman he shared a vision quest with once told him the Civil War shouldn't have lasted more than five years. It was already going on a decade, on and off. The movers and shakers at this gathering were almost certainly aware of all that, and they'd only gather for something momentous.

"What else is going on around here, Cookie? Anything that might have attracted such a hall of fame?"

Cookie shrugged. "Ain't heard nothin'. Just been here a few days myself. There was that war a few months back."

Lacy frowned and started to amble away.

"Oh wait, Mr. O'Malley." Cookie's enthusiasm got the better of him once more. "I guess I did hear one thing. That Injun that started the Battle of Deadwood is still on the run somewhere in the Black Hills. Maybe they're afraid he's gonna do it again? I dunno though...I thought the Sioux wanted his scalp more than the government did, but...well...I don't follow these things so much. I'm just a cook."

Lacy nodded, gave a half smile, and went off to annoy some of the more famous faces he spied around Deadwood.

Cookie didn't mind. He'd just talked to one of the most famous people in the West. And he was gonna make O'Malley and the rest one hell of a feast.

"Hey, little girl. Are you okay?" Wyatt Berry Stapp Earp stood in the yard of Dingler's Whirligigs. His brother Morgan eyed an autogyro and was considering a ride, but the ever-cautious Wyatt had cast his aspersions as hard and silent as death.

Wyatt had left Morg to stare at the New Science devices and headed toward a small figure east of the shop when a young girl, maybe twelve or thirteen years old had just wandered out of the woodline. Her hair was a mess, her dress was tattered and filthy, and there wasn't a spot on her face, arms, hands, or feet that wasn't covered in dirt.

"I said are you okay, miss?" Wyatt repeated, closer now. But he knew she wasn't.

Morgan followed right behind. "Holy Hell! What happened to you?" The more hot-headed of the Earp brothers drew his Colt and looked around for trouble, but didn't see any.

The girl looked up at the Earps and recognition flashed in her eyes. Then she fainted dead away. Wyatt caught her before she hit the ground.

"What's for dinner, Cookie?"

"More like what *ain't* for dinner, Mr. Johnson!" Cookie smiled. "I got elk, pheasant, taters, onions, carrots, rabbit. No liver, though."

Johnson's mouth curled in a snarl.

"Er, sorry, Mr. Johnson. I didn't mean to assume nothin'."

Johnson held the snarl for a long pause, enjoying watching Cookie squirm...then broke out in a laugh. "Haw! You think I *want* more liver? I've had enough liver to last three hundred lifetimes."

Cookie laughed back, nervously. "I reckon you have, at that."

There was a brief awkward silence, then the tension and the horror of "Liver Eatin'" Johnson's tragic past broke like ice on a lake, and the two guffawed like fools.

"Tell you what I could really go for," Johnson eventually managed. "Somethin' sweet. Gonna have anything like that?"

Cookie smiled from ear to ear. "Sure do, Mr. Johnson. Bass Reeves brought in all the fixin's for an apple pie. I've already got the crusts bakin'."

"Liver Eatin'" Johnson leaned in and sniffed. "It's gonna be a good day," he grinned. "Yup. I've got a good feelin' about it."

Millicent didn't clean up well at all. The baths were all taken— both from the illustrious guests in Deadwood and the inevitable soiled doves competing for their attention. So Doc Taylor and his assistant had to make do with sponging her down. It didn't take much.

"She's malnourished, Mr. Earp. She needs a good meal. And a bath. But I've seen worse. That hair o' hers is gonna take some real trimmin' to clean up, but she won't let me touch it. We don't know what she...what kinda...trauma...she went through out there. There are mercenaries still out on the prairies from the battle. Prospectors hidin' from the Sioux—and the US Army— the Black Hills are off-limits, you remember. And then there's a whole mess of Indians looking for payback despite a truce most of 'em didn't sign on to in the first place."

Wyatt frowned, studying her. That was all likely. There was a lot of violence and ignorance in all parts of the world, of course, but there was an extra dose of hard feelings in South Dakota territory right now.

"But . . . I don't see any signs of . . . well, violence." Doc put his kit away and sighed. "Physically, she seems fine. Unless she's got a head wound. That hair's more tangle than a briar patch. I'll check her again after she gets a bath and we can untangle it a bit."

Wyatt nodded. But something wasn't right. He couldn't quite put his trigger finger on it, but it nagged at him like his old school marm. "How long was she out there?"

"She said her parents died during the battle sometime, but that was a couple months ago now. From the look of her, I'd say she's only been wanderin' a week, at most. She's thin and her color's off, but nothin' a young thing like her won't recover from right quick."

Morg pulled a piece of peppermint from his pocket, unwrapped it from a clean cloth, and handed it to the girl. "She just needs some hot food and maybe something to get her mind off whatever happened to her for a while, right, Millicent? You got any skills, girl?"

Millicent snapped her head toward Morgan Earp fast enough to startle the three men and answered instantly. "I can cook."

"Cookie, it would be a great favor to me and my brother if this little gal could help in the preparation of the victuals." Morgan Earp smiled. Wyatt stood behind him, rolling the cigar in his mouth back and forth, pondering.

Cookie looked Millicent over. He could use a little help with such a big feast. And a favor for the Earps? Well, that was something, wasn't it? "I'd be happy to, Mr. Earp."

Morgan went to pat Millicent on the head, but she pulled away quickly. "Well, I understand. Now you help Cookie here for a few hours and make sure you get yourself fed. My brother an' I will check on you after this meeting and figure out how to help." He flipped Cookie a double eagle and headed toward the meeting house. Wyatt stared a moment longer then followed.

Heart of gold, that one, Cookie thought about Morgan Earp. Hot-headed, if the newspapers were to be believed (and Cookie did), but that's how it was with those passionate types, wasn't it? Everything was Heaven or Hell with them. Not much Limbo in between. Morgan's brother though? That one had a serious streak the size of Kansas.

Cookie looked over his new help. "Okay. I'm sorry, girl. I didn't catch yer name."

"Millicent. You can call me Milli." She looked with wide eyes at the boiling pots, spitted meat on campfires, and Dutch ovens Cookie had set up in the empty lot west of Broadway. There was a house near there where all the bigwigs were talking, but it was too small to feed them inside. That would come promptly at six. The Chinese the agents hired had already set up long tables with red-and-white checkered tablecloths.

"Milli it is. So you can cook, you say. How about checkin' on that stew then? See if the taters are soft yet. Oh, and are you hungry? Dinner's not for another hour, but some of it's ready. You look like you could use a little somethin' to tide you over till then."

Milli shook her head. "No. I'm not hungry." She walked over to the stew and stared at it intently. She took up one of Cookie's big wooden spoons and began to swirl it around the rich brown broth.

Her back was to him so he couldn't see her face, but he winced a little at the debris in her hair. Cookie wasn't the most hygienic person in the West, but he took pride in his work and tried not to let too many stray hairs wind up in his food. "Mind your hair there, girl. We don't wanna serve up dirty grub."

"Oh no..." she whispered. "We wouldn't want that..."

Stone looked at the dead braves. Each one was twisted and contorted, as if something had wracked their bodies from the inside. They'd been here a few weeks. He chuckled slightly. You'd think being Death's right hand, he'd know exactly when a man passed. But that's not how it worked.

The bucks hadn't been touched by animals. That was a dead giveaway that whatever had happened to them was less than natural. He sniffed. Something smelled off. Dead flesh was a constant, so he could filter that out easy enough. This was something else. Something pungent but subtle just below the surface...maybe congealed in their veins.

He poked one with a jagged fingernail, hard enough to pierce the skin. Dry black blood poked from the surface. More like dried paint sticking out of an artist's tube than blood. He sniffed his finger.

There it was. That's what he was looking for. The good stuff.

Stone stood. His dead knees creaked and popped as much as the dried leather of his gun belt. One of the braves had the scrap of a white dress in his belt. Maybe kept it as a souvenir. Maybe just used it to wipe the snot off his nose. But it was Milli's. She'd been here.

It wasn't the first group of dead Indians he'd found in the Black Hills. There were several others, all contorted and twisted up like these. Some, he could tell, had met with Milli. Others seemed to have keeled over soon after eating the local game.

This was one powerful little monster.

The gathering at Deadwood was a big nut to crack, though. There were a lot of goody-two-shoes and troublemakers down there. Some of them even had enough mojo to give Stone a little trouble.

And it was *his* job to be trouble. It was his job to make sure the so-called heroes didn't foul things up for the boss. It was his job to plug 'em when they got too big for their britches.

"Let's see what you can cook up, little girl," whispered Stone as he climbed back on his mare. "I'll handle the leftovers."

Whatever the meeting was about, it turned contentious. Cookie watched as the Earps walked out of the house on Broadway and quietly talked among themselves. The Ranger sat alone on the porch, whittling a sharp stick out of pure frustration. The agents congregated in their own little clique, occasionally glancing over at the Ranger. The dime-novel heroes, Lynch, Van Helter, and McGrew, left town—Cookie shoved his worn copy of *Perdition's Daughter* back in his pocket, disappointed. He was hoping to have them sign it.

"How's them pies comin'?" asked "Liver Eatin'" Johnson, clearly starving. He was a big man. He dwarfed the table and blocked Cookie's view of the meeting.

"They'll be fresh and hot right after the main course, Mr. Johnson! They're lookin' good."

Johnson patted his belly. "Can't wait." Then he noticed Millicent. "Say, who's your new help here?"

"Her name's Millicent. Don't know her last name. The Earps found her wanderin' the woods, I think. She's helpin' out for a while. I think maybe the Sioux...well...I don't know what happened to her. She don't talk much."

Johnson sniffed the air. Leaned in closer to Milli, who was across one of several firepits and surrounded by the smells of cooking meat, boiling stew, raw onions, and more. Cookie thought he had a good sniffer, but Johnson's senses seemed almost preternatural.

"The Sioux, you say?"

Cookie harbored no particular ill-will toward any race or creed. "Well, I don't know. Coulda been anyone. Or, um, no one. I don't actually know what..."

Milli said nothing. She just kept her back to the two men and stirred the stew.

Johnson took a step closer, peering at the back of her head. He frowned and looked over at his assembled peers just twenty yards away and scattered throughout the yard.

The mountain man stroked his chin. His frown switched to a sharp smile. "Y'know, I've got a case of something I'd like to share, given the rare nature of this meal and all these luminaries. Something of a certain vintage that's hard to get out here in the middle of the Sioux Nations." Johnson winked. "It's with my mule over in the livery. Can I borrow your girl to help me haul it back?"

Cookie nodded. He could use a drink after this long hot day. "Sure thing, Mr. Johnson. Milli, would you mind helpin' our friend here?"

Millicent turned from the stew pot and looked Johnson square in the eyes. "Not at all, Mr. Johnson. Show me the way."

Stone sat on a little rock on the southwest side of Deadwood. There was an empty lot with several long tables and a passel of men and women standing about waiting to eat. There was also a cook manning several large pots, spits, and cook fires. But no Millicent.

Stone leaned back and rested, more out of habit than any bodily need. He knew whatever was about to happen would be interesting, at least.

"It's right over here, girl," Johnson said as he entered the livery. He glanced about to make sure no one else was around and headed toward the back of the large, dark building.

Milli followed, innocently.

All the animals were outside. There was nothing here but hay and horse shit. Johnson looked around for a second, then circled back around Milli, trapping her in the corner. His hand moved slowly to his belt.

A man calling himself Agent Sam Jones told Cookie to start serving. Cookie had to laugh a little at the fake mustache peeling slightly off one side of his face in the hot August afternoon, but the tone of the man's voice wasn't one to be trifled with.

"Yessir," Cookie nodded. *Now where's that girl?*

"Liver Eatin'" Johnson pulled a long Bowie knife from his belt. "I don't know what you are, but I know you ain't no little girl."

Milli blinked in confusion. "I don't... Momma said..."

Johnson took a step toward her. "What did Momma say?"

Milli turned her head slightly. "Momma said Daddy was bad. He had to go."

Johnson's eyes narrowed. "An' the war was an excuse to get rid of 'im, wasn't it?"

Milli's eyes snapped to the mountain man's. "She kilt him. Kilt him dead. Pa keeled over right in his stew. Then she dragged him out and put a few bullets in him. Said the Sioux did it."

Johnson pondered for a moment. "How'd she kill him?"

Milli smiled. "I toldja. The stew."

"I know a lot about Injuns, little girl. I know their habits and their ways, and I know their legends."

Now it was Milli who took a step closer. Her smile broadened, showing long, pointed teeth that had grown an inch in the last minute.

"One of them legends is about the poison woman," He continued, never taking his eyes off the girl. "The Sioux believe that if you poison your husband, you'll come back as some sorta..."

Milli's eyebrows rose in anticipation . . . and though it was dark in there, her eyes looked clouded. Black as coal.

"Thing."

At that Millicent's *entire jaw* unhinged, revealing an unholy maw of spiny teeth!

"But I've killed 'things' before . . ." Johnson grunted.

Millicent's black fingernails erupted from her fingertips, black blood dropping as they ripped apart the flesh around them.

The mountain man heard footsteps behind him, back toward the door to the livery.

"WHAT THE HELL?" Cookie yelped as he walked in on the mad scene.

Johnson turned his head to see who had interrupted his killing time, giving the thing that had been Millicent the opportunity she needed to strike. Her long dark claws ripped into "Liver Eatin'" Johnson's thick beard and dug into his throat. They came out dripping bright red blood.

If Cookie's jaw could unhinge like Millicent's, it would have hit the floor. He simply gawked in fear as his senses rebelled against what his treacherous eyes told him was playing out in the darkness of the livery.

"Oh, Cookie," it said. "I wasn't ready for you yet. You have such a feast to serve. Guess I'll have to do it myself now!"

Millicent leapt across the room at the cook, her jagged nails pointed like the tines of a pitchfork at his throat—and stopped in midair an inch from his flesh. "Liver Eatin'" Johnson held her ankle with one hand while his other stayed tight on his own torn throat. "*Kill it . . .*" he rasped and pointed with his eyes at Cookie's hand.

Cookie looked down. Maybe there was a God, because he still held his meat cleaver.

The cook swung halfheartedly . . . he'd never harmed a living *person* in his life. He hated to kill what was once a little girl, but his reflexes and fear took over.

The blade bit deep into Milli's left arm. Black blood dripped from it and hit the floor, the fresh hay sizzling beneath it.

She barely winced.

The odd scene held for what seemed an eternity . . . Cookie standing there with his meat cleaver in Millicent's arm, she on one leg, her other held by Johnson, and the mountain man on his knees with one hand on his throat and the other on Milli's ankle behind him.

Milli, or the thing that lived inside her now, laughed out loud at the absurdity of it all. Then she jerked her leg free of Johnson's grip and danced about the livery, slashing at Cookie with her talons as she herked and jerked demonically on the blood-spattered hay.

"You're right," she hissed at Johnson, but kept her dead black eyes fixed on Cookie. "I am a poison woman. But not how you might think. This girl poisoned no one. Her momma did."

Johnson rolled over on his back to face the horrid thing. Cookie backed up against the opposite railing, holding his meat cleaver hopelessly before him.

"Momma became a poison woman after she killed Daddy. But then that war with Raven came. Her supplies didn't last a week and all the game was gone."

Johnson sneered. Cookie's mind reeled.

Milli danced now, twirling her gore-stained dress obscenely. She was a full-on demon now. Sunken eye sockets and obsidian eyes. Yellow, veined skin oozing pus from numerous cuts and gashes. Oversized claws. And that massive, unhinged jaw full of rotten, spiny teeth.

"Momma was always protective of this little one. That's why she did it. And that's why she kept the stew coming day after day. And why she walked a little funny afterwards..." Milli held up a foot... topped with scraggly black and yellow toenails.

She smiled at Cookie and licked her own toe. "Any kind of meat tastes good in a stew, doesn't it, Cookie?"

Horror grew on the chef's face as he realized what Milli was saying. "Your... mother... fed you her own..."

"Oh yes! Such delights!" Milli danced again, kicking the rapidly fading Johnson in the leg as she twirled about. "This little one didn't know what was happening, but as she faded, I grew. Finally, Momma died, and she and I went out into the wilderness and became one. So many young braves tried to *help* me. We became one with *them* too!"

Milli moved with ferocious speed into Cookie's face, her vile spittle landing on his cheeks as she spoke. "How about that? They tried to *help* me." She trailed a claw down the front of his shirt. "Most of them, anyway. But they all died."

Hot piss ran down Cookie's leg.

"IT MUST HAVE BEEN SOMETHING THEY ATE!" Milli rushed in with her massive maw to rip Cookie's throat open. He somehow managed to dodge, causing her to bite hard into the railing behind him.

The cook took a haphazard swipe with his cleaver... and felt it fly out of his sweaty hand. He dodged past her and ran in terror, but found himself trapped in a horse stall with Johnson.

"*Kill... it...*" Johnson repeated.

"WITH WHAT?" Cookie screamed in panic.

Millicent hurled herself at Cookie. He threw his arm up for protection and felt her horrid teeth sink into the bone. He grabbed the back of her head with his other hand, trying desperately to pull her off, but to his horror, felt his fingers sink deep into mush where there should have been solid skull.

Milli released her jaws and pulled back. She bent over, almost a curtsy, and let her hair fall forward, showing her prey the hideous hole in her head and the green pus dripping out of her exposed brain. "That's where the good stuff comes from," she laughed.

Cookie felt the world spin. How was any of this possible?

The demonic child pulled a small piece of pus-stained gray matter from the hole in her head. "That's what I've been putting in the stew all day!" she cackled, delighted to finally reveal her secret ingredient. Then she roared back into Cookie's face once more. "THEY'RE ALL GOING TO DIE! EVERY LAST ONE OF THEM!"

Cookie fell to his knees, wiped the poison off his hand onto his apron.

"The greatest heroes and those who might have been! They're going to choke on it, Milton! They're going to choke and dance and die in such beautiful agony!"

Something snapped in Milton's mind. She knew his name. Of all he'd seen, somehow that was the final straw. He rose, picking up Johnson's Bowie knife as he shuffled to his feet.

"No," he spoke softly, at first. Then with more confidence. "No one, and I mean *no one*, messes with my table..."

"I'll have some of the stew." Wyatt Earp motioned with his head at the big pot, now sitting cold by the fire it had been simmering on all day.

"I'm afraid it didn't turn out," Cookie smiled apologetically.

Wyatt noted Cookie's left arm was in a sling and he had on a fresh wipe apron, far cleaner than the one he'd been wearing earlier. "That's a shame," Wyatt replied. "I was looking forward to it."

"Meat spoiled. Might have killed every one of ya," Cookie laughed nervously.

Wyatt nodded slowly. "How's that girl? She okay."

A thin voice came from behind Earp. "She moved on."

Wyatt turned to see "Liver Eatin'" Johnson, a bloody bandage wrapped around his throat.

"Cut myself shavin'." He half grinned. "A lot."

"Mmm hmm," Wyatt replied. "Well, what else is good?"

"Everything. Everything else is good," Cookie said proudly. "Especially the apple pies. Have some of them elk loins, and I'll bring you a slice in a few minutes, Mr. Earp."

Wyatt nodded and loaded up a plate...slowly. The cautious law dog cogitated and looked carefully about for anything untoward, but nothing stood out. Finally, he decided that whatever had happened there had already played out. He even sensed it had played out right. He didn't know how he knew that, but he did. He'd been party to some strange occurrences himself the last few years.

"Pie it is, Cookie. I'll be waitin'."

It was near 10 p.m. The gathering had ended, and those who were still around had moved on to the Bella Union for drinks. Cookie was still in the empty lot, preserving what he could to sell tomorrow and cleaning up his pots and pans.

"How'd you do it, cook?" came a voice like gravel from the darkness. A tall, gaunt man in a ratty brown coat stepped out of the gloom.

"Wha—" Cookie jumped. After today's events, he was still more than a little jumpy.

Stone looked the man up and down. "How'd you kill her? Average man like you. Nothing special. Ain't even heeled."

"What're—who are you?" Cookie instinctively felt for his cleaver, but it was nowhere to be found.

"Doesn't matter. But tell me. How'd you do it? Or was it one of those...*heroes*." Jasper Stone said the last word with a sneer most others usually reserved for the lowest of creation.

Cookie drew himself up. Stood straight. After today, if he was going to die, he was going to die with his spine straight. "She ... it ... fucked with my food. I may not be much, whoever you are, but one thing I am ... I'm the cook. She had a hole in her skull just the right size for a Bowie knife. An' I know how to cut aroun' bone."

Stone chuckled. Then he laughed. Loud and hollow, like it was coming from the inside of a grave.

When he was done he looked at the cook all over again. "I oughtta kill you for that. She was gonna make this easy. Kill 'em or make 'em sick. Take out the whole lot at once. That's my job, y'know. Killin'. Those who keep pesterin' the thing that thinks it's my master. And anyone else who gets in the way."

Stone leaned in close across the carving table. "Or anyone else I just feel like killin'."

Cookie stood his ground. Running really wasn't an option anyway.

Stone pulled back. Almost relaxed. Thumbed his gun belt and thought about it for a few seconds. Then he seemed to reach a decision. "But there's a lotta trouble a street over. And you made me laugh. So I guess today's your lucky day, cook."

Milton glared right back at the monster before him. A whole world of terrible things splayed open before him like the guts of a sick elk.

"It's Cookie."

A TALK WITH MY MOTHER

Charlaine Harris

I sat on a bale of hay and stared at the horses in their stalls and the cars parked in the other half of the stable. Weren't enough horses to fill it up any more, and visitors wanted to put their cars somewhere safe. Not that our little town had many visitors. When there were strangers, they stuck out. Strangers didn't seem to understand that. I laughed a little, and I wiped the wetness from my face. I knew what I had to do next. I had to talk to my mother before anyone else got to her.

I stood. The corral and the parking area were both empty, to my relief. I took a deep breath and stepped out of the shadowy stable, looking up at the sun. About four o'clock.

It was a good time of day to find my mother alone in the house she shared with her husband, Jackson Skidder. Mom had dismissed the kids from Segundo Mexia's one-room school two hours ago. She might have dropped by the grocery, but then she would have gone home. Mom often took a little time to relax before she started supper.

Jackson, who was my mother's husband, but not my father, would be out and about attending to one of his businesses. With any luck, I'd have enough time to talk to Mom alone. Tell her what I'd done.

I felt a little off plumb as I walked from the stable to the house. It was not far, a block and a bit from Main Street, but my feet didn't seem too well connected to the rest of me.

I remember somewhere along that walk, someone said, "Hey, Lizbeth," and I spoke back. Don't know who it was or what I said.

When I'd unlatched the gate in the fence and stepped onto the stone walkway to the porch, I pressed my lips together so hard they hurt. This was going to be very hard. I forced my feet to move forward, onto the porch. I took care to wipe my feet on the mat. Mom was rigid about stuff like that. I had dust all over my boots. Plus, I smelled like horse.

I used my special knock.

"Come in, Lizbeth," Mom called. "If you've wiped your feet."

Mom and Jackson have a nice house by Segundo Mexia standards: one big room, two bedrooms, and a bathroom. I had done some of my growing up in this house. There was still a bed in the second bedroom for me, though I had my own place now.

Mom was sitting in her easy chair with her feet up on a stool. She'd been snapping beans. She put the bowl on the table beside her and scooted forward as if to get up.

"Stay still," I said, motioning her down. I bent to give her a hug and then sat right opposite. I not only reeked of horse, but I had death hanging around me. I could feel it, almost smell it. I didn't want Mom sensing that.

But Mom smiled at me, though I already saw some doubt creeping in.

Mom's name is Candle Rose, and she's real pretty, and she's smart, and she has what Jackson calls "integrity." I think that was the clincher after he first noticed her. Jackson wasn't put off by Mom having a ten-year-old. If he had misgivings, he'd kept em well hidden.

And in all the years I'd watched em, they'd gotten along real well.

Mom kept the house neat and straight, and she ran things the way lives ought to be run. She was a good cook, and meals were on time. Jackson had bought her a big wood stove, after she'd turned down an electric stove. (Our electricity is what you might call unreliable.) Jackson worked hard, never came home drunk, and didn't visit whores. He gave Mom respect.

"Lizbeth, how you doing?" Mom's eyebrows had drawn together, and her smile was long gone. She knew something was wrong. But I couldn't just plunge right in.

So I shrugged. "Okay," I said. "You?"

"Teaching kids is not as easy as it used to be," Mom said. "Especially now that I've got twenty-four, all different ages. And especially now I'm in my thirties."

Mom was young to have a grown girl like me. I'm eighteen, and her only child; Mom had me when she was fifteen. She'd had a hard row to hoe. Her mother and father had kept me during the week while Mom rode the bus to the training course for teachers.

Mom had not married, hadn't even considered it, for most of my childhood. I'd asked her why more than once. She'd finally told me, "After—you know—what happened to me, I was real man-shy. That's the first reason. For another thing, I loved you so much I couldn't be with any man who didn't love you, too. Who might just put up with you because he wanted me. Who the hell wants to be with a man who thinks I ought to be grateful for the privilege of sharing a bed and an income? I figured I'd rather pay my own way than be dependent and beholden." Though these were bitter problems, Mom had smiled at me as she closed that conversation forever.

I understood how much she loved me.

I felt that love now, and wished I had the words to tell her how hard I returned it. But I'm not good with words. I'm more of a doer than a sayer. As I looked at her, the sunlight from the window glinted on a white thread in the black river of Mom's hair. It would be a blow to her pride when she noticed that.

"How is Jackson?" I asked, because she was looking at me funny. It was kind of a waiting look, kind of anxious. Moment was approaching when I had to speak up.

"He's well. You know that man never gets sick. He was saying just the other day it had been too long since you two had been out hunting together."

"I'll be glad to go hunting any day he picks, if I don't have to work." If Jackson Skidder had ever thought I was a burden, he sure hadn't shown it. "You know I love to hunt."

"Oh, Lizbeth," Mom said, shaking her head. "You love your guns."

That was the truth. I loved the bolt-action Winchester my grandfather had left me. He'd carried it and used it through many skirmishes, and it had a history of accuracy. I also loved the matching Colts Jackson had given me. I wore my sidearms everywhere, and I'd just put the Winchester in its rack by the door where it kept company with Jackson's rifles.

Of course, I was not the only gal in Segundo Mexia who liked to hunt. And I was also not the only gal who was a good shot. But I was one of the few who made a living with my guns.

Tarken had taken me onto his crew when he'd had a vacancy. (When there's an opening on a crew, it means someone died, nine times out of ten. I'd taken Callum's place when his wounded leg got infected, which is what killed him.) Not many doctors left now, after the flu, and the banks failing, and no crops for a while.

"I love the work," I said. "I got a knack for it. Galilee and Martin and Tarken say so." So had Solly, until he got killed on a run to Mexico.

"I guess the money is okay?"

"The money isn't bad." Every now and then, I slipped into the house while she was gone to hide some money in the secret hole in the wall in my old room. I was sure she knew that.

"You all have a job lined up?"

"Tonight. A run to New America. Piece of cake."

Mom sighed. "I wish you'd get a regular job with some nice people."

But she knew I couldn't have borne to teach school like her, or work in a shop, or take care of a house and kids and cooking and laundry—the never-ending work of keeping a family running—like my neighbor, Chrissie. "Me and the Colts and the Winchester, we work together," I said.

Mom shook her head and got up to start supper. Looked like that would be chicken and rice and the green beans. In quick movements, she dumped the snapped beans into a pot of hot water and added a dollop of bacon grease.

"Heard you were seeing Tarken after work," Mom said, taking care to be turned away from me when she said it. She tried to sound casual. She was poking around trying to find out what was wrong with me. Trouble with a man would always be the first suspicion that sprang to her mind.

"It's a new thing. Me and him hit it off."

"*He and I* hit it off," she said, in her "teacher" voice.

I had to smile. "Yes, ma'am. He and I hit it off."

Mom knew better than to ask any more questions. Our crew guarded cargo, be it people or goods, as we moved it on its way to wherever it needed to be, by means of Tarken and Martin's big truck. The two men had put it together out of parts from this and parts from that, and they worked on it every day.

The Tarken Crew took refugees—almost all from the area Mexico had annexed in the 1934 war—and ran them up to New America, the plains north of Texoma. Sometimes we took goods from New America down to other towns in Texoma—which used to be Texas and Oklahoma, more or less. Every now and then we went east to Dixie.

Sometimes nothing happened on these trips. Sometimes we were attacked by bandits, or Indians, or wild dogs. Sometimes our employer decided not to pay us.

And on those occasions, I got to work with the Winchester. Or my Colts. Depending on distance.

"You let us know if we need to do anything," Mom said, still thinking about me and Tarken. She meant that she and Jackson would hire a church for a wedding or make him marry me if I got pregnant...if that was what I wanted.

Mom was pretty sensitive about the consequences of men and women getting together. Some people hadn't been kind to her when her stomach began to show. Because Mom was pretty and smart, they were sure she felt superior to them. Which was not true. But people are like that—they know what *they'd* feel, and they're sure you have to be the same way.

If Mom had been ugly and dumb, no one would have thought twice about her condition, my opinion.

"I don't think you need to be worried about Tarken and me," I said, to close the door on that subject. Now she'd turned her back again to add something to her cook pot. I must start talking about today.

I wanted to walk out of the house so bad, but I would not be a coward.

"Listen, you know Skelly, over in Cactus Flats?" Easing into it. "Jose Maldonado, everyone calls him Skelly, though. Owns Elbows Up?"

"I went to school with Jose," Mom said, real slow. I could tell she was wondering where I was going with this. But she wasn't going to rush me. "He inherited that bar. And the hotel next to it. And he usually has a worker or two."

By "workers" my mother meant "whores." Mom said that

whoring was hard work, and the men and women who chose to make a living that way deserved to be treated with courtesy. To my surprise, Jackson agreed with her.

"Skelly's always had a great opinion of you. Did you know that? You taught his nephew, Roberto. He turned out real good."

"I've had a few Robertos," Mom said over her shoulder. "One had the last name Maldonado. Smart kid, good with numbers."

I nodded. "That's the one. Anyway. Dan was over in Cactus Flats making a delivery for his folks, and he dropped into Elbows Up, and Skelly gave him a message for me." Dan Brick and I had grown up together.

My mother turned away from the stove, and put her hands on her hips. That meant she was giving you serious attention. It also indicated she didn't like what she was hearing. "What was the message? Just go on and tell me."

I took a deep breath. I tried again to think of any way I could delay this talk, any way I could just *not have it*.

I straightened my spine and went on. "Skelly told Dan that the man who'd raped you was in Cactus Flats. Skelly recognized him. He told Dan to let me know."

Mom's face froze. She stared at me without a blink or a twitch or a frown. I didn't think she was breathing. "Mom," I said.

Finally, my mother nodded, in a jerky way. "I understand," she said. She took off her apron. Looked like she was going somewhere. But instead, she just sat in her chair again clutching the apron. She waited for me to say something else.

"So I went over to Cactus Flats late morning," I said. "I rented a horse at the stable. Vangie, the gray mare? It only took me a couple of hours to get there." I started to say something about Vangie being a good horse, and then I just shut my mouth. Took a deep breath.

My mother made a "come on" gesture with her fingers.

"First thing, I saw Cal and Maria," I said. Cal Trujillo was the sheriff in Cactus Flats, and Maria Hannigan was his deputy. Cal was the better tracker, Maria the better shot.

"They know you," Mom said, which was an odd thing to say. I figured she meant they'd be coming after me.

I shook my head. "Cal just nodded at me, and shut the door to the sheriff's office. Not before Maria pointed at Elbows Up."

Mom drew in a deep, shuddering breath.

"It was when the sun begins to slant, and the bar door was

open, but I couldn't see inside. There was a fancy car parked outside the hotel, and you know where the saddle shop was, went out of business last year? There was a big banner tacked over the door, said 'The Great Karkarov, Mystic and Magician.'"

Oleg Karkarov was a grigori, one of the wizards who'd fled with their leader, Grigori Rasputin, all the way from Godless Russia. When the old tsar and his family had made it to the boats, the grigoris had made their escape possible by magic, or so I'd heard. Given Karkarov's age, it was more likely his dad had been the original refugee.

Course, not all of them could work for the tsar. Those with less talent had to make a living, same as the really good ones, who were healers or killers or weather controllers. The most hapless of the grigoris had little traveling shows that moved through New America and Texoma. Like regular magicians, grigoris performed slight-of-hand tricks. Unlike regular magicians, grigoris also produced illusions and did other amazing things with their power.

One of the things this grigori, Oleg Karkarov, had done was bespell a pretty girl in a rural town. Then he'd raped her. Then he'd left town, never minding that behind him he'd left a miserable girl who would never be the same...and her child.

Mom turned her palm up, asking me to break my silence, to let her know what had happened in Cactus Flats. She wanted this talk to be over as much as I did. I saw how wide her eyes were.

So I resumed telling the story.

"The door of the bar was open but, like I said, it was too dark inside for me to see the customers. So for a while, I sat on the porch of the general store right across the street, and I waited. Ralph came out to sweep, or so he said, but I think he wanted to make sure it was me, and find out what I was doing there. He went back inside after he'd moved the broom around a little and talked to me. He turned the sign to say *Closed*."

I snorted, remembering. That had made me feel kind of good and kind of bad. I already had a name in that town.

"You have a reputation," my mother said, like she was an echo in my mind.

I hadn't realized Mom knew that.

I shrugged. You were only good as long as you shot first and accurate. If people were scared of me, all the better. They might live.

"I got tired of sitting on the porch, and I could see the alley behind Elbows Up was in shade, so I decided to move. I got Vangie some water and relocated."

"I recall that their outhouse is back of the bar," Mom said.

"Yep. Skelly has plumbing indoors, but he just only lets the ladies use it."

I think Mom would have smiled if this had been an ordinary story, but her mouth only twitched a bit.

"You waited between the back of the bar and the outhouse."

"Yes. I waited."

"For God's sakes, Lizbeth, tell me he didn't rape you." Mom's hands were shaking.

I should have known her mind would go there. "No, Mom. No!" That was a sickening idea. I'd thought of many things he might do to me if he got the chance, but I'd never thought of sex. So since I'd first held a gun, I'd practiced to be the fastest, the sharpest, the most accurate.

"What happened?" Mom said, almost yelling.

"I shot him dead."

And that stopped her again, brought back the frozen look. "You killed him?" she said, in a whisper, just trying to make sure. "For real?"

"Yes, Mom. I killed him."

"You're sure?"

"Four shots before he hit the ground," I said, tapping the point right under my breastbone. "Course, I went and checked."

"Oh my God. Oh my God."

I don't think Mom even knew she was talking.

I nodded. Confirming to her it was true, that she should believe me.

Mom had thought of another thing to worry about. "You're sure it was him?"

I grabbed a hold of my patience, before I said something I'd regret later. Took a deep breath. "Yes, ma'am. He had blond curly hair and blue eyes, like you said." I'd inherited the curly and the eyes, but my hair was black like Mom's. "And I asked him."

"Asked...?"

"I said 'Are you Oleg Karkarov?' And he said, 'One and the same, pretty girl.'"

"And then you said...?"

I blocked that out. "I didn't say nothing. I drew."

Mom's eyes were as wide as they could get. "Did he try to hurt you?"

"He started saying some words, and he grabbed at a pocket in his grigori vest." Oleg Karkarov had reached into one of his many little pockets. He'd pulled out a pinch of green powder. He'd twisted his wrist to fling it on me. His lips had been moving the whole time, spell words.

He'd been fast. But I was faster.

"I got him first," I said, remembering how smooth it had been, my Colt in my hand. "I shot him. *Bam bam bam bam.*" I looked away from her.

"So none of his powder touched you?" She reached over and took my hand. "You weren't harmed?"

I shook my head. "I was fine."

Mom shuddered. "So after he fell, what happened?"

"Then. Hmmm. Well, I heard a lot of yelling from inside the bar, and I think there were people starting for the back door to see what was going on. So I got on Vangie and rode away."

Mom hardly knew how to feel. "This was today?" she asked, almost at random.

It felt strange to realize that yes, it was the same day, and yes, I had really shot Oleg Karkarov, and here I was telling my mother before anyone else could.

Just that moment Mom's door flew open. We both jumped a mile.

For a second I thought it must be Cal, maybe having decided he should arrest me after all. But it was Jackson, and he was in a state. Though what kind of state, I could not have told you.

"Candle!" he said, not yelling but not quiet, either. "Candle!"

Then Jackson saw me sitting opposite Mom and holding her hand, and I didn't know what he was going to do. With some relief, I watched him relax bit by bit.

"I'm glad you come to see your mother," Jackson said, well in control of himself.

Jackson and I are more alike than my own mother and me. He's not a big man with words, either.

"As soon as I could," I said. I left out the half hour I'd spent in the Segundo Mexia stable when I'd returned Vangie to her stall. I'd shivered and shook like I had the influenza. 'Fore I could screw up my courage to head for Mom's.

"You done telling Candle about it?" Jackson said.

"Just did."

"Candle?" Jackson asked. "You okay with this?" I couldn't say his voice was gentle, it never was, but it was as soft as it ever got. He only used that voice with my mother. It was one of the reasons he was the best present our little family of two had ever gotten.

"I'm thankful Lizbeth is unhurt. About the rest of it, I don't know," Mom said. She shook her head, and then she got up and went to the stove to stir something, add salt to something, whatever she had to do to keep her back to us while she got her face straight.

"Lizbeth, how are you?" Jackson asked next. Though he moved stiffly, still wary of the situation, he went to his chair and sat.

"I feel pretty good," I said, stiffening my back. "I done my job."

"*I've* done my job," Mom muttered.

I smiled at Jackson. "Yes, I've done my job."

And my stepfather smiled back. I'd hardly ever seen him smile. "You did," he said. "You're a good daughter, Lizbeth. And a fine gunnie."

"Thank you." Jackson didn't give out many compliments, so I valued that.

There was an empty second. "I got to go," I said, and I stood.

"Wait," Jackson said very quietly.

I looked down at him.

"You checked to make sure he was dead?" Jackson said.

"I did."

"Four before he hit the ground, I heard?" The smile flickered again.

"Yes." I held my hands in a circle to show Jackson how small the spread had been.

"I'll send a donation to the burial fund in Cactus Flats," Jackson said. "Don't need to spend the town's money putting that piece of shit in the ground."

It had the makings of a joke, the "piece of shit" when Oleg Karkarov had been gunned down outside an outhouse. But I wasn't in a jokey frame of mind at the moment.

"I got to be getting along," I said. "Thanks, Jackson. Mom, I'll see you soon." I wanted to add, *I hope you're not mad at me. I hope you don't think I'm going to hell.* But right now, I just couldn't ask her those things. Maybe I wouldn't ever be able to.

As if she'd known what I was thinking, Mom faced me. "We will never talk about this again," she said. "Ever." She wasn't angry at me. She was sad I felt I'd had to kill a man because of her.

"Ever," I agreed.

As I was on the path out of town and up the hill to my place, I remembered him coming out of the bar, the shock of seeing him so much my likeness. Slight but sturdy, slender jaw, big eyes, thick curly hair. Short.

And I'd said, "Oleg Karkarov?"

"One and the same, pretty girl." At that second, his eyes had widened. He'd realized he needed to defend himself.

And then, as I'd raised the Colt, I'd said, "Dad."

THE GREATEST HORSE THIEF IN HISTORY

D.J. Butler

July 1932

"Sugar beets, is it?" The man standing behind his own screen door might have been fifty years old, a few years older than Hiram himself. He dressed better than Hiram, in a button-down shirt and high-waisted trousers, though the calluses on his hands betrayed the fact that his work, too, included manual labor. His face was screwed into a tight and bitter shield.

He looked angry, but he didn't look like a thief.

A creek splashed over rocks behind the house. In the background, across fields heavy with wheat, the town of Heber lay sprawled across the valley floor. Beyond it stood snow-capped Timpanogos.

"Someone tell you I'm a beet farmer, Mr. McCrae?" When Hiram came to a town giving away food, word tended to spread ahead of him. Elbert McCrae was the last man on his list to visit.

McCrae nodded. "A man can only fill his belly with sugar beets so much."

Hiram nodded. "That's why I stopped on the Provo Bench and traded the beets for bread and beef. Can I come in?"

McCrae hesitated, but opened the door. "The Provo Bench, huh? You know, they call it 'Orem' now."

"After the railroad man. I just can't bring myself to use some of these new names. Slow to change, I guess." Hiram set down the crate of groceries he carried to kick the dust from his Red-wing Harvesters and beat more dust from the legs of his denim overalls with his fedora. He gestured at the Double-A sitting on the gravel drive. "My son?"

McCrae squinted. "Looks Indian."

"He's Navajo." Hiram nodded. "Parents died, and my wife and I took him in."

McCrae grunted. "May as well bring in the whole family. I do appreciate the groceries."

Hiram beckoned to Michael. The boy slid out of the front seat of the truck and scampered up the porch, slipping in through McCrae's front door in front of Hiram with a wooden crate full of groceries in his hand.

"Thanks for letting in the help, Mr. McCrae," Michael said.

"You ain't that much help," Hiram grunted.

"I drive, don't I?"

It was true. Hiram's fainting spells made him uncomfortable driving more than short distances, so Michael drove. If the state legislature did what it was threatening, and started requiring a license from drivers, would Michael qualify?

Hiram pushed away the thought.

"You drive," he agreed.

They set both boxes on a small table in McCrae's kitchen. The table was just big enough to hold the crates on its white and green enamel top without McCrae raising its wings. "You got ice in that Frigidaire, Mr. McCrae? The bacon is cured, but the beef isn't."

"I got ice. I got food, too, comes to it."

Hiram put the beef in McCrae's large porcelain ice box. There was room for it, so he loaded the bacon and vegetables in as well. Despite McCrae's claim, the ice box held nothing but ice and what Hiram had brought. "I'm glad you got food. And I'm glad I can bring you a little extra, Mr. McCrae. I'm just here to help."

"Report to Salt Lake about my habits, is that it?" McCrae frowned. "How much am I drinking, am I attending church services, what exactly does an unmarried man like me living up in the Uinta Mountains do for fun? Come to meddle in the behavior of the working man?"

Hiram shook his head. "You're thinking of Henry Ford. I don't care what you're drinking or whose company you keep, I'm just here to help. We're all supposed to pitch in. Believe I heard Mr. Roosevelt himself suggest that."

"That's your job, is it? To pitch in?" McCrae snorted.

"It's my ministry, I guess you'd say." Hiram shrugged. "My *job* is to grow sugar beets."

McCrae collapsed onto a soft chair, his bitter energy suddenly gone. "I'm sorry. I just...I worked all my life, Mr...."

"You can call me Hiram. Hiram Woolley. My boy is Michael."

McCrae nodded. "I worked all my life, Hiram. I ain't comfortable taking help."

Hiram sat on the sofa opposite. Michael sat beside him, bouncing slightly and drumming his fingers on his knees. The boy could stand to have his hair cut. For that matter, Hiram probably could, too.

"I don't just bring food," Hiram said. "Sometimes I help solve family disputes. Dug a well over in Price last week. I do what I can to be of assistance, when I don't have to plant and harvest. Maybe I can help you find work, Mr. McCrae."

McCrae stared at the hardwood floor.

"Horse ranching, isn't it?" Hiram asked.

McCrae grunted. "Only ever owned one or two at a time, myself. But until last week, I was foreman on one of the local ranches. You really want to help?" McCrae nodded toward the back door, eastward. "Go talk to the owners of the Flying Z, get me my job back."

Hiram sat quietly, hoping to hear still, small voices of guidance. He didn't.

What to do? He had to help McCrae if he could. But the same neighbors who had sent Hiram to find Elbert McCrae had also suggested that McCrae might be a man who deserved to lose his job.

McCrae stared at him. How long had Hiram been silent? "I was told the Flying Z lost a herd," Hiram said.

"Five hundred head."

"The Oldhams figure it's your fault the horses escaped?" The Oldhams owned the Flying Z.

McCrae laughed bitterly. "Worse than that, Hiram. They think I stole 'em. Thirty years of honest work under my belt and a spotless reputation don't matter. They think I made five hundred horses just disappear. That'd make me the greatest horse thief in history, I expect. And hell, I'd be off in California or Texas, spending the money. Instead, I'm here, knocking door to door and asking for more work."

"You don't look like a guilty man," Hiram agreed.

"And yet they won't hire me back," McCrae said. "Nor will any of the other ranches. And there's no work for me in Heber, not even at the tack and saddle shops or in the slaughterhouse. Everyone figures me for a horse thief."

"I'd like to help." Hiram balanced his sweat-stained fedora over one fist as if it were a hat jack, looking out the window at the bleached blue sky. "You have any idea what happened to the horses?"

McCrae opened his mouth, shut it. He looked at Michael briefly, frowned, and then stood, pacing back and forth. "I don't like to say."

"I'll go talk to the owners of the Flying Z," Hiram said. "Whether or not you tell me anything else. But the more I know, the more I can help."

McCrae stopped his pacing and stared at Hiram. "Yeah," he said, "okay. It was Indians."

Indians? Hiram tried to avoid looking astonished. "The Utes? Uinta and Ouray Reservation? It's been a long time since the Utes rustled any horses."

"I didn't say it was them." McCrae cleared his throat. "And I can't say I really know one kind of Indian from another, begging your pardon, but I see the Utes from time to time, shopping down at Heber, or passing by at the Flying Z. They drive cars, they wear jeans and boots."

"Surprise," Michael muttered.

"The horse thieves looked...old-fashioned," McCrae continued. "Horseback. Paint and feathers, the whole thing."

The heliotropius in his pocket, the red-streaked green stone with so many useful properties, lay still; McCrae practiced no deception. Hiram felt a vague sense of disquiet. "I'll go talk to the owners."

"Of course, we'll give Mr. McCrae back his job," Ada Oldham said. Her husband and co-owner of the Flying Z, Ira, stood with his head and shoulders under the hood of his vehicle, grunting his agreement. "Just as soon as we get back our horses."

"He says he didn't steal them," Hiram said. "I believe him."

"He said Indians in war paint took the horses." Ada wore her hair in a simple bun and dressed in calico. She and her husband were working on their Fargo truck together. The two-story ranch house must have had seven or eight rooms, judging from the outside—the Oldhams were doing well, but didn't dress or act rich. In other circumstances, Hiram would have liked them very much, but now he felt waves of distrust radiating from Mrs. Oldham, and, tightening his own stomach, he tried not to radiate it right back. "You believe that, too?"

"I believe he isn't a liar." Hiram watched Michael bounce from side to side in the front of his own truck, the Ford Model AA. "Is he a drunk?" The former foreman had seemed a little defensive about his drinking habits.

"The man is a teetotaler, as far as I know," Ada said. "Raised Kentucky Baptist. But really ... war paint?"

McCrae hadn't exactly said "war paint," at least not to Hiram, but there was no sense picking a needless fight. "You got any maps?"

"What kind of maps?" Mrs. Oldham asked. Under the hood of the Fargo, Mr. Oldham banged metal against metal and cursed mildly. "If you're looking for a highway, there aren't any. That's why we came out here to the Uintas to run our horses. Get away from the big towns like Provo and Ogden. Even Heber's getting too big for my Ira's taste, these days."

"Just horses?" Hiram wondered.

"Also cattle." Ada shrugged. "It was horses that got stolen."

"All the maps you got. The older, the better," Hiram said. "If you had any maps from when you first bought the land, I'd be especially happy to look at those."

"What are you thinking, exactly?" She eyed him with suspicion.

"Mr. McCrae saw something," Hiram said slowly. Then he dodged her question with a slight evasion that didn't quite amount to a lie: "Maybe if I look on the maps, I'll see what it was."

"Like a rock formation he took in the darkness for an Indian in headdress?" Mrs. Oldham suggested dryly.

"Yes," Hiram said. "Something like that."

"I'll give you all my maps," Mrs. Oldham said. "Only remember, I'm not looking for an explanation. I'm looking for five hundred horses."

"I get your five hundred horses back, will you hire Elbert McCrae again?"

"Of course."

He waited with Michael by the truck while Ada Oldham went into the ranch house. The boy looked at Hiram with his dark liquid eyes and smiled. Hiram smiled back and tried not to let the sudden pang of loss, such as came over him every time he thought of his wife, twist that smile into a frown.

"So Mrs. Oldham seems to accept the idea that Indians might be thieves," Michael said. "Only she doesn't believe in the war paint."

That ended Hiram's nostalgia, and he tousled the boy's hair.

Ada Oldham returned; her facial expression was softened. "I only got the one, or at least, only the one I can find."

Hiram spread the map over the hood of his Double-A. Michael joined him and looked at it over Hiram's shoulder, standing on the running board and hoisting himself high into the air on the mirror.

"We're here?" Hiram indicated a rectangle on the map.

"No, that's our neighbors. Our house wasn't built when this map was drawn. We're here." Ada Oldham pointed. "And the horses were penned here."

She pointed at a meandering line. Above it, in a white space, were written the words *Carre Shinob*.

"Carre," Hiram said. "I'm no good with languages, but that looks French to me. But Shinob...I don't know. What is that?"

Ada Oldham shrugged. "The man who sold us the land gave us the map, and the map came with those words on it. I have no idea what they mean. The line there is the creek, and that's where we had the horses penned. The space under those words is a ridge above the creek."

"The French trappers got as far south as Utah, back in their day," Hiram said. "Provo's named after one of them."

"I taught a little school, back when I was Miss Halstead," Ada Oldham said. "And I think I remember enough French to know that *carré* is a square. That long, high ridge looks nothing like a square. But you're welcome to go look around it all you like."

"Bit far from the house, isn't it?"

"You gotta go through Heber. We only moved the horses

there this year; it was McCrae who suggested it. He scouted out all our land and said he thought that was the best grass. Used to keep the horses just across the road here."

"Thank you." Hiram handed back the map.

Since they were passing through Heber anyway, Hiram stopped and sent a telegram to his friend Mahonri Jones at B.Y. High in Provo. Mahonri was a librarian who loved a good riddle, and if his own library didn't have the answer, he could walk up the hill to the university.

As Hiram and Michael bounced up the rutted road between high ridges, nearing the creek where the Oldhams had kept their cattle, the late summer sun began to sink.

"You were in charge of packing the truck," Hiram said to his son.

"We have blankets and water and sandwiches."

"What do we have for light?"

"A flashlight and an oil lantern. Did you pack the gun?"

"Go ahead and check," Hiram suggested.

Michael looked into the glove compartment, finding the revolver and the spare full moon. "Shall I make sure it's loaded? Maybe shoot a couple of fenceposts for good luck?"

"You let me handle the gun," Hiram said. "You're thirteen. You get the flashlight."

The road ended at the gate of a rail fence that abruptly blocked off the canyon. The fresh darkness of mountain evening filled the canyon before them. Hiram and Michael both climbed out of the Double-A. Hiram tucked the revolver into the back of his belt, and brought along the oil lantern and a box of matches.

Michael solemnly carried the flashlight.

"Can I climb it?" Michael asked.

"Stay close to me."

They climbed the fence. Oil lantern lit, Hiram took slow steps. He breathed in the pine-scented air and, following the burbling creek, looked for horses. He saw plenty of fresh droppings, green, compact balls of recently-digested grass, but none of the beasts themselves and no gap in the fence through which they might have gone. McCrae was right; the grass here was tall and lush, and the stream looked year-round and abundant. And somehow, the horses were gone.

The ridge staring down from above the canyon was bare of trees for its upper half. In the nearly moonless night, its bulk was a shadow blocking out the enduring stars of the northern sky. Hiram found himself standing still, staring at the ridge, with the hair on the back of his neck standing up.

He pulled his fedora down tighter and scratched the back of his neck to make the feeling go away. It didn't.

"Michael, does Carre Shinob mean anything in the language of the Dine?"

Michael's Navajo was limited—he'd been a baby when Hiram and his wife had adopted him—but he had learned a few words. "The people live really far south of here, Pap."

"I know."

Michael circled his adopted father without slowing down as they talked. "I don't think Carre Shinob means anything."

Hiram nodded. He felt a flutter in his chest, and the hair on the backs of his arms was standing up as well. "Are you tired?"

"It isn't late, Pap."

"Shall we hike up that ridge?"

"We'd see better stars up there." They didn't see great stars anymore on the farm in Lehi; Salt Lake was just too close, and Utah Valley was filling up with farms. But on new moons, Hiram liked to drive Michael out west toward Tooele, where the sky was as dark as it had ever been for Jim Bridger.

They hiked up the slope. As they gained elevation on its flank, Hiram saw that the ridge hunkered down into a saddle and then rose to a final promontory before dropping into the two streams that had carved it.

"Up there." He pointed, and a shiver ran up his spine.

"Pap," Michael said. "I have a funny feeling in my stomach."

Hiram did, too. It was a feeling he'd felt the one time he'd ridden the tilt-a-whirl in Salt Lake, a sensation that reminded him of falling. "Let's both keep our lights on," he told his son. "That way we can always see each other."

The night air was crisp in the Uintas, even in August, but the hillside was steep and Hiram was sweating by the time they reached the saddle. He shook sweat out of his fedora, wiped his forehead on the back of a sleeve, and then rolled both sleeves up past his elbows.

Michael stuck close to his side as he caught his breath. The boy shone the watery yellow beam of his flashlight in all directions, but especially up to the top of the promontory.

"There's no one up there," Michael said.

"Right," Hiram agreed. "Let's go have a look."

At the height of promontory was a flat patch of bare earth, bordered by a handful of weathered stones and a few stubborn bushes, barely larger than weeds. In the center of the stones lay a low pile of rocks, oblong in shape, about seven feet by three.

A pile of rocks such as you might lay over a body in a shallow burial.

"What is this place?" Michael's voice trembled.

Hiram shivered, but not from the chill; there was no wind and he was sweating. A sensation like an electric current played along his spine. He wasn't especially sensitive, not like Grandma Hettie had been. The veil had been thin for that old woman, and there were moments when past and present alike, as well as the movements of spirits and angels, seemed to be an open book, written for her exclusive reading. Hiram didn't have that.

But neither was he an insensate clod. A spirit waited atop this hill.

He stooped to examine the rocks and saw that some had been disturbed. He crouched to poke in the earth where the stones had been removed and found a strange set of objects: a scrap of canvas cloth, a large animal claw with a hole drilled through it, one leather glove with the tips of the fingers and thumb cut off, and a strip of paper.

Unfolding the paper, he found an improbable signature: *Brigham Young.*

Hiram stood and took a slow breath. Should he take Michael back to the truck? But the boy was already nervous; surely being left alone in the truck would terrify him, despite his bravado.

Hiram could come back another night, but it was a long drive from anywhere he was willing to sleep, and besides, a spirit that was here tonight might not be here tomorrow.

"Listen, son." Hiram knelt, to be able to look Michael directly in the face as they spoke. "I'm not going to lie to you. I think there are spirits on this hill."

"More than usual?" Michael asked.

Hiram nodded. "But remember, a spirit has no flesh and bone, and cannot hurt you. No matter what it shows you, it can't make you do anything. And if you want it to go away, you can cast it out in the name of Jesus."

"I remember." Michael swallowed. He was a brave boy. Hiram tousled his long hair and Michael smiled faintly.

"I want you to turn your flashlight off, but hold on to it, and keep your thumb on the switch."

"I can do that." Michael turned off his flashlight, and gripped it with both hands. "Are you going to turn off your lamp?"

"No," Hiram said. "I'm going to use it to try to talk to the spirit."

Michael swallowed so hard that Hiram could hear his Adam's apple move. "Why?"

"I want to help Mr. McCrae get his job back."

"You think the spirits might know where the horses are?"

"Yes."

Michael nodded.

What on earth was the scrap of paper signed by Brigham Young? A contract, an old deed to the land? A missionary commission? An order for wheat? Hiram shook his head.

He set the lantern on the ground beside the oblong heap of stones.

"I can tell you're here," he said.

Nothing. The air was still. A hundred yards away though he was, Hiram thought he could hear the bubbling of the stream.

"This must be a lonely place. Don't you want to talk?"

The stars shone down, cold and now queerly unfamiliar, as if Hiram had forgotten his years of star lore, or had been transported to an alien world under a different zodiac.

"That's my lantern on the ground. I know you can see the flame. If you can hear me, make the flame dance. Don't try to put it out, just move it."

The air was still. Hiram fixed his eyes on the lantern.

"Just move the flame. Just a little."

The flame jumped. As if struck by a sudden gust of wind, the flame snapped sideways for a split second before returning to its normal, upright posture.

Michael jumped, too, pressing himself against Hiram's side.

Hiram wrapped an arm around Michael's shoulder. "Very good. Now I'm going to ask you questions. If the answer is yes, make the flame move again. Gently, you don't want to put it out." But what to ask?

Michael shivered, and Hiram drew him close.

"Is there more than one of you?"

The flame moved.

"Are there fewer than ten?"

The flame moved.

That was a relief. However much the idea of a ghost discomfited Hiram, the idea of a multitude of ghosts was much worse.

"Are there two of you?" Nothing. "Three? Four? Five?"

The lantern's flame moved.

Strange, though. The heap of stones was the size and shape of the grave of a single person.

"Are you all men?" Nothing. "All women? Both men and women? Men, women, and children together?"

The flame moved.

Hiram frowned. "Are you a family?"

The flame moved.

"Pioneers?" Hiram asked. "Mormons?"

Nothing.

"Indians?"

The flame moved.

Hiram pressed the ghosts in this slow fashion, eliciting additional information. The Indians hadn't died in this spot, but had been moved here. Asking about revolutions of the stars, he thought he got the information that they had been here for seventy years—that made 1865, which was consistent with the signature of Brigham Young, who died in 1877.

He stabbed in the dark, but couldn't land on a question that threw any more light on the paper.

"Two weeks ago, horses were stolen from the valley below this ridge." Hiram paused. "Did you take them?"

The flame moved.

Michael was shaking.

"Will you give me back the horses?"

Nothing.

Hiram took a deep breath. "Will you trade the horses with me?"

The flame moved. The ghosts would trade.

But how to find out what to trade?

"Pap," Michael said softly, a hint of a whimper in his voice, "is that you running your fingers through my hair?"

Hiram's hand was on Michael's shoulder. He grabbed the

lantern in his other hand and raised it high; as if disturbed by unseen fingers, the boy's hair moved about on his head.

"Turn on your flashlight," he told his son, trying to keep his voice calm. "We're going back to the truck."

They finished out the night in a rented room in Heber. Hiram was awake two hours after falling asleep, with the peep of the egg-yolk sun through the paper blind. Michael, despite coming down from Carre Shinob trembling with nerves, slept another four hours.

He was thirteen years old, and Hiram let him sleep.

No response came to the telegram that day. Hiram examined the objects more closely. He learned little, except that the glove was not of home manufacture—it had a tag stitched inside it, faded now into illegibility. He bought a pair of long leather shoelaces at the mercantile and threaded one through the claw, which he then wore around his neck, right alongside the chi-rho talisman that protected him from enemies.

The scrap that contained actual legible words—the name Brigham Young—was the least comprehensible thing to him. He considered driving back up the ridge with a shovel and unearthing whatever lay beneath those stones, but if the spirits involved—and there were definitely spirits involved, and not just spirits, but the ghosts of dead human beings—were disturbed, then digging up the grave would only disturb them more.

They had offered to trade with him. No, that wasn't quite right, he had asked whether they were willing to trade and they had indicated yes. Or perhaps, the one of them that was speaking had indicated yes. He shouldn't assume he'd been speaking to the same spirit the entire time, since he hadn't asked.

But then that spirit, or another of them, had ruffled Michael's hair.

Had they wanted to trade for his son? Or had they wanted to take Michael? They had said they were Indians. Hiram and his wife had adopted the boy because he was without family—Hiram had been close to the child's father in the Great War—and because they'd been unable to have family of their own. Not all Indians were happy with white people adopting Indians—did the dead Indians want to take Michael away from him?

Would that involve them killing Michael?

Hiram shook the thoughts out of his head. He needed more information. Short of digging up the grave...

"Are you okay staying here tonight?" he asked Michael. "We'll lock the door, and I'll leave you here with milk and graham crackers and all the pulp magazines the mercantile has? As long as they're not *too* lurid, that is."

"I don't know, Pap." Michael grinned. "I can handle some pretty lurid stuff."

With the sun still up, Hiram climbed up into the saddle of Carre Shinob. There he built a little fire and brewed himself tea, using a packet he always carried in the Double-A, hidden inside a folded state map he never used. His grandmother had called the tea "the devil's snare," but she'd taught him to use it. The muddy brown infusion made from the jimson weed opened the mind to the universe. To an unprepared mind, that let in chaos—hallucinations, clowning, madness. To a prepared mind, it could let in revelation.

He put the tea in his thermos flask, just a single cup. It would be enough. He put his hand into the glove, and the claw around his neck. He clenched the scraps of paper and canvas in his gloved hand, and he stood beside the tumulus.

Watching the sun sink, he emptied his mind of all thoughts. He inhaled, focused on Michael's safety, reminded himself that the boy was in a bright room eating graham crackers and reading detective stories, and exhaled, letting go of that concern. He did the same with thoughts of McCrae's belligerence, the Oldhams' indifference, his own physical safety.

With the stage of his mind empty, he placed onto it the questions he had. Who were the ghosts waiting there? What was their connection with the physical objects he held? Why had they taken the Oldhams' horses? What would they want in return for releasing the beasts?

He drank the tea—hot or cold, it was disgusting, and Hiram wasn't one to sweeten anything with sugar.

Then he lay down on the grave.

It wasn't comfortable, but it was necessary. This, too, was an old technique he'd learned from his grandmother. Solomon had practiced it, she'd told him, sleeping in the Temple of the Lord until Jehovah himself appeared. The Greeks knew it, and the old

Arabs. Mind open, heart focused on his questions, Hiram Woolley lay on the rocky mound and waited to see ghosts.

He touched the Saturn ring on his finger. It was made of lead,
forged by Hiram himself from a simple mold, and scratched by
him with the sign of Saturn while that planet was strong in the
skies. Saturn ruled melancholy, and dreams, and insight.

He fell asleep.

Hiram saw a man on a horse. Around his neck, the rider
worse a necklace of teeth, claws, and bones. Several of the talons
might have passed for the one Hiram had found on Carre Shinob.
Two young Indians, a boy and a girl, led the horse by its reins,
and the man sat stiffly, staring down at them.

Hiram looked down at himself. Wool trousers, muddy boots
that weren't his. But he wore fingerless leather gloves on each
hand—gloves he recognized.

Whose eyes was he seeing through? Whose memories were
these?

He looked again at the rider, and realized with a shock that
the man was a corpse. His legs were strapped to the animal and
his back was strapped to a plank that rose from the saddle behind
him, the whole arrangement keeping him upright in death. The
dead man's fist was clenched around a sheet of paper.

A sheet of paper that had once been signed by Brigham Young?
But why would a dead man carry such a thing?

To prove his status? To prove to his ancestors, or to his gods,
that he, too, was a mighty chief, a person worthy of a friendship
with Brigham Young, famous chief of the Mormons?

It was only a guess, but if felt right to Hiram.

He stood on a high bluff, but this was not Carre Shinob. A
wide valley full of yellow grass stretched out to the west. This
was not the Uintas, it felt more like Beaver or Parowan, with
lower hills and cultivated land.

He heard weeping. There were words, but not in a language
he knew.

Looking about, he saw that a man standing beside him also
wore a wool suit, and had the craggy face and pale hair of a
northern European. Everyone else on the scene, maybe as many as
fifty people, was Indian. Hiram knew enough Navajo to recognize
their dress and a few of their words, and this was another people.

The two weeping children led the horse to a hillside tomb, a small natural cave that had almost been bricked in with stones and mortar. Indian men untied the corpse and carried it inside.

But the glove? It remained on Hiram's borrowed hand, outside the tomb.

And there was no canvas in sight.

Here was only part of the answer to Hiram's riddle, at best.

Brother Morley, the other European man said in an urgent whisper, *you cannot allow this to happen!*

Allow what to happen?

Shut your mouth, Hiram found his body saying. *Do you want another war?*

The other man was sullen, silent.

Then let them have the foolish traditions of their fathers. I will speak my eulogy and keep my vow.

Let them have their traditions, aye, no matter what?

No matter what.

The dead man arranged, the Indians stood in front of his tomb. Two women stood in the open doorway itself, and though the others fell silent, they continued a feverish chant under their breaths.

One of the men nodded to Hiram.

Colorow was a great man, Hiram said. *He made war on the Mericats and the Mormonee, and he was a mighty leader in war. Then he made peace with the Mormonee, and he was mighty in peace as well.*

The Indians nodded, satisfied.

Then the warriors standing to either side of the chanting women stepped forward. With long knives, they slit the women's throats.

Hiram wanted to scream. The body whose eyes he borrowed panted and sweated, but did nothing.

Could this be a lying vision? Jimson weed was called the devil's snare for a reason, and could send dishonest dreams, as well as true ones.

But no, Hiram had a strong mind, and he was prepared.

And the vision had answered some of his questions.

The killers laid the two murdered women—sacrificed women—inside the grave with the chief's body. As they finished bricking up the opening, the onlookers returned to weeping and song.

Hiram still wanted to scream, but he forced himself to keep watching.

With the tomb sealed, the two wailing children were led forward. With a shock, Hiram realized that theirs was not the obligatory crying of a professional mourner, or the general sorrow of someone whose tribe has lost a leader, but was caused by real terror.

They knew what was coming.

Then sacrificers drove long iron spikes into the stone to either side of the tomb. They shut iron collars around the necks of the two children, and then with short chains, they shackled the children to the tomb.

The dead chief's tribe turned and walked away, singing.

The man with the gloves and his white companion went with them.

The cries of the shackled children rose piteous to a deaf heaven.

Coming up out of the jimson weed trance, Hiram felt cold. He ached from the rocks and his blood pulsed sluggishly in his veins, ineffective against the freezing Uinta night.

He couldn't let himself come up, he needed to see more.

He tightened his fists around the scraps of paper and canvas.

More, I need to know more.

He forgot the cold, and sank again.

He found himself under a swollen moon, standing on the same high ridge beside the Indian chief's tomb.

You stood the earlier passage, Hiram was saying. He leaned closed into the face of the craggy blonde man he'd seen before. *The earlier passage was worse.*

In that murder, and heathen sacrifice, are worse than grave robbing, aye. The other man was furious. *But don't pretend that what you're proposing now ain't a sin, just the same.*

They're asking us. His brothers. It isn't robbing, it's just moving the dead, to keep him safe, preserve his honor.

Hiram pointed at four Indian men as he spoke. Everyone wore long wool coats, and their exhaled breath puffed up in tiny clouds.

The blond man shook his head, shoulders slumping in surrender, and Hiram and the others got to work.

With slow movements and chanting a song Hiram didn't understand, the six men knocked in the stones that bricked up the chief's tomb. Hiram and his fellow white man stood back, and the Indians crept into the tomb holding a white canvas sheet.

When they emerged, there were three bodies in the sheet.

Them, too? Hiram asked, pointing at two small skeletons lying outside the tomb. Years must have passed, because the flesh had all fallen—or been eaten—from their bones, and the collars around their necks had fallen off, together with their skulls.

The Indians nodded.

Hiram helped gather up the children's bones. Picking up one of the skulls—the boy's?—he found it still covered with a thick mop of black hair. He ran his fingers through it and felt tears trickle down his cheeks.

They bundled all five skeletons into the canvas and then together the six men hoisted the bones up onto the back of a buckboard wagon. Hiram climbed into the seat and took the reins, shushing his uneasy horses.

Where are we taking the chief? he asked.

North and east, one of the Indians said. *Far. A place called Carre Shinob.*

Hiram drove into Heber with ache in his bones and disquiet in his stomach. A chief had died and been buried somewhere in the west, and then reburied here. The man's grave had been disturbed by McCrae and the Oldhams' horses, and his ghost had taken the herd.

The chief would give the horses back, but after seeing the man's funeral, Hiram's fear that what he wanted in return was the life of his son Michael intensified.

A light in the telegraph office drew him to park there in the gray dawn light, setting the handbrake of the Double-A and shuffling into the creaking wooden building. The clerk's desk was vacant, and Hiram stood gratefully in the heat of a coal stove in the corner, feeling its warmth slowly burn away the frost that had sunk into his bones.

The clerk dragged himself to his place behind the desk, blowing his nose through a drooping mustache and into a yellowed old handkerchief. "I got a pot of coffee, if you want some."

Hiram shook his head. "Thank you for the stove, though. I only stopped in because my boy's still sleeping, and I wanted to see if I'd had an answer."

"Oh yeah, you're the fella with the queer words. I gotta say, you look more like a farmer than a...whatever kind of man would be sending telegrams like that one."

"I *am* a farmer. Beets. Down at Lehi."

"That explains it. Let me check."

"Thank you."

The clerk dug into his clip stand of messages and came up with one. "Here you go, came in last night while Jensen was working. He didn't have an address to send it on to. Looks like your answer's just about as strange as your question."

"I planned to come in to pick it up." Hiram tipped the clerk a precious nickel and took the telegram. The telegram was from Mahonri, and it was much longer than the question. Mahonri behaved as if he had an unlimited budget for sending telegrams; since Hiram was the beneficiary, he couldn't complain.

Carre Shinob is legendary place where chief Walkara's bones were moved. Walkara also known as Colorow and Walker as in Walker's War. Most famous horse thief in history rustled 3000 horses in California in a single day. What are you doing up there?

"Thank you," Hiram said again, and headed for the boarding house.

"They think I'm crazy at the slaughterhouse," McCrae grumbled. The foreman carried a large bag slung over his shoulder and grimaced from the weight as he climbed the ridge to Carre Shinob.

The bag was full of horse bones.

"Did you tell them you wanted to make soup?" Hiram squinted at the sky. In the evening's last blue-gray light, a sheet of glowering clouds gathered. In the east, over the higher Uintas, he saw lightning flash, and then the ensuing thunder crawled past him.

That should help, if anything.

But the storm made him even more glad he'd left Michael a second night in the boarding house.

"Yeah, I tried your joke. That's why they think I'm crazy."

"Well, if this doesn't work, you don't get your job back, and then I guess you're out of options, and you'll have to leave town. So as I see it, the opinion of the slaughterhouse crew shouldn't worry you much."

"And if I do get my job, I stick around, and I get the reputation of an eccentric who makes horse soup."

"You could have told them the truth," Hiram suggested.

They reached the saddle of the ridge, and McCrae set down his sack. "And what is the truth?"

Hiram set down his sack, which contained wooden rattles, a small hand drum, and a square of sheet metal, bowed over to squeeze it in. "Some would call it magic. My grandmother would have denied that."

McCrae spat thick phlegm into the dirt. "And what would *she* have called it?"

Hiram looked up at Chief Walkara's grave mound. "She'd have said that when you need to get something done, you do what works. A cunning woman or a cunning man is just somebody who knows what works."

"I guess on the whole I'd rather be known as the fella who wants to drink horse soup. Shall we get this started, then?"

Thunder rolled across the ridge, fat drops of rain splattered on their faces, and Hiram nodded. The heliotropius was said to be able to call rain. Sadly, it had no power to *dismiss* rain clouds.

They commenced at the far end of the ridge from the relocated bones of Chief Walkara. With the peals of thunder becoming more frequent, until they almost seemed to roll over the top of each other, the two men inched down the ridge. Elbert McCrae shuffled slowly, shaking his head and trying not to look at Hiram.

Hiram danced, kicked his toes into the softening dirt. He also whinnied and snorted, making all the horse-like noises he could.

McCrae carried the sheet metal, and he flexed and shook it. The sound he made was closer to the thunder's noise than to the sound of actual horses. Hiram beat the drum, shook the rattles, and clapped his hands in turn. It was his best imitation of the sound of a running herd, but it was rude and childish at best.

Would it be enough?

He kept his eye fixed on the tumulus, but saw nothing.

As they climbed toward the site of the grave, McCrae traded the sheet metal for the sack of bones. He shook his head. "That's the weakest damn horse imitation I ever heard, Woolley."

Hiram chuckled. "I'm trying, but I'm more of a mule and truck man, myself."

"A horse sounds like *this*." And then McCrae began to neigh and whinny for all he was worth.

And he really *did* sound like a horse.

They climbed the promontory prancing together. At the top, rain mixed with hail pounded down on them as they trotted three times in a circle around the stones, McCrae scattering the bones from his sack all over the knob of earth.

Then Hiram stopped, and McCrae stopped with him. The foreman wore a surprisingly cheerful grin.

"We brought you these horses, Chief Walkara!" Hiram cried, addressing the low mound of stones.

Lightning flashed, illuminating the top of the hill—it was still empty of life other than the two men.

"We brought you these horses to trade!" Hiram added.

The rain had become entirely hail. Hiram shivered. He felt cold, tired, and suddenly alone. He was too cold from the mere weather to be able to feel whether there were spirits present, and there was no way he could light a lamp in these conditions.

"We give you *this* herd!" He tried one last time. "We ask you to bring back the Oldhams' herd!"

Nothing.

He sighed.

"That's it, then." McCrae kicked at the muddy earth. "Well, foolish as I feel, I appreciate the effort."

Hiram nodded. They trudged down off the promontory Carre Shinob, heading down the saddle toward the valley below.

Lightning flashed.

McCrae sucked breath in past his teeth. "You see that, Woolley?"

Hiram raised his eyes. "What?"

Lightning flashed again. The valley below them was full of horses. Not phantasms, but flesh and blood beasts, huddling together beneath the trees to shelter from the storm.

"He brought them back," Hiram murmured.

Lightning flashed a third time. Hiram smelled horses surrounding him, felt their heat as they passed, and heard the thunderous rattle of hooves on the ridge—and yet the ridge held not a single flesh-and-blood horse.

At the high end of the valley, standing just outside the rail fence penning in the horses on that end, Hiram saw a band of Indians. He only saw them for a moment, but he saw them clearly and he knew their faces. He'd seen them before.

He'd seen their funeral.

But now all five sat on horseback. Chief Walkara faced Hiram with one arm raised over his head, holding a spear in greeting.

Hiram raised his own arm in return, and then the Indians were gone.

The heat, smell, and sound of the phantom horses passed with them.

"I'll be damned," McCrae said.

"I don't think so. Anyway, I hope not."

McCrae took two steps away from Hiram, as if mere proximity would damn him. He cleared his throat. "What do I...what do I tell them?"

Hiram felt tired. "Mrs. Oldham said she wasn't looking for an explanation. She just wanted her five hundred horses back. She said she'd hire you right back."

"She'll think I stole them."

"Tell her we found the Indians. Tell her the Indians weren't from around here, but they were famous horse thieves, and we bought the horses back. That's the simple truth, as I see it."

McCrae nodded slowly. "And if she asks what we paid?"

Hiram began trudging down to his truck. "*Then*, Mr. McCrae, I would consider telling a lie."

THE DOCTOR AND THE SPECTRE

A Doc Holliday Story

Mike Resnick

The date was November 8, 1887.

Doc Holliday lay on his deathbed in the Hotel Glenwood in Glenwood Springs, Colorado, struggling to breathe. Suddenly, he opened his eyes, and the hint of a smile crossed his lips.

"This is funny," he said, and died.

According to most of his biographers, including Ben T. Traywick, Gary L. Roberts, Sylvia D. Lynch, and E. Richard Churchill, those were the last words ever spoken by the notorious gunman, and there is no reason to doubt them.

But would you like to know *what* the dying gunfighter thought was funny?

April 23, 1887. It was almost midnight. Kate Elder was down in the hotel's bar having a drink, while Doc, his body wracked by tuberculosis, lay on their bed, trying unsuccessfully to get some sleep.

Suddenly, he heard the door open, but the footsteps were too heavy to be Kate's. He reached carefully for his holster, slid his gun out, and swung his feet to the floor.

"Hold it right there!" he growled.

"Oh, damn!" said a masculine voice. "You're not her."

Holiday pulled a match out of his pocket with his free hand, struck it against the rough surface of the bed table, and lit the lamp that resided there.

And stared.

And frowned.

"Who the hell are you?" he demanded. "In fact, *what* the hell are you?"

"Isn't it obvious?" came the reply.

"Not to me," said Holliday, staring at the tall white skeleton wrapped in a black robe and carrying a wicked-looking scythe.

"I am the Spectre of Death."

"You took long enough getting here." Holliday showed little surprise. "I've been waiting years for you. Okay, how do we go about it?"

"You misunderstand," said the Spectre. "I've made a clumsy mistake."

"What the hell are you talking about?"

"You're the famous Doc Holliday," said the Spectre. "I was sure you'd be downstairs gambling." It paused, finding its words. "I have come for Kate Elder."

"Don't be silly!" snapped Holliday. "I'm a lunger who's been dying for years, and she's in perfect health."

"Nonetheless, it is she who I've come for."

"You leave her alone!" growled Holliday.

"Why?" asked the Spectre curiously. "Surely you're not going to argue that you love her. Hell, you're Doc Holliday—you've never loved anything but your gun and your cards."

"I've always had a woman," replied Holliday.

"*Had*, not *loved*," said the Spectre. "And especially not this one."

"She takes care of me," Holliday replied, uncomfortable about even mouthing the word "love."

"Well, I'm sure you can find someone else," said the Spectre, turning toward the door. "I'll go downstairs and claim her now."

"Don't do anything foolish," warned Holliday.

"I'm just doing my job." The Spectre spoke with no show of anger or malice.

"And I'm just doing mine!" Holliday aimed his pistol at the hand that held the scythe and pulled the trigger.

"Now look what you've done!" The Spectre held up its hand for Holliday to see that his third and fourth skeletal fingers were completely shattered.

"Didn't seem to hurt you," noted Holliday.

"Of course not!" growled the Spectre. "But the force of the

bullet, coupled with my missing fingers, knocked my scythe clear out the window."

"So pick it up on your way back to wherever the hell you came from," said Holliday sardonically. "Which had better be soon."

The Spectre shook its head rapidly. "You don't understand. If someone touches the scythe—"

Before he could finish the sentence, a horrible scream rose from the wooden sidewalk below Holliday's second-floor window.

"That was *your* fault, John Henry Holliday!" The Spectre pointed at him accusingly with his good hand. "I've got to retrieve my Scythe of Death before anyone else can lay a hand on it or trip over it in the darkness. Even the slightest contact with it is fatal."

Holliday indicated the gun still directed at the Spectre. "Our business isn't finished yet."

"This encounter was just an accident," said the Spectre. "I have no business with you."

"Yes, you do."

The Spectre frowned. "What are you suggesting?"

"Take me instead of Kate."

"Why should I? You're dying anyway."

Holliday got to his feet, walked over to the Spectre, and pointed the gun at its head. "But not necessarily alone," he said.

The skeleton stayed silent as he contemplated Doc's proposal. "You for Kate Elder?" he said at last.

Holliday nodded.

"All right." The Spectre gave Doc a resigned sigh. "It's a deal."

"Okay," said Holliday. "Give me a minute to get dressed and we can go."

The Spectre shook its head. "Not yet."

Holliday frowned. "Why not?"

"You have one more man to kill yet."

"Who?"

"I am forbidden to tell you," said the Spectre. "But you'll know him when you see him."

"And then you'll come for me?"

"As soon as I can work you into my schedule."

"It's a deal," said Holliday. The Spectre began extending its hand to cement their agreement with a handshake, noticed its shattered fingers, turned, and walked out the door.

☆   ☆   ☆

Weeks passed. Then months. November 8 arrived, and Holliday lay on his bed, from which he had not risen for almost two full days.

Kate Elder sat in a corner of the room, reading a book and waiting for the inevitable. Finally, she stood up, walked to a bucket of water, rinsed out a cool compress, and laid it across Holliday's forehead.

"It's too soon," he rasped.

"What?" she said, straining to hear him.

"I've still got to kill someone."

She sighed and shook her head sadly. "Delirious," she muttered, and walked back to her chair.

Holliday thought back on all the men he'd killed—Frank McLaury, Tom McLaury, Mike Gordon, Frank Stillwell, Jim Austin, Ed Bailey, Kid Colton, the ones with no names or faces that he could bring to his fevered mind—and decided that he'd more than held his end of the deal. But he sure as hell couldn't see how he was going to kill one more man before the Spectre came back for him.

He thought he heard a sound near the door, and tried to prop himself up on an elbow to see if it was the Spectre with a new game plan, or perhaps the man he was supposed to kill—but his strength, what little remained of it, failed him and he collapsed back onto the bed.

"Is something wrong, Doc?" asked Kate solicitously.

"No," he rasped hoarsely.

"Can I get you anything?" she continued. "Anything at all?"

He stared at her, the woman who, on different occasions, had broken him out of jail, sworn out an arrest warrant against him, supplied him with guns, and even backed him up in a fight.

"Just keep on being my Kate," he whispered.

She was about to answer him, realized that she didn't know quite how to reply to that, and settled for smiling. Nodding her assent, she went back to reading her book.

Holliday closed his eyes again, and thought back across the tapestry of his life. What would have been the odds, he wondered, when he was twenty years old and a serious dental student, that over the next decade and a half he'd be wanted for murder in four different states, or that he and the Earp brothers would take on their enemies in the single most famous gunfight in history—or that he'd wind up at age thirty-six, unable to stand on his own power, in a bed in the middle of Colorado, which wasn't even on a lot of maps when he was a kid?

Or, he added mentally, *that I'd be lying in a hotel bed in a room with one of the more notorious women in the West, wishing that my number was up and scared that it isn't.*

Kate got to her feet and walked to the door, where she paused and turned to Holliday.

"I'll be right back," she told him, holding up an empty flask. "I'm just going down to the bar to fill this up."

"Go." Holliday mouthed the word, but nothing came out.

He closed his eyes again, then opened them a couple of minutes later when he heard footsteps approaching.

"Back already?" he tried to say, but again, no words emerged.

"Good afternoon, Doc," said a masculine voice that seemed vaguely familiar. "It's been awhile."

Holliday made a supreme effort and opened his eyes. Standing at the foot of the bed was the Spectre of Death.

You're early, thought Holliday.

Actually, I'm a few days late, answered the Spectre. *I hope you haven't been in too much pain.*

I can't feel much of anything, including pain, replied Holliday.

Be grateful for small favors, said the Spectre.

I haven't killed anyone since last we met, Holliday admitted.

I know, answered the Spectre. *It was determined by the Celestial Record Keeper that you'd never be strong enough to do so. Anyway, the paperwork's all done, the permissions have all been granted, and I'm here to take you now.*

Good, said Holliday. *I've been ready for weeks. Months, even.*

You see? said the Spectre, its lipless, fleshless face contorted in a nightmare version of a smile. *Not everyone has a reason to fear me.*

I've never feared much of anything, Holliday confessed.

Just then the door opened and Kate reentered. She walked over to the bed, laid a hand on Holliday's forehead, then went to her chair, sat down, picked up her book, and started reading.

Son of a bitch! thought Holliday. *She can't see you.*

Certainly not, answered the Spectre. *She belongs to this* world.

But I *can see you.*

You're more than halfway inside my domain already, explained the Spectre.

The hell I am, said Holliday. *I'm laying in a bed in a godforsaken little town in Colorado.*

Only the unimportant parts of you, said the Spectre.

Okay, said Holliday. *Let's get this show on the road.*

That's what I'm here for, said the Spectre.

Quick question, said Holliday. *Do they play poker where I'm going?*

Beats the hell out of me, answered the Spectre.

Holliday frowned. *What are you talking about?*

I'm just your guide between worlds, said the Spectre. *I live in the in-betweens.*

Some guide! snorted Holliday.

Some dentist! shot back the Spectre.

I was a damned good dentist! said Holliday angrily. *I lost my clients because I kept coughing and bleeding on 'em, not because I couldn't fix 'em.*

I know, answered the Spectre gently. *And now, are you prepared for the voyage to that Other Place?*

I've been ready a long, long time, said Holliday.

Then let's go!

Holliday tried to sit up and swing his legs over to the floor. The movement was barely discernable.

I can't do it, he announced.

I'll give you a hand, said the Spectre, reaching out for him.

Holliday looked at the Spectre's hand, missing most of its third and fourth fingers from when he had shot it in April.

Ain't you healed yet? he asked.

Not a problem, answered the Spectre. *I don't feel pain. You know that.*

He tried without much success to grab Holliday's arm and help him up to a sitting position.

Maybe you don't feel pain, said Holliday, *but you don't grip too well neither. Better use your other hand.*

I can't, said the Spectre.

Why the hell not?

The Spectre held up its other hand. It was missing the thumb, the forefinger, and had a large ugly hole in the palm.

What happened? asked Holliday.

It seems that unlike you, John Wesley Hardin had no interest or desire to come with me.

Yeah, that sounds like John Wesley, agreed Holliday. He paused for a moment. *So what do we do now?*

I'll think of something, said the Spectre. *After all, it's my job. I've messed up the Holliday file enough as it is, trading you for the lady in the corner, then making a deal you couldn't keep. I'm not about to screw it up a third time.*

So, like I said: What do we do now?

We sit here and wait. Something will come to me.

Holliday opened his eyes for the last time. He looked briefly at his less-than-elegant surroundings and at the woman reading in the corner—the woman who defied every assumption the world had made of her. Then Doc turned his gaze to the skeletal creature standing at the foot of the bed, awkwardly holding its Scythe in the shattered fingers of one hand, frowning as it concentrated on the seemingly insoluble problem confronting it.

A hint of a smile crossed Holliday's dry, cracked lips.

"This is funny," he whispered aloud, and died.

The date was November 8, 1887. Kate Elder lived until November 2, 1940.

DOTH MAKE THEE MAD

Jane Lindskold

"We hear you're looking for work."

Prudence's hand slid to where one of her six-guns rested, hidden by the folds of her skirt. The man looked respectable enough, as did his companions, but a woman on her own could never be too careful.

"Depends on the work," she replied guardedly.

The man flushed from his stiff collar up. "My apologies. My name is Wayne Chambers. I am the head of a committee that is seeking to hire a schoolmistress for the town of Copper Creek, New Mexico. May we be seated? We can explain over a meal—on us, of course."

Prudence nodded politely. About a half hour earlier, she'd learned she lost the teaching post she'd interviewed for to a newly arrived Boston miss whose blond curls and cultured accent were her best qualifications. She'd retired to the hotel dining room to consider her options, and now options had come looking for her.

Orders were given that made the waitress, who'd sniffed over Prudence's previous request for coffee and a buttermilk biscuit, brighten considerably. She returned promptly with a heaping plate of biscuits and a pot of fresh coffee. Prudence helped herself as introductions went around the table. Wayne Chambers proved to be Copper Creek's banker, as well as its mayor. His companions were Reverend Jenkins and Sheriff Dixon.

"And you," said Wayne Chambers, glancing at a paper in his hand, "are Miss Prudence Bledsloe."

"That's right," Prudence replied. She knew what they were seeing—a severe-looking young woman with brown hair whose most distinguishing features were brown eyes so light some had called them yellow. "I'm originally of the Smoky Mountains of Tennessee. I don't have much in the way of formal credentials, but I can read, write, and cipher well enough to teach your children. I know history and geography. I'll admit, my ancient languages aren't the best, but I can get by with the basics of Latin and a smattering of Greek. I speak and read Spanish, as well as some German and French. I know my Bible front to back and back to front."

"So we were told by Mayor Walters," Chambers said. "We'd asked him to inform us who their selection committee would have chosen if Miss Clarke had declined the position."

Sheriff Dixon, who'd been slathering strawberry jam on one of the biscuits, explained, "Y'see, Miss Bledsloe, we heard they were interviewing, and came to ride drag on their herd. We lost our schoolmaster a few weeks back to an accident, and didn't have time to advertise for a post if the term was to start on time."

"Whoa, now, sheriff," interjected Chambers. "You're putting the cart before the horse." He turned a professional smile on Prudence. "Copper Creek, which we represent, is about two hundred miles from here."

"About two hundred miles from anywhere," muttered the sheriff. Prudence didn't think she was meant to hear, but then she had extraordinarily good hearing.

"The majority of our population does work related to the mines. However, we also have a timber mill and various commercial concerns. Additionally, we are attracting homesteaders who have found the area salubrious. Although we are not served by a rail line, we have hopes for the future. In the meantime, there is a regular stagecoach service."

Reverend Jenkins took over. "Copper Creek boasts a good one-room schoolhouse, newly refurbished. Although the schoolhouse does double duty as the town's meeting hall and chapel, most times, it is the schoolteacher's domain."

They went on, talking up their little town, never knowing that Prudence would actually prefer a small town to a larger metropolis. True, she'd be required to teach children as young as five—even younger, if one included the inevitable three- or four-year-old who was often sent along with an elder sibling to get them out from being underfoot at home. Prudence's older students would include those who would be considered adults in a year or so, but Prudence didn't mind the variety. This was the sort of schooling she herself had had, when she'd had any formal education at all.

"We can offer," Mr. Chambers concluded, "a reasonable salary, in addition to room and parlor board with a respectable widow."

"How about stabling for my horses?" Prudence asked. "I have two."

The men exchanged glances, but when they learned that Prudence would ride to her new post, thus saving them coach fare, they agreed that stabling and reasonable fodder would not be an excessive request.

Prudence asked a few more questions, just so she wouldn't seem too eager, but she'd already made up her mind. That the three interviewers didn't ask more questions of her, she put down to the recommendation of the local school board. After the plates were cleared away, she carefully reviewed the proffered contract, then signed.

"We'll be in town for another two days," Chambers concluded. "If you wish, you may ride out with us then."

Prudence accepted, knowing that the men were offering their protection, but thinking wryly that, if trouble came, she was more likely to be protecting them than the other way around.

The day after her arrival in Copper Creek, Prudence stopped by the stables to check on her horses, Buck and Trick. As she was leaving, she was met by a freckled minx of about nine, with bright copper curls and shining green eyes.

"I'm Eileen Murphy," the girl said. "I'll be one of your students. I think you're gonna be nicer than Mr. Hale. Meaner, too, but that's all for the good. This is one of those times when the friendship of one who shares the blood of those who chase the sun and moon will be helpful."

Eileen darted off before Prudence could even think of a response to this peculiar greeting. Shaking her head, she moved on to inspect her new domain.

As promised, the schoolhouse had indeed been recently refurbished. The walls were freshly whitewashed, and the chalkboard looked to be new. Prudence wondered what had necessitated the replacement of a considerable number of floorboards toward the front of the room. Flooding, perhaps? But the roof looked sound. Maybe someone had spilled paint and replacing the floor had been easier than scrubbing it clean. Mayor Chambers *had* said there was a lumber mill near town.

Prudence dismissed this minor mystery and set herself to inspecting the stationery cupboard. The former schoolmaster— Samuel Hale—had left a number of books, including his lesson plans from prior years. The course of study was surprisingly ambitious, especially for a one-room schoolhouse in the middle of nowhere, but Prudence decided that, with a little cramming, she'd be up to it. Her own education had been, if nothing else, eclectic, and one of the advantages of being mostly solitary, as she had been these last few years, was that she'd had ample time to read.

When, on the first day of the term, Prudence's scholars filed in, she was immediately struck by two things: how strained many of them looked, and how impossibly well behaved they were. Now, it was natural enough for returning scholars with a new teacher to be on their best behavior—but it was equally natural for at least some to test the limits. Prudence had expected the latter, especially since their former instructor had been a man of some years, while she was a young woman.

"As all of you already know, I am sure," she introduced herself, "I am Miss Bledsloe. I have met some of you already, after services or about town. Nonetheless, I think we should begin with roll call. When I call your name, stand up and tell me something about yourself. Let us begin with the youngest scholars."

The little ones, with their charming shyness as they stammered out their names and ages, should have broken the tension. Instead, they augmented it. Mary Filmore, age six, broke into tears when she accidentally introduced herself by her nickname, "Daisy." Two other members of the infant class rose to their feet, then stood in wide-eyed terror, name and age forgotten as they stared glassy-eyed at their new teacher. Prudence pretended not to notice when siblings on the benches behind coached the infants through in their replies.

The middle students did better, but the way they recited name, then age, offering nothing more, reminded Prudence of military drill. Finally, she started asking a question here and there: "Your father's the Reverend Jenkins, isn't he?" "I believe I met you at the dry goods store when I was shopping with Widow Schuler." "Your mother takes in sewing, I think. Your frock is quite a credit to her."

These questions relaxed the scholars, perhaps too much, for when the roll call reached the oldest scholars, a lanky young man whose efforts to grow a mustache made his upper lip look soiled, finished his recitation of "Filbert Ditwaller, age sixteen. My pa came here to work in the mines, and I helped with the diggings this summer" with a pert "and, frankly, I'd rather be there now, than stuck in here."

"I am certain," Prudence replied coolly, "that your parents know best."

She'd forced herself to swallow a more sarcastic retort. Indeed, in a more usual schoolroom, she would have said something quite tart, then set Filbert to spend his recess chopping wood, but these students were already nearly frozen with fear.

And it's not as if they know enough about me to realize that there is actually something to be afraid of, Prudence thought ruefully.

Then she remembered Eileen Murphy's peculiar comment and wondered.

After roll call, Prudence put the older students to written exercises up at the chalkboard, while she ran the younger ones through their rotes. From his lesson plans, Prudence had gathered that Mr. Hale had been an advocate of public recitation. By the end of the morning, Prudence had taken the younger children through their alphabet and counting; the middle children through their times tables and required they read a short passage aloud.

When Prudence released her scholars for lunch, she was certain of two things: the children were exceptionally well drilled, and Mr. Hale had been a believer in both the ruler and the cane. Many a child, after fumbling a letter or number, a phrase or figure, had flinched, drawing back his or her hand inadvertently as if to avoid a blow. Some had actually extended a hand for the anticipated strike.

Nor did the scholars relax when Prudence's most severe penalty was a request that they begin again. Clearly, as they saw it, it was only a matter of time before the pain began.

☆   ☆   ☆

Over the next few weeks, Prudence garnered more about her predecessor. Samuel Hale had been a true believer in the value of education. As the best educated man in Copper Creek, he had set himself above everyone else, although he did condescend to socialize with the minister and the banker, always making clear he was doing them a great honor by sharing his elevated presence with them.

By all accounts, Mr. Hale had been a sternly charismatic man, supremely capable of wooing others to his belief in his own superiority. When asked why he had settled in an isolated town like Copper Creek, Hale had explained that he was a true advocate of democracy and desired nothing more than to elevate those without education to where they might someday join him among the select.

Prudence thought that it was more likely that Samuel Hale knew his belief in violent corporal punishment for the least infraction would earn him rebuke in a larger, more enlightened community. Even those who advocated "Spare the whip and spoil the child" would surely hesitate at caning a six-year-old until her legs bled merely for mixing up the middle of the alphabet, as had been done to Daisy Filmore. Punishments should fit the crime, and only Mr. Hale thought his fit.

Nonetheless, Hale's despotic rule had continued until near the end of the previous school year. Rebellion came when Ralph Bolton, one of the older boys, had refused to stand meekly by while his little brother, Charlie, was caned for forgetting that six times six is thirty-six. Springing forth, Ralph had torn Hale's walking stick from the indignant teacher and broken it over his knee.

As Ralph headed for the door to take Charlie home, Mr. Hale had ordered the door barred, threatening unspeakable retaliation if he were not obeyed. Then, before his horrified students, Hale had seized a chunk of sapling from the wood pile and beaten Ralph about the head and shoulders until the youth had fallen unconscious. The doctor had been summoned, but there was little he could do. Ralph had lingered for several weeks before dying from his injuries.

Mr. Hale wasn't charged with murder, as he might have been, but he had been told his services would no longer be needed.

After that, the accounts varied. Everyone agreed that Samuel Hale had raged that he would take his revenge, but whether his death was an accident, as Prudence had been told, or suicide, as some had hinted, Prudence could not confirm. What she did learn was that Samuel Hale had died in the schoolhouse, and that the extensive renovations had been necessary to remove the mess. There had even been talk of closing the school entirely, and making do with dame schools to be offered in various homes. However, the town fathers of Copper Creek were ambitious for their town, and a school was necessary for proper standing. Moreover, Prudence gathered, they felt that failure to reopen the school would encourage the scandal to linger.

But they made sure to go far afield seeking a teacher, Prudence thought. *No wonder those children looked so frightened. Coming into that schoolhouse, with all the desks returned to their neat rows, must have been like walking back into hell.*

Some women might have grown nervous when they learned that where they stood—although on different boards—a man had died, possibly by his own hand. But Prudence wasn't "some women," nor even most women. She'd seen things and done things that would make the fate of Samuel Hale seem pale and tepid. So, mystery solved—so she thought—she turned her attention to teaching her students not only the four R's, but also that although failure had consequences, those consequences need not be paid for in shame and pain.

Some of Prudence's students grew to love her for being strict without resorting to cruelty. Prudence even grew friendly with most of the older girls, although she was careful to present herself as a mentor to them, rather than a pal.

Others, especially the older boys who had almost admired Samuel Hale for his brutal strength, the way boys often admire a successful bully, resented having to obey a "weak as dishwater" woman. Prudence dealt with their rudeness and rowdiness with ease. These "almost men" were nothing compared to roughnecks she'd come up against in her wanderings.

Rather than argue with the big boys, Prudence set them physical chores to wear them out. When a few refused to carry wood or water, she gently chided them by demonstrating what a mere woman could do. This was somewhat unfair, for there was nothing "mere," about Prudence, but what the boys didn't know wouldn't do them any harm.

Nonetheless, when Filbert Ditwaller—the ringleader of the troublemakers—failed to show for school one day, then a week later the word came that he'd run away, probably with riders escorting a load of ore, Prudence felt relieved. Without Filbert to egg them on, the other troublemakers would certainly be better behaved.

But then Josie Garcia, daughter of the hotel's cook, vanished after lipping off to Miss Bledsloe over an incomplete essay. Next, Henry Schuler, grandson of Prudence's landlady, disappeared after failing to show up for some afterschool tutoring his grandmother had arranged with her parlor boarder. Mrs. Schuler remained as polite as ever, but Prudence heard her sobbing every night when she thought no one could hear.

Prudence began to feel apprehensive both for the children, and for herself. First, she tried searching after dark, using techniques that would have horrified the dwellers of Copper Creek. However, she found neither hide nor hair of any of the missing children. What Prudence did learn, she wasn't about to share, for the knowledge would only increase her own danger. Both Henry and Josie had gone to the schoolhouse shortly before they'd disappeared. Quite likely, that building had been their final destination.

Prudence inspected the schoolhouse carefully, inside and out, wondering if a secret door or hidden room might have been added during the reconstruction after Samuel Hale's "accident." She was in the woodshed, knocking at the back wall, when she was surprised by Sheriff Dixon—an event that in itself showed how worried she'd become. The last time someone had snuck up on her, she'd been five and playing hide-and-seek with her brother, Jake.

"I was thinking," Prudence said, stammering and, to her dismay, even blushing, when the sheriff's shadow darkened the door, "that if we cut a door through here, then no one would need to go outside to fetch firewood. The children have been telling me how incredibly deep the snowdrifts pile up."

"True enough," the lawman drawled, his tone mild, but his eyes narrowed in suspicion. "There's just not enough thaw between storms. Come spring snowmelt, though, you'd be surprised at what we discover."

"I'm sure," Prudence replied inanely, bending to pick up the kindling basket. "It's probably too late in the season to cut a door now. Maybe next year, when the paint is being freshened."

"Maybe so," Sheriff Dixon said, reaching for the basket. "Now, why don't you let me carry that kindling for you?"

But, for all his politeness, from that point on, Prudence was all too aware of how often the sheriff's gaze, eyes narrowed between deep-cut crow's feet, followed her as she made her way about Copper Creek.

When Rosemarie Dubois, a gentle girl of fourteen, vanished after failing her Bible recitation, Prudence's apprehension turned to fear, not only for her missing students, but for herself. People began to look at her sideways. During religious services, despite the chapel being crowded, Prudence sat with a gap on either side of her. Only the fact that Prudence had always comported herself with propriety in public, and that she was boarding with Widow Schuler, who swore (incorrectly, as Prudence herself knew) that Prudence could not have left the house without her knowing, kept anyone from making a direct accusation.

That and the fact that, to this point, no sign of missing children—alive or dead—had been found. The winter snows drifted deeper. Prudence knew that if, when the thaw came, bodies were found, questions would be asked. Judging from how the victims had been chosen, there would be evidence pointing to her. People would believe the accusations that would inevitably follow. After all, their last schoolmaster, a pillar of the community, had beaten a boy to death with a piece of firewood.

Lacking confidants, Prudence found herself talking to Buck when she took the horse out for exercise.

"I could run," she said, "but I don't much like the thought of leaving you and Trick behind. Besides, if I run, I'm never going to be able to stop running, and I'm hermit enough as it is without being barred from every town and ranch. Sure, the West is wide, and has plenty of empty space, but rumor has always had broad wings, and these days it has the telegraph as an ally. Let's face it, there just aren't that many young women with yellow eyes."

Buck snorted, then whickered as he caught scent of another horse. Prudence had already noticed Sheriff Dixon riding a discreet tail. Doubtless if she let on she'd seen him, he'd say he was just keeping an eye on her, as a courtesy, that was all.

Knowing she was out of earshot, Prudence continued her soliloquy. "Worse yet, I don't dare let anyone get so worked up that I find myself facing a lynch mob. Won't make matters any better that I'd probably live through being hanged. The consequences of that just might make being accused of mass child murder seem mild. Besides, who am I fooling? I can't leave those children to be picked off one by one. The only solution—for me and for them—is to find out how this is happening. Then I can reveal the truth or leave a trail of clues so that someone else figures it out. Sheriff Dixon isn't stupid. He just lacks my specialized knowledge."

As she reined Buck around back toward town, Prudence considered what she should do. There was an obvious culprit, but how could Prudence prove her case—especially since everyone in Copper Creek knew for certain that he was dead?

Despite the number of scholars who began to be kept home on the slimmest excuse of weather or illness, Prudence had her stalwarts. First to arrive each morning were Eileen Murphy and her brother, Dylan, freckles faded now, noses pink with cold. They were both middle students, nine and eleven. After her strange statement at that first meeting at the stable, Eileen had shown herself nothing other than a very usual student with a fondness for books of fairytales. Her brother, Dylan, had the makings of a naturalist, and Prudence had started letting him take home some of the illustrated natural history texts.

On the heels of the Murphys came the three Taylor siblings: Faith, Hope, and Charity. Hope was a boy of twelve—a scrappy lad who began every school term proving himself with his fists to those who thought "Hope" was only a girl's name. His older sister, Faith, was one of the girls Prudence would have been happy to count a friend. Charity was nine, intensely proud of having graduated from the company of the "littles." Then came Mary "Daisy" Filmore, with her older brothers, Edward and Daniel. As Prudence stood on the porch, ringing the final bell, the stragglers raced in, brisk and red cheeked from their run.

Each scholar greeted Prudence politely but, as they settled into their seats, Prudence became aware of an unusual air of expectancy. The children kept glancing at each other, not with dread, but with pent-up excitement. Finally, after the morning prayer and Bible verse, Faith, the eldest present, raised her hand.

"Miss Bledsloe, we need to talk with you—about the missing children."

Prudence stiffened, wondering if they were about to accuse her. "Why me? Why not Reverend Jenkins or Sheriff Dixon or Mayor Chambers?"

Faith shook her head, the motion echoed by all the rest. "They wouldn't listen. John and Elizabeth"—she motioned with her head toward the minister's son and daughter—"tried to talk with their father, but Reverend Jenkins told them they were overwrought. He, at least, really believes in God and devils. If he won't listen, why would the sheriff or the mayor?"

Prudence managed a slight smile, although her heart was still pounding unreasonably fast at what felt like a near miss. "Very sensible. All right, I'll listen, but I reserve the right to take your problem to the proper authorities, if that's what I feel is needed."

Faith looked at Dylan Murphy. "Go on. Tell her."

"Did they tell you anything about Mr. Hale?" Dylan Murphy rose to his feet as if called upon to recite a lesson. "How he, uh..."

"Had an accident?" Prudence arched her eyebrows to indicate she was open to other explanations.

"He didn't. I mean, have an accident. He..." Dylan gulped, but continued after Faith gave him an encouraging smile. "You know how me and Eileen get up early to help our da about the stables? Well, I finished first, and was going bird's-nesting. There're swallows who like the eaves here at the schoolhouse. When I got here, I saw the door was open. It shouldn't have been, since school was out for the summer..." He gulped again, then finished all in a rush. "I went to check, even though I was right scared I'd find Mr. Hale there. Well, I did, and there's no way what happened was an accident. He'd drawn all over the chalkboard and the floor: weird letters, full of angles. He had cuts on his arms and face. There was a ruler sticking out of his chest."

Dylan paled and covered his mouth with his hands as if trying not to vomit. Eileen took pity on him, and turned a pleading gaze on Prudence.

"You've got to believe this bit, Miss Bledsloe. Dylan doesn't tell tall tales. He told me everything, even after the grownups suggested that he keep quiet. He said that the worst part was that he could swear that Mr. Hale was still alive, alive and grinning at him, grinning wide like he'd won some tremendous prize."

When Eileen fell silent, tugging her brother down to sit next to her, the scholars from littlest to biggest stared at Prudence.

Certainly at least some of them were waiting for her to reassure them, to tell them that they were excessively imaginative or, in the words of Reverend Jenkins, "overwrought." As easy as it would have been, Prudence couldn't do that. She paused long enough for them to feel sure she was carefully considering what Dylan and Eileen had confided, then she inclined her head solemnly.

"Very well, I believe you. Why tell me?"

"We don't know who else to tell." Hope's voice broke with simple desperation. "No one would believe us about how evil Mr. Hale was when he was alive. Then we had the bruises to show. They just said Mr. Hale was strict, that he had our brightest futures in mind. Why would they believe us now that he's dead?"

Since Prudence had entertained similar thoughts, she could only nod. "Very well. Tell me everything you know—even what you guess."

Now the words tumbled out: reports of too-coherent nightmares, of whispered threats that, if they didn't keep up with their studies, Mr. Hale would return to give them a proper "schooling." How, before he had disappeared, Henry Schuler told Dylan Murphy that Mr. Hale was trying to make him come to night school to catch up on his lessons. How Rosemarie Dubois had taken to sleeping with her Bible, but how her mother had forbidden her to do something so disrespectful of the Good Book, and, then, the very next day, Rosemarie had vanished. The tales were all outrageous, all—given what Prudence suspected about Samuel Hale—too much a confirmation of her fears.

When the scholars had finished their reports, Prudence sent them outside for morning recess. They dashed out with lighthearted enthusiasm, the burden of their special knowledge transferred from their shoulders to hers. Only Eileen Murphy lingered.

"What will you do, Miss Bledsloe?" she asked, her expression far too wise for a child.

Prudence spoke her half-formed thoughts. "Mr. Hale doesn't seem to care about me, only about the students. If I am to reach him, then one of the students must be used as bait to bring him out of hiding. I don't know if I dare do that—both for the child and, quite honestly, for myself."

"Because people are talking," Eileen responded seriously. "Most of us have spoken up for you, but there are those—the lazy ones who don't want to come to school, the scared ones, those big boys who don't like that you don't respect them as nearly men—who feed the nastier gossip. But those of us here today, we all trust you. If you ask, any one of us would act as bait. You see, we all stood by when Ralph Bolton was killed. That haunts us as much as does Mr. Hale."

"Guilt's a powerful force," Prudence agreed, knowing how true that was from long experience. "But why do you all believe I can do something about Mr. Hale?"

Eileen answered Prudence's question with one of her own. "Did I ever tell you I have the second sight? There is a time to set a wolf to guard the flocks."

She grinned impishly, tugged her knit cap over her red curls, then skipped from the room to play in the winter sunshine.

Although Prudence protested, Charlie Bolton insisted that he be the one to act as bait.

"Mr. Hale killed my brother. And he hates me worse than he does the rest, 'cause not only did I get shut of him, he lost his job because of me and Ralph. He might suspect a trap, but if it's me, he won't be able to hold back."

"Won't your parents be keeping a close eye on you?"

Charlie's lips pressed into a thin line. "Not a bit. They've gone strange since Ralph died. I think they blame me."

Or if they don't, you do, Prudence thought. *Another reason to take the risk. I won't have this child bearing that burden.*

"Very well, Charlie," she said. "Start reciting those times tables. If you mess up around times six, I'm going to speak very sternly to you. I might even give you lines."

One element of her plan that Prudence had not confided to the students was that it included permitting Samuel Hale to capture Charlie. She needed to track the schoolmaster to his lair if she were to have a chance to find the other children—children she felt certain were still alive, if not entirely sane.

So it was that when Charlie, moving as if sleepwalking, came trudging across the packed snow and entered the schoolhouse, Prudence locked the schoolhouse door behind them both. Then, a shadow among shadows, she drifted after the boy. Behind the teacher's desk an opening gaped amid the new floorboards.

Prudence felt no doubt that this was the precise location where the hate-maddened schoolmaster had shed his own blood. The opening led to a staircase that twisted around itself in a jagged spiral with angles like those of summer lightning.

Putting one hand on the bannister, Charlie stepped into the dark mouth in the floor and began his measured descent. Afraid that this uncanny portal might exist solely for the boy, Prudence waited only until Charlie's head had vanished beneath the floor, then hastened to follow, matching her steps to his, so that it would sound as if only one person paced the metal treads.

The sides of the spiraling stair were lined with thousands of elegant leather-bound books, each of which bore the name of Samuel Hale on the spine. Samuel Hale on geometry. Samuel Hale on Shakespeare. Samuel Hale on the Roman Empire. Samuel Hale on pedagogy. Samuel Hale on occult knowledge. No title repeated twice, each volume a testimony to the wildly impossible dreams of an ambitious man.

After a descent that seemed to continue for hours, the stair ended at the doorway into nightmare version of a one-room schoolhouse. Chained to uncomfortable iron desks were the missing scholars: Filbert, Josie, Henry, and Rosemarie. Eyes dull, the four children recited in cacophonous unison fragments of the rotes they had failed in Prudence's class. Every time they made a mistake, fire flared around them and they screamed—an action that caused more flames, more screams, more errors. Despite this, not a one showed a single blister or even reddened skin. They remained neat and tidy, a teacher's ideal of perfect students.

At the front of the classroom, Mr. Hale stood at a podium more suited to a fine university rather than a one-room schoolhouse. He was much more handsome than Prudence had expected: tall and stately, clean-shaven, his golden hair shaded with silver at the temples. Only his eyes hinted at his revenant existence, for their natural color had been replaced by the dancing orange-red of an infernal furnace. Hale's body showed none of the mutilations he had inflicted upon his mortal form, although perhaps his dark broadcloth suit hid the scars. His left hand gripped the podium, with his right he held a ruler that he tapped in cadence with the scholars' recitations.

When Charlie hesitated at the doorway, Mr. Hale's head swiveled. The motion was inhuman, a twist like a doll's head that involved neither neck nor shoulders. The expression of evident scorn made his handsome features ugly.

"Times six still giving you problems, Charles?" Hale boomed in a deep, sonorous voice. He motioned for Charlie to seat himself at a vacant iron desk where the chains shifted in anticipation of their prey, like rattlesnakes waiting to strike.

When Charlie obediently stepped over the threshold, the rattling chains struck out at him. Prudence grabbed the boy by the collar and swung him behind her. The chains struck her with enough force that she staggered, but their fanged heads could not piece her winter clothing, although her favorite cloak would never be the same. The chains hissed in metallic disappointment and coiled back, granting Prudence a brief second during which she could attend to Charlie.

Prudence's grip had broken whatever spell that had held the boy. He began screaming in terror, and might well have frozen where he stood, but Prudence pushed him onto the stairs.

"Charlie! Run! Leave this to me."

Charlie didn't hesitate to argue or offer heroics. As he fled, his footsteps rang against the stair treads. Alert to any pause that might indicate that Hale's magic had freshly ensnared the boy, Prudence's sharp hearing caught a muffled thudding from far above. Prudence realized that this was someone pounding on the schoolhouse's locked door. Time was running out—at least if she wished her own secret to remain undiscovered.

Prudence stepped into the schoolroom, placing herself between the four youngsters and Mr. Hale. "I have come for my scholars, Samuel Hale."

"*Your* scholars?" Hale sneered. "I have sacrificed myself to Knowledge, thus I claim these four, body and soul. Who are you, a weak and undereducated woman, to challenge me? I went to Harvard! I went to Yale! You would coddle them, *love* them, pamper them to their eventual detriment."

"Undereducated I may be," Prudence replied coolly, "but weak… Well, now. You're just showin' your own ignorance."

With that, she began her change. Human was only one of the three forms that Prudence Bledsloe could call her own. The other she chose most often was that of a wolf. One of the joys of living in the western wilds was that, unlike "back East," a pawmark barely merited notice. But there was a shape that rested between, a form that no one—not even the one who wore it—could term other than that of a monster.

This was the shape Prudence chose now: the shape of the werewolf. For this encounter, she had not thought it wise to rely upon her guns, for she did not know how far the sound of shots fired might carry. Nor did she know if bullets could harm the undead thing into which Mr. Hale's knowledge of the dark arts had remade him. She'd long learned to choose her attire so there would be no unseemly tearing when she changed. Pleats on both skirt and blouse spread to accommodate her altered build.

Although she did not wish to use her guns against Hale, as a werewolf, Prudence possessed natural armament. Her mother had warned her about the dangers of tasting either human flesh or that of wolves but, whatever else Samuel Hale might be, he was no longer human—nor was he a coward. As Prudence's form reconfigured, Hale lifted high the ruler he held in his right hand, the straight edges glinting like razors. He lunged at her, stabbing for her heart as once he had stabbed into his own.

The ruler blade found its target, slicing through Prudence's bodice, deep into her heart. Hale shrieked in satisfaction but, although Prudence shuddered at the impact, swallowing a howl of agony, the ruler was not silver. The wound could hurt her, it *did* hurt her, but it could not kill her. She forced her transformation to continue until she stood in her new form: wolf head atop human torso, that torso covered with fur and possessed of much larger hands that curled from the weight of claws. She still possessed a woman's long hair, caught in a bun, still a woman's figure, but these softening touches only made her seem more a monster.

"Yellow-eyed daughter of Fenris!" Hale declaimed, leaping back from Prudence with inhuman agility. "I hoped to weaken you before you had gained your monstrous form. Do you think that I, high-priest of Knowledge, do not know what will harm you?"

Prudence was perfectly certain that Hale did know what could harm werewolves. However, he'd already demonstrated that he had no silver weapons. What could he do to her?

Holding his razor-edged ruler high, as a wizard might his wand, Samuel Hale declaimed in a steady rhythm that recalled the rotes he set his students. Prudence's Latin wasn't very good, but she knew a spell when she heard it. She braced herself for what might come.

A hissing clatter caused Prudence to wheel to one side, although she took care that she did not turn her back on Hale. The iron chains were sliding from Filbert Ditwaller, releasing him from his bondage. As the hulking youth staggered to his feet, his glazed expression transformed into one of purest malice—a malice Prudence knew instinctively was Hale's own, for no boy could be capable of so much hatred toward one whose worst offense was a refusal to grant him an adult rank he had not yet earned.

Samuel Hale had chosen his weapon well, for Prudence would not harm one of those innocents she had risked so much to save— nor could she risk that in his eagerness to grab hold of her, Filbert might unintentionally injure one of the three still entrapped. Darting past Filbert, Prudence gathered her skirts and loped down the aisle toward the back of the classroom. Chortling madly, his malice colored with something like lust, Filbert stalked after her, chunky hands outstretched to grab Prudence, his lips moving in an obscene parody of a kiss.

Even with her bulky werewolf's form, Prudence possessed a degree of grace, and easily dodged the youth. If she could hold off Filbert long enough for those above to arrive, well, her own doom would be assured, but she had never expected to live a long life. That was rarely given to monsters such as herself. At least the children would be saved.

But Hale's perfidy did not stop at turning Filbert into an extension of his will. He was laughing now, laughter which punctuated an insane lecture.

"Do you know, Miss Bledsloe, why silver is necessary to harm a shapeshifter? Do you know why we needed to reach the modern era for silver to become a truly effective weapon?"

Prudence noticed that Filbert's attack became less focused as Hale spoke. The youth still followed her, his hands reaching out to grope, but the motions lacked intensity. If she could keep Hale's attention split, she might be able to avoid injuring Filbert.

Intensifying the drawl she had brought with her from the mountains of Tennessee, a drawl she had trained herself to speak without, Prudence replied, "Well, now. No, I can't rightly say I do. My mama jus' told us that silver weapons can be fatal to our kind, and that we should take care when we must carry silver coin and suchlike."

In response, Hale's own accents became more precise, more

blueblood. "Silver affects werewolves because it is the moon's metal, polishing to shining white, tarnishing to inky black. Just as the moon is the orb of change and can rule the shapeshifter, so the moon's metal is the only one that can do lasting and permanent harm to a ferocious monster such as yourself."

"That's right sensible," Prudence said, making her tones unctuously impressed. "I ain't never heard such a way of seein' it."

And she hadn't. Maybe someday she'd spare the time to find out if there was anything to Hale's theory but, at the moment, Filbert had backed her into a corner while Hale chanted in Latin again. This time she recognized the words for silver and for Moon and knew to fear the worst.

Had there been moonlight outside the windows before? Prudence didn't remember, nor did she particularly care. There was moonlight now, wide silver beams that were being sucked in by the razor-edged ruler Hale held in his right hand. But what he held wasn't a ruler anymore. The ruler had transformed into a pistol—a pearl-handled model, a bit effete compared to the six-guns that Prudence herself preferred—but definitely a pistol and one that she did not doubt would shoot silver bullets. Heck, Hale probably wouldn't even need to worry about reloads.

"The lore that silver can harm shapeshifters includes references dating as far back as the Middle Ages," Hale lectured. "However, its usefulness as a weapon is a modern development. This is because silver is comparatively soft—at least when compared to steel. Silver makes a fine ceremonial blade, but is hardly practical for repeated use in battle. Bullets, however, can be made of even softer metals, such as lead."

He leveled the pistol at her, taking careful aim. "Prudence Bledsloe, I command you, accept the moon's kiss and die!"

But Prudence was not about to stand there and wait for him to pull the trigger. A skilled shot herself, she knew how often amateurs misjudged even carefully aimed shots. What she couldn't risk was that Hale's aim relied less on his ability with a pistol than upon black magic. She leapt onto the nearest desk, so that Hale's shot, rather than penetrating her heart, passed through her skirts.

Filbert had stopped moving, forgotten as Hale struggled to reorient the unfamiliar weapon. Prudence leapt from the desk onto the youth, knocking him flat so that a chance shot would not harm him. Then she raced away, leaping erratically from desktop to floor, rolling in the aisles, doing everything she could to keep Hale from drawing a bead on her. Her task was complicated in that she tried to keep the three children, whose droning recitations and erratic screams had continued throughout the confrontation out of the line of fire. Hale's next shot missed, but the one after perforated her dress's mutton-leg sleeve, another drilled a hole through the bun that rose behind Prudence's wolf's ears.

Hale was so focused on shooting Prudence, that he didn't notice that the werewolf's erratic progression had a purpose to it. Leap by leap, she was drawing closer to him, well aware that even an unpracticed marksman could hit at close range. Hale cackled madly as he leveled the pistol, aiming for her snarling wolf's muzzle. Rather than dodging back or side to side, as Hale clearly expected, Prudence dropped to her hands and knees. Her long skirts kept her from moving easily on all fours, but her forearms were strong enough to hold her as she kicked off with her feet against the floorboards and leapt at the schoolmaster.

First, Prudence tore the pistol from his hand and threw it across the room. Then she gripped the schoolmaster's skull in one clawed hand, and braced his spine with the other. Bending his neck, she bit down through gristle and spine until the laughter abruptly stopped. There was no blood, for what remained of Samuel Hale held neither blood nor tears nor pity. Nonetheless, the eyes in the nearly severed head remained horribly alive and the mouth continued to declaim.

"Nothing shall end my triumph over death!" Hale shrieked.

"You sure?" Prudence drawled as she tore Hale's head free from the shreds of flesh and tendon, then threw it so that it smashed into the chalkboard and broke into flinders. The eyes rolled free from the shattered bone, their unholy light gleaming for a final long moment before going out—hopefully forever.

Before the scholars awoke from their daze, Prudence hastily reverted to her human form, then draped her cloak to cover the damage to her attire. She was unchaining Rosemarie when she heard pounding feet on the treads of the supernatural stair. Charlie ran directly to Prudence, clutching her skirts to reassure himself that all was well with her. A few paces behind, Sheriff Dixon paused wide-eyed in the doorway, Reverend Jenkins peering around him.

"When I heard you'd given Charlie lines, I feared the worst," the lawman explained, "as did Reverend Jenkins. I kept watch and, when I saw you go toward the schoolhouse, I paused long enough to bring the reverend—for not only did I wish to catch you in the act, I needed a reliable witness. What the hell is this?"

Momentary eloquence lost, the sheriff gestured to where the shriveling but still recognizable corpse of Samuel Hale sprawled headless on the floor of his dark temple to knowledge. Reverend Jenkins sprinkled what was probably holy water on Hale's corpse. If he sprinkled a little on Prudence as well, she forgave him.

The minister continued the sheriff's account. "When we arrived at the schoolhouse, the door was locked. We peered through gaps in the curtains, and it seemed that the building was empty. We were inspecting the woodshed and outbuildings when Charlie threw open the door and shouted for us to come with him. Can you tell us what has happened?"

Prudence stood tall within her cloak, doing her best to look schoolmistressish and prim. "I believe the Bible has words that speak to the case of Samuel Hale far better than ever they did to that of Saint Paul."

The sheriff looked confused. Reverend Jenkins gave a dry cough that was not quite laughter. "I believe I know which words you mean."

"Well, I don't," Sheriff Dixon said. "Mind enlightening me?"

As one, minister and werewolf quoted, "'Much learning doth make thee mad.'"

SUNLIGHT AND SILVER

Jeffrey J. Mariotte

The trip west from Trinidad, Colorado, should have been easy, but a stinging rain had fallen after Caleb Willows set out. The trail turned slick, the wagon's wheels caught in the mud, and by the time he camped that first night at the base of Purgatoire Peak in the Sangre de Cristo Mountains, he already regretted accepting the commission. His horse was miserable, he was miserable, and he figured whatever he earned from the job would be spent replacing the animal and laying in enough firewood to keep his home warm, because he wanted never to be so cold again.

Having anticipated problems with the weather, Caleb had packed his equipment carefully in its cases, then wrapped the whole in oilcloth to keep it dry. He'd placed it in his buckboard, directly behind his bench so it wouldn't slide around. He wished he could have treated himself the same way.

The second day dawned frigid but clear, and with the morning sun at his back, throwing his shadow out past that of the horse, he worked his way up the mountain toward Naciemento.

He had been on the road for less than an hour when he saw a single figure ahead of him, on foot, carrying a saddle, a rifle, and a knapsack. The man heard him and turned around, waiting. Caleb slowed the wagon and eyed as bedraggled a human as he had ever seen. Wet mud caked the cowboy's boots and dappled his jeans. Even his once-proud wide-brimmed hat drooped shapelessly around his head.

"If you're headed—well, anywheres, I'd sure appreciate a ride, mister," the cowboy said.

"Hop aboard," Caleb replied. "I have business in Naciemento. As far as I know, that's the only place this road goes."

"That's more or less where I'm headed. Heard tell there might be some work up that way."

"Not ranch work, I don't think. I believe there are some farms around town, though."

The man put his things in the buckboard's bed, taking care not to get mud on Caleb's gear. "I'll take what I can get. I got busted out of the outfit I was with, and somebody told me there's someplace hirin' up the mountain."

"Well, you're welcome to ride along with me. I'm Caleb Willows."

The cowboy climbed onto the seat beside Caleb, tugging off a leather glove and offering his rough, weathered hand. "Nate Murdock," he said. "Thanks for the hospitality." He put the glove back on as he sat back. "That rain yesterday 'bout drowned me in my boots. The horse my old boss guv me slipped on a wet rock, busted her leg somethin' fierce. Bone stickin' out through her flesh. Pain she was in, this far away from any doctorin', tweren't but one thing I could do for her. Hated to do it, and not just because it left me afoot. But she's sleepin' peaceful now, out of pain forever."

"It's the right thing to do," Caleb agreed. Just the same, if his horse had broken a bone, he wasn't sure he'd be able to do it. He had a rifle in a scabbard lashed to the bench, but he was no shooting man. A scholar and an artist, he bought his meat from a butcher. He had packed the rifle mostly for show, to discourage potential robbers. And he had heard bears stalked these mountains.

Murdock was an amiable enough passenger, and they chatted along the way, reaching Naciemento at midafternoon. Although not quite September, early autumn colors carpeted the slopes surrounding the town: bright yellows, rich oranges, deep browns, and reds so vivid they almost hurt the eye. Not for the first time he wished he knew a way, short of hand tinting, for photographs to capture the true colors of nature. He saw the world with a photographer's eye, and had often said that of all the senses, he prized vision the most. He would rather be struck deaf, or be unable to smell or taste or even feel, than lose his sight. Only his eyes truly mattered.

He let the remarkable view delay him for only moments, though. The sun had reached its zenith, and then some, and he wanted to be able to work before it vanished behind the western peak. He urged the horse forward, and soon they reached the town proper.

"Ain't the friendliest place, is it?" Murdock observed.

He was right. People on the street glanced at them and hurried on their way, but offered no words of welcome, no smiles. Caleb felt under suspicion from the moment of their arrival. He noticed that the town's one church, a large adobe structure, looked abandoned, with scorch marks shooting up its outer walls. He saw two saloons, a few stores. Down a side road, he spotted a laundry and a place that might have been a brothel.

"No, it's not," Caleb said. "Are you sure about looking for work here?"

"A man's got to work, he wants to call himself that," Murdock answered. "I'll find somethin', or keep movin' on. Thanks again for the lift."

"You're welcome. If you're ever down in Trinidad, look me up. Caleb Willows Photographic Arts, on Commercial Street."

"I'll do that." Murdock hopped down, grabbed his things from the back, and stood in the street, turning in a slow circle, as if unsure which way to go.

Caleb missed him already. Given the sense he got that Naciemento didn't particularly welcome strangers, he appreciated the man's friendliness all the more, as well as the sense that he knew how to use that rifle he carried.

His client, Hodding Benson, had given him directions back in Trinidad, and soon he pulled up in front of the Benson homestead. It was a small house at the edge of town, with a lush garden behind it. Mounted on the wall beside the door was a bell, nearly the size of Caleb's head. Something to use to call in their child at suppertime, he supposed.

Too bad they'd never again need it.

The day's relative warmth had vanished, as if Nate Murdock had carried it with him, and Caleb cursed the cold as he carried his equipment into the house. But it was warm inside, for which he was grateful. Hodding Benson explained, "I left it chill for three days, as must be. I started a fire just this morning, as you suggested."

"Good," Caleb said. "Has the house a basement, or another windowless space that I can close off? I need a working space with as little light as possible, and another, where we'll pose her, with as much light as possible."

"A contrarian, then," Benson said. "There's a parlor you can close off, and I believe the most light comes in through the girl's bedroom windows."

"Good, good. We can pose her on her bed, if you like. Or we can bring in a lounge or chair from some other room, if you'd rather. I think it best if she's sitting up, to some degree."

"Then a chair might be most natural," Benson suggested.

"As long as it's of adequate size. Some subjects are not easily posed."

"I'll help with her."

While Caleb made additional trips out to the wagon to bring everything in, and got his darkroom gear set up in the parlor, Benson carried a chair into the bedroom, drew back the curtains, and went to fetch Addie, his daughter.

As Caleb had feared, she was hard to pose.

Benson hadn't left Naciemento until the day after she'd passed, and it had taken him a full day on horseback to reach Trinidad. Upon his arrival, he had made inquiries, and wound up hiring Caleb for the job. But Caleb hadn't been able to leave until the next day. So four days had elapsed. Benson had kept Addie cold, but Caleb had warned him that she shouldn't appear frozen, so for the last several hours, he'd been warming her. That had the unfortunate, but unavoidable, effect of stiffening her in a different way—one he hoped would leave her slightly more malleable.

As they worked to prop her in the chair facing the window, a favorite doll clasped in her hands, Benson gasped. "Your hands," he said. "Did you suffer frostbite on your journey?"

Caleb looked at his hands; he was so accustomed to the black fingertips and dark nails, caused by the silver nitrates he worked in, that he tended to forget about them until someone else noticed. "An occupational hazard, I fear," he said. "The photographic chemicals stain them. They're always that way."

Benson nodded. "Guess so. How does she look?"

"We're close," Caleb said. "Have you a cross, or any other religious articles that you'd like to be in the image with her?"

"We don't truck in those things here," Benson said sharply.

Caleb couldn't be sure if by "here" he meant in their home, or in Naciemento, with its one vacated church.

"Fine, then. Perhaps you could wait in another room, now. I shouldn't want to be disturbed while I work."

"Of course," Benson agreed. "Her mother's been beside herself. She's resting now; she's hardly left her bed for days. I'll look in on her. Call if you need anything."

When Benson had left the room, Caleb rearranged Addie. He angled her chin up a little, as if she'd heard something outside. Taking a spoon from an equipment bag, he used its handle to pry her upper eyelids open and to push the lowers down. Dampening his fingertip with saliva, he rolled her eyeballs until the pupils were in their proper position. With the sun reflecting off them, she would look almost lifelike. He'd had to paint eyes to appear open in the past, and it never looked quite real.

With her in place, he hurried back to the parlor, racing the sunlight. In the darkened room, with a cloth spread to keep out any stray light, he worked quickly, by feel. He poured collodion on a sheet of glass, turning and tilting it this way and that, expertly coating it. That done, he closed it in a box and carried it through the house, to the bedroom. As he went back and forth, he heard a woman's weeping from another room, and the soft rumble of Benson's voice trying to soothe her.

Back in the bedroom, he pulled forward the focus window, inserted the coated plate, and closed it with a snap. He took one more look at the girl—eleven years old, petite, with dark tresses that held natural waves, large dark eyes, and full lips—and opened the aperture.

Later, he presented Hodding Benson and his wife, Madeleine, with an albumen print showing their daughter holding her doll. He had captured her, he thought, in blacks, whites, and every shade of gray. They were pleased; she looked, Madeleine said, "Almost as she did in life."

"That's the point," Caleb explained. "A camera is a kind of time machine. It freezes a moment in time, and then that moment is forever in the present. Never gone, never lost, it's always now."

"Can you stay the night?" Benson asked. "It's too late to leave. You can take Addie's bed; we'll put her out for the night, and bury her in the morning."

Caleb had hoped for such an invitation. He didn't want to

stay in the dead girl's bed, necessarily, but neither did he want to spend another night in a tent, out in that weather.

"That would be most appreciated," he said. "I'll be no trouble."

"Before you go, let me ask around," Benson offered. "I expect I can drum up some more business for you."

"Here in Naciemento?"

"We're suffering an influenza epidemic," Madeleine said. She rubbed her nose, red and raw from days of crying. "It's been terrible. So many gone."

Caleb turned back to her husband. "You didn't tell me!"

"You didn't ask," Benson pointed out. "You asked if she was disfigured, as if by accident or misadventure. It was nothing of the sort."

"Still, you should have told me."

"No harm done," Madeleine said. "We aren't sick, and she can't harm you now."

Caleb looked out the window. Full dark had descended, and a fierce wind blew. Leaving was out of the question.

Besides, if so many had passed, he might be in a position to earn enough here to make the trip more than worthwhile.

He stayed that night, and attended the burial in the morning. No one spoke of God, nor did Caleb see any clergy. Hodding Benson mumbled a few words over the open grave—Caleb thought he heard "Ashes to dust, dust to clay," but that didn't make sense—as a few other townsfolk stood in a ring around him, chanting in a language that Caleb had never heard before, sibilant and strange.

Benson introduced him to some other families, and he ended up staying for three more days. The dead were mostly children, seemingly scores of them. Their grieving parents wanted tintypes; cartes de visite; and albumen prints, for albums, or frames with braided locks of hair and other treasured objects. Although reluctant to let him into their homes, they wanted the service that only he could provide. Others closed doors and shutters when they saw him coming, and if those houses contained more of the dead, he would never know.

During daylight hours, he worked without pause. Move to another home, set up, pose the departed, prepare the plates, make the image, print it, and then start all over again. He felt a sense of tragedy wrap around him like a stifling cloak on a scorching day. All those children. People died every day, he knew. Children, too. But he had never had to confront it like this, so many, all at once. It wore at him, made his heart feel heavy in his chest.

He expected that he would never get the sour-sweet smells of death and flowers out of his nose, and that he would conflate the two forevermore.

And he thought the town the oddest place he had ever been. Each house had a bell, like the Bensons' had, but he never heard them toll. The people he met seemed friendly enough, but strangers never spoke, only looked away when they saw him. The sun rarely penetrated skies like molten pewter, and the air never warmed. Every minute he stayed, he couldn't wait to get away. But before he left Naciemento, he had made as much money as in a good month, back in Trinidad.

At home, the photographs from Naciemento brought Caleb Willows some measure of fame. Wealthier residents hired him to memorialize their children while they were alive, and to make records of weddings and other occasions, as well. For those without the resources to spare, a photograph of a dead loved one was a necessity, lest that person's face fade from memory with time. Caleb's studio on Commercial Street grew, he took on assistants when necessary, and his reputation spread.

He considered it his due. He had, after all, studied in New York under Mathew Brady, Jeremiah Gurney, and Alexander Gardner. That training had prepared him well for his career, and he had resolved to take his talents west, to a place with less competition and unlimited opportunity. He had hoped to make his living in portraiture of the living, and perhaps to make excursions into nature, to photograph scenes of the West that heretofore had only been shared through paintings and etchings. But the dead kept him busy.

He found himself wondering sometimes if Nate Murdock might drop by. He'd enjoyed getting to know someone so unlike himself—a real westerner, not some eastern transplant like himself. But he had never seen the man again after dropping him off on Naciemento's main street.

One evening in late winter, a few months after that Naciemento trip, an assistant named Elspeth dusted and straightened the photographs displayed in the shop's front window. As she did, she made a little noise in her throat, then said, "That's odd."

"What is?" Caleb asked.

"This photograph. I could have sworn there was a child on this chair before."

"There is," he said.

"There's not."

Had she gone blind, or been imbibing spirits? He stormed over to the window and snatched the frame from her hands. Soft light fell through the window from outside, onto the print. "You're right..." he began. Then he let the sentence trail off.

He studied the image he had made of the Benson girl. Addie.

All it showed now was a chair, empty but for a doll seemingly forgotten there by a child who'd wandered off.

"There must be some mistake," he said. "Did you replace this one with another?"

"Never!" Elspeth cried. She was young, in her teens, and her fair cheeks flushed when she was angry or embarrassed. She had only been in his employ for a couple of weeks; he'd found it more than passingly hard to retain help. "I don't like those images of the dead. I only touch them when I absolutely must."

"Well, I never took this one," Caleb said. "Put it in back; I'll have to find something else to replace it in the window."

He had, by now, taken enough photographs of the dead in Trinidad to fill the window many times over. But clients passed by the studio on a daily or weekly basis, and he didn't want to remind them of their losses. Instead, he used the Naciemento images to promote that particular service.

He went to his files. He had made multiple prints of each—those he sold to the families in that bizarre little town, and others for his own use. But when he found the prints where Addie Benson should have been, she was missing from them all. Only the doll remained, on the chair where he knew he had posed the dead girl. As much trouble as that had been, he wouldn't have misremembered it.

Nor would he have wasted his efforts photographing an empty chair. But he held in his trembling hand the proof of it.

He studied the other prints. Most appeared as he remembered them, but on another—he thought it was a boy named George, eleven years old, who he'd posed with his favorite drum—the image of the boy had faded to a ghostly shade of itself, through which could be seen the sofa on which he'd lain.

Caleb had several prints of this one, as well, and the same effect showed on each.

He knew photographic technique as well as anyone, he believed. He didn't understand the chemistry behind it all—he knew how to mix and use the appropriate chemicals, but he was no experimenter or inventor. Possibly this phenomenon was due to some flaw in his chemicals, or the way he stored the prints. He didn't think so, but he was at a loss for any other explanation.

Back in New York, Caleb had seen some of William Mumler's "spirit photographs," in which ghostly images appeared around those living beings who posed for them. If trickery had been employed, Caleb couldn't spot it. The war had seemed to increase the public's appetite for word from beyond the veil of death—little wonder, since so many knew someone who had gone to battle and never returned. He had never heard of vanishing subjects, though.

He wondered whether he should report it to the photographic section of the Cooper Union for the Advancement of Science and Art, in New York. Union experts could examine the photographs and perhaps discover the explanation that evaded his own grasp. In the end, he decided against it; he couldn't bear the thought of being labeled a fraud by those experts he so respected.

More weeks passed. Each time he looked at those prints, more of the children had faded away. Never the adults; they remained as distinct as ever. But the children disappeared, with only whatever object he had posed them with—a spray of flowers, a hoop, a favorite hair bow—remaining to indicate they had ever been there at all.

Then one day, he had another visitor from Naciemento. The man introduced himself as Jacob Banister. "You came to Naciemento in the early fall, and photographed some of our townsfolk," he said.

"That's right. Memoriam photographs." He wasn't sure whether he should say anything about the vanishing images.

"Can you return?" the man asked. "My son . . . there's been another wave of illness, and nobody in our town has your skills, or your knowledge of the necessary processes. I want a photograph of my son, before it's too late, and I know others will want them as well."

Caleb didn't want to spend another few days like the last time, working from dawn to dusk capturing images of one dead child after another. But only the photographs he'd taken in Naciemento were subject to the mysterious fading; if the trip gave him the opportunity to figure out why, it would be worth it.

Besides, the last one had paid well. He agreed to leave the

next morning, and Jacob Banister thanked him, then headed back home.

In the morning, Caleb loaded his things into the buckboard, shoved his rifle into the scabbard, drew on a hat and a coat, and left Trinidad behind.

Once again, the weather turned while he traveled. The calm, sunny day turned windy. Clouds whipped in from the north, heavy and dark. As he climbed higher into the hills, snowflakes started falling. They were featherlight at first, but then turned wet, sticking to Caleb's coat and to the ground. Before he finally reached Naciemento, the drifts were two feet deep, sometimes more, and the snow kept coming. He'd made it in a single day, but darkness surrounded him. He would have to start in the morning.

The town seemed little changed. He ascribed the nearly empty streets to the snowfall, which was taking on blizzard proportions. Gaslights burned in some windows, other houses stood dark.

The weather did nothing to improve his spirits. He was wet, chilled to the bone. Even the horse shivered. Caleb was growing to hate Naciemento. This would be his final trip to the godforsaken place, he swore.

He found the Banister home, where Jacob and his wife Eliza mourned the loss of their son, John. When they invited him in, he explained that he couldn't begin work until the morning. They'd expected as much, and had prepared a room for him.

In the fresh light of morning, Caleb posed John with a favored ball and bat. The print came out perfectly, he believed; young John looked almost glowing, as if he could step out of the image and engage the viewer in conversation. Well satisfied, the Banisters introduced Caleb to neighbors whose infant had succumbed just the day before. Once again, he worked tirelessly to meet the demand of so many deaths.

After several days, he ran out of dead children to photograph. The epidemic had passed, and he was free to return to Trinidad, his pockets stuffed. But he had one more thing to do before he left.

He rode to the Benson house, climbed down from the wagon, and knocked on the door. At first, no one came. He pounded harder, and finally heard footfalls on the other side. The door creaked open and Hodding Benson stood there, looking somewhat older than he had before. His hair had gone gray in the interim, perhaps from grief.

"Mr. Willows!" Benson said. "I heard you were back in town."

"So you remember me?" Caleb asked.

"Of course. You're the photographer, from the city."

"So I am. And do you recall why I visited before?"

Benson nodded. "To take a photograph of our dear Addie."

"And did I do so?"

Benson laughed nervously, as if facing a madman at his own door. Perhaps he was, Caleb thought.

"But of course you did," Benson said.

"And did I then photograph dozens of others, over the next few days? All of them victims of the influenza epidemic that swept through your town?"

"Indeed you did. And you've just done it again, haven't you?"

"I did. It's not a pleasant task, and one I won't do again. The next time an illness strikes here, you'll have to find another photographer."

"Oh," Benson said. "Hmm. That's unfortunate. You won't change your mind? We'll always pay you well."

"I can't do it anymore. I refuse. There are others who can do what I do."

"It's up to you, I suppose," Benson said. "But unfortunate, just the same."

"There's something else I wanted to talk to you about, Mr. Benson, if I might. May I come in?"

Benson looked over his shoulder, as though someone behind Caleb might be able to shed some light on his odd behavior. He glanced back over his own shoulder, then said, "I suppose."

He backed out of the doorway, and Caleb went inside, stomping snow off his boots.

"Do you still have the photograph?" he asked. "May I see it?"

"I don't believe so," Benson said. "No."

"You don't have it? It's the only image of—"

A child's voice sounding from the parlor interrupted him. "Who is at the door, Father?"

"It's just a man I know," Benson said.

Caleb had been sure the Bensons had only the one child, only months ago. They could have had another in the interim, but not one as old as this one sounded.

Then the child—a girl—stepped into the entryway. "Go on to your room, Addie," Benson said.

"Addie?" Caleb repeated. "Another Addie?"

"Another?" Benson asked. "What do you mean? It's just our Addie."

"But she was... I don't understand."

"What's to understand? You've seen children before."

"But not..." Caleb wasn't sure how to say it, in front of the girl. He remembered those big, dark eyes, the waves in her hair, even her lips, cherry red now instead of pale in death. "Never mind," he said. "I-I have to be going."

"As you will," Benson said. He followed Caleb to the door, and stepped outside. As Caleb climbed into the wagon, Benson started ringing the bell beside the door.

"What are you doing?" Caleb asked. "Stop that infernal ringing!"

Benson ignored him. He kept ringing the bell. From other homes, more bells began to ring.

Caleb urged the horse on. The sooner he got out of this place, the happier he would be.

But as he traveled down the town's main street, people started flooding into it, blocking his passage. He recognized many of them; the families he had met on his first visit. Parents who had been grieving the loss of their children glared at him.

Worse, those children were with them.

He had spent more time looking at the children than at their parents. Posing them, exposing the plates, developing the images, making the prints. Then their photographs had surrounded him in his studio—until they had faded away. He knew the face of every child he'd photographed on that trip.

And he recognized them now, surrounding his buckboard, some of them still with the earth of their graves dusting flesh and hair and clothing. The horse balked, sidestepped, then simply halted and refused to move again. Too many people filled the street. They didn't say anything to him, but seemed to whisper in that bizarre, sibilant tongue he remembered from Addie's funeral, sounding like nothing more than dozens of hissing snakes.

"See here!" he shouted. "Move aside! Out of my way!"

No verbal response came, but the townsfolk swarmed closer. Caleb realized with horror that some—the families he had photographed for on this visit—carried the prints he had made for them. He reached for his rifle. A man—Caleb recognized him as the father of a pair of twins who had both passed on the same day, during his first trip—leapt onto the buckboard and wrested the gun from his grip, hurling it far from the wagon.

"What's the meaning of this?" Caleb demanded. "Let me pass!"

Then the children clambered onto the wagon. Small hands grabbed Caleb's clothing, his hair, his flesh. He tried to bat them away, but they outnumbered him. They hauled him from the wagon and into the mob, where adults joined in. Caleb struggled in vain as they bore him toward the now-open doors of the seemingly abandoned church. Inside, candles glowed.

Caleb screamed, fury and terror warring within him. The townsfolk seemed oblivious to his cries. They carried him inside the church. There was nothing left of God in the place. The pews had been piled in a corner, along with the altar.

Then they forced him to his knees, at the front of the church. Before him, hanging on the wall in a cruel mockery of crucifixion, he recognized Nate Murdock. The cowboy's flesh had mostly been eaten away, but enough remained to give an impression of the man he'd been. His chest had been ripped open in the shape of a cross. His misshapen hat, clothing, and boots lay on the floor nearby.

All around him—on easels, leaning against the walls, or just lying on the floor—Caleb saw the photographs had made on his previous visit. In these prints, though, the children hadn't faded away.

Or they had come back—as the children themselves had.

A couple of men tore Murdock's corpse from the wall and tossed it unceremoniously to one side. Caleb saw that it had hung from a sharp hook, like a butcher's meat hook, mounted to the wall and driven through the cowboy's back.

As he knelt there, held down by dozens of hands, the hissing whispers swelled into chants. The families of the recently deceased came forward, along with the children who Caleb had photographed before. Each child claimed his or her own portrait, and the new families replaced those prints with the ones Caleb had just made.

Caleb started screaming again as realization dawned on him. His photographs weren't meant to memorialize the children of Naciemento. They had a more devilish purpose. They were totems in an ungodly ritual—a ritual that would bring the dead back to life.

With all the photographs in place and the way cleared, they lifted him up once again. Fighting, struggling, trying to writhe away from the hands, large and small, carrying him toward that hook, he understood.

Part of that ritual included sacrifice.

The chanting voices rose to a feverish pitch. They turned Caleb around, lifted him near the wall. He wanted to close his eyes, but he couldn't. He took the scene in, as if through an open aperture, and it inscribed itself upon his soul in his last moments—the parents, the children, his photographs, the candles. The open church door on the far side of the crowd, offering an escape he would never know. He saw it all in black and white and shades of gray.

Every shade of gray.

Then the hook bit into his flesh, and agony blinded him.

And even in death, his eyes stayed open.

PINKERTON'S PREY

Frog and Esther Jones

George E. Hoinschauffer cradled his glass, staring mournfully at the rotgut liquor the refreshment-car bartender had poured him in response to George's request for whiskey. Instead of a rich, amber color, the liquid in his glass shone clear, with only a light brown tint. Where George hoped for an intense bouquet of floral and smoky scents, it assaulted his nostrils with the odor of rotting barley.

"Problem, George?"

From the barstool next to George (and slightly above, given their difference in height), Leonard Neilson looked at him with a wry smile. George shook his head, but said nothing. Neilson shrugged, then tipped his own glass into his mouth with an easy grace that George at once both envied and reviled.

The two men could not have been more dissimilar to look at. Whereas George was short, somewhat pudgy, and certainly balding, Neilson looked tall and lean, and had a thick crop of salt-and-pepper hair peeking out from under his hat. Both wore vests, but where George's had the crisp-clean look of new silk, Neilson's had been made of coarse woven cotton, and showed fray about it. Both wore white shirts underneath; George's had been cleanly pressed, Neilson's had possibly been laundered sometime in the last month. Neilson wore a faded, dusty derby; George's balding pate shone bare.

"The trick," Neilson said, "is to let it hit the back of your throat while spending as little time as possible on the tongue.

This ain't the sipping whiskey you New York folk are used to; this here is to be drunk *solely* for effect."

George nodded, then tried bravely to mimic Neilson's smooth shot. He felt the liquid burn his tongue, then the back of his throat. The rancid-barley finish bloomed in his gullet and coated his mouth; he came up coughing.

"There it is," said Neilson. "I like you, George. You're a game sort of fellow. Most of you hoity-toities tend to get upset when presented with a beverage such as this."

"Hoity-toity?" said George. "I've seen what we're paying you for this job. You've no call to—"

"Whoa, there. I am an *employee,* Mr. Hoinschauffer. A servant of the Pinkerton Detective Agency, which in turn has been hired by South Mountain Mining, Limited. You've seen what the agency is getting paid for my services; I get a percentage, is all."

"How much of a percentage?" asked George, curious.

"Enough to keep me in bad whiskey. Not enough to keep me in good," said Neilson.

George had little response to this, so the two men sat for a while in silence. Neilson seemed perfectly comfortable with that and motioned to the bartender for another round. George felt increasingly awkward sitting next to Neilson and not conversing.

"So...do you think Lorents is actually coming?" George asked as the bartender refilled Neilson's glass.

"Ha!" said Neilson. "George, for the last three months Randall Lorents has hit every one of South Mountain Mining's payrolls. This here is number four. What in the world makes you think he's going to stop?"

"Well, maybe he knows we hired you to—"

"I sure's fire hope not!" said Neilson. "The anti-summoner branch of the agency does *not* like to advertise its activities. George, he don't know I'm here. And he sure as hell don't care. Not only is he going to hit this train, I would place five dollars that he does so in the next"—at this, Leonard Neilson pulled a rather nice, if worn, pocket watch from his vest—"three minutes."

George's back stiffened, and his eyebrows rose at this sudden pronouncement. "Three minutes!" he said.

"Yup," said Neilson calmly. "That's when we'll be in the Lido Gap. Most likely place for an ambush." Neilson turned back to the business at hand as George stared at him in disbelief. The tall Pinkerton simply slammed the second glass of whiskey down, offering no further explanation.

"But—shouldn't you—I mean—three minutes! Shouldn't you be *doing* something?" said George. He'd always known the train would get robbed, but the sudden immediacy caused goosebumps along both his arms.

"Like what?" asked Neilson, calmly.

George could not believe the insufferable laziness before him. "Mr. Neilson, your agency is contracted with South Mountain Mining to protect its payroll from Randall Lorents and—"

"No," said Neilson. His voice was quiet, but it held a cold edge that arrested George's power of speech, "it ain't."

"It isn't? Then why are you here?" George found himself stunned by the man's demeanor. The Pinkerton Agency had a reputation for getting the job done, not for this. "You have to—"

"Read your contract again, George. It says absolutely rat-squat about protecting this here payroll."

"But—"

"No," said Neilson, gesturing again to the bartender. The squealing sound of brakes suddenly intruded upon the conversation, and George snatched at the bar as the sudden deceleration nearly threw him from his stool. Neilson, however, appeared to handle the shift with a peculiar grace.

"That's them!" said George. "Go!"

Instead, Neilson calmly repeated his gesture to the bartender. The man held the bottle, looking at George, but poured.

George's irritation grew, and he felt his face going red. "You cannot simply sit here and drink while—"

"George," Neilson said in that low, cold voice. "That's exactly as I intend to do. And do you know why?"

"I cannot imagine," said George, his volume raised, "what madness would cause you to—"

"The why," said Neilson, his voice staying calm, "is because the Anti-Summoner Division of the Pinkerton Detective Agency never contracts to *stop* a robbery."

"But—" spluttered George. His frustration began to turn to panic as the sounds of shouting, and sporadic gunfire, echoed down to the two men from the front area of the train. Someone had to *do* something.

Neilson threw back his third shot of whiskey, then waved the bartender off a fourth. "George, I am a single man. I am equipped with both a .45-caliber revolver and a lever-action rifle. I flatter myself that I am proficient in the use of these tools. But this train is, as we speak, being robbed by Randall Lorents. A summoner, equipped with the ability to draw on the boundary between our worlds to power his magic. He can move forces and things about as he wills or summon entities from outside our world to his side as allies. And he has planned this robbery out. He is ready."

"Yes!" cried George, seizing the moment. "That's why *we* hired you."

"You hired the agency because the Anti-Summoner Division has a demonstrated record of returning bounties on summoners. Bounties, Mr. Hoinschauffer. Not protection. The only way to deal with a summoner is from as great a distance away as one is comfortable making the shot. I have no intention that Lorents know anything until my bullet pierces his skull, which is why we are here enjoying one another's company instead of getting killed like a pair of fools."

Cheering erupted from ahead of them, and soon after a half-dozen men rode fast past the car, heading back down the tracks out of the Lido Gap, in the direction from whence the train had come. George's anger gave way to fear as the summoner and his men passed within feet of George's own person, separated only by thin dining-car windows.

Neilson stood from his stool and walked behind George to the door of the refreshment car. George could only watch as the Pinkerton grabbed his rifle from where it leaned up against the wall. Neilson nodded at the bartender, and then stepped outside. From behind him, George heard the bartender politely cough. The noise catapulted George into motion at last. Anger surged back, covering up his fear as he slapped a bill on the counter and moved to follow the Pinkerton.

Neilson had stepped off the train and moved three cars down, to a stable car. As George stormed toward him, the tall man unlatched and pulled back the door, before leading his own horse onto the bare dirt.

"Well," said Neilson in his matter-of-fact tone, "They took the bait. *Now* I can get to work."

George knew he wasn't in control of himself. He let the anger direct his words, losing any semblance of being a proper gentleman and pointing furiously at the hired gun. "*That's* your plan? Go after them?"

"Well," said Neilson, pausing for a moment, "yes, I reckon that when you boil it to its core, that's my plan. Go after them, find myself a nice little perch overlooking whatever valley they choose to rathole up in, and kill me a summoner. There's some parts at the end involving getting paid and spending a fair amount of time with the ladies at Miss Sandy's up in Buffalo Creek, but you've struck at the heart of it."

"I'm coming with you," George said, firmly trying to regain control of this situation.

"Well, now," said Neilson. The Pinkerton removed a cheap-looking cheroot from inside his vest and placed it in his mouth. "That does strike me as a singularly terrible idea. I would advise against it." He struck a match.

George let his semblance of self-composure give way, and he yelled at the target of his ire. "Mr. Neilson! You, sir, are contracted with South Mountain Mining, Limited, of which I am a representative. I have already observed you idling your way through a robbery, and now you announce that your plan is simply to ride off into God-knows-where to do God-knows-what before you claim that you have completed your end of the contract. I will not have this, sir. If my company acknowledges your performance, it will be because I have witnessed it, as I no longer trust that you intend to act in good faith!" He stared at Neilson, trying to display his resolve. Instead, his hands shook, and his breaths came only by panting.

Neilson rose an eyebrow toward George for several seconds. Then he took a deep draw from his cheroot and held it for a moment. The Pinkerton tilted his head backward and released a billow of smoke upward to the sky, then looked back down at George.

"George," Neilson said, still in that calm, low voice. "You are a damned fool. But I reckon that's just your nature, and there's little to do about it. And I also reckon further that there ain't a way I can stop you mounting up and riding after me when I go. That is, no way short of shooting you here and now, an act to which I ain't inclined. So, get your horse and let's get on with it."

George straightened his jacket, regaining his aplomb. By his tally, he'd actually won this round with the imposing Pinkerton. He stepped toward the stable car, and as he began to enter he heard Neilson's voice behind him.

"But, I will remind you again that the Pinkerton Agency has no contract to protect anything here. That's the payroll, sure, but that also means I ain't obligated to save your fool self when you do something stupid. My job is to kill Lorents. All the rest is gravy, far as I'm concerned."

In the privacy of the stable car, George allowed himself a flash of panic. He was about to go after a wanted outlaw—a summoner of great power—with no training, a single derringer pistol, and this lazy, indifferent man at his side. But he could not let Neilson get the better of him, and *he* had been tasked with seeing to the payroll.

"Your warnings are noted, Mr. Neilson," George said, hoping his fear did not show in his voice. He led his horse out of the stable car, then huffed and clambered into the saddle. "Now, shall we be off?"

Neilson's method of tracking completely mystified George. He'd read several stories, in the digests of New York, of men who could tell the path of an enemy by no more than a bent twig, or a subtle imprint. He'd secretly delighted in the tales of men who could put their ear to the ground to find a herd of buffalo, or an enemy troop of cavalry.

But Neilson did none of these things. He did not dismount. He simply . . . rode. The two men kept a steady canter, around this rock and through that valley, based on some guidance that George E. Hoinschauffer simply could not understand.

It was not until the sun began to approach the horizon that Neilson dismounted. He tied his horse to a tree and gestured for George to do the same. He handed George a bucket, then pointed at the small stream running through the valley.

"Fill it, and let it warm a bit before you give it to the horses," Neilson said.

"Shouldn't we push on?" asked George. "They got a head start on us, and likely they're still going." He peered ahead, trying to get a sense of their next destination.

"Not likely," said Neilson. "They're just on the other side of that ridge, there." The tall Pinkerton pointed to a small ridge to their . . . North? South? In these hills, George had lost all sense of direction.

"How do you—"

"Because the tracks sent them down there, and I pulled us over here tonight. Unless I miss my guess, you should keep your eyes on that ridgeline."

Neilson rubbed down the horses while George fetched the water. Upon returning, George saw a thin stream of smoke from the other side of the ridge.

"Now, that's about right," said Neilson.

"We caught up to them?" George said, still bewildered.

"They left that train at a full gallop," said Neilson. "Gave them a head start, sure, but it was still a damned fool piece of riding. Winded their horses. Never ride a beast that *fast* unless you don't need him to go very *far,* you see?"

"Oh," said George. The pulp-digest heroes galloped everywhere, but what Neilson said made perfect sense.

"So, tonight we'll go without a fire," said Neilson. "No sense letting them know where we are. They'll be getting drunk. Successful robbers *always* get drunk. Tomorrow morning, when Lorents is hung over and stumbles out his tent to make water, I'll be up on that ridge with a rifle. He clears his tent, I shoot him in the head, contract fulfilled. Nice and simple."

This plan sounded like it offered minimal risk to one George E. Hoinschauffer while providing a reasonable chance at recovering the payroll, and therefore he found it acceptable. The two lay out their bedrolls as the sun descended and gave way to night.

"Where *did* you learn how to track like that?" asked George. "The agency is known for hiring skilled men, not training them."

"Rode with Buford back in the war," said Neilson, calmly.

"General Buford? You wore the blue?"

"Don't sound so surprised," said Neilson. "Not every rough-and-tumble horseman put on a gray uniform. And Buford was one of the best."

George nodded. "Well, that explains why you'd spend your time hunting summoners," he said after a moment.

"How do you figure?" asked Neilson, a note of genuine curiosity in his voice.

"Wasn't Buford there on the First Day at Gettysburg? When that Reb general—what was his name—Heath? Heth? The man summoned a devil to kill General Reynolds."

"Oh, that mess?" asked Neilson. "I guess so. But it ain't like we had no summoners either; that demon killing General Reynolds was just a fluke. Don't believe what you read in the *Times*; summoning's just a tool, like being good with this here rifle. Some folk use it to rob, some to help. The agency pays an extra twenty percent if you go after summoners, and a man who can shoot from a long range makes a good living that way."

That had to have been about the most positive thing George had ever heard anyone say about the practitioners of the dark arts. As to the rest, George found himself disappointed. He wasn't sure why; every other business that men engaged in, his own included, they did so in pursuit of money. Why should being a Pinkerton be any different? And yet, it felt like a life this dramatic should have an equal amount of drama motivating it. Instead, it turned out Neilson functioned like every other man. You offer to pay him, he does a job.

"Now," Neilson said. "If you don't mind, we have something of an early morning tomorrow, so best we turn in."

And with that, the Pinkerton rolled over onto his side and promptly began to snore, leaving George to stare up at the stars as they began to peek out through the twilit sky.

As he did, his thoughts began to turn. This man had waited through the robbery back at the train. Oh, he'd given his reasons, such as they were, but he'd ignored his real purpose. He'd allowed George to come along with him only after George held his contract hostage. And he'd been careful to warn George that George might not live through this little trip.

Now, maybe Neilson was playing straight. But all George had as firsthand evidence was a fire on the other side of the ridge, and that said little about who had started that fire or how. And if Neilson put a bullet into George, and then regretfully reported him as a casualty, he could claim the contract complete. After all, George was a man who'd been well and duly warned of the dangers and ignored them to his detriment. South Mountain Mining would pay the Pinkertons, the Pinkertons would pay Neilson, and Lorents would remain at large.

The more he lay there, wrapped in his own thoughts, the more George knew he was right. Neilson had no intention of claiming a bounty or filling a contract. Not when all he had to do was kill George.

George drew the small derringer he kept in his vest pocket, cocked it, and pointed it at the back of Neilson's head.

No.

He had to be sure. If he were going to murder the man, in the middle of the night, while effectively lost, then he'd need to *know*. He slipped the hammer back down and stood from his pallet, leaving his questionable companion at rest.

Then he began to walk up to the ridgeline, using the moonlight as his guide.

Once atop, he looked over a small cliff and saw three large tents made of thick canvas down below, arranged in a wheel-spoke pattern. A stovepipe poked its way through the top of each tent's roof, happily puffing its smoky release to the night.

How in the hell had they—thought George, then interrupted his own train of logic. *Right. Summoner. That bastard can bring the comfort to them; no need to weigh a horse down with a sleeping roll when you can simply summon a full tent with a bed inside.* The thought that Randall Lorents and his bandits lived a life of comfort, regardless of where they were, irked George to no extent. The bandits in the digests always lived lives of hard misery, not this kind of portable luxury.

An owl hooted, flying above George. Another, which sounded as though it were perched up the ridge from George, hooted in response. Then a third from below the ridgeline. George couldn't remember if he'd ever heard owls communicating like this, and wondered whether the species was particular to—

And then he found himself in a tent.

No showy flash of light accompanied his teleportation. No slow bending of time, and no sense of anything out of the ordinary happening. One moment, he pondered the sounds of the owls around him. The next, he was sitting on the ground, within the confines of a canvas tent, looking directly at the little Franklin stove in its rear.

"So," said a voice behind him. "You'd best introduce yourself and tell me why you should live through the night."

George tried to spin around, but it was a difficult maneuver while still seated on the ground. Instead, he executed something of a graceless half-fall, half-spin maneuver, coming to rest on his elbows facing the front of the tent and the man who stood in it.

Whoever had drawn Randall Lorents's wanted poster had done a spot-on job. The bandit stood tall and broad shouldered. His face was coated in stubble, and his dark hair had been slicked back along his head. The faint smell of booze lingered about the tent, but Lorents did not appear mightily affected.

"I, uh—I..." George said.

"You don't look much like a bounty hunter," said Lorents.

"I'm not," said George. "I am a duly appointed representative for South Mountain Mining."

"And you are here to...what, exactly?" asked Lorents. "Negotiate with me? Is there something you have that I'm not already taking?"

"Uh..." George, still trying to get his grasp on the situation, improvised. "Yes, exactly. The company has authorized me to offer you a, well, let's call it a tribute of sorts. One hundred dollars a month. No risk, no work, just a nice, easy cash stream, and you let our payroll through."

Lorents stared, then stood up and clapped slowly.

"That," said Lorents, "was a very smart play. You saw the opening, and you went for it. I do believe I am impressed at your level of gumption, Mr. Representative. But I know when a man right in front of me is lying. Given your situation, I take no particular offense to it, mind you. Now, you *are* a representative of the company, that much is true. So, the question becomes...what will they pay to get you back? And, come to think of it, who the hell else is out here with you? Because they sure as damnation didn't send you after a summoner packing only this little toy."

George's derringer appeared in Lorents's hand. George patted at his vest pocket in futility as Lorents stuck the small pistol under his belt, crosswise in the front.

"So, let's see. Boys!" Lorents shouted.

A couple of gruff-looking men stepped into the tent. Lorents gave them a quick gesture toward George, who shortly found himself hauled to his feet and dragged outside.

"You men keep a watch on our Company Man, here. I need to look for something else."

And, with that, Lorents sat on the ground and closed his eyes. From atop the ridge, George once more heard the hooting of owls.

"A *Pinkerton*," said Lorents. "Now *that* makes sense. Let me guess: long bullet in the morning, kill me before I have a chance to get my Sense up? George, you are traveling with an awful clever man, and it is to my great benefit you had to see me for yourself. Now, let's take care of this."

Lorents took out a stick and scribbled some symbols on the ground. George looked at them, but could not make sense of the strange, angular writing. Lorents then took out a large hunting knife and stepped to George. A lance of pain shot through George as Lorents quickly opened a sizable gash through both shirt and flesh on the back of George's left forearm. George inhaled through clenched teeth, desperate not to show weakness before this predator.

"I am sorry about that," said Lorents. "But I need me some blood, and better it come from you than me. Now, step over here. That's a good lad." The two goons dragged George over to the markings, and Lorents held George's arm above them, shaking it so that he bled onto the script. George saw an additional three men stepping out of their tents to watch as his blood dripped to the earth.

"That'll work," said Lorents after a moment. Then he took a deep breath and, after only a moment, the prone, snoring form of Leonard Neilson, Lorents's assassin-to-be, appeared on the ground, laying atop the symbols. George felt his last shred of hope vanish, as he knew now that nothing was going to save him from captivity and likely death at the hand of these bandits.

Neilson, bereft of his warm bedroll, gave a snort, then groggily opened his eyes.

"Well," said Lorents to the waking Pinkerton, "likely you weren't imagining that the two of us would ever converse."

Neilson sat up straight, blinked a couple of times, looked around, and saw George held captive. He gave a half shrug.

"Nope," said Neilson to the bandit, still blasé. He fetched one of his cheroots out of his vest pocket, then struck a match and lit it, taking a deep draw. "I can't say as this here falls under the category of Plan A."

Lorents gave a chuckle at this. "You're a man knows how to keep his demeanor, Mr. Pinkerton. I respect that."

Neilson shrugged, taking another puff off his cheroot, then looked past Lorents at George. "Mr. Hoinschauffer," he said, "I ain't too sure what happened, but I reckon you and a mighty large dog have recently engaged in unnatural relations with one another. Do you have a mind as to how exactly you plan on living through this here predicament?"

Lorents turned back to George with a wry smile on his face.

He gestured toward Neilson with both hands, as though encouraging George to answer.

George could think of nothing. He'd ceased to hope, and merely hung his head, then shook it.

"Right," said Neilson. "Well, I am sorry about that, George. I do believe that this is your fault, but still I ain't pleased at the consequence."

"I would imagine not," said Lorents.

Then Neilson whispered something. George couldn't hear what it was, and apparently neither could Lorents, as the big bandit crouched down to look at Neilson up close.

"What was that, Mr. Pinkerton?"

Neilson didn't say anything. He didn't move, except to look Randall Lorents, master of dark magics and scourge of South Mountain Mining, directly in the eyes and smile.

Then George's derringer, ensconced in the waistband of Lorents's pants, simply discharged itself into Lorents's leg.

"Son of a—" Lorents shouted, as he staggered back up with his good leg.

"Mr. Lorents, what I said was," said Neilson, rising to his own feet, "you half-trained bandit summoners never seem to think about what others can do to you. No defense. You thought you had a captive in front of you, and you left yourself wide open."

The owls hooted once more from behind George, closer now than they had been before. In front of him, Neilson slapped Lorents on the leg, directly on the wound. Then he pushed up his left shirt sleeve with his bloodied hand, coating a tattoo that appeared to be more of those strange symbols. As the feathers of the owls rustled above George's head, a massive bear appeared between Lorents and Neilson, pushing Lorents to the ground. Now in George's line of sight, the owls dove for the ursine combatant. The bear easily swatted down one owl, then another, but the third dove for its face, clawing at the bear's eyes. The big animal reared back on both legs, roaring, as the sharp talons blinded it.

"Jesus!" said the big man holding George's left arm. The goon to George's right remained silent; neither appeared motivated to move into a fray between the two summoners.

Lorents had his eyes closed. George couldn't tell what exactly he was focused on, but he felt a surge of hope as Neilson sidestepped around his ursine companion with his revolver drawn. Behind

Lorents, a gateway opened in the air, and something massive and shadowy formed on the other side. But Neilson's gun belched fire and thunder, and Lorents's body simply crumpled to the ground as the portal behind him closed without anything emerging.

The other bandits, including the ones holding George, finally reacted. Judging by the panicked noises the ones next to him were making, George figured they knew any move would be pure desperation.

Each one reached for his pistol. None of them cleared their holster.

Neilson didn't even move the barrel of his gun; he simply pulled the trigger five more times, and the bandits all fell with Neilson's lead in their skulls.

George staggered backward from the carnage, stumbling to the ground.

"You, you're—" he said, looking at Neilson and gibbering.

"A summoner?" asked Neilson, calmly thumbing bullets back into his revolver. "Yes, I am. The Pinkertons don't hire non-summoners to chase summoners; that would be suicide. But we don't let it be known, as folk don't really like summoners now the war's over. And we certainly don't want them we're chasing to know what we can do. So, it's agency policy to keep this secret, you understand."

"Well, yes," said George, thinking about it. "That makes sense. And you've collected your bounty, here. Well done, I suppose."

"No," said Neilson. "You don't understand. The agency *does not allow it to be known*. Generally, we ain't accompanied on these little expeditions. I did try to discourage you, George. Told you not to come. Then, after that didn't work, I tried to do things the way the agency *tells* people we do them. Tried to get the long shot on Lorents without showing my powers off. But you mucked that too, didn't you?"

"Well," said George, "I'm sorry about that. But you should know that I'm very pleased with your eventual result."

Neilson sighed. He shook his head as he slapped the revolver's cylinder back into place. Then he pointed the big hand-cannon point-blank at George's face, and George felt his stomach drop in a sudden rush of understanding.

"No," said the Pinkerton, one final time. "You're not."

THE RELAY STATION AT WRIGLEY'S PASS

Derrick Ferguson

Sebastian Red paused at the Wakarusa River for two reasons. To let his horse, Ra, rest and take a long drink of water. The second, and equally important, was to get his bearings.

It had been quite a while since he'd been in this part of Kansas. And while getting lost rarely happened to him, it still was a possibility. As a rule, Sebastian generally tried to stay out of Kansas. He found Kansans in general to be a cantankerous lot. But the purpose that brought him here was dire enough that Sebastian could put aside his dislike for the locals.

He slid off the large bronze stallion, ran his hand down along his body until he reached the ebony tail—a match for his mane—and gently slapped him on his rump. Ra trotted over to the river and bent his head to drink. Sebastian Red pushed back his sombrero, shook his head to allow his dreadlocks to hang around his shoulders. Small silver and gold coins the size of pennies and hand-carved wooden idols the size of his thumb were woven into the dreadlocks, but not as decorations. They were protective charms, blessed with prayers and enchantments by his wife while she braided them into his hair the night before he left her and their daughters.

Sebastian Red squinted at the sun, fixed his position, and contemplated where he was in relation to his destination. He reckoned another two hours or so would bring him to the relay station at Wrigley's Pass. It was a destination he'd never expected to willingly go to.

Sebastian heard the soft crackling behind him at the same time Ra did, and the horse's warning whinny sounded at exactly the same time he whirled around, smoothly drawing the huge black seven-shot revolver from the well-worn holster on his right leg. One hand hovered over the hammer of the Leone Nightmaster while Sebastian waited until he knew for certain he would be firing upon an enemy.

The man and woman emerging from the thicket didn't look dangerous. But long ago Sebastian learned that out here, everything and anything could be dangerous. "That's far enough. State your names and your business."

The man raised both hands to shoulder height, standing in front of the woman. From their style of clothing, Sebastian took them for easterners. "We're not armed," the man said tentatively, but with no fear. "May we approach?"

"Yeah. But slowly." Sebastian lowered his gun, but did not replace it in the holster.

The man and the woman walked toward him. Slowly, as commanded. "My name's Finch. Harry Finch. This is my wife Melody. We're from back East. New York."

"I can tell. What are you doing all the way out here? And unarmed at that."

"I don't know anything about firearms. I hired a man to guide us out here. A day ago, he robbed us, took our wagon," Finch said, embarrassment clearly below his calm words. "He did leave us food and water, though."

"You're lucky he didn't blow your fool heads off."

Finch managed a half-wry smile. "That's what he said as he rode off. Said that it was a sin to kill fools and women, and that's why he left us alive."

Mrs. Finch looked at Sebastian Red. Dressed in his buckskin, the wide-brimmed, sweat-stained sombrero with the tall conical crown, necklaces gold and silver woven together hanging around his neck, she seemed to regard him as if he were something escaped from a carnival show.

"You still ain't said what you're doing all the way out here in the middle of nowhere," Sebastian asked, to get her eyes off of him.

"We were on our way to the relay station at Wrigley Pass."

Sebastian Red's eyes narrowed, and the hand holding the big

black revolver raised again slightly. "Why you want to go to that station? What you know 'bout it?"

And Mrs. Finch spoke up. "We've heard stories."

"Lotta stories about a lotta things. What stories you heard about that station?"

The Finches swapped looks before the husband answered for the both of them. "There's a stagecoach we want to catch there. We understand it's a stagecoach that can take you anywhere you want to go."

Sebastian returned his gun to the holster. He rested his left hand on his other weapon, a scabbarded sword. "Depends on where you want to go. I heard tell that stagecoach may drop you off somewhere you might not cotton to."

"We'll take that chance," Melody Finch replied in a voice leaving no room for Sebastian Red to continue to debate the subject. "And it seems to me we've answered enough of your questions, mister. How about you answering some of ours?"

"Fair enough. I'm Sebastian Red, for starters." He walked closer to shake Finch's hand.

"And what's your business in these parts, Mr. Red?"

"Luckily enough for you, I'm on my way to the station."

"Is it close?" said Mr. Finch, finally getting in a word.

"Not more than a couple of hours. Mrs. Finch can ride on my horse while we walk, Mr. Finch."

"That's mighty kind of you."

Sebastian shrugged. "We're goin' the same way. No trouble on my part."

Melody Finch spoke up again. "And are you going to Wrigley's Pass Station to meet the stagecoach, Mr. Red?"

"Me? No, ma'am. That stagecoach can't take me to the place I want to go. Least not yet."

"Then why are you going there?"

"There's a man I need to see. Got some business with him."

Melody looked at the gun and sword riding on his hips in well-worn holster and scabbard. "Are you some sort of gunfighter, Mr. Red?"

"There's some who might call me that. Me, I only fight when there ain't no other way out of a situation."

"A bounty hunter, then?"

"I hunted some bounty in my time. Reckon I'll hunt some

more. But my business with this man don't got to do with no bounty. Now, I suggest we get moving while we still got plenty of light. We'll have time for palaverin' when we reach that there station."

"That's it?"
"That's it."
Sebastian stood on the left side of Ra, lightly holding the reins. Finch stood on the stallion's left. Mrs. Finch rode sidesaddle, holding onto the wide pommel.

The relay station consisted of four buildings, all constructed from lumber. The main building, the stable, the outhouse and a storage shed. It wasn't as dirty or as run-down as other relay stations Sebastian had seen, but then again, this wasn't a relay station like those others. Finch assisted his wife in dismounting from Ra while Sebastian lifted his voice; "Hello the station!"

After about two minutes the front door opened and a stocky, full-bearded man stepped out onto the porch. He squinted at the trio and the horse through square-framed glasses. He shouted back, "Who be ye?"

"My name's Sebastian Red and this be Mr. and Mrs. Finch. We ask the hospitality of the station."

"Come on ahead, then. Hospitality has been asked and so must be given."

"Seems like a whole lot of jibber-jabber," Finch said. "We could have just walked up and knocked on the door."

"And very likely been blown outta your shoes by a shotgun blast through the door. Back East, them politenesses are what you do. Out here, you stop a respectful distance from any dwelling and make yourself known first." Sebastian let go of the reins and pointed at the stable. Ra trotted in that direction.

The trio walked up to the main building and went on in, the two men removing their headgear as they crossed the threshold. The building had a genuine wooden floor—another surprise. A fire crackled merrily in the fireplace. A communal round table occupied the center of the room. Several comfortable chairs had been placed around the fire. More sat by the window where those waiting for the stagecoach could look out if that was what they wished.

The bearded, bespectacled man stuck out a hand. "Name's Conroy. I manage this here station."

Sebastian took the older man's hand, looked at him narrowly. "Pleased to know you. How long you been managin' this station?"

Conroy looked back at him just as narrowly. "Quite a while, Mr. Red. Quite a while. Come on in and make yourselves to home. It ain't fancy, but it keeps out the cold and the wet and that's enough."

Finch shook Conroy's hand. "You've got food and drink, I assume?"

"Got a pot of slumgullion on the stove. You're in luck. I caught a couple of rabbits in my traps last night, so there's fresh meat in it. There's water and there's corn liquor to drink. Name yer cherce."

Mrs. Finch was quick to say; "We'll both have water!" Her husband nodded in confirmation, but judging by the expression on his face he'd cheerfully have accepted the corn liquor.

"Save the corn liquor for me," Sebastian said. "Stage is due in tonight, isn't it?"

"You know it is. Otherwise you wouldn't be here. Tonight is the first night of the full moon this month, kee-rect?"

"That it is."

"Then the stage will be here."

Sebastian nodded. "Excuse me while I see to my horse." He replaced his sombrero on his head as he went back outside. He didn't go out alone. Conroy followed him.

"Mr. Red."

Sebastian turned back around. "Mr. Conroy."

"That was a silly question you asked me back there. About how long I been managin' this station. You can make a good guess. You got a touch of The Sight. I can tell. Knew it the moment I clapped eyes on you. Not much, though. A smidge of it, sure. Enough to give you the edge in your profession, I warrant."

"As you say, just enough. You've got a good deal more of it, I wager. Born with it?"

"I was. Me mam had it and her mam before her and so on. You?"

"Learnt how to use it in my travels here and there."

"It lettin' you See anything now?"

"Such as?"

"Is it?"

Sebastian shook his head.

Conroy sighed. "Back before I became manager here and was out roamin' around doing what men do when they roam wide and free, sometimes The Sight wouldn't work for me. And when that happened I knew somethin' awful bad is about to happen. But The Sight wouldn't let me See what it was because The Sight is wiser than me and knows I would take a hand in tryin' to change what it is I saw. An' right now The Sight ain't working for me and that hasn't happened in more years than I'd care to tell you. What be your business here, Mr. Red?"

"Waitin' on a man."

"You gonna kill this man?"

"I would prefer not to. But I don't think he's going to leave me much leeway in that regard."

"You huntin' him for bounty?"

"Nope."

"Then what you want him for?"

"That's between him and me, Mr. Conroy. And I'd be obliged if'n you just leave it at that."

Conroy nodded. "Your business is your own. Go on and see to your horse and then come on in for a drink. I do so hate drinkin' alone and somethin' tells me that you got a lot of interesting stories to tell, Mr. Red."

The slumgullion was better than most Sebastian had in the past. This was a rich, full-bodied stew with plenty of flavor thanks to the herbs and spices Conroy grew out back in his own little garden. The Finches ate two bowls of stew apiece with little of the high-falutin' easterner's table manners Sebastian expected them to demonstrate. The Finches ate like folks who were hungry and not ashamed of it.

Sebastian set aside his own bowl, burped long and loudly to show his appreciation for the meal which brought a wide grin of appreciation to Conroy's lips. "Where's that jug of yours, Mr. Conroy? Good meal like that deserves a good drink."

"Be right back." Conroy pushed his chair back and walked across the room to the left and went through a door. Sebastian reckoned his sleeping quarters were behind the door.

Finch sat back in his chair and patted his full stomach with both hands. "Have to admit, that tasted a lot better than I thought it would have just by looking at it. Who would have guessed the old guy is such a good cook?"

Sebastian took out a long, thin black cigar from a pouch hanging from the belt holding up his pants. His other belt, the one with his weapons, hung on the back of his chair. "Out here a man learns to be his own cook."

"Which do you prefer, Mr. Red?" Mrs. Finch wanted to know. "A man's cooking or a woman's?"

"Depends on the man. Or the woman, ma'am." Sebastian lit his cigar and gave her an amiable smile.

Conroy returned with a large brown jug he placed on the table between himself and Sebastian. "You won't find better corn liquor for fifty miles around. Mainly because it's the only corn liquor you're gonna find for fifty miles around!" Conroy cackled gleefully at his own joke as he hunted up a pair of glasses.

"When will the stage be arriving, Mr. Conroy?" Finch asked.

"It'll arrive sometime after the moon comes up, Mr. Finch. It'll be here, that's all I know for certain. As to an exact time... well, the driver of the stagecoach has his own schedule he follows, and he ain't never took me into his confidence on that score. You best make yourself comfortable and resign yourself to waitin'."

"Is there someplace I could lie down for a bit?" Mrs. Finch stood up. "I'm so frightfully weary."

Conroy paused in lifting his full glass to his bushy lips. "I don't have cots and such since them that come here only come to meet the stage. But I can offer you the use of me own bed. Go right on through that door. I beg your pardon in advance for the appearance and the odor."

"I'm sure it will be just fine. I just need to stretch out for a few minutes. Come along, Harry."

Finch offered his wife his arm and walked with her to Conroy's quarters. The door softly closed behind them.

Sebastian and Conroy exchanged knowing looks. "How long you reckon it'll be before he's back out here?" Conroy cackled.

"Judgin' by the way he was eyein' that jug, about two minutes after his wife's head hits the pillow. She's about all done in. She almost fell asleep twice while eatin' your slumgullion. She'll be asleep in no time." Sebastian drained his glass, reached for the jug. "Fine stuff you got here, Mr. Conroy. Whereabouts you get your liquor from?"

"Make it myself. Got a still in the storage shed. Don't got nothing worth storing, so I built me a still in there. The manager before me wasn't a drinking man, I suppose. Beats the tar outta me how a man can be manager of this station without liquor or a woman to pass the time."

"How do you pass the time?"

"I likes to read. Sometimes one or more of the passengers that get off the stage will have a book they'll leave with me. When I was younger and better lookin' occasionally a woman would stay with me for a bit until she got enough gumption to go on out into the world and see what it had to offer her." Conroy took another drink. "That ain't been for a while, though. Still, it ain't bad out there. Folks will come along to take the stagecoach, and they'll tell me about what's goin' on out there in the world, and I figger I'm better off here."

Sebastian poured himself another drink, sipped half of it. He rested his forearm on the table, slowly twirling the shot glass in his long fingers. "How long you been here, Mr. Conroy? Really?"

Conroy's lips pressed together tightly. He poured himself another drink, tossed it down. He looked squarely into Sebastian's eyes, opened his lips—

The bedroom door opened and Finch slipped back into the main room, slowly and quietly closed the door shut. He turned around, grinned at the two men, rubbed his palms together. "I certainly hope you gentlemen haven't finished off that jug."

"If'n we do, I got two more, young feller. C'mon over and getcherself a snort."

He didn't have to tell Finch twice. He sat down and accepted the shot glass Conroy seemingly produced out of thin air. He reached for the jug, but Sebastian's hand intercepted him. "Looked to me like your missus didn't want you drinkin', Mr. Finch. You wouldn't be the type that cain't hold his liquor, are you? You the type that gets cantankerous and wanting to fight once you got some liquid courage in you?"

"Me? No. I can hold my liquor just as well as you can, I warrant. It's just that Melody's right religious. Don't hold with drinking or gambling or dancing. Got even more so when we lost the baby."

Sebastian Red removed his hand, satisfied. Finch poured himself a drink, raised it in salute to the two men and downed it like a professional.

"You say you an' your missus lost a baby, Mr. Finch?" Conroy asked. "I'm sure sorry to hear that."

Finch shrugged. "Thank you. It happened two years ago. Melody and I...we've become kind of numb to it by now. Funny how for the first six months or so we couldn't stop crying and just wanted to hold onto each other and not let go. Then one day we woke up and...we just went on with our lives."

"What brings you out here to meet the stagecoach?" Sebastian asked.

"One of Melody's friends heard stories about this station and the stagecoach. Both of us are well off. Our parents left us with enough finances so that I only had to work when I wanted to. I'm a lawyer by trade. We were able to hire people to investigate these stories and, once we were satisfied as to the truth of them, we sold our house, all we had to come out here and meet the stagecoach."

"And where is it that you expect the stagecoach to take you?"

Before Finch could answer, there was a loud hullabaloo outside; "Hello the station! Can a man come in and enjoy the fire and a bite of food?"

Conroy laboriously got up out of his seat. Twilight had come on fast, but there was still enough light to see the man standing outside. Sebastian and Finch couldn't see him from where they sat, but Conroy obviously was satisfied. "Put your rig in the corral over there and come on in." Conroy left the door open. "Busy night."

Sebastian didn't pay attention to him. He looked at Finch. More accurately, at the expression on Finch's face. "What ails you?"

"That voice. I could swear I've heard that voice before. Recently, in fact. It—"

"Everybody just stay where you are, and this won't have to go off and kill somebody."

A stocky, wide-shouldered man filled the doorway. His fat lips curled in a malicious smile. The gun in his hand punctuated his demand.

"You son of a bitch!" Finch slowly stood up.

"You know him?" Conroy asked.

"Of course I know him! This is the man we hired to guide us out here! He robbed us and left us to die!"

"Now, now, that ain't quite so, Mr. Finch. I left you and your missus food and water, didn't I? I knowed you warn't far from this station, and you made it here, didn't you?"

"No thanks to you! If Mr. Red hadn't found us and helped us here—"

The man's eyes shifted to Sebastian. Eyes full of caution and maybe just a little bit of fear. "Mr. Red? Sebastian Red? You be Sebastian Red?"

"I be."

"Looky here, Mr. Red...I got no quarrel with you. You got no quarrel with me. Let's keep it that way. Deal?"

"Way I see it, long as you got that gun pointed in my general direction then that qualifies as us having a quarrel, mister...?"

"Sheffield. Art Sheffield."

"You can put that gun away. Neither Mr. Conroy nor Mr. Finch are armed. You act like you got some sense, now, and put that gun back in the holster."

"Think maybe I'll just get back in the wagon and keep on goin'. That—"

The bedroom door opened as Melody Finch burst into the main room. "You better not be out here drinking, Harry! I told you—"

Sheffield, startled, swung around and fired. Mrs. Finch screamed as the bullet smashed into the frame of the door next to her ear, showering her with slivers of wood and dust.

Sebastian's right hand went out for his sword and drew it from the scabbard. He came up out of his chair, bringing the sword up in a flawless cut that sliced the barrel of Sheffield's pistol clean off. It fell to the floor with a clank. And then Sheffield felt the edge of cold steel against his Adam's apple. "Might as well drop the rest, partner."

Sheffield complied. Finch ran over to see to his wife. She was frightened, shaken but unharmed.

"What do you intend to do with him?" Conroy asked.

Sebastian looked thoughtfully at Sheffield. "If it were upta me, I'd kill him like the weasel he is. But it warn't me he abandoned. It was them." He waggled his head in the direction of the Finches. "It's up to them to have the say." He plopped Sheffield down in the nearest chair.

Conroy went over to assist Finch with his wife. The two of them helped her to a chair by the window while Finch looked her over. "None of those wood chips seems to have done any damage, thank God."

Conroy pressed a shot glass into Mrs. Finch's hand. She shook her head, tried to give it back. "I don't drink."

"Go on and take it, ma'am. A shock like you just had, you need it."

Mrs. Finch argued no further and tossed back the drink with an alacrity that matched her husband's. Held out the glass in Conroy's direction. "Another," she said simply. With a wicked grin, Conroy obliged and Mrs. Finch downed the second drink as fast as the first one. Finch observed all this with quiet astonishment and Sebastian Red reckoned that the right religious Mrs. Finch had pulled a cork or two in her time. She handed the empty glass to Conroy and glared at Sheffield. "It's *him*," she hissed. "The animal that robbed us and left us to die."

"That he be, ma'am." Sebastian kicked the pieces of Sheffield's gun out the door and closed it. He still held his sword in his hand. Five feet of shining single-edged death. The hilt banded with leather and the pommel crafted in the shape of an armored gauntlet holding a rose, wonderfully worked in silver and ivory. A breathtaking piece of craftsmanship. "What do you want to do with him?"

Mrs. Finch looked confused. "I don't understand."

"It was you he robbed and left out there to die. You get to decide what happens to him."

Mrs. Finch's eyes widened. "You can't be suggesting that we kill him?"

Sebastian shrugged. He returned his sword to its scabbard where it locked in with a soft click. "I would."

Mrs. Finch looked up at her husband. "Harry?"

Finch turned hard eyes on Sheffield. He contemplated the frightened man for a few long minutes before speaking. "Melody and I got here okay. Maybe a little tired, a little scared but we got here, and that's what's important. We gave up all our worldly possessions to be here to ride on the stagecoach. That's all I care about. Melody's not hurt, so I'm willing to call it square."

Sebastian nodded, sat down next to Sheffield and poured himself another drink. "That's a good man right there, Sheffield. Called him a fool, didn't you?"

"Reckon I did."

"World could use more fools like him and less fools like you."

"One thing puzzles me," Finch walked over to where Sheffield sat, stood glowering down at him, fists on hips. "Why'd you come here when you knew this is where Melody and I was heading?"

"I didn't plan on coming here a'tall! I intended to be miles away from here by now. I can't figure how I got turned around like that."

Conroy chuckled. "Yeah... during the nights when the stage is due to come, the land around the relay station gets kinda strange, twisted around. Folks have been known to sorta lose their way."

"I don't wanna be here! I don't wanna ride that stagecoach!"

"Don't you fret about that. You don't want to ride the stage, you don't have to. It only takes them what wants to be passengers." Conroy pushed the jug over to Sheffield. "Have a drink, stay in that seat, stay quiet, and you'll come out of this okay."

Finch returned to his wife and Sebastian returned to his seat, eyeing Sheffield who plainly was delighted to find himself not under a sentence of death.

"How long you been robbin' folks?" Conroy asked.

"Four, five years."

"Couldn't find honest work?"

"Don't like honest work. Easier robbin' folks like them." Sheffield jerked his head in the direction of the Finches. "There's a lot of greenhorns like them. But I always leave 'em food and water. I don't gun down helpless folk."

"I just bet you don't," Sebastian chuckled with grim humor. "You done some backshootin' in your time. I can tell."

Sheffield wisely said nothing. He poured himself another drink.

"Hello the station!"

Upon hearing this new voice from outside, Sebastian sat up straight in his seat. "About time," he muttered. He finished off his drink, stood up and reached for the belt with his weapons, buckled it around his waist. "There's the feller I been waitin' on. You folks stay in here."

Sebastian walked to the door, opened it and stepped out onto the porch, immediately went to the right so that he wasn't illuminated in the light streaming from inside. Conroy followed Sebastian, lanterns held in each hand. "Told you to stay inside, Mr. Conroy."

"Still got my job to do, Mr. Red. Stage will be coming in soon and lanterns got to be lit."

"There's liable to be some shooting."

"I knows how to duck." Conroy busied himself lighting the lanterns while Sebastian Red regarded the three men sat astride horses a few feet from the relay station. The man in the middle squinted as his eyes adjusted to the sudden light. "Hello the station!"

Sebastian spoke up. "Hello right back atcha, Farrell."

Farrell didn't seem surprised at all. He just reached up to scratch his cheek, let out a low laugh. "Y'know, I woulda been disappointed if you hadn't been here, Red. You been doggin' me for what, a month now? You come by your rep honestly, I give you that. You start out huntin' an hombre, you don't stop until you got him. How'd you know I was comin' to the relay station?"

"You shouldn't be so free telling your hopes and dreams to whores, Farrell. They ain't got none, so why should they care about yours?"

Farrell laughed again. "Yeah, I been dreaming about riding this stagecoach ever since I heard about it when I was a boy. Thought about riding it a passel of times. But it warn't till I killed me that lawman out in Wyoming that I bent a serious mind to it."

"I know all about that lawman. He was a friend of mine. Left behind a wife and three young'uns." Sebastian's voice darkened. "You're not gettin' on that stage, Farrell."

"I got two guns backin' me up. Between them, they done kilt a dozen men. You countin' on that old man and that dude to side you?"

Sebastian turned to see Finch and his wife crowding the doorway. Conroy hadn't moved since lighting the lanterns.

Out of the corner of his eye, Sebastian saw Farrell's hand go for his gun. And his men followed suit. Sebastian threw himself to the left, drawing his seven-shooter. The big gun boomed. The man on Farrell's left flew backward out of his saddle as if he'd been hit in the chest with a cannonball.

Farrell's first shot slammed into the wall of the station behind Sebastian as he dropped into a crouch. Sebastian fired again, this one taking the hired gun on Farrell's right. He fell out of his saddle.

Farrell fired again, the bullet smashing into the porch not more than a few inches from Sebastian's head. He rolled, got to his feet, fired but missed. Farrell unloaded his guns cursing, obviously unnerved by Sebastian's speed and agility. He fought to keep his frightened horse under control while trying to get a bead on Sebastian.

The second man snapped off a shot from where he lay. Sebastian's shot hadn't killed him, just hit him in the shoulder. Sebastian made sure he killed him with his next shot. It hit the hired gun right in the middle of his forehead.

The other two horses fled in panic, and Farrell's horse tried to do the same, but he kept the animal facing the relay station as he attempted to get a clear shot at Sebastian.

Sheffield burst from the station, wrapped beefy arms around Sebastian. He bawled, "I got 'im! I got 'im! Kill 'im! Kill 'im!"

Sebastian leaned forward, lifting Sheffield off the ground, then whirling around, so that Sheffield's back faced Farrell just as Farrell fired, Sheffield took the bullet meant for Sebastian squarely between the shoulder blades. He screamed and dropped to the porch. Sebastian finished him with a bullet in the throat.

Farrell fired once more, the shot going wide, but Sebastian, without any further distractions, placed his bullet right where he wanted to for months. Farrell cursed as he tumbled to the ground. Farrell lay on his side, reaching for his gun, a few feet away, however, Sebastian kicked it away as he approached. Farrell rolled over on his back, breathing hard. "Dammit, Red. This ain't no way for a man to die, lyin' in the dirt."

"Who said you's a man?" Sebastian put a bullet in Farrell's brains. He twirled the big gun lightly back into the holster as if it weighed no more than a feather. He turned and walked back into the station, stepping over Sheffield's body.

Conroy, standing on the porch, turned as he heard the creak of Sebastian's boots on the wooden floor, his horror-lined face a portent to what lay before them. Finch sat on the floor, legs outstretched in front of him, his wife's head resting in his lap. The front of her dress was dark with blood. Her eyes were half-open and her mouth almost appeared to be smiling.

"She caught a stray shot from one of them owlhoots," Conroy said.

"That's why I told you all to stay inside." Sebastian knelt down next to Finch. "You got my deepest sympathies, Mr. Finch. I didn't want nobody to get hurt save that man out there. I'd even have let those two gunnies of his go if'n they hadn't drawed on me. I didn't even want Farrell dead. I just didn't want him getting on that stage. Guess I should have known the only way to keep him from doing that was to kill him."

"I don't blame you, Mr. Red. We should have stayed inside. But when the shooting started, Mr. Conroy and I hit the floor, but Melody froze. Almost as if she had to see it all. Why? Why did she have to see it, Mr. Red?"

Sebastian and Conroy looked at each other and neither of them knew what to say.

The unmistakable sound of a stagecoach approaching gave them the way out.

"It's time," Conroy said, as he looked up at the full moon.

Sebastian followed Conroy outside. The moon had been hidden behind thick, inky clouds. They parted and the silver moonlight poured down on the relay station, almost bright as daylight.

The stagecoach made the ground under their feet quiver as if came closer. Bigger than any stagecoach Sebastian had ever seen, and trailing ribbons of azure fire, the iron wheels rumbled like the wheels of some ancient war chariot. Drawn by ten massive horses, black as death with red eyes and hot blue steam for breath. A heap of luggage rested on the roof, held down firmly by a netlike mesh. The stagecoach pulled up to a halt in front of the station with much cursing and yelling from the driver. Faces looked out of the coach windows. Sebastian couldn't rightly tell how many passengers there were. None of them got off.

The shotgun messenger turned his head to look down at Sebastian. It did not surprise him that the man had no eyes. Just empty black sockets.

The driver spoke to Conroy, ignoring Sebastian. "Got any passengers for me tonight?"

"Thought I did. A man and a woman. But the woman's dead."

"Mayhap the man would like a ride."

"I dunno. But we can find out." Conroy raised his voice. "Mr. Finch! The stagecoach is here!"

Finch stumbled out of the station like a man in a dream and made his way over to where Sebastian and Conroy stood. The stagecoach creaked and sighed like a living thing as the ribbons of azure fire faded away. "It is real."

"That it is, boy," Conroy said. "Best git aboard. It doesn't pay to keep the driver waitin'. He's got a schedule to keep."

"How can I go without my wife?" Finch said in a slightly

dazed voice. "We planned this together. It was our dream together. What sense does it make for me to go on now? Melody's dead. Our baby is dead..."

"Your missus wouldn't want you to waste your life grievin', Mr. Finch," Sebastian said gently. "Mr. Conroy's right. You get on that stage and get on with your life. Where ever it takes you."

"Are you getting on, Mr. Red?"

"Me? Naw. Like I told you before, I came here for one reason." Sebastian nodded in the direction of Farrell's body.

Finch turned to Conroy. "Why don't I stay here with you? Surely you could use some help here? I've got nothing to go back to. Melody and I sold everything, gave it all away."

Conroy shook his head. "There's only one station manager, son. That's all this relay station ever had. That's all it will ever have."

"Then let me take over. You get on the stage."

Conroy looked hard at the younger man. "Don't think I won't take you up on the offer, son. I been doin' this job a powerful long time, and I'm 'bout due to retire. You sure about this?"

"I am."

"I ask because the job must be exchanged willingly. Both have to agree to it. I agree to give it up. You agree to take it on?"

"I do."

"Then take my hand."

Conroy extended his and Finch took it. The air around them shimmered and it was as if Sebastian saw them through a hazy film for a second before they snapped back into focus.

"Now you say, 'I relieve you, sir.'"

"I relieve you, sir."

"I now stand relieved." Conroy let go of Finch's hand. "That's it then. Look under the mattress on my bed. You'll find a book that'll explain your duties."

"Come on if you're coming," the driver said. "I got a schedule to keep."

"Just a minnit." Conroy smiled, nodded at Finch. "Thank you, son."

Finch simply nodded back. Conroy stepped over to Sebastian to shake his hand. "Pleasure meetin' and drinkin' with you, Mr. Red."

"It's been an honor knowin' you, Mr. Conroy. May your road be free of incident."

Conroy grinned, nodded and walked over to the stagecoach. The door swung open of its own volition and willing hands reached out to help Conroy in.

The driver directed his next words at Sebastian. "You would do well to come with us, Sebastian Red. It is not an opportunity for many men to be given a way to escape their fate. This could be yours."

Sebastian shook his head. If he was surprised that the driver knew his name, he didn't show it. "Like I said, I had no intention of riding your stagecoach when I come here. Still don't. Go on your way, driver."

The driver nodded while the shotgun messenger showed black teeth in a diseased grin. The driver cracked his whip and the stagecoach moved off, picking up speed as it did so. Conroy's hand and arm briefly appeared in a final wave before obscured in a cloud of dust.

And then it was gone.

Sebastian Red sighed.

Harry Finch asked him, "So, what now?"

"Let's find a suitable spot to bury your missus first. Then we can find another spot as far away from her resting place as possible to bury these others. Then you need to get that book Mr. Conroy mentioned and get to readin'. I 'spect you got a lot to catch up on."

Finch nodded. "And you, Mr. Red?"

Sebastian Red smiled slightly. "I got a lot more road to ride, friend. A lot more."

NOT FADE AWAY

Cliff Winnig

Joan Stark dropped the saddlebags onto the dirt road and slumped against the wooden sign. She'd carried them maybe ten miles since Lulu had died. Relieved of her burden, she felt she might float up into the blue Arizona sky. Only the June sun pressing down on her kept the soles of her boots on the earth.

Even her men's clothes—which she always wore for riding, and most other occasions, truth be told—hadn't made the walk bearable. The heat and her saddlebags' weight had dragged at her. She'd run out of water and jerky five miles back.

Her only dress now lay by the gunnysack beside poor Lulu's corpse with all the other useless stuff, and good riddance! She'd taken only what she needed most: coffee pot, matches, spare bullets for her Colt, and little else. Her Bowie knife she kept at her hip, like her gun. She'd left the spare horseshoes and suchlike back with the horse. No point in any of it.

Lulu, mouth flecked with foam, rose again in her mind. Joan squeezed her eyes shut, but that just brought her right back. The bright desert circled them, closing in. The horse beneath her buckled and fell.

This will not do. Joan opened her eyes wide, willed it all away. Forced it. After a few moments, she succeeded. She was back in the present, alone in the afternoon heat.

The desert broke things down to their smallest components. She could feel it. Her grief became anger became mere annoyance. Her feet ached. Her legs ached. She needed a drink. Water too.

125

Joan stared at the stretch of empty desert between her and the actual town named on the sign and scowled. *Why the hell do they put these signs so damned far out of town?*

"Well," she said aloud, her throat dry. "Not a crazy long walk, at least."

She could make it. She had to.

She thought about the Thing Behind Her. It did not rest. It had caused her to push Lulu even when the horse took ill. Lulu's death was one more item on its tab.

Got to keep moving. Joan peeled herself off the faded sign and took her first real look at it. It had originally read LOST VALLEY, POPULATION 340, but someone had crossed through both name and number with chalk so that it now read TRUTH, POPULATION 1. Some of the chalk had rubbed off on her shirt, but she didn't bother wiping it. Too much effort. Stiffly, she knelt down and retrieved her saddlebags, which still smelled of Lulu and would for weeks more.

As she rose, Joan focused again on the task at hand. The sun would be setting soon. She needed to be indoors before that happened. She hoped she would get along with the one other person in Truth, but either way she couldn't be out here alone.

Besides, she needed to find and warn that person about the Thing Behind Her. Her fault, and thus her responsibility.

Joan shuddered once, momentarily cold even in the devil's own heat.

Late afternoon shadows stretched across the road and crawled their way up the abandoned church, general store, and two-story whorehouse on the east side of the street. They were cast by the hotel and the combination dentist's office and barbershop facing them.

Joan barely glanced at either set, or at the dozen or so buildings beyond them. She went straight for the stream dead ahead, just past the edge of town. She didn't see any sign of the one other person in Truth, but she carried her saddlebags with her the whole way anyway, wary for any movement.

Joan knelt when she reached the water's edge. The stream smelled pure and fresh. The last of the sunlight sparkled on the swift-moving water. She shrugged off the saddlebags and plunged her hands into the cool of the stream. She drank from her cupped palms, not bothering to pull out her tin cup from its home by the coffee pot.

She took a long time drinking her fill and washing her hands and face, but not too long. She knew the Thing Behind Her drew nearer with every breath, every heartbeat. *Has it found poor Lulu yet? Probably. Will it stop there to dine? No, I don't imagine it will. The coyotes will have her, and it will keep coming.*

Joan sank the pain of that truth into the deep chambers of her heart, where it became a dull ache, a stone to be carried within her.

Keep moving. She threw the saddlebags over her shoulders and stood. Across the stream, maybe two hundred yards further on, a gentle slope rose to meet the darkening sky. The plain, square entrance to a mine stared back at her, hollow and black. She wondered if the sole remaining person in Truth had the claim to that mine, had chosen not to give up, even after everyone else had left. That would be a dangerous man.

She considered crossing the stream and skirting the mine. She could follow the trail the road became and leave Truth behind her.

No. It would not do to meet the Thing on the open road. And I'm hungry, with no time left to hunt.

So Joan turned back to face the dark town, as hollow, in its own way, as the mine.

A breeze came with the quickening dark and blew through town toward the stream. Joan smelled nothing of horse nor man, just the aroma of chalk dust. When she drew near the center of town, she saw why. Someone had drawn people all over the place: peering through the windows, draped across chairs on porches, lying on the ground like the shadows of invisible men. Two even sat in front of the saloon playing a game of checkers. The arm of one player started on his seat, dropped to the sidewalk boards, and reappeared on the table to hold one of the pieces. Some figures showed details of clothes and face, as if drawn from life, but most were faded, vague impressions of whoever they were meant to represent. She hadn't noticed them on her way through town, so intent had she been on her thirst and the stream that promised to slake it.

The urge to flee gripped her again, but she could feel the Thing drawing closer. She had no time.

Joan looked around for a place to spend the night, a place

she could fortify. The whorehouse was tempting. Unless someone had stripped it bare, there'd be lamps and oil for the use of
nocturnal clientele. She'd spent many a night in such places as
a paying customer. There was always one whore who wouldn't
mind, and usually two or three to choose from. It had led to her
moving on rather quickly from more than one town, as word got
around, but even that had been a harmless enough excitement
compared to her current straits.

She examined the shadowed building for a minute. Whore-
houses had their many windows, their myriad ways of entrance
and egress. This one looked pretty typical that way. *Hard to defend.*

She looked past the general store to the church. Since the Thing
Behind Her had started dogging her trail, she'd never tried spending the night in a church. There'd never been an abandoned one
on offer, either. This one had large doors, but it doubtless also held
pews she could shove against them. While her mother had been
Jewish, her father had been Lutheran, originally from Hamburg.
Probably it would be all right. The Lord would surely forgive her for
seeking shelter there, despite the Thing being her own damned fault.

"The church it is." Before she could change her mind, she
climbed the three steps to the building and threw open the doors.
They were unlocked.

Inside, dust motes flew in the last of the sunlight streaming
through a window somewhere above her. The rays landed on
the plain wooden cross on the far side of the room, making it
glow. Joan didn't know whether that was a good or a bad sign,
but she stepped inside.

Everything seemed intact. The pews stood in row after empty
row and led to a plain pulpit. A closed Bible lay atop it. A small
slate board on the far wall read "Gen. 6:4" for the weekly sermon,
in faded but still-legible chalk. The windows along both sides
were designed for raids by hostile Indians: tall but narrow, with
gun slots forming crosses. They were all shuttered. The Thing
could maybe pound its way through, but it wouldn't be able to
slither. A small but ornate organ sat to one side, the only item
that smacked of indulgence. It looked new. Joan wondered if it
had even been played before the town was abandoned.

When her eyes had adjusted to the gloom, she started briskly
down the center aisle, not bothering to remove her hat. A door
near the back led to a side room, off to the right. She'd have to

check everywhere to make sure she could secure the place. There wasn't much time. If the church wouldn't work, she needed to know right now.

A scampering noise caught her attention. Her head snapped in that direction, and she saw that far door swing shut. *A small animal? A coyote? Or have I just missed the only other resident of Truth, Arizona?*

Joan dropped her saddlebags and sprinted down the rest of the aisle, then tore right toward the door. She threw it open and looked around. A cramped vestry doubled as an office. A writing desk and two wooden chairs filled most of the space. A figure had squeezed itself between the desk and a chair, taking advantage of the shadows that lay thick over the whole room. If it hadn't been so pale, Joan might have missed it.

She put her hand on the Colt but didn't draw. "I see you, so you might as well come on out. I won't hurt you, but I'll warn you, I've got a gun. I can defend myself."

"Go away!" The high voice came thin but clear from under the desk. "Leave me alone."

A child.

Joan raised her hands, palms out, and took a step back, so as not to panic the kid. "All right. I'm just looking for a place to stay the night."

"You've got the whole town for that. Leave me alone!"

Might as well ask. Local knowledge and all. "Other than this church, is there another safe place? I mean, one I can defend."

The child didn't answer, but Joan heard her adjust her position some.

Joan lowered her hands, but didn't rest one on the Colt again. "I ask because—"

"You know about it? Then why'd you come here?"

Joan raised an eyebrow. *She doesn't mean the Thing. She can't. That's behind me.* "My horse died. It's nighttime. I've got troubles of my own."

The kid poked a bright blonde head up from behind the chair. *A girl, maybe ten, maybe twelve.* She had sun-bleached hair, but oddly untanned skin. "What sort of troubles, mister?"

Joan chuckled. Despite the Thing Behind Her, despite Lulu's death, despite this strange kid and her ghost-haunted town, it came back to that. "Ma'am, not mister. My name's Joan. Joan Stark."

Another hesitation, then: "Margaret Ross. Not Maggie. Not Peg. Margaret."

Joan held out her hand. "Pleased to meet you, Margaret Ross."

The kid stared at her for maybe a full minute before she unfolded herself from behind the chair. She wore a faded blue dress, no shoes, and a haunted, hungry look. Joan wondered when she'd last eaten.

Nonetheless, Margaret strode up like it was her house and shook Joan's hand. Joan had maybe a foot on her, but Margaret looked her in the eye. Her handshake was as strong as a boy five years older, and stronger than some men she'd met.

"You can't go anywhere else in town, Joan. It ain't safe."

Joan nodded. "I think we ought to barricade the door. Help me move the pews?"

"I can do that myself," Margaret said, standing straighter. "But you can help me."

After they'd shoved a couple of pews in front of the doors and checked all the windows to make sure they were secure, Margaret did something unexpected. She lit an oil lamp and asked Joan to hold it. Then she led Joan all around the perimeter inside the church while grasping a stick of chalk. The whole way, she stared at the floor where it met the outside walls. Joan saw that a single line of chalk lay along the entire length. It followed the shape of the church rather than a circle, but she knew a magical barrier when she saw one. *I guess I shouldn't have worried about getting struck down entering a church, at least not this one. This kid knows her witchcraft.*

Margaret touched up the line here and there. When they reached the front doors, she reconnected a stretch Joan had smudged with her boot when she'd come in.

Now that Joan was examining things more closely, she saw a handful of chalk drawings of people among the pews. When they got back to the vestry, she saw two figures, quite detailed, on the wall to either side of a boarded-up window. Margaret approached them with reverence, careful, Joan noticed, not to touch either one while she examined the floor beneath them. The figures were drawn from behind, but the faces were in partial silhouette, as if they were gazing out the now-boarded window.

When Margaret finished her task in the room, Joan met her

gaze. "Did you draw those?" Joan nodded her head toward the pair. "They're good."

Margaret looked stricken for a moment, before a blank look fell into place like a door slamming shut. "No. And before you ask, none of the others in town neither."

Joan shrugged. "All right. Just making conversation."

"Well don't." Margaret brushed past her into the sanctuary, where she put the stick of chalk on the pulpit next to the Bible. "Sorry. I don't mean to be rude."

Joan followed her in and sat down in the front pew, facing Margaret, who fished for something from behind the pulpit. The girl brought out an old sack, a hunk of cheese, and a large jug, then came to sit beside Joan. She placed everything on the pew between them.

"It ain't much, but I'll share. We'll need to find food tomorrow, though." Margaret opened the bag, and Joan saw that it held communion bread.

Joan glanced at her saddlebags, still lying forlorn in the aisle. No food there. "I thank you."

Margaret nodded. "Then let's eat. Afterward, you could tell me about your troubles, if you please."

The kid didn't offer to say grace, so Joan didn't either. With her Bowie knife, Joan sliced the cheese in half. The jug held water from the stream. Not as cool as what she'd had earlier, but just as pure. The communion bread was stale, dry as dust, and hardly filling. She wondered how old it was. She'd never had any before, hoped she wouldn't again, if it was like this.

After they'd finished the cheese and as much of the bread as they could stand, Joan took one more swig of water before she began. She'd been wondering how to tell her tale, especially to a kid, but she decided the unvarnished truth would be best. "I had this friend who was married, and—"

A thud and a creaking sound came from behind them, as of something very heavy stepping on wood. They both spun around. Two more thuds, then a pause, then a pounding on the door, loud. Once, twice, three times.

Joan looked back at Margaret, saw she was crouched on the floor, behind the pew. "Get down!" the girl hissed. "It'll peer in through the crack."

Joan did just that. The noise had stopped. Perhaps whatever

was outside was looking through the narrow gap between doors. Perhaps it was just waiting.

They crouched in silence for several minutes. Joan knew this wasn't the Thing Behind Her. That was large, true, but not heavy. Light as feathers, in fact, like smoke on the wind. Whatever this thing was, it was the kid's monster, not hers.

As no more sounds came from the front, Joan grew impatient. Her limbs still ached from riding, her fall, and the ten miles she'd walked. They were beginning to scream at her now. *Surely it must have left. Could it have flown off?* Finally, she whispered, "I think it's gone."

Margaret glared at her. "Shhh!"

Another pounding came, and this time the doors shuddered. Whatever it was, it was throwing its bulk against them. *Wham!* Again. Behind them, the chalk rolled off the pulpit and clattered onto the floor. *Wham!* The wooden doors creaked with the impact, but they—and the pews blocking them—held, though barely.

Joan drew her Colt and held it close to her cheek, aimed toward the ceiling.

"Bullets won't stop it," Margaret whispered. "Just wait. It'll give up. It probably can't come in here anyway."

"Because of the chalk?" Joan whispered back.

Margaret gave her a funny look. "No. Because it's a church." She waved away Joan's next question, glaring her into silence.

A minute more, and they heard three huge footsteps from the front of the church, then nothing. Apparently, it had gone.

Joan released a breath she hadn't known she was holding. "Okay, kid. Maybe you should tell me about your own troubles first."

Margaret frowned. "I thought you'd heard. Ain't that why you were seeking shelter?"

"No, like I said, I got troubles too."

"All right, but the chalk ain't for that thing. That's just the golem. Chalk won't stop it, only walls."

"Then what in the hell is the chalk for?" Joan used the Colt to point to the nearest bit of the border.

"That thing down in the mine!" Margaret was the picture of frustration, like any fool should already know the town had two monsters, only one of which couldn't cross chalk. "That good-for-nothing golem was supposed to take care of it, but it didn't. It didn't do squat. I mean, look at the town. Just look!"

And that did it. Something came loose in Margaret, and she fell into Joan's arms like a drowning man, her face already soaked with tears.

Joan held the sobbing child, but she didn't really think about what she'd been saying, about there being two monsters on top of her own. No, all she could think was, *This kid doesn't weigh a thing. She don't look that thin, but she'd float right down that stream if she fell in.*

Joan knew it wasn't just an impression. She'd found yet another unnatural thing in Truth.

Joan got the story out of Margaret bit by bit, but, in the end, she had all the pieces.

The silver mine, like the town, was pretty new. Three brothers had staked a claim and worked it hard. Other prospectors had started to come, but they hadn't found any veins nearly as promising, not yet anyway. Still, word had spread. The town was on the cusp of booming when it happened.

Joan didn't get the exact details, but Margaret said they'd found a forest down there in the mine. That didn't seem to make any more sense to Margaret than it did to Joan, but the girl insisted it was true.

Something had come out of that forest, something ancient. And hungry.

"My pa was the preacher here," Margaret said. They sat in the front pew again, facing one another, no longer touching. Margaret had composed herself. "But he had an old book that weren't about Jesus or even no Christian. Instead, it was about this Jew, in a city back East, across the ocean."

"Prague," Joan said.

Margaret's face lit up. "Yeah! That's it. He said the man was from Prague!"

"Rabbi Judah Loew ben Bezalel."

Margaret cocked her head sideways. "You sure know a lot about this."

Joan shrugged. "My ma was Jewish. She taught me stories." *And more than that, but it hasn't been much help of late.* "She told me about the golem. The rabbi made it to save the Jews of Prague, but he couldn't control it."

Margaret nodded briskly. "That's what Pa said, but he said he could do better, being a Christian. He could improve on it." She looked down, spoke to her feet. "But it didn't work. It couldn't stop that thing turning people to chalk. Faster if it bit you, but sooner or later either way."

And there it was. There weren't chalk drawings all over town, just victims of whatever had come out of the mine. Worse, Joan knew who the two people in the vestry had to have been. *Poor kid. How long has she been holed up here, watching what's left of her parents fade away?*

"The golem tried," Margaret said, "but it couldn't do nothing about it. Went kind of crazy after that. That's why it comes around. Like maybe it's got to fight someone."

Joan started. She felt something in her chest, an unknotting. Hope. Something she hadn't believed she'd ever feel again. "It wants a fight, you say?"

Margaret looked up and faced her. "Yeah. It's like a mean drunk, comes around spoiling for it."

Joan wondered how much this kid knew about mean drunks. She hoped it was just from her pa's sermons. "Maybe it can help us, after all."

Margaret shook her head. "I done told you, it ain't no good against the thing from the mine."

Joan offered a sympathetic look. "I'm sorry, Margaret. That's not the only problem this town has now. I brought something with me."

Margaret narrowed her eyes. "Your troubles."

Joan nodded. "Like I said, it all started with my friend." She paused, sniffing the air. There it was: sulfur and frankincense. *Speak of the devil, even in a church.* "Damn."

Margaret wrinkled her nose. She'd caught it too. "What's that smell?" She looked at Joan as if maybe she were the source.

Joan stood and turned to face the doors. "My troubles. They've found us. Quick, get the lamp."

To her credit, Margaret didn't ask any more questions, just hopped up and grabbed the lamp off the pulpit. Joan retrieved her saddlebags and opened the one with her box of matches. She struck one and began lighting the candles at the head of the church. She knew only one thing besides walls that slowed the Thing down, and that was light.

By then, the smell was impossible to ignore. Margaret was

looking around in all directions, white-knuckle gripping the lamp in front of her chest with both hands.

"Come on out, honey," the Thing whispered. The voice came from the front doors, but also from beyond the boarded-up windows to their right. Despite its whispering, they both heard it clearly enough. The Thing was large, and its whole self vibrated when it spoke. It didn't talk with Prudence's voice, or even that damned wizard Hank's, but "honey" was what Prudence had called her. "I got something for you. Come look."

"What is that thing?" Margaret squeaked, her voice thinner and reedier than before.

"Like I said, it started with my married friend."

"You cheated with her husband?"

The unvarnished truth. "No, she cheated on him. With me."

Margaret glanced at her sideways, but she didn't say anything. Perhaps this whispering monster outside made a good distraction.

I should consider always waiting for times like this to bring it up. Joan took one of the candles out of its holder and went to stand by Margaret near the first pew.

The Thing outside kept whispering, but a bunch of things at once, a susurrus that now came from the front and both sides of the church. *Damn. It's grown.* Joan heard "honey" and "love light," another term of affection Prudence had used.

"Well, I don't know about that," Margaret said after a pause, while the sound outside gradually rose and the smell gradually worsened. It took Joan a moment to realize Margaret was still talking about Joan's affair with a woman. "I just know you shouldn't covet another man's wife."

Joan chuckled. "That's the truth. I wish I hadn't. This thing wouldn't be here right now."

Margaret moved closer to Joan. She looked small and terrified. "I'm ... I'm kind of glad you did, Joan. You wouldn't be here neither if you hadn't."

How long has the poor kid been alone? Joan nodded once, teeth gritted. "Let me know in an hour if you still think so. That is, if we're both here to talk about it."

Now the Thing Behind Her—which had become the Thing All Around Them—started pounding on the church wall. It banged on the front doors. It smashed against the windows. It drummed on the slanted roof above them. It didn't sound like the golem trying to get in. That had been the pounding of fists. This was more like giant waves crashing one after another, like thunder getting close.

"What *is* it?" Margaret cried, looking up at the ceiling.

"Don't know exactly. Something her wizard husband called up when he found out about us. He got jealous." It had gotten so loud outside, she had to shout.

"That's one heck of a jealous man. Must have come from Cain's line."

Joan thought of the tall man, darkly handsome but mean, so no temptation at all for her. Prudence had married him for his money, and because her parents approved. "Might be, Margaret. Might be."

With one final blow, the window above the church doors shattered. In poured the Thing. It roiled and curled about itself like smoke from a volcano, gray and black and red with rage, with a thousand bright green eyes looking everywhere, searching for targets.

Joan held the candle before her at arm's length. Without needing to be told, Margaret raised the lamp. The part of the Thing that had entered the church rose up like a wall, a huge wave, green eyes all fixed on the two of them now. It screamed in inchoate rage. It hated freedom to act, freedom to sin. It hated everything, everyone. Most of all, it hated Joan.

The wave crashed down upon them, parting only for the lights they held. They moved to stand back to back. Each waved her flame around in arcs, keeping the Thing at bay. It glared at them from everywhere.

"What do we do?" Margaret screamed over the churning cries the Thing spewed out. "We won't last the night."

"I have an idea," Joan said. "But we need to leave the church."

"Okay. It's not like we can stay here forever."

Joan looked down at her feet. She saw the floorboards and part of the front pews, before they vanished into the body of the Thing, spread out around them like a dome. "We need to follow the aisle outside."

They moved slowly, carefully. They each had to focus on moving their light here or there between themselves and the Thing, which kept putting out tendrils. Eventually they made it to the front of the church. Using her weight, Joan pushed the pews out of the way while Margaret held the Thing at bay.

When Joan had finished and opened the doors, the girl hesitated a moment before she stepped over the line of chalk. But only a moment.

Then they were outside, where the Thing was a howling maelstrom around them. Jade-colored eyes spun so fast that they blurred, each one a shooting star on its own course through the red-gray-black of its amorphous body.

"Now what?" Margaret cried.

"Depends," Joan said. "Which way you think that golem went?"

"The golem?" Margaret shot her an angry look. "What the heck is that gonna do for us?"

"Its job. Besides, I'm half Jewish. Maybe that's extra incentive."

Margaret pointed with her lamp. "That way. Toward the stream. It lurks near the mine, for all the good it does."

Joan nodded grimly. *Well, I'm bringing two monsters together. Might as well bring all three.*

It was a bit like dancing, how the two of them swirled and swung their lights all around, as they made their way down the street. The Thing picked up the dust and hurled it, causing them to cough as they moved. Margaret's dress fluttered this way and that, her hair like a crown of fire. Joan wondered that she didn't get lifted into the air, given how unnaturally light she was. She also wondered when the girl would begin to tire. Like her, though, she seemed to be buoyed by terror alone, at least for now.

With a splash, Joan backed into the edge of the stream. Though it didn't soak through her boot, she almost slipped and fell. That would have likely doomed them both. She stepped back to the shore.

"What now?" Margaret screamed.

"Yes!" The Thing cried, its first coherent word since they'd left the church. "What now, honey? You can go no farther, and your love lights will soon go out."

Joan glanced at the oil lamp. It still shone brightly, but maybe a little dimmer than before. Her own candle had burned down considerably, although the flame hadn't wavered in the unnatural wind, perhaps because it was sacred. That wouldn't matter in the end, though. Neither of them had light enough to last until morning.

The Thing reared up until it was no longer a dome around them, but a circular wall. Joan saw a patch of sky above, the myriad stars spread along it like chalk marks on velvet. It was taunting her. Showing her a way out she couldn't take. *Though perhaps the kid. Margaret's so light, maybe I could get her out with one good toss. If I aimed right, she could land in the stream. I'd have to throw down my candle, use both hands.* She knew what would happen to her next.

Still.

"Margaret," Joan shouted. "I think I can get you out."

Margaret bashed an especially eager tendril directly with the lamp. It burst into smoke, and the stub retreated. The Thing's howl of rage grew louder in response. "How?"

"I can throw you. You're light. I don't understand it, but you're really light. I could throw you up and over, and you could run away, far away from the mine and the golem and my troubles, which I am so sorry to have brought to you here and would take away again."

Margaret shook her head. "Don't you understand?" With her free hand she reached up and grabbed a lock of her own hair, held it out. "I'm not blonde, not normally, and I've got olive skin, like you."

Joan's brow furrowed as she looked at the pale child. "But—"

"I'm *fading*, Joan. I've seen the thing from the mine. It's a curse on the whole town. Even if I leave here, I'll fade. That's the truth. That's why I renamed the damned town. Sorry. It *is* damned. That's why I said it."

Joan just stared at the child, so worried about swearing in the face of her own extinction, about being the good preacher's daughter, an upstanding example for her community of one.

No, Joan realized. *Her community of two. She cares about what I think of her.*

A tendril wrapped itself around Joan's neck and pulled, hard. *What a fool I am. I forget what's important, what's all around me.* Joan knew that, too, was truth.

She tugged the tendril with her free hand, but it dragged her back to the waiting eyes. Margaret's stricken face receded. Joan tried to position the candle to burn the tendril, but it kept shifting, even as it kept its chokehold. She waved the candle in circles. She couldn't quite get it to a spot where it wouldn't also burn her.

This is it. It finally has me. I just hope it will be too sated to take Margaret too. She could hope that, she knew, but she also knew the Thing couldn't be sated. It would consume all of creation.

More tendrils grabbed her arms, pinned them to her side. They lifted her off the ground and drew her toward the maelstrom. Her hat blew off and was consumed. Her head would be next, she knew.

The Thing screamed in triumph, a long, ululating sound, deep and high at once.

Then it just dropped her, tendrils curling into itself.

Joan drew in a breath. Her lungs spasmed as they filled with the dusty air, but something got through. She drew a second breath.

Her eyes focused on Margaret, facing away from her. She'd plunged her lamp into the maelstrom and now dragged it along like a dredge behind her.

The Thing was screaming all right, but in pain.

Joan grinned as she stood up, despite her own pain. "That's a great idea, kid. Maybe with both of us doing it, we could get somewhere." She looked down at her candle and cursed. It had gone out in the fall. With her matches back at the church, she'd have to light it from the lamp, which meant pulling that back out. Another opening for attacks, this time on both of them.

Might as well tell the kid now. Joan took a ragged breath and stepped toward Margaret.

The Thing screeched and all but a dozen eyes vanished into the maelstrom. Margaret pulled the lamp back out and turned to Joan. "I didn't do that, did I?"

Joan shook her head. "No. It's looking at something other than us now."

From the direction of the stream, they heard a tearing noise, and another scream from the Thing. They shared a puzzled look, as the rest of the eyes vanished from sight. Another tear came and another, and the wall that encircled them became a wall to one side.

They backed away from the stream and from the Thing, now locked in combat with a silent clay giant. The golem, for that's what it surely was, had reached rough, misshapen hands into the Thing and pulled out fists of the stuff. Whenever an eye came free, the golem threw it to the ground and stomped on it.

The Thing lashed at it with tendril after tendril, then tried to smother it with its own flesh, all to no avail. The golem had no breath to smother, no heart upon which to focus its jealousy. It probably seemed to the Thing that it was being torn apart by nothing at all.

In short order, the Thing had diminished so that it no longer loomed over the golem, which itself had to be twelve feet tall. Soon the golem towered over it. Then it stood over the quivering remains. The last remaining eye looked away from it and found Joan. It narrowed in rage before the golem's foot came down, obliterating it.

Being a creature without a soul, the golem did not speak nor utter the smallest of victory cries. When it had finished its task, it stood totally still. Then it turned toward Margaret and Joan.

"Run!" Joan called, and turned to do so, but the kid just stood there.

"Ain't no point," Margaret said. "You can't outrun it. I've seen people try."

Without hardly noticing she'd done it, Joan dropped her lifeless candle and drew her Colt. She fired as the golem stepped toward them, hitting it square in the chest three times. Big chunks of clay flew off with each impact, but it didn't slow down.

"That don't work neither," Margaret said.

"You've seen people try that too, huh?" Joan didn't wait for an answer. She fired again, backing up to give her some space, this time aiming at the face. The first shot missed, but the second blew off one if its eyes. It didn't seem to care. At least, it didn't slow down.

The golem raised its arms when it reached the edge of the stream, but by then Joan and Margaret had backed up maybe twenty yards. They couldn't outrun it, the kid was right about that, but it hadn't started running yet.

Joan peered closely at the golem's emotionless face. She had one bullet left. She'd been lucky to take out one eye, and she wasn't sure she'd get that lucky twice. Naturally, her spare bullets were all back at the church with her matches and everything else.

The golem sped up now. Joan backed up faster, not wanting yet to turn and run, given the futility. There was something nagging at her. Something about its face.

Joan changed direction, backing toward the west side of the street. The golem turned to track her and, in so doing, faced directly into the moonlight. *There. Something written in chalk on its forehead.*

And she remembered. The golem was powered by the Hebrew word for "truth." The way to stop it was to remove the first letter, which changed it to the word for "dead."

"The trouble is," Joan said aloud. "I can't read Hebrew." She shrugged, bone weary. "Well, it's all I've got."

Joan stopped backing up. She took the Colt in both hands, aimed at the left side of the word on its forehead, and waited for it to get closer. From her left, Margaret was calling to her, telling her to hide, to try and make it inside a building, but Joan ignored her.

The golem got so close that Joan aimed nearly straight up. It raised its hands, making them into a pair of fists. Joan waited. It leaned over her, so as to aim its killing blow.

Joan fired.

One of the fists got in the way. Though she blew it to bits, the other one came down. She dodged to the left, saw it smash into the dirt.

Still the golem didn't utter a sound. Even a scream of pain or frustration would have been oddly reassuring. The silence, she knew, was the silence of death.

Now Joan ran. She dropped the useless gun and sprinted away from the golem, toward a house where Margaret stood in the door, calling her name. Joan reached out to her, wondering even then if it were Margaret's own house she ran toward. Then the golem grabbed her leg with its remaining hand and pulled her into the air.

The town and stream and star-filled sky flew around her as she was lifted upside down toward the golem. For a moment she worried that it would eat her, but then her logic told her no, it would probably just dash her on the ground, maybe crush her for good measure.

"Run, Margaret! Run! Get away from here!" she screamed. The golem lifted her above its head so that she dangled in front of its good eye. It paused there a moment, regarding her with its immobile, passionless face. She saw the ragged chunk her bullet had blown off. She saw its good eye, which was a bit of quartz, and she saw the Hebrew word for truth in that strange, boxy script.

Looking at it upside down, she remembered something else her mother had said about Hebrew: they wrote it backward. *Hell. Even if I'd hit it, I'd have blown off the wrong letter.*

Then the face flew away from her as the golem raised her up, ready to throw her down to the ground.

Joan twisted in its grip. It had her by one leg, just below the knee, so that joint screamed at her when she moved. She managed to get a swing going, though. She turned it into a back and forth movement.

When it threw her down, she flew at it in an arc. The whole time, her eyes focused just on that mysterious letter, farthest on the right, and she reached for it. Stretching, straining.

Her thumb jammed painfully into the golem's face. Her forehead smashed into its chest. She went head over heels, landed on her boots, careened forward, and rolled.

She wound up on her back, panting, waiting for the killing blow.

But the golem didn't move. It would never move again.

When she had her breath back, Joan sat up. Her knees were killing her. Her head screamed. She nonetheless found the strength to call Margaret's name.

No response came. Joan tried again and again. Finally, when she had no more breath left, not even for crying, she faced the truth. She was alone.

Joan searched the house, of course, and more of the town besides, calling Margaret's name the whole time. She also looked, as much as she didn't want to, among the chalk remains for another silhouette, one that would be painfully familiar. She didn't find a trace.

At length, as the sun crept toward noon, she faced the inevitable. She faced the mine.

Joan ate a full meal, scrounged at the general store, drank her fill at the river, and took care of her other needs before she forded the stream. She brought her Colt, fully loaded, and her Bowie knife, though she knew neither one would do any good. She brought the stick of chalk from the church. She left the Bible.

Joan had the lamp with her—she'd found it by itself inside the house, still lit—refilled and burning bright. She held it in her left hand and the chalk in her right.

The day had already grown hot, so entering the mine was cool and refreshing, though not like the stream had been. The tunnel sloped gently down, largely straight. She only had to crouch a little to follow it. Doubtless the brothers who'd dug it had been taller than her.

She didn't call out. There was only one way it could have taken Margaret, if it had taken her at all. No sense in alerting it to her presence any more than her lamp already did.

After a while, the passage branched, but one branch only went a dozen yards. Joan took the other, and that's when she found the forest. It was strange enough that she paused a moment, holding the lamp close.

Leaves of stone, as if carved into the ceiling and along one wall by some crazed but highly skilled sculptor. Fossils of vanished ferns. They looked tropical. She had trouble picturing Arizona ever having been like that, but here it was. Had she found the remains of Eden? She couldn't have. That was supposed to be by the Tigris and Euphrates.

She followed the tunnel as it changed, from straight into a downward spiral. Everywhere along the walls and ceiling and floor, the plants intertwined with one another. Joan had traveled all over the western part of the continent, but she recognized none of them. *What antediluvian world once thrived here? How long ago?* As she descended, she formed the impression the brothers must at some point have stopped searching for silver and simply dug deeper into that primeval forest.

Joan reached Margaret without warning. She rounded more of the spiral, intrigued by the birdlike creatures that had appeared on and beneath the branches and leaves, and there the child sat at the end of the tunnel.

She was translucent now, her dress as well as her skin. She looked back at Joan with wide, empty eyes that didn't focus.

Next to her stood a feathered reptilian form, or the shadow of one. Even in the light, its body was dark as tar, the feathers more an impression of flight than anything else. Only its chalk-white teeth shone bright.

The creature focused on Joan and charged.

This works or it doesn't. Joan dropped to one knee and drew a solid line with the chalk across its path, then scuttled backward out of range.

The beast stopped at the line, jaws snapping. These too, Joan noticed, did not cross.

"Well," she told herself as she stood painfully up. "That's half the battle."

She walked up to the creature, stopping maybe a foot away,

and held the light up to its face. It didn't flinch. "You're out of your time. The Flood is long gone now. It's our time. You should be at your rest. How can I help you?"

It thrashed about, as if it understood her speech and found it unsettling, then returned to glare at her with its tar-black eyes. It couldn't pass the barrier. No part of it could.

But I can. Slowly, Joan put the lamp down on the floor of the cavern. She glanced at Margaret, who lay on the dirt now, transparent. She could see where the girl would leave her chalk impression.

Joan returned her attention to this strange shadow of an antediluvian beast.

Then she leapt.

She drew a line over one of its eyes before it twisted its head and caught her. It snapped its jaws across her chest, though it didn't pull her anywhere, just clamped down. The teeth tore through clothes and flesh, but they didn't rend. Instead it felt like dozens of ice-cold knives slicing into her. Joan felt weaker, tired, exhausted really, but in no more pain than she'd already been. With careful deliberation, she found and crossed out its other eye.

Now it did lift her off her feet and shake her back and forth. Joan saw her own flesh begin to fade. Its color drained until it was as pale as Margaret's had been when they'd met. Then it got paler still. She let herself go limp, and the blind beast stopped thrashing enough for her to focus on its body again.

"Maybe this." She drew a line across its neck, slitting its throat with the chalk.

The beast didn't so much drop her as fall apart around her. It became dirt, then dust, then nothing at all. By the time Joan crashed onto the shaft floor, it was gone.

But it had left her something. Joan's color was back. In fact, her skin glowed. A black light poured from it, drowned out the pure light of the lamp. She felt the tug of the ages, a call across time into a wild past, one she could reach out toward, could fall into. She knew now where the souls of Truth, Arizona, had gone, and she longed to join them with a kind of mindless abandon.

No. Margaret deserves a life here, now. I can give her that. I can use this light, transform it.

Joan rose. She stood tall, head against the top of the shaft, free of the pain from her long walk, her many falls, from the abuse she'd put her body through for the last many days of running, then fighting. She approached the dying child and laid her hands upon her.

"Where will you go?" Margaret sat on the front steps of the church and turned toward Joan, seated beside her. She passed back the bottle of whorehouse whisky that Joan had let her take one—and only one—sip from. The girl hadn't coughed and sputtered, so Joan figured that wasn't her first sip of whisky. *Probably not the only thing her pa didn't know about.* Still, the kid was too young for drink. Plenty of time for that when she grew up, now that she would grow up. She'd never be a teetotaler, that much was clear.

"Don't know where I'll go," Joan said. "Up to Deadwood, maybe. You?"

"Got an aunt in Tombstone, Pa's younger sister."

Joan nodded. She put the bottle back in a saddlebag. She'd have to keep track of how full it was. "I'll take you."

Margaret gave her a quizzical look. "Ain't that a bit out of your way?"

Joan shrugged. "Tombstone's still Arizona. That makes it a local stop, right?"

Margaret grinned. "I suppose it does."

Joan stood, offered the kid a hand. Without hesitation, Margaret accepted.

THE SPINNERS

Jennifer Campbell-Hicks

The Spinners resided in a ghost town under big prairie skies. Eloise rode in on a main street reclaimed by grasses. Hitching posts and broken shutters marked what used to be the feed store, the smithy and the sheriff's office.

Wind gusted through grass with a sound like a hundred rattlers. Eloise pressed a hand to her wide-brimmed hat, while the long braid of her hair whipped around her. Her horse snorted and pranced.

"It's all right." Eloise dismounted and rubbed his nose. "This place gives me the willies, too. It doesn't feel solid, like it might blow away."

She stayed on foot and led the horse toward a decrepit saloon with holes for windows and a hawk's nest on the eaves. The horse planted its hooves and refused to go any closer. When it reared and almost kicked Eloise, she backtracked to tie him to a hitching post that wasn't rotted through.

"Don't you run off," she said. "You do that, and I'll be stuck here."

Satisfied the horse would stay put, Eloise returned to the saloon. Her spurs jingled and her boots clomped up three steps and across a wooden porch to a door that creaked on rusty hinges.

The place smelled like a barn. Animals had left behind nests, scat and bones. Sunlight shafted through broken windows onto dust-covered tables and chairs, some overturned, some splintered or missing legs. Broken bottles littered the floor. Behind the bar was a mural of a tree, bare branched and bristling with brambles.

Eloise's heart quickened.

This was the place.

After months of searching, on a horse she had stolen from her father's ranch, with money she pinched from her father's safe, with impossible hopes in her heart, she had finally arrived.

"Hello?" she said.

A voice came from the shadows like the rumble of an avalanche. "Why are you here?"

Her hand flew to Peter's gun on her belt. Beside it hung the knife that had once belonged to her sister, Annie—buried in the ground these last ten years. None of Eloise's belongings, it seemed, were her own. The most important—her heart—she had given to Peter, only to have it die alongside him.

What did that leave her with?

"Show yourself," she said.

"Why?"

"I'm here to deal. That's what you do, right? You make deals."

Outside the saloon, clouds crossed the sun, and the shadows deepened. They swirled and slithered across the walls, and an eerie sense of déjà vu came over Eloise, that of a recurring dream of shadows and darkness, and of falling into darkness, falling so long and so far that she would never hit ground. She shivered as the shadows coalesced behind the bar in a semiopaque silhouette that was humanlike, but also not.

Was it one silhouette, or many? Her eyes couldn't focus on the shadows long enough to count. They dissolved and reformed, and through them, the branches of the bramble tree mural appeared to sway in a breeze.

"Saints alive," Eloise muttered.

She lifted her hand from her gun and crossed herself. Bullets would no more harm this shadow than a drop of water would douse a raging forest fire.

"Name your desire," the voice said.

"My husband," Eloise said. "Peter."

"You want him back."

"Yes."

"He is dead."

"Is that a problem?"

Eloise waited, tense and anxious. If they said no, she was out of options. She would return home and do as her father

ordered: marry one of her many suitors who were more inter-
ested in someday inheriting her father's ranch and riches than
in Eloise herself.

She didn't want them. She wanted Peter, dear Peter, the sheriff's
son, with his blue eyes and kind smile, who loved her for her.

"What price will you pay?" the voice asked.

"I'll do anything."

A pouch appeared on the bar. That was how it seemed to
Eloise. One moment, the pouch was not there, and then it was.
It was made from an animal skin unknown to these parts, blue
and pearly, as if from a mythical sea serpent or dragon.

"Take it," the voice said.

"Where'd that come from?"

"We spun it. From another Earth. A different Earth."

That made Eloise uneasy, but she meant what she said. She
would do anything, pay any price. She tied the pouch to her belt.

"There's a cave in the mountains," the voice said. "Go due west
through a steep pass, into the shadow of a mountain shaped like
a buffalo. Fill this with what you find there and bring it to us."

"If I do, you'll give me Peter?" she asked, but outside, the
clouds dispersed. Sunlight pierced the saloon and flooded the
dark corners. Eloise squinted against the sudden light. When she
looked again, the shadows were gone.

For five days, Eloise rode west through the mountains. The
terrain was rocky and steep. Travel was slow. She hoped when
this was over, she could find her way out again.

The stores in her saddlebags ran low, so she packed late
spring snow into her water flask and set snares to catch rabbits
and squirrels.

Each night, when she set the snares, she recalled hot summer
days when she and Annie and Peter had done this together. They
once caught a quail with beautiful speckled feathers. Annie had
wanted to cook it. Of the two sisters, she was the rough one, more
like their father than soft-hearted Eloise, who begged for the bird's
release. In the end, Peter resolved the argument by cutting the snare.

"She always gets her way!" Annie said.

If only that were true, Eloise thought as she sat by the campfire, wrapped in a horsehair blanket. If it were true, she wouldn't
be here with only her memories for company.

Three days more, and she found the cave, an open wound in the skin of the world. Wind moaned through the dark gap. She couldn't see farther than a couple feet inside. What had the Spinners sent her to find? Gold and treasure? A mystical object? A special plant or fungus? Would she need to defend herself from a bear or cougar?

Brave Peter and reckless Annie—even her father—would have charged in, but Eloise remained cautious. The cave entrance faced west. In a few hours, the sun would drop and pierce the gap, and then she would see.

While she waited, she snared, skinned, gutted and cooked a squirrel, and forced the stringy meat down her throat. She didn't miss the suitors or the pressure from her father to choose one, but she missed good food, hot baths and the comfort of her bed. If this worked, she would have all that again, with Peter. They would be happy.

The sun arced across the sky and sank into a dip between two peaks. Liquid gold light spilled into the cave.

It was now or never.

For courage, Eloise drew Annie's knife in one hand, rested her other hand on her gun, and marched inside.

Eloise returned to the town of no-name and tossed the iridescent pouch onto the saloon bar.

"I did what you wanted," she said.

The shadows formed. Eloise expected it this time but was no less unnerved. They opened the pouch and breathed in its contents, if a shadow could do such a thing.

"Ahhhh," the voice said.

"The cave was empty," Eloise said, "except for air. You could get air anywhere."

"Not air. Perfect nothingness. Only one with nothing in their soul could enter the cave and collect it."

She felt chill. The Spinners had gazed into her soul and found nothing. This is what had come of losing Peter.

"Why do you want nothing?" she asked.

"Something can only come from nothing."

She didn't understand. If she asked for an explanation, she wouldn't understand that, either.

"Where is Peter?" she asked.

"He awaits you at home, but know this: We cannot spin the dead back to life. Some barriers are impossible to break. We spun him here from a world like this one but different. He will not be as he was."

Eloise remembered the warning, right up until she saw Peter in the doorway of their small house, on their corner of the ranch with the creek and rolling hills, his blue eyes and tender smile as they had always been.

Good days followed. The suitors left and no new ones came. Eloise's father welcomed back his son-in-law. No one asked questions. Perhaps that was part of the Spinners' magic. Eloise seemed to be the only one to remember Peter lay buried under the willow tree by the creek, beside her mother and Annie.

"How did we meet?" Peter asked one evening on their porch, while he cleaned his rifle and Eloise polished a candlestick.

From her rocking chair, she watched a brilliant orange sunset. Gnats swarmed over the creek, and birds darted among the gnats. On such a perfect summer night, the days of Peter's absence seemed distant.

Except sometimes at night, she still dreamed of falling into darkness, and then sometimes, Peter asked about this world and their life together—a reminder that while he was Peter, he wasn't *her* Peter. She suspected those things were linked, like a horse and its cart, and that if she could make Peter happy, the dreams would end.

"We were children together, you and me and Annie," she said. "You would ride in from town, and we went on adventures. We learned every inch of this land. Then Annie died, and you stopped coming."

"How did she die?"

"She fell from her horse and broke her neck."

Even now, the memory hurt of the impossible stillness of a girl who was always on the move, her eyes sightless and glazed, lips parted in frozen surprise, blood in her long strawberry blond hair. As for Peter, she couldn't judge what he was thinking.

"When did we meet again?" he asked.

"Five years later, at the town harvest festival. It was like we'd never been apart." She took his hand. "You proposed a year later. You built this house for us."

"I've never been much of a builder. My father said I have too many thumbs and not enough sense."

That was the most he had said about his past in a while. Eloise wanted more, but he fell silent, and she didn't push.

The last sliver of sun vanished behind the hills, and a cricket chirped near the creek. More joined it, and more. As a child, Eloise had opened the bedroom window to listen to their songs until Annie grew annoyed at the "racket" and slammed the windows shut.

"What makes that noise?" Peter asked.

"Crickets."

"What's a cricket?"

"It's an insect. It rubs its legs together to make the chirping noise. You didn't have crickets before?"

"No. I don't like them."

"Neither did Annie," she said. "This place must be different for you."

"In some ways, yes."

Peter didn't cry. Her Peter hadn't been a crier, either. But in that moment, he was unguarded, and Eloise saw his grief.

"Are you happy here?"

She hadn't meant to ask that, but the words were past her lips before she could stop them. She was happy with him, but what if he did not feel the same? What if the Spinners gave him no choice in coming here? What if she had selfishly obtained her happiness at the expense of his?

He looked at her.

He told her.

His answer sent her back to the ghost town.

The mural of the bramble tree was gone, and a real tree grew in its place. The trunk burst upward through the wood-paneled floor. Black branches, bristling with spikes, thrust toward windows and into the eaves.

From the branches dangled shapes—cloth dolls, no bigger than Eloise's hand, with yarn hair and black stitching for their eyes and mouth. Hundreds of dolls covered the tree like strange fruit. Instead of apples or peaches, the tree was growing tiny girls and boys.

Where had the dolls come from? The tree, too, for that matter.

Eloise had last stood here mere months ago, but judging by the trunk's thickness, this tree was decades old.

Impossible.

She laughed.

Peter was dead, yet he lived. That alone proved that *impossible* was, in itself, an impossibility.

"Why have you returned?" asked the voice.

Eloise saw no shadow figures, but there was a presence whose weight pressed down on her, and she was frightened. She wished Peter was with her, but her father had needed his heir at the ranch. Besides, this was her mistake to fix, not his. She had slipped away in the night and only told Peter afterward, in apologetic letters delivered by Pony Express.

"You know why I'm here," she said.

"Do you think so?"

"You chose a specific version of Peter to—what do you call it?—*spin* to this world. You know what he left behind."

"His son."

Eloise spat her distaste for the shadows. "You separated a parent from a child. That was cruel. What did the boy think when his father disappeared?"

She hoped her righteous anger would sway the shadows, yet she also felt guilt for her own part in this tragedy. She had orchestrated her husband's return without a thought to his own desires.

Because of that, she owed him. Peter wanted his son. *Their* son, though she had not met the boy. She and her Peter had wanted children, but the sickness took him away too soon.

The dolls twisted subtly so they faced Eloise with their frozen smiles. She would not allow them to frighten her.

"Give him back his son," Eloise said.

"You want the boy?"

"I demand him."

"You must pay a price."

"I won't return to your cave of nothingness."

"That is no longer the price."

"Name it," she said, while she thought, *What do you want, you devil? You trickster?*

"Bring us the innocence of a child," the voice said.

"What?"

Her anger faltered.

The voice repeated.

"I don't understand," Eloise said. "How do I do that?"

Why would she do that? To steal a child's innocence was to erase a bit of goodness and purity from the world, to snuff out a small light against the darkness.

The voice didn't answer. The presence that had weighed on her lifted. Suddenly the dolls were just dolls, and the tree just a tree. This time, the Spinners had left nothing on the dusty bar for her to collect and carry what they had tasked her to find.

Eloise searched aimlessly, with no plan except to keep moving until a plan presented itself.

On clear nights, she lay with her saddle for a pillow, stared at the stars and thought about worlds where Peter and Annie were alive, where she and Peter had started a family together, where they shared the memories of their son's birth and his first steps and his first words. She yearned for such a world with a desire so strong it hurt.

Peter knew their son, but she did not. Did he have her eyes or Peter's? What color was his hair? Was he smart or athletic, a daredevil or a bookworm? Would he recognize her as his mother? Would she love him as her own?

Such questions consumed her. Weeks passed. She wrote more letters to Peter, telling him how much she loved and missed him and how she dreamed of the day she would be in his arms again. Summer did battle with autumn, lost and retreated to gather its strength for next year. Prairie grasses browned. Dry leaves crunched under her horse's hooves.

Eloise wandered from town to farm to ranch and wondered how to take a child's innocence, and whether she even should. She had lost her own innocence on the day Annie died. Who had taken it, she wondered, or had it evaporated into nothing, like dew drops on a hot day?

The next town was like every other one: a main street, buildings, horses and wagons, goods and services, a way station amid the ocean of grass. In this one, townsfolk crowded in the street around wooden gallows, hastily constructed, meant to be torn down when its purpose was fulfilled.

Eloise hitched her horse and walked over. She had witnessed a hanging when she was fourteen years old, and the man whose neck had cracked was a thief who stole cattle from her father.

This man who marched to the gallows had his hands tied behind his back. He was pale but stoic, determined to face death with bravery.

"What did he do?" Eloise asked a woman in the crowd. She wore a homespun dress and apron, and looked at Eloise, in her dirty men's garb, with suspicion. "I'm traveling. Passing through. I just rode into town."

"He killed his wife's lover," the woman said.

"That's a hanging offense?"

"It's murder, ain't it?"

A man with a deputy's star on his chest fitted the noose around the neck of the murderer, who searched the crowd until he found a person he was looking for. His lips formed the words *I love you*.

"Papa!" cried out a young voice. "Papa, papa!"

"Saints alive," Eloise said. "He has a child?" Without thought to the consequence, she cried, "Stop! You must stop!"

Murmurs from the crowd followed her as she pushed her way to the gallows. The child's cries rose above all. Eloise climbed onto the wooden platform. Her eyes found the child, a girl clutching a doll.

The deputy on the platform unholstered his gun. "Whoever you are, you get outta here. This ain't none of your business."

"You would deprive a child of her father. That makes it my business, and the business of all decent folk."

He pointed his gun. "You wanna get shot?"

Eloise knew she should stand down, that this wasn't her mission, but she couldn't stop. "Do you want to kill two people today? Exile this man from your town, if you must, but don't ruin this child's life. I beg you."

The girl sniffled.

The deputy cocked his gun. "Last chance."

Eloise looked not at him but the girl at the base of the platform. Her tear-streaked face radiated fear and hope, and something else. Innocence.

The innocence of a child.

Though it tore her heart, she knew what she must do. To reunite Peter with his son, she must tear this father and child apart.

"I'm sorry," she said and stepped aside.

The deputy holstered his weapon. He kicked at a latch, a trapdoor opened and the condemned man fell through.

The girl screamed as her father spasmed and twitched at the end of the rope. Eloise stared through the opening of the trap-door, and she imagined herself falling into the darkness beneath, like in her dream. Vertigo seized her. Her balance failed, her foot slipped off the gallows platform and she tumbled over the edge, several feet down into the dirt. No one moved to help her.

This is my fault, she thought as she lay there with her guilt and grief, while another internal voice said, *There was nothing you could do.*

Then it was over. The crowd loosened like a frayed knot and came apart. The girl was led away by an older woman. Eloise watched the body be cut down and tossed onto a cart.

An object lay beside her. She picked it up. It was the girl's doll, hair made of corn silk and eyes and mouth of black thread. It was a childhood treasure, but the girl had walked away without it, changed forever; no longer in need of such a thing.

Eloise cradled the doll as she walked back to her horse. She tucked it into her saddlebags with the tenderness that its former owner might not know again in this lifetime.

She rode from the town as fast as she could and took the doll to the Spinners.

Their son's name was Simon. He was four years old, with blue eyes and strawberry blond hair. For the first time since the deaths of her mother and sister, Eloise was part of a family. Laughter lived in their home by the creek. She had thought when Peter returned she could not be happier. She had been wrong.

The day was chill and the ground soft from a recent snow. Peter had gone to town. Eloise and Simon tended to the chickens, and they made a game of blowing out clouds into the winter air.

In the afternoon, Eloise had Simon practice riding on old brown mare named Milly. To test his knowledge, she had the boy tell her how to saddle and bridle the horse, and corrected him when he didn't get it quite right. He hugged his arms around her neck as she hoisted him into the saddle, and she adjusted the stirrups for his short legs.

"Hold the reins like this," she said and positioned his hands on the soft leather strip.

"I know that."

"What else do you know?"

"I know how to ride."

"Oh, do you?"

He nodded solemnly. He was a serious boy. "I've known how to ride forever. Since I was three. But not on horses like this. Horses here ain't proper."

Did the horses he knew have wings? Or six legs? Or red eyes? She didn't ask because she didn't want him to think too much about before. Simon was young and would forget he had lived in any world but this one.

"Milly is a proper horse," she said. "She likes carrots. When we're done practicing your riding, you can feed her one."

The anticipation of giving Milly a treat made Simon forget about anything else. He squeezed his boots into the horse's flanks. Milly responded by plodding forward a few steps and stopping to munch on dry grass between two patches of snow.

Simon kicked the horse's flanks. "Come on, horse," he said, but Milly ignored him. Eloise sensed his frustration. He had told her he could ride, but Milly wouldn't cooperate with his declaration. He kicked harder. "Go, horse! Go!"

All at once, Milly went. She shot off like a bullet with Simon bumping along atop, yelling, "Help!"

Eloise ran after. "Simon!"

She yanked up her skirts to free her legs. She wished she could wear men's pants here, as she did on the trail. She ran fast, but she couldn't catch a horse at full gallop. Her only hope was that Simon would control the animal, which was unlikely, or Milly would turn around on her own.

Simon started to slip.

"Aunt Eloise, help!"

Eloise watched, terrified, as Simon tilted to the right and his left foot parted from the stirrup and he tilted farther and farther until he crossed some invisible barrier and jolted out of the saddle entirely and toppled headfirst toward the ground.

For a heartbeat, Eloise was a girl again, watching a horse rear and buck and throw her sister from the saddle.

Forgetting when she was, she screamed, "Annie!"

Her feet were too slow, her boots seemingly encased in lead, but she reached the motionless figure at last and knelt beside him. Milly, having rid herself of her passenger, slowed and walked back toward the barn.

Simon cried, his whole body shaking. He clutched his left arm to his chest.

Despite herself, Eloise felt relief. He was alive.

"Are you hurt?" she asked. She reached for him, but he jerked away. "It's all right. Does your arm hurt? May I look at it? It's all right. I'm here. Your mother is here."

"You're not!"

The words stung her. "I am."

"You're not!"

In her earlier panic, she had not noticed what he had named her when he called for help. Now she remembered.

"You said Aunt Eloise."

His eyes were watery and helpless. "Father says I must call you Mother and not Aunt. Please don't tell him."

"I'm not your mother?"

He shook his head.

"Annie?" she asked.

He nodded miserably.

Stunned, Eloise looked out at the winter landscape without seeing it, and without hearing another word of Simon's, or his sobs as she lifted him in her arms and carried him to the house.

Her world was not as she had believed. Peter had kept secrets and had persuaded Simon to do the same.

Why had he not been honest? She hitched a wagon to Milly, who had returned to the barn, calm and oblivious to the chaos she had caused, but Eloise could not find that same calm. She drove the cart with Simon in the back to town to see the doctor. The long trip gave her thoughts time to settle into two new truths.

The first made her sad, that the Peter with whom she now shared a life was not her husband. In his world, Annie had lived. Eloise had separated her sister from her husband and son. She had destroyed their family.

The second truth filled her with rage: Peter had lied to her, but she couldn't believe he did it of his own accord. He had to have been coerced in some way.

Eloise knew who had done the coercing—there was only one possibility—but not why. She had to know why. For that, she would have to make one last visit to the Spinners.

☆   ☆   ☆

A hundred children or more filled the streets of the town with no name. They ranged from toddler to teen. Boys and girls. White, brown and black. They played games with balls and sticks, and chased one another around the blacksmithy, and dug in the dirt, and stood doing nothing more than staring at a bug or a tree. They talked and yelled and laughed and cried.

Bewildered, Eloise walked among them. She might as well have been invisible for the interest the children showed in her.

This was wrong. The wrongness wasn't just a gut feeling. It had gravity to it, a solid presence that was more *there* than the buildings around her and the ground she stood on. Every instinct told her to leave, but she couldn't. Not until she had answers.

An older girl with brown braids sat on the steps of the old general store, engrossed in a dime novel. On the cover, a cowboy pointed his six-shooter at a green alien creature with a huge head.

"Good morning," Eloise said.

"Mornin'," the girl said.

Eloise wasn't invisible, after all.

"How did you get here?" she asked the girl, who shrugged without looking up from the dime novel. "Where are your mother and father?"

"Ain't got no mum and dad."

"Everyone has parents."

She shrugged again.

"Where are you from?" Eloise asked.

"Over there."

"I don't understand."

Shrug.

"What do you mean, over there?"

The girl looked up. Her irises were so dark as to appear black. She pointed at the saloon.

"You came from that building?"

She nodded and returned to her reading.

No children played on the saloon's steps and porch, as if by mutual agreement this area was off-limits. The bramble tree had doubled in size since Eloise had last seen it. The tree and building had gone to battle, but the battle was over now, and the building had given its surrender. Branches thrust through windows, walls and the roof—gnarly, knotted wood, bent into clawlike shapes.

This was the source of the wrongness. The feeling became

more concentrated as Eloise approached the saloon. Climbing the steps to the porch felt as if she climbed a mountain.

Inside, the sounds of the children silenced. Eloise heard only her own breathing. The air smelled of rotten things. The tree trunk took up half the space. Roots crawled across the floor. Eloise stepped over them. She stared at the tree for several seconds before she realized the dolls were gone.

"You have returned," said the voice.

"What have you done?" Eloise demanded. She looked for a shadow figure behind the splintered bar but saw none. "Why is the town full of children? How did they get here?"

"That is not your business."

"It is my business. What do you mean to do with them?"

"What we will."

"I take it back," Eloise said. "The deals we made. All of it."

"You cannot undo what has been done."

"You gave me a husband and child who are not my own."

"He made a deal with us. In coming here, in doing what he did, he fulfilled his part of it."

That took Eloise's breath away. Peter had dealt with the Spinners.

"What deal did he make?"

"Only he can say."

"I asked. He turned away and would not speak."

"Then you will not know."

She clenched her fists in frustration. "If he has fulfilled his part, send him home. Send them both home. Will you do that?"

"We will on one condition. Your life, freely given, to spin where we please."

Incredulous, she said, "You would do to me what you did to him?"

"Yes."

Only then did Eloise understand how neatly she had walked into their trap. Was this what had happened to Peter? Had he lost Annie or Simon and made a deal to bring them back, only to discover that in seemingly getting what he wanted, the Spinners had used him instead?

Her own Peter had been loyal and loving. He would have done anything for his family. This Peter would have done the same.

In her mind, she saw the man who was not her husband, and

his son Simon, with her sister's strawberry hair. It was them, or her. That was her choice. Which meant there was no choice at all.

She bowed her head in defeat.

"Send them home," she said. "I am yours."

"It is done."

The tree shivered, then shook. The roots undulated, while shadows spun faster and faster. A roaring filled her ears, louder than her pounding heart.

The tree glowed from within, a cold light like which she had never seen before and could not have described even if a gun were put to her head. The light spread from the core to the branches to the brambles, but it did nothing to illuminate the room.

Eloise gaped. She forced down a scream. Was this what Peter had seen? And Simon?

A sinuous root caught her foot. She tumbled backward and expected to hit ground, but she didn't. Shadows swallowed her. The saloon and tree vanished. In darkness, she fell and fell, and closed her eyes and waited for impact.

THE STOKER AND THE PLAGUE DOCTOR

Alex Acks

"I don't give a shit about the hazard pay. I'm not doing it," the stoker, a man named Eli, snapped.

James, the depot agent, crossed his beefy arms over his chest. "You think you got a choice?"

Theodore watched them argue with annoyance. He felt seconds slipping away like sand grains through his fingers, each one perhaps representing the last breath of some unfortunate man or woman's life. He'd gotten as far as Cheyenne City, Wyoming, on regular freight trains, his space assured by the fact of his rank. But there were no trains scheduled out to anywhere near his next stop for well over a week, and that was far too long. He'd tried to acquire an engine and a stoker for the journey, but he didn't have the sealed orders that would allow him to demand it. And thus, this stupid argument.

"You're damn right I got a choice," Eli continued. "You can have me whipped all you like, but that still won't make me wake the fire."

"Maybe I'll have you up on charges. Insubordination. How about treason?"

Theodore cleared his throat. The other two men looked down at him, as if they'd almost forgotten he was there. His diminutive height had been of use to him in the past, when it came to sniffing out secrets and remaining unnoticed by bullies. Now, with the clock ticking on the mission he'd set for himself, it had become a burden that made everyone underestimate him, from the surgeon general to these utter morons. "There is no criminality in refusing to volunteer for an unsanctioned journey." As tempting as it was to lie in pursuit of the greater good, he was far too honorable of a man for that. "But I will promise you a favor. A heavy one."

"Ain't a favor big enough in the world to die for," Eli said. "Not even from one of *you*."

Before Theodore could respond to that implied insult, a muffled shout sounded through the half-open door that stood nearby. "I'll take the job!"

"Who was that?" Theodore demanded.

"No one—" James began.

Theodore yanked the door open, summoning forth a wash of cool, earthy air. Wooden stairs led downward, and he followed them. James, cursing, was right behind him. In the claustrophobic basement of the train depot, there was a single, small cell made of iron bars, and a redheaded, pale man inside. A fist-sized cage of copper wire that flared with the living heat of a spark hung over his heart on a chain—he was a stoker, then. The man's eyes widened as he looked at Theodore and took in his apparel: long black coat of a particular cut, a silver watch chain peeking from his pocket, and black leather gloves.

The man jerked back from the bars, crossing himself as he said: "Plague doctor."

Theodore was used to being treated with a sort of cautious respect, often laced with fear by those who mostly knew plague doctors by reputation, but this man looked like he'd seen a ghost. On the other hand, Theodore did not care. He only needed someone who would get him where he needed to go. He looked at James, whose ruddy complexion had become an apoplectic maroon. "Well, is this man a stoker?"

"That's Leon O'Connell. He's a damned murderer. Killed one of yours, even," James said. "Just waiting for the damper to come through next week, and then he won't be my problem anymore."

"I don't care." So this stoker deserved to die. Expediency meant in this moment that it didn't matter. Theodore looked back at Leon, and the man shivered under his gaze. "I can't call on a favor large enough to save you from the hangman. Do you still volunteer?"

Leon squared his shoulders and stepped back up to the bars. "I'll take being under the sun again before I die."

"You will release him into my custody, then," Theodore told James.

James hemmed and hawed, cussed and wheedled, but Theodore would not be moved. Lives were at stake, and he wasn't above reminding the depot agent where plague doctors fell in the hierarchy of the Army on the Frontier. In that, it didn't matter that the surgeon general hadn't sent him.

James at last unlocked the cage. As Leon stepped out, Theodore pulled off one of his gloves and reached up to touch the man's face. He felt in that instant the warm vitality that rang through all stokers, and tasted metal and oil and smoky fire. For that instant, he held Leon's life in his hands, and the power of it was both intoxicating and displeasing—there was nothing wrong with the man's health, for all he deserved to die for his crimes. Theodore nudged him with his power, enough to twist his gut a little. Leon staggered back satisfactorily, clutching at his stomach.

"The fuck was that?" Leon gasped.

"Disease," Theodore said shortly. "If you run, if you kill me, you will be dead in three days, and it won't be peaceful."

James guffawed into Leon's horrified silence. "Let's get you to your engine, then."

The old 4-2-0 had seen better days—its cattle guard bent and pitted with rust, all of its paint covered with soot or long since blasted off by sand. And that's all that waited on the tracks: the single locomotive, surrounded by rolling ropes of August heat.

Being in the light had at least pushed the feeling of sickness away from Leon's gut and left him filled with energy; the living spark of soul and metal and fire caged at his neck—which had guttered low while he'd been in his cell—flared hot back to life against his skin. He felt whole for the first time in weeks, with the tracks humming nearby, thrumming with the song of dozens of locomotives large and small as they worked across the country. He rested a hand on the locomotive and felt it stir; it was tired, aching, so unlike his old partner that it made him ache, too. "Not expecting to come back, huh," he said to the plague doctor.

"The lack of faith isn't mine," the little man snapped. He crossed his arms over his barrel chest, his black eyes sparking in his sallow face. "Is there anything else you need before we depart?"

"Just the destination."

"Owlwood." At Leon's confused look, the plague doctor added, "The spur out past Whitewood."

"That's a long fucking trip," Leon observed. Fine by him, because it was that many more days of life, that many more days to try to figure out how to escape the doctor's witchcraft and the law.

"Did you have somewhere else to be?"

Leon laughed and climbed up into the locomotive like it was the scaffold to the noose. But damn, it felt good to have the heavy iron around him again. He was dimly aware of the plague doctor behind him as he rested his hands on the engine's heart and felt it stir in response. "Just one more time for both of us," he said, coaxing. He opened the cage at his throat one-handed and guided the spark down into the engine's heart, where it flared into full, hot life.

The locomotive wheezed unsteadily through its bent stack, like an unsteady snore. Its great heart beat slowly, unevenly, then began to speed as the machine woke. Engines were monsters made by man; they couldn't be truly alive, no matter how much blood and flesh got folded into the metal. But with half a stoker's soul and fire, they became the mightiest animals to ever shake the earth. Leon felt the engine's elemental awareness, its wordless, fatigued questioning and pains, and did his best to reassure it: one more time.

The locomotive understood, gathered itself, and began to accelerate down the track, wheels screeching as the rust stripped from them.

Leon sat down on the splintery bench seat, his chest heaving and head swimming. Maybe it was another symptom of having been out of the sun for so long, but he was tired. He glanced at the plague doctor, still standing at the end of the engine compartment. A few narrow chests had been stacked up in the limited space, presumably the doctor's belongings and, Leon hoped sincerely, supplies. "Got some water in there?"

Wordlessly, the plague doctor flipped the lid on one trunk and offered him a canteen.

"You going to keep standing there the whole time? It's a long trip."

"I didn't expect it to be comfortable." But the plague doctor sat on the bench across from Leon, carefully avoiding touching him.

Leon drank the lukewarm water. "Your lot doesn't normally travel alone." Plague doctors were too valuable to send off without a cadre of soldiers, particularly when there were some areas of the frontier where people had strong feelings about witchcraft or shamanism.

"It's no concern of yours."

"Is what we're headed into also not my concern? Because I'd like to know if I got a different kind of agonizing death waiting for me."

The plague doctor tilted his head. "Your supervisor said you were a convicted murderer. Who did you kill?"

Leon bared his teeth. "Jumped a train off the track. On purpose." When the man offered him no reaction, not even a slow blink of the eyes, he continued, "Army train. Taking cannons and Gatlings out to the cavalry so they could cut up more Indian women and babies. And yeah. One of you."

"Not merely a murderer, then. A traitor," the plague doctor said coolly.

"Proud of it," Leon said. He felt a stab of sorrow, thinking of the locomotive he'd destroyed in the process. The great machine that he'd been partnered with since he'd gotten out of the army school at sixteen, the source of the metal he'd used to make his spark, had deserved better. And maybe that word gave him a lick of sick guilt, just because he'd been beaten into a shape that was supposed to feel that way since he'd been taken in. That just kindled his resentment.

There was no pity or understanding in the plague doctor's face, but no anger either. He was a blank slate, and Leon saw only his own belligerence reflected back in the man's black eyes. "There was a choleric outbreak in Owlwood, of unusual proportions. This requires investigation. You will very likely die there, and deservedly so."

Leon considered the plague doctor's face, still round with baby fat. "And you'll be stuck. Pissed someone off, did you?"

They did not speak again until they reached Owlwood.

Owlwood was a hell-on-wheels town, the sort made of equal parts rail workers, drifters, gamblers, and whores. These spur towns sucked up rail company money like milk from a tit, kept afloat only to justify building the line out this far into the god-forsaken plains. Hell, the first building visible, across from the platform that would someday be a rail depot—if the town didn't just dry up and blow away—was a saloon that should have been belching gun smoke and whiskey fumes and shouting drunks out into the packed dirt that stood in for a street.

Except that Owlwood lay silent as a crypt, save for the hiss of wind in dry grass, the metallic squeal of an unoiled wind-mill, the hum of flies. The trees that presumably gave the town its name were a dark smudge on the horizon, marking the Owl River. As the wind shifted toward the locomotive, it carried the stink, the sour throat-choke of rot in the sun.

Leon felt the locomotive's unease and offered it comfort he did not feel. It was probably for the best that he needed to lay the great machine down; he sang it the traditional lullaby with a throat scratchy with death scent and pulled his spark back into its cage to rest.

The plague doctor stood on the platform, his arms crossed over his round chest, his smooth chin dipped.

Leon rasped at the stubble on his own and wondered if he could ask for a shave, but he doubted it. Traitors didn't get sharp objects.

"They all dead?" he asked.

"Not all," the plague doctor said. "There's still life in the town. I've come in time." He pulled a set of manacles from his pocket.

"Is that necessary?" Leon asked.

"I'll leave you out in the sun, if you prefer."

"I could help you."

"I neither want nor need further aid from a traitor."

The urge to throw a punch tightened Leon's fist, but he also still felt that twist in his gut. He was a dead man in so many ways, but whatever the plague doctor had done to him would probably be the worst. He let the man chain him to the platform railing, full in the sun so he could enjoy the light at least, for all the light felt thinner up in Dakota Territory.

Theodore ignored the stoker as he prepared himself for the hunt. Most of the supplies in his trunk would wait until he knew what exactly he was dealing with, but certain things were unquestionably required: hand mirror, silver scalpels, a few pre-cious glass tubes for the inspection of fluids, and his mask. The plague doctor's mask hadn't changed much over the centuries, but for the beak being repurposed. Theodore's training and talents in the arcane arts made him immune to all but the most evilly conceived diseases; the mask's true purpose was to help him sniff them out. As always, he felt a curious relief settle over him as he pulled on the mask. The glass lenses of the eyes warped the world outside slightly, to a truer form. But more importantly, he felt the relief of having his face covered, the assurance that no one could now look at him and think they saw something he was not.

It was a relief, really, to not have the soldiers trailing him. He was tired of their jokes and comments, just as he was tired of arguing with his colleagues—who had known him since he'd been delivered to the army school—what his proper name was. What a time he had come to in his life, that he was happier to travel in the company of a traitor and murderer.

He set out into the deserted dirt swathes that stood in for the few streets of Owlwood, seeking out the signs of life he had felt at the edge of his awareness. This took him to a small house, its walls uneven and filled with gaps, at the end of one of the streets. He did not bother to knock as he went inside.

The air was thick and close, and he smelled the sickness—and vomit, blood, and shit—along with the exhalations of the living. The back room of the house contained a bed with two Chinese women. They shivered under a thin blanket despite the heat of the day that already had sweat collecting in the small of Theodore's back.

One of the women opened her bloodshot brown eyes and saw him, an unsteady little scream escaping her mouth.

"I am here to take your sickness away," Theodore said, though she looked too ill and feverish to understand, if she even spoke English. He pulled off one glove and rested his hand on her clammy forehead, letting his awareness fall into her body. The disease was superficially like cholera, he felt immediately, but twisted into something new and even more deadly. He forced the miasma of it into a single mass and pushed that through her blood. All it took was a little flick of one of the silver scalpels to open a vein in her arm and let the filth of it ooze out, shit-brown and smoking.

He wiped the miasma away with a bit of cloth and bound her arm up with another. When he met the woman's narrow eyes again, they were still fever bright, but recognition lived in them now. "Where do you get your water?" he asked.

With a shaking voice, she told him.

One by one, Theodore visited each shack that still had a living person in it; there weren't so many as that. At each, he drew out sickness, asked after their water, and told them all the same thing: drink beer for now, do not touch the well, and wash yourself thoroughly. Most of the population seemed to be common laborers, Chinese salted with Irish, not unusual for this area.

He passed by the churned, bare dirt of a mass grave, buzzing with black flies. His feet dragged a bit by the end of those visits, an unfortunate consequence of having done so much healing. But he'd known this would happen, when he'd found the discarded plea for help in the surgeon general's wastebasket. And this was no better nor worse than what some of the more famed plague doctors of the corps had done in the past. He knew he was as strong and competent as his peers—more so, even—and this would be his ultimate proof of that fact.

As he mounted the platform, the murderer Leon spoke to him: "Mind giving me a drink of water again?"

He'd almost forgotten the man was there. Theodore pushed his mask up so he could wipe the sweat from his face. Loyalty to one's part in the great machine of American progress; that lesson had been the drumbeat of his life. But Theodore couldn't quite find it in his heart to think that a condemned man must suffer more. It did not sit well with his principles as a healer; perhaps that was why his colleagues thought him soft.

He gave Leon the water canteen again and released one of the man's hands so he wouldn't have to contort himself around the railing to drink. "You about done?" Leon asked.

The question, and the concern in it, caught Theodore off guard. "With the healing, yes. Next, I will capture the disease itself, which is best done at moonrise."

"You should rest until then," Leon said.

Motivated, Theodore was certain, by the desire to not die in agony if the plague doctor happened to collapse and leave him chained at the platform. "I'll consider it," he said dryly. He didn't think he could sleep, with the presence of the disease still weighting down the air. Instead, he retreated into the engine where he could gather his materials and prepare; sunset was only a few hours away. As a happy side effect, it meant Leon could not attempt further conversation.

Theodore might have fallen asleep on the splintery bench in the locomotive for a short while, but the oppressive heat left him feeling suffocated. He bore his implements for the battle to come out to the town's well; the seven silver spikes were so heavy he could only carry them two at a time.

"I could help you with those," Leon offered, from where he remained chained to the railing. Theodore ignored him.

The last thing he carried in the fading light of sunset was a bag of salt mixed with silver filings and crushed abalone shells. He used that to draw a circle around the well, adding the appropriate arcane symbols at the compass points. He lit his lantern and set it on the ground nearby, where it cast warped shadows and splashed light across the glittering white-pink salt.

He felt the miasma as the sliver of moon rose, like the deep rumble of an earthquake, spread out in the water underground. Theodore took his one precious vial of quicksilver from his inner pocket and smashed it against the side of the well.

The disease, drawn inexorably by power and silver and the compass points, rose from the well in a great cloud that blotted out the stars and choked off the light of Theodore's lantern. He felt a familiarity to the structure of its form, as he had before, like it had once been cholera but had undergone some demonic transformation. Theodore picked up his hammer and the first silver spike. The miasma beat against the invisible wall made by the salt circle, shrieking and whistling at a pitch no one but a plague doctor could hear.

He stepped across the circle, careful to keep the hem of his coat from disrupting the salt.

The disease crashed down on him like a wave. It felt like warm treacle against the armor of his coat and mask, held at bay by the carefully etched symbols of protection on the inside of the leather. With a mighty effort, Theodore heaved the weight back and stabbed the first spike into it. Between breaths made harsh with effort, he pounded the spike through the miasma and into the ground. He recited: "I swear by Apollo the Healer, by Asclepius, by Hygieia, by Panacea, and by all the gods and goddesses, making them my witness, that I will carry out, according to my ability and judgment, this oath and this indenture..."

The miasma screamed as Theodore picked up another spike and hammered it home again and beat the doctor bruisingly on his shoulders and chest. Sweat soaked Theodore's shirt and gathered at his chin. He tasted salt with each breath. As his muscles burned and a deep ache built in his hands, he continued, "I will use treatment to help the sick according to my ability and judgment, but never with a view to injury and wrongdoing..."

Some plague doctors preferred Christian prayers, but Theodore had found the old oath more powerful to keep his mind and energies focused on the disease despite all fatigue.

His words ran out as he took up the last of the spikes. The disease, pinned but still flapping like a malevolent sheet in unseen winds, slapped him back hard and sent him stumbling. His foot hit the salt circle and smudged it. Immediately, the black thing began to stream for the opening, stretching and thinning to snap where it was pinned. With a hoarse shout, Theodore plunged the seventh spike into the pulsing mass and struck with the hammer.

The miasma let out one last unearthly shriek, then went still, twitching feebly. Dizzy and panting, Theodore forced himself into motion, walking around the circle widdershins seven times. The small circle felt miles across to his aching legs. At the seventh circuit, he pulled up the dregs of his power, already depleted from so much healing earlier, and took out a glass vial from his pocket, mercifully unbroken in the struggle. He touched it to the seventh spike.

All seven of the spikes went black with tarnish. The disease vanished in a soundless explosion that threatened to knock Theodore flat. When he held the vial up, it was filled with something dark and viscous and undeniably evil.

And now that he could see it so concentrated, it carried a terrible veneer of familiarity.

Sickened, he took up his lantern and stumbled back to the rail platform.

"You ain't dead, are you?" Leon asked. He knew the plague doctor wasn't dead. He could see the man's chest rising and falling from where he'd sprawled across the platform, seemingly too exhausted to move further. A little glass vial had tumbled from his fingers and lay nearby. No, the more important question was if he was awake.

The answer to that seemed to be no.

Carefully, he edged along the railing until the manacle around his one wrist caught. The plague doctor hadn't bothered chaining his other hand back up in the afternoon. Leon was a tall man, with long arms. If he leaned as far as he could, his full weight pulling his wrist against the manacle, he could just reach the plague doctor.

Slowly, barely daring to breathe, he began to pull the doctor's coat aside, going for the pocket he knew contained the key.

His gut twisted around the promised agonizing death in three days, but Leon had taken a lot of time to think, sitting out on the platform. There hadn't been anything else to do, other than twitch flies away and watch the plague doctor's comings and goings. He'd tried every trick he knew to ingratiate himself with the fat little bastard, and he might as well have been howling at the moon for help. So he'd concluded, sometime in the afternoon, that if he was going to die anyway, he'd take the pain if it meant not living out his last moments in a dank cellar. And who knew, maybe he could make it far enough west to get to Indian lands. Maybe if he didn't get shot on sight, one of their shamans would be willing to help him if he told his story about the derailed train and his death sentence. It was more hope than the alternative.

His fingers found the key. The plague doctor's eyes flew open behind the mask and he grabbed Leon's wrist with his leather-gloved hands. Leon jerked back, and only succeeded in dragging the man closer. It gave him a new idea: He heaved again, and they were suddenly in fighting distance, and Leon had all the advantages even if he could only use one hand. He twisted free of the plague doctor's grasp and got his hand around the man's throat. "Take your curse off me, you little bastard."

The little man mutely shook his head, his leather-coated fingers scrabbling for purchase on Leon's arms.

"You know I'm a killer. I'm not even going to feel sorry for notching another one of you fuckers. Take your curse off!"

The plague doctor stopped prying at Leon's fingers and started shaking, but it wasn't fear—he was laughing, silent and horrible.

With his high-pitched voice curiously tinny through the apparatus of his mask, he wheezed, "I know...you're lying."

The cold that shot through Leon had nothing to do with magic. His grip relaxed. "The hell did you say?"

The plague doctor pushed his mask up, revealing an expression of horrible merriment. "I know bodies. Your liver's about drowned in drink, and that didn't happen whilst you were locked up. You were no doubt drunk when you derailed that train. You're no willful murderer."

"You're the liar!" Leon kicked the little man, the motion halfhearted rather than savage. He felt naked before the doctor's dark eyes. After weeks of telling the story, he'd almost convinced himself it was the truth, building himself into a new Leon who might be a hero. Now it had all collapsed like a house of cards, and the plague doctor...had stopped laughing.

He'd propped himself up on one elbow. "Why lie about it?"

"I was dead either way," Leon said. Trapped in the wreckage of his train and wishing he'd died, he'd had a lot of time to think. What had stuck in his head was the last thing he'd heard, coming out of Fort Laramie—a preacher going on and on about Indian removal being wrong, shouting to be heard over a jeering crowd. Leon had added a few drunken curses of his own, not because he cared, but because he felt like shouting just then. But in the wreckage, with blood slowly soaking through his shirt, he'd found himself thinking back to the army's so-called school where all the stokers went as soon as they were found. And he'd thought about nights hearing the kids younger than him crying and knowing some of them had come from reservations and thinking maybe they weren't being done any favors. He'd been saved from the breakers and a short life in the mines, himself, but he'd also never seen his family again.

And he'd wished, in those despairing, bleeding moments, he'd had the bravery to make that kind of choice, instead of just losing control of his partner locomotive on a curve, driven too fast by whiskey dizziness, and finding them all irreparably thrown to the earth.

He sat down on the platform, the boards still warm from the sun. "Doesn't matter anyway, if you put a disease in me."

"I might have lied, as well," the plague doctor said. He took the key from his coat pocket and offered it over to Leon.

"Fuck you." But Leon took it and undid the manacles. He chafed his sore wrist as he glared at the little man. It would serve him right if he gave him another good kick and ran off with the locomotive now. "I'm going to fucking leave you here."

The plague doctor picked up the vial from platform and laid back down, holding it toward the moon like he might see through it. It was black as pitch in his hand. "Do you know what this is?"

"Your balls," Leon said, sullenly.

But the plague doctor didn't even seem to be listening to him. "The disease I took from the well. And I know that it was put there by the hand of man. Now that I have it, I can tell that it isn't natural. It was . . . modified. By another plague doctor of the Army on the Frontier. Not the surgeon general himself, I don't think . . . it doesn't smell of him. But one of his close confidantes."

"You can do that?" As if the plague doctors weren't terrifying enough already.

"Oh yes. Though it's a terrible, evil thing to do. We're supposed to use our power and knowledge to heal, never to hurt. And yet." The plague doctor turned the vial in his hand. "Our people have been friends with disease since we first set foot in America, you know."

"What are you going to do with it?" Leon asked. Why was the man telling him this—and why did he care?

"I'm supposed to bring it back to the medical corps, to be examined and classified and cured."

"But?"

"But I'm not inclined to violate my oath and help turn another unseen monster loose."

"So you're going to destroy it?"

"Destroying something like this isn't as easy as moving it or capturing it," the plague doctor said, and sighed. "Without a gathering of plague doctors to help, it would be very dangerous. Most likely deadly." He turned his face to look square at Leon, something new in his dark eyes, an invitation for Leon to understand.

Leon had wanted to believe that he would sacrifice himself for principles that he hadn't really possessed. This odd little man offered him a new choice: face possible martyrdom instead of claiming it retroactively. Leon felt like he stood at the edge of a cliff. It terrified him.

It was a second chance to be the Leon he wanted to believe he was.

"You got a name?"

"What?"

"Don't fancy waltzing down to hell with someone whose name I don't even know."

The plague doctor laughed. "Theodore."

"All right, Theodore." Leon smiled, and it felt strange and free, like he was taking his first breath in weeks. "Where to?"

BIGGER THAN LIFE

Steve Rasnic Tem

Dawson never had many friends. Not that he disliked company; he just didn't have the talent for it. He'd say the wrong thing, or they'd say the wrong thing, and then there'd be a scrap, and by the end of the night he'd either be in the local calaboose with acquaintances he couldn't abide or heading out on his own again, living the hermit's life.

What he truly needed, he believed, was a wife, but he had no better luck with romance than he had with friendships.

"No sir, what you need is some tin," the grizzled prospector said, stirring the fire.

Dawson hadn't been aware he'd spoken aloud. But he was so tired, and the San Juan mountain air so chill, the campfire had him near hypnotized.

"That's money, to a greenhorn like you. You get yourself some money, and the compadres and the females are bound to come around. Grab yourself a root and try some of this." Old Tate passed the stick with what remained of the burnt squirrel. It was mountain squirrel, and bigger than the ones Dawson was used to back East, but skinned and blackened like that it could just as well been a rat. Still, he hadn't had a hot meal since that first day off the train in Denver two months ago. Dawson picked up one of the potatoes on the edge of the fire and took a bite, then leaned in and commenced gnawing on the squirrel.

Tate looked sheepish. "Now it ain't *my* business—long as you do your part with the claim, I'm happy to give you a share—but

177

could you tell me what all them marriage proposals is about? You ain't addle-headed, is you?"

"Well." Reluctantly, Dawson put the meat down. "I reckon love is a kind of madness, as the poets say. But I've been alone most of my life, and I'm damned tired of it. I'm flusterated with the whole business, to be frank. A man needs something bigger than hisself, and that means a family, a house and kids—the whole kit and caboodle."

"Oh, I get that. But askin' every woman you meet if she'll marry you? That farm gal yesterday was a grandma—looked like she were on death's door. Seventy if she were a day! Besides, she had money and property. A bit above your bend, I'd say."

"Love knows nothing of age or class. She were still female, weren't she? Not a lot of women in these mountains. Love is a gamble—I'm trying to improve my odds. I don't much fancy the idea of dyin' alone."

"I bet you ain't heard many yeses!"

"I reckon I just need the one." He paused, turning the stick with the carcass between his hands. "Marital bliss is a big thing, and that's what I'm aiming for. Something big enough to swallow me up. You ever feel that way, Tate?" The prospector grunted. "Well, the war was like that. Big and angry and eatin' men— young'uns and old codgers alike—alive, sometimes spittin' them out with parts missing. They tell me love can be like that, too, and marriage, 'cept it don't kill you. Mostly." Dawson went back to his meat.

Something woke Dawson up in the middle of the night. He sat up quickly and stared around, confused for a moment as to where he might be. This happened to him all the time. He'd moved around a great deal since he first left home to join the 23rd Virginia Volunteers, sleeping under a different sky almost every week. Then, after the war, there'd been farm work down South, and a little ranch work in the Midwest, all the while still wearing pieces of his Confederate uniform until they rotted off and showed his scars. If folks took offense at the uniform, or the scars, he'd just move on. If they asked about the war, he declined to discuss it.

That's when he decided to get married. He'd tried every other job, so why not? But he was aging fast, and God knew when his days would be over, so he commenced asking every likely match and more than a few that weren't. Married women, fresh young maidens, women with babies sitting with their husbands in church. Why not? He kept hearing it was a free country now. Maybe the marriage wasn't happy. Maybe the husband wanted to get rid of her. He reckoned they could always say no.

"Will you be my own?"

That's the way he put it. He thought it sounded sweet that way, although apparently not everybody agreed. He was run off more than once, jailed a few times, threatened, beat up, shot at. But anything worth having was worth taking a risk.

He'd read in the newspapers about the gold found in Colorado, and then the silver. People were going out there to find their fortunes. And wives were expensive, or so he'd been told. Soon as he saved enough for the train trip, he was on his way. He spent a few nights drunk in Denver before journeying south and west into the mountains, arriving one hot day in Rico on the Rio Grande Southern.

He kept staring into the Colorado dark trying to get his eyes to adjust. There were things moving around out there, but he couldn't rightly tell what they were. He still wasn't used to the western nights. On cloudy evenings, they were the blackest he'd ever seen. The few glowing embers left in the fire didn't help none. If anything they lit up just a hint of things he probably wasn't meant to see.

Then there was this low, far-off moan that shook the ground. Dawson could feel it moving up through his feet and kissing his spine. Was that what woke him up? He afeared it, whatever it was.

"That's the bolter," the prospector said groggily from under his blanket. "It's when you don't hear him is when you should worry, which I reckon is most of the time. Lonesome sound, ain't it? Calling for his mate 'cept his mate ain't there. I never hear tell of two of 'em together."

"Bolter?"

"Slide-rock bolter. It's like a, well, a mountain whale."

"Who you trying to fool, old-timer? Whales die out of the water. I seen them, rotting up on the shore. Besides, whales don't make a sound. Afore the war, I spent a year on a square-rigger out of Boston. Heard them whales splashin' aplenty. But they were mute, not like a dog or a donkey."

"You just never heared them underwater, talkin' sweet to their ladies."

Dawson barked a laugh. "Like me, you mean? You're a crazy old man. Is that the kind of tall tale you tell flatlanders?"

Tate shook his head vigorously. "Now I didn't say whale. I said *like* a whale. Different critter entirely. Bolter's bigger than a whale, I reckon. But they's a likeness. Shaped like the world's biggest teardrop, and up front surely the world's biggest mouth. Two giant eyes you don't notice till they opens, and all that skull plate above, like a cliff. It's even got a big tail like a whale, 'cept the bolter's got a bunch of hooks under the tail, like fingers, so it can clamp itself on top one of them steep mountain sides. It hears something below, something loud enough to bother with, it lets go and slides down the mountain mouth open, gobbling up pert near everything in its path: trees, rocks and all, and whatever folks unlucky enough to get in the way."

Dawson wasn't believing a word of this, of course. He figured the old prospector had been wandering these mountains alone too long, more evidence of the ravages of the unmarried life. But still, Dawson had to wonder how the fellow had all this worked out in his head. "So, you got him—the bolter—down the mountain. How does he get back up again?"

"Best part." Tate grinned. "It's them finger things under his tail. They's strong. They dig into the dirt and the rocks, and they drag him back up the slope a little bit at a time, and they anchor him to the top again until he's ready for his next meal. Now a good night to you." The prospector rolled over and covered his head.

Dawson studied the night some more, and eventually must have fallen asleep. The next thing he knew he was peeling back his lids to a fresh fire of sun.

All that next day they did more digging, widening and deepening the tunnel the prospector had made in the side of the mountain, shoring it up with timbers as they went. It's what they did most days. Dawson didn't mind the work much, though he didn't know how he'd feel once they got deeper under the ground. Dawson liked it much better when sometimes Tate would take the morning off, and they'd go scrambling around the slopes, looking for traces of silver ore where the ground had sheared away, or picking through the remnants of a recent slide for whatever they could find. Tate had almost a biblical faith in his claim, but couldn't stop worrying there might be something better only a short hike away.

On one of those mornings, a few days later, Tate found a rusted pick, along with the twisted remains of a coffee pot, a tin cup and a few scraps of cloth. He crouched down and started pawing through the piles of torn ground.

Dawson held back a bit, uneasy. "What you looking for now?"

"This poor feller's bones, if any are left, and maybe something to tell me who he was."

Dawson looked around. "You think Utes, or claim jumpers?"

"Utes ain't no bother, not since that 'greement took this land out of their reservation. We're in a *slide*, son. Can't you *see*? I reckon this be bolter work."

Dawson looked left and right, finding the edges of the disturbance, and then he gazed straight up the incline to the cliff above. A wide path of nothing led away and up the slope as far as he could see: no trees or other plants, no rocks of any great size, as if a giant spoon had scooped the top off the ground. He squinted. The top of the mountain looked perfectly normal as far as he could tell.

Dawson frowned at Tate. "If there's a giant so-called bolter hanging up there at the top of the peak, how come I can't see him? In fact, I looked at a lot of these mountain tops, and I ain't seen nary a one!"

"You can't take my word for it, a new feller like you? You gotta question everything?"

"What, you ain't got no answers?"

The prospector sighed. "You seen a horny toad, ain't you?"

"Heard of 'em."

"Well, it's like that. Them bolters got a hide on 'em looks like rocks and ground. They blends right in. You could be standin' right on top of one them bolters and not even know it!"

Dawson looked down at his feet and shuffled nervously, looking for some sign of the giant creature he might be standing on. He scowled at old Tate. "Ah, you're just fooling." He waited for a response. Getting none, he said, "Ain't you?"

The next day they took the wagon down to Rico for supplies. Rico was a relatively new place in the world, first born out of whatever wealth could be squeezed out of fur trapping, then later that crazy passion for gold, and then silver out of the

Blackhawk and Telescope mountains. Hell, "rich" was right there in the town's Spanish name. Folks in these parts weren't much for philosophizing; they knew exactly why they were there.

Tate had a long list for the general mercantile: beans and hardtack, flour and Arbuckle's coffee and bacon and those love apples in a can the old prospector loved so much. But Dawson had his own plans for while Tate filled that order. He'd been working so hard up in those mountains, he hadn't had much time to check out the local talent.

He'd spent the day before getting ready, washing that old red shirt of his in the creek, pounding the dirt out on the rocks and then draping it over a squaw apple bush to dry (hopefully getting some of that sweet perfume on it as well). And this morning he shaved—first time since he'd been in the San Juans. It was a torturous operation, and he come out of it with a few nicks which he hoped would add character to his admittedly plain-headed appearance.

First thing he did was ask an old pod outside the mercantile where they were hiding the women. The feller grinned and pointed him toward a smart-looking house down the street, a bed house for a bunch of calico queens. Now Dawson wasn't a prude, even though he'd been saving himself for the right woman. He believed in forgiveness and second chances, and figured there was nothing wrong in calling at a whorehouse, even though it wasn't the usual way courtship occurred. He picked one out and went upstairs with her and when she tried to get his clothes off he kneeled down and said, "Will you be my own?"

She looked down at him—he'd thought she was young, but from that angle she looked as old as his ma—and said, "I'm whatever you want me to be, honey. Long as I get paid."

"Well, I got no money."

"Then how were you going to pay for sex?"

"I'm saving myself for my one and only," he replied.

Next thing Dawson knew, some old rusty guts had pushed him out the front door all the while scolding him for wasting the lady's time.

Undeterred, Dawson went on down the street to where there was a little church. In the yard outside that church, there were tables and chairs and some kind of supper was being served. Dawson sidled up to a table full of women and sat down, tucked a napkin inside his collar, and grinned at the woman sitting next to him.

"Excuse me," she said. "I don't think I know you. Are you a member of this congregation?"

Dawson ducked his head, reached out and took her hand firmly in his. "I could be, if you would agree to be my own." He was so focused on his new love—the rising red in her face only an improvement in her appearance—he didn't notice those tall blue-skins closing in until it was too late.

Tate laid another strip of bacon across Dawson's swollen cheek and examined the results. "You can leave that on awhile, but you get blood on it, it's your breakfast, not mine."

Dawson didn't know how late it was. It might have been dark out, but he still couldn't see too well to know for sure. He'd slept some, but he didn't know how long.

"Thanks for saving me."

"It were pure chance, son. I give up on you, to speak plain. I heard about that dustup at the whorehouse, and then them shenanigans at the church. Hell, boy, you can't mess with them Presbyterians. Some of them folks is *fully armed*.

"I can't get atwixt you and the locals. I need them folks for my supplies. I was on my way out of town, quick as possible, when you run right into the wagon makin' your escape from all them church people. I wasn't there to save you, frankly."

Dawson smiled up at Tate from between two slabs of bacon. "Well, anyway, thanks for not turning me in."

"Oh, I didn't reckon they'd had time to put up no reward money yet." He cackled as if that was the funniest thing anyone'd ever said.

An hour or so later, they peeled the bacon off Dawson's face and fried it up for dinner. Tate even cracked open one of those cans of love apples to celebrate Dawson's survival. Dawson tried to relax some, but he was feeling all jumpy, sorry that he might have caused trouble for Tate. Sorrier still for the state of his social life. Clearly, his attentions weren't welcome in the town of Rico. He wondered if there was any place in the world where they would be.

The night itself seemed to hum in nervous sympathy. There was a constant rustle in the brush, the ticks and flaps of bugs. The air was warmer than it had been in weeks, and the gnats and horseflies were out in their aggravating multitudes. Dawson was ready to jump out of his skin. Even Tate, seemingly too old to worry, looked cautious, moving thoughtfully and deliberately as he cooked their meal.

Suddenly Tate raised his head and stared at that stretch of darkness between them and the town. "Did you hear that?" he murmured.

"Hear what?" But then there was a clang, and a progression of muffled thumps like boots in sand. And if Dawson wasn't mistaken, a voice or two.

"Just wait. Move away from the fire." Tate slipped off into the shadows.

Dawson backed into the taller brush away from the campfire. For a moment, he thought he heard that same low moaning as the other night. It made his toes itch inside his boots. But maybe he was imagining things because he didn't hear it again. Some birds exploded from the top of a nearby tree, and he pissed himself a mite.

More voices and steps in the darkness beyond the campfire. Old Tate reappeared, panting. "Luddy mussy, Dawson," he whispered. "It's them damn Presbyterians. We got to get you out of here."

Two tall gents in their Sunday-go-to-meeting best stepped into the edge of the firelight, guns drawn. A number of grayish shapes pushed out of the gloom behind them. Tate reached into the campfire and drug out a burning stick and began swinging it around his head, shouting at them. Dawson ran away into the darkness and stumbled, catching his balance before he fell on his face. He staggered around until he found himself down the slope below the campsite. He looked up the hill and watched Tate still swinging the fiery stick as a large number of men approached. Everybody was shouting: warnings, threats, maybe even a growl or two. Maybe even a roar. The ground began to shake apart, and Dawson fell to his knees.

There was that tremendous moan again, but closer, louder as it descended the hill. Dawson thought of a train, or a herd of cattle stampeding in panic. And then there was the noise that drowned out everything in a calamity of rocks and dirt and trees flying past him down the mountain. He threw himself face first in the dirt and put his hands over his head.

He heard the men scream and glanced up. A massive cliff of

gnarled rock and ground suddenly filled the sky, a savagerous maw opening at its center and sucking all those poor souls inside. Tate's flaming stick bounced harmlessly off a vertical snout higher than four men, momentarily illuminating a gigantic blood-filled eye.

Dawson could hear Tate calling his name from somewhere above. "Outta there!" the old man screamed. But Dawson felt staked to the ground. Some things were too big for a man to reckon with. The war taught him that, if anything. He hugged himself tight and made himself stare directly into the massive face of the oblivion coming to take him out of this world.

But then that damned bolter finally stopped. Dawson figured it just let gravity take its course—that's how the big old thing got down the mountain. Something like that plows up a lot of ground, and eventually that's going to stop even something big as a whale. And like any whale, this thing was a big bag of blubber, with no arms or legs, so not much it could do once it stopped.

Relieved, Dawson got out of its path and scrambled up on a big mound of rock and dirt at least ten yards away. He dusted himself off, giddy over his last-second reprieve, and tickled at the prospect of now watching the second part of Tate's tale unfold, the part where the bolter uses those hooks on its tail to drag itself back up the mountain. Now that was going to be a sight to see and quite a tale to tell his grandchildren! And didn't he have just the perfect perch for witnessing it all? He just hoped it wasn't too dark to make out the details.

But then he felt that rumbling under his feet. He thought at first it was just the ground shaking from the bolter's laborious ascent, but it hadn't started back up yet. In fact it appeared to just be staring at him with them huge, lovestruck eyes! And Dawson of course would understand that look more than most.

The ground rumbled again, and Dawson looked down just as a massive eye opened up beside one of his boots. He stared back at the bolter and not only understood, but sympathized. If you've been calling out for your mate for years, it was only natural justice that some night she would answer.

It almost lessened his terror as the bolter's mate shook off more of the dirt covering her face, dropped open her jaw, and swallowed him whole. Almost. And as Dawson felt himself sucked down into his digestive demise, he couldn't help thinking he wouldn't be in this fix if just one of them gals just said yes.

DREAMCATCHER

Marsheila Rockwell

She was at it again.

Father Grady had just left the Petersen homestead, making his rounds bringing Holy Communion to parishioners who lived too far out from Salina, Kansas, to come to Mass on Sunday, and he carried in his hand another one of Morning Star Woman's sacred hoops.

Dreamcatchers, some whites called them. When he'd worked in the newly formed Diocese of Duluth back in Minnesota, the Ojibwe there had called them *asabikeshiinh*, which he believed meant spider. It made sense—they looked like webs, and he understood they were meant to "catch" the bad dreams of infants and children and allow only the good ones through the hole in the center, guided down to the child by the hoop's single feather.

Superstitious nonsense, of course. Blasphemous, even.

Which was why he'd confiscated the sinew-and-willow circles at every home he'd found them in and thrown them out with the trash. But somehow, they kept reappearing, despite his lectures to the good people of the Diocese of Concordia that the best way to keep their nights trouble-free was to recite the Prayer to St. Michael, which Pope Leo XIII had added to the Low Mass just a few years earlier, in 1886. Of course, it took time for changes in Rome to make it across the ocean, let alone out onto the Great Plains, and he was one of only a few priests serving this area— more now that Bishop Scannel was actively recruiting from other dioceses—but still woefully insufficient for the sheer number of

187

miles that needed to be covered. There were parishioners, like the Petersens, that he only saw once every other month because it took him that long to make his rounds in between his regular duties at the church.

Plenty of time for the displaced Ojibwe woman to get up to mischief.

He'd heard her story from several of the homesteaders out here—she was the wife of a Duluth railroad worker who'd taken ill in the cold and moved south for his health. Unfortunately, the marginally warmer winters here had not been enough to counteract whatever ailed the man, and he had died soon after, leaving his Indian wife with a house in the middle of the Smoky Hills, a horse, a rifle, and little else. She hunted her own game and grew her own produce, trading for dry goods and other things she needed by providing herbal remedies to the community.

In other words, potions and talismans, like any good witch.

Father Grady could almost forgive the Petersens for accepting another dreamcatcher from the Indian woman—Sarah Petersen was a young mother with a colicky baby and no other women nearby to help her with the tasks of raising a newborn. Anything that might alleviate the child's squalling and allow for even a modicum of sleep would no doubt be welcome in their household.

But at what cost? Relying on Morning Star Woman's charms instead of the Lord's mercy was one step down a slippery slope that led right to the gates of Hell, and it was his responsibility to keep the Petersens—and all of Salina's faithful Catholics—firmly on the straight and narrow.

What had started as merely an annoyance could quickly become a battle for the souls of Salina. He needed to face his adversary head-on and confront her before it got to that point.

After all, she'd been the wife of a white man in a prosperous northern city. She must have more than just the veneer of civilization; something of the white man's ways must have stuck with her. Surely she could be reasoned with.

Father Grady looked at the dreamcatcher in his hands. He'd taken this newest one from Sarah Petersen and told her not to accept another, on pain of mortal sin. She'd tearfully acceded.

Now he crushed it between his palms until the leather-wrapped willow snapped. Then he tore it in two, ripping the sinew webbing apart and tossing it to the ground beneath his horse's hooves.

Satisfied that there was one less of the Indian woman's fetishes in the world to tempt his parishioners, he turned his horse's head and made for the western hills where he knew she lived.

Behind him, the hoop's feather floated to the earth, landing atop the ruins of the dreamcatcher before a gust of prairie wind caught it and blew it far away.

Morning Star Woman sat on her porch waiting for him when he arrived, though it was twilight and she couldn't have seen him approaching. Her dark silhouette on the front stairs gave him a momentary chill.

"Good evening, Father," she said in near-perfect English as he brought his horse to a halt and dismounted.

"Good evening, ma'am," he replied politely, walking toward her. Lamp light shone from inside the open front door, illuminating something in her hands. As he neared, he was nonplussed to see it was another dreamcatcher.

"*Waaban-anangokwe*," she corrected. "You are from *Onigami-ising*, like me. Surely you can use my name?"

Onigamiising was the Ojibwe word for Duluth; it meant "place of the small portage." In point of fact, he was only from the Diocese of Duluth, which encompassed ten counties in northern Minnesota, and not from the city itself, but he didn't think the distinction was worth making.

"My apologies. I never properly learned your language; I'm afraid any attempt I made to pronounce your name would mangle it beyond recognition."

She caught him looking at the dreamcatcher.

"You like it? *Onizhishin*."

"Yes, it is pretty," he replied, recognizing the phrase.

Morning Star Woman laughed, a surprisingly pleasant sound.

"That's not all *onizhishin* means, Father. It means something is good. That it's right. It's as it should be."

"Well, I'm afraid I have to disagree with you about that, ma'am," he said.

Morning Star Woman's head turned so that her face caught the light, and Father Grady saw that she was far younger than he had expected. Probably only in her late twenties, and dressed in buckskin rather than black robes. Certainly not the crone he'd been envisioning, though he supposed that biblical witches were never actually described thusly—that depiction came from fairy tales. In reality, witches were far harder to identify and far more dangerous.

"Oh?"

"Your charms to chase away bad dreams are against church teachings, ma'am, as I suspect you may already know. I can't allow you to continue giving them to my parishioners. You're endangering their souls, whether you intend to or not."

"On the contrary, Father. I'm trying to keep them *out* of danger."

"I'm glad to hear that. It means we have the same goal."

The Indian woman inclined her head, but said nothing.

"I need you to give me your word that you'll stop making them."

"No."

Father Grady was taken aback. He hadn't expected her to refuse. He tried again.

"Then I need you to stop giving them to my parishioners."

"Parishioners?"

"The Catholics. The ones with the crucifixes and the rosaries. If you want to keep giving them to the Protestants out here, or the heathens, well, they're not part of my flock and there's nothing much I can do about that. But I have to insist you leave the Catholics out of it."

"You want them to have no defense against their nightmares?"

"I want them to rely on the Lord Jesus Christ, His Blessed Mother Mary, and Saint Michael the Archangel for their defense. Not some Indian superstition. I want them to rely on their *faith*."

"Have you considered that if their faith were enough, they wouldn't have turned to me in the first place?"

"They need to strengthen their faith, not abandon it in favor of trinkets."

"And what are your crucifixes and rosaries, if not trinkets?"

Father Grady pursed his lips.

"I'm not here to debate theology with you. I'm here to secure your promise that you will leave my parishioners alone. If you truly care about protecting them, you'll do as I ask."

Morning Star Woman smiled, and the expression was somehow less pleasant than her laugh had been.

"Of course, Father. We will see if your Saint Michael is as effective as Spider Woman at keeping the night terrors at bay. And if he is not? You know where to find me."

☆   ☆   ☆

It was another month and a half before Father Grady made it back to the Petersen homestead, and by the time he got there, he was dreading what he would find. A mysterious hemorrhagic fever had run through the community, taking the lives of several children and elderly residents, but not before causing them to hallucinate horrible creatures attacking them. Father Grady had sat with one young boy as he was in the throes of such a vision—the priest had never been to an exorcism, but he'd heard them described, and felt like he was in the middle of one as he prayed the Prayer to Saint Michael over the boy and tried to calm him, right up until the moment the child opened his mouth and vomited blood all over the both of them before collapsing back on the bed, dead and staring, his face contorted in terror.

The Halperns had had half their cattle slaughtered by what the law was calling a wolf pack, though no one had seen wolves do this kind of damage to steers before—literally tearing the carcasses to shreds and leaving the meat behind, uneaten.

Butch McCafferty had taken his shotgun and shot his entire family before putting the barrel in his own mouth and blowing off his head.

It didn't escape Father Grady's notice that each household was Catholic. They had one other thing in common, too.

They were all homes he'd confiscated dreamcatchers from.

So it was with some trepidation that he approached the Petersen house, not knowing what horrors awaited him.

Sarah Petersen greeted him at the door, all smiles.

"Hello, Father! How are you?"

Father Grady blinked in surprise. This, he had not been expecting.

"Tired," he said honestly. "How are you and Ted? And the little one, Mary Rose?"

"We're well, Father," Sarah replied, ushering him into the small kitchen and gesturing for him to sit while she poured him some coffee from a tin pot on the cast iron stove. Mary Rose's cradle was near the stove, no doubt for warmth as the evenings were beginning to turn crisp. The baby was lying in it, sleeping peacefully. "I'll fetch Ted. He's out back."

When she was out of the kitchen, on a hunch, Father Grady got up from his chair and crossed over to the cradle. For a moment, he was afraid he might find the child dead, her seemingly sane mother actually out of her mind with grief tending to a corpse as though it were still alive and nothing in the world was wrong. It would fit with everything else that had been going on in Salina this month.

But, no, little Mary Rose was in fact sleeping like a proverbial angel, her cheeks as pink as her namesake flowers. Father Grady was about to turn away when a flash of color caught his eye. He reached down and pulled the woolen blanket back to reveal one of Morning Star Woman's dreamcatchers clutched in Mary Rose's chubby fist.

"I'm sorry, Father," Sarah's voice sounded from behind him. "I know you said it was a sin. But I just couldn't risk it. Not with everything that's been happening."

Father Grady covered the baby back up before straightening and turning back to the young couple.

"It's all right. I think God understands," he said.

He thought he did now, too.

"Do you mind if I stay here for the night? It's too late to travel any more this evening, and I need to head farther west in the morning."

"Of course, Father. You're always welcome."

Father Grady smiled and thanked them. After a simple dinner of soup and bread, he lay down in their extra bedroom—the one that Mary Rose would share with any siblings she might someday have—exhausted and sore. He was asleep in moments.

At first, his slumber was dreamless, a welcome respite from the nightmares of the past month. But then figures began to slowly coalesce out of the darkness, countless slavering demons with claws like razors and red, glowing eyes. They advanced on him hungrily, and he realized that he stood in front of Mary Rose's cradle, the only buffer between her and the demonic horde. He held up a crucifix, its crucified Christ weeping blood. He began to recite the Prayer to St. Michael in a trembling voice, all the while wondering if he should instead be chanting the Commendation of the Dying.

The monsters did not even pause.

The first one had nearly reached him, was pulling its arm back to swipe at him with its razor claws, when suddenly Morning Star Woman appeared before him, holding up a staff to block the demon's blow.

Its claws bounced off the slim wooden pole as if the weapon were made of iron. Then there was a flurry of motion as the demon attacked the Indian woman in earnest, but she fought it off, her staff moving faster than Father Grady's eyes could follow. Behind him, Mary Rose began to cry.

He turned and quickly gathered the child from the cradle, glancing over his shoulder as he did so. He saw another of the demons rake its claws across Morning Star Woman's thigh. She went down to one knee, still fighting valiantly, moments away from being overwhelmed.

Father Grady would not waste his chance. He took the baby and ran.

And woke with a start, sweating, to see the sun creeping through a crack in the gingham curtains that covered the room's small window.

Time to go.

Morning Star Woman was waiting for him on the porch again when he arrived.

"Father," she said. "I thought I'd be seeing you soon."

"What have you done to my people?" he demanded, eschewing niceties. His parishioners had not been terrorized until he'd demanded she stop handing out her charms to them. Ergo, she must have cursed them in retaliation, perhaps hoping they'd do as the Petersens had done, ignore his edicts and come running back to her, regardless.

"What have *I* done? You are the one who removed them from my protection."

That brought Father Grady up short.

"Wait. You're claiming you're *not* the cause of these atrocities being committed against my parishioners?"

"I was the only thing standing in the way of those atrocities. Do you not know what haunts this land?"

Father Grady frowned.

"What are you talking about?"

"The blood of many who have died by violence stains these hills. Their spirits do not rest. They seek out the living to share their torment. The *asabikeshiinh* kept them at bay, away from the families—the children—who had no part in the taking of innocent lives. But you removed them, and let the *maji-manidoog* have their way. Now they stalk the land freely, sowing destruction wherever they may."

Father Grady had seen that destruction with his own eyes, and seen it bypass the Petersen's homestead as if their lintel had been painted with the blood of the Passover lamb. He could not doubt her words, as contrary to his faith as they were.

"Then return their dreamcatchers, so the spirits will let them be."

"It is too late for that. The evil has grown too strong for the *asabikeshiinh* to hold it back—even those who are now covered by their protection will not remain safe for much longer. You saw that for yourself last night."

Father Grady's eyes narrowed.

"How could you know about that, unless you were behind the attack?"

"Not behind it. Trying to stop it." And she lifted the hem of her buckskin dress to reveal four long gashes along her thigh.

Father Grady felt a chill wash over him as he realized the woman was telling the truth. Then he thought of little Mary Rose. The idea of that sweet baby succumbing to the evils he had seen sickened him. He could not let that happen.

Would not.

"Then what are we to do? If neither my faith nor your beliefs can stop this scourge, how can we protect these people?"

"We must go to where the evil is strongest. Only there can we fight it."

As was becoming common with this woman, her response was not what he expected, but what choice did he have but to trust her wisdom in the matter? She had been right before, and he hadn't listened, and his people had paid the price for his obstinance. No, he would swallow his pride and heed her words this time.

"Very well. Lead the way."

She had a pack already prepared, and her horse was out back, saddled and ready to go. She led them deeper into the switchgrass-dotted hills, which had gotten their name because of the blue-gray haze that hung over the bluffs and rock formations at sunrise and sunset, like smoke from hundreds of campfires. Father Grady wondered if it weren't in fact the *maji-manidoog* bound to the land here by the crimes committed against them. Just a month before, he would have dismissed the thought as superstitious nonsense. Now it made him shiver.

He followed as Morning Star Woman eventually led him into a ravine, still in shadow though the sun was nearing its zenith. Sandstone walls the color of new flesh rose above them, closing them in, funneling them toward darkness. Father Grady wanted to reach for the holy water in his pack, and was suddenly sorry that he'd given the last of the consecrated host he carried with him to the Petersens in the sacrament of Holy Communion. Carrying the body of Christ with him during this venture would have given him great comfort. He never carried the blood with him, as it was too easily spilt, and too easily absconded with, should he encounter thugs along the way, who would view it as just wine, and so drink it unworthily. And since the body, blood, soul, and divinity were present under both species, it was not necessary for his parishioners to receive or for him to travel with both.

Still, even a sip of the unconsecrated wine would not go amiss right now.

"We have arrived," Morning Star Woman announced abruptly.

Father Grady looked up from his musings to see that the ravine had ended in a gaping black hole surrounded by spindly yucca plants with leaves like well-honed knives. The horses whinnied and balked; it was clear they would not enter. Their riders would have to go on foot from here.

He and the Indian woman dismounted. That was when he noticed the rifle she slung across her back, and the odd walking stick she grasped, sharpened at one end. What good would either of those things do against spirits, he wondered?

She led him into the cave, which was several degrees cooler than it had been in the ravine. Father Grady shivered again, and told himself it was just from the cold.

It took a moment for his eyes to adjust to the darkness, but Morning Star Woman stepped surefootedly through the gloom, as if she could see without the benefit of light.

Or as if her moccasined feet knew this path well.

A sense of foreboding filled Father Grady, but by that time the Indian woman had guided him through the curving tunnel into a wider cavern lit with torches. In the center, suspended between two pairs of massive stalagmites and stalactites, waited a man-sized wooden hoop.

Morning Star Woman turned to him, dropping her walking stick and pulling the rifle off her back. She pointed it at him.

"That's far enough, Father."

He looked at her accusingly.

"*This* is how you intend to fight?"

"It is the only way to stop the *maji-manidoog* from preying on the people. It was by your actions that they were allowed to grow strong enough to do so. It must be by your action that they are pacified."

He wondered if he could grab the gun from her before she could get a shot off. He had no doubt the weapon was loaded.

She must have seen his thoughts in his eyes, for she took a step backward, leveling the rifle.

"I need you to go stand in the hoop, Father."

"And do what?"

"You are to become the people's dreamcatcher."

He didn't know what that meant, but he'd seen the effects of what the *asabikeshiinh* had been holding back from his parishioners. He didn't particularly want to face whatever caused those effects.

"What if I refuse? Let you shoot me?"

"I can shoot you and yet not kill you, Father. I would rather you did this willingly—the protection will be stronger then—but it will work even if I have to hang you up unconscious and bleeding."

The idea of being unconscious didn't sound so bad. But she must have read that in his face, too.

"You would not remain asleep for long, Father. Once the dreamcatcher is finished, you will be awake forever, enduring the horrors of the *maji-manidoog* so that your people no longer have to. You will be following in your Christ's footsteps. A . . . martyr, I believe is the word?"

What she said made sense. It would be his penance for bringing this plague on his parishioners in the first place. And it was his duty to protect them, and their immortal souls.

Even at the cost of his?

He thought again of Mary Rose.

May God have mercy on him.

"Fine. I'll do it. Willingly."

Morning Star Woman did not lower the rifle.

"I need you to go stand in the hoop, Father," she repeated.

He did as she asked.

"Now stand with your arms and legs spread so they are touching the hoop, as if one limb is pointing toward each of the four winds."

He did as she instructed, wondering how she was going to bind him to the hoop. Surely she'd have to put the rifle down to do so? He could still escape then, if he chose. He didn't have to commit to this path, after all.

But she did not put the rifle down. Instead, he felt a tickling sensation at both wrists. Glancing to his left, he was appalled to see dozens of hairy black spiders swarming over his hand, weaving webs to hold his arm in place. Looking to his right, he could see there were spiders there doing the same, and others at both ankles. Then he could feel the scurrying of their legs across the back of his head and neck as they wove a loop around his throat, connecting his head to the arc above him. Other spiders were at his waist, attaching it to both sides of the hoop, and still others at his groin, attaching that to the bottom of the hoop. When they were finished, he was anchored to the circle at eight points, and could not move, like some bizarre parody of the crucifixion. Webbing stretched between the anchor points, sticky and glistening in the torchlight.

"We are almost done, Father," Morning Star Woman said.

She slung her rifle over her back and picked up her walking stick.

"There is still the matter of the hole, to allow the good dreams through."

So saying, she took the sharp end of the stick and plunged it into his abdomen, pushing it through until it protruded out his back. Father Grady screamed in pain.

He screamed again when she pulled it out. As blood flowed, he thought again of Christ on the cross, pierced by the Roman soldier's spear.

"The *maji-manidoog* will be coming soon, drawn by your blood. I must go." She paused for a moment, regarding him with dark eyes. "This is a good thing you do."

She turned and walked from the cavern then, leaving him alone in the flickering light of the torches. As he waited, unable to move, the pain in his midsection consuming him, he thought he saw movement on the edges of his vision. His eyes darted left, then right.

Nothing.

In the distance, he heard a faint rumbling. It took him a moment to realize the Indian woman must have sealed off the entrance to the cave.

He would never be rescued. Never be found.

Except by the *maji-manidoog*.

When they came, he was not ready. They appeared as dark shapes, a few at first, then dozens, then hundreds, walking through the cavern walls toward him, their eyes glowing red, like in his dream. Some seemed human in form, but others seemed like animals, and others yet were amorphous.

The first one reached him, hesitated. He could feel hunger radiating off it like heat. It wanted his blood. Wanted him. But it was wary of the webbing.

Finally, its hunger overcame it and it stepped forward. As the blackness touched the glistening white web, it dissipated, and a memory of being violated at the hands of Cheyenne braves washed over Father Grady, pain and terror and horror and shame rocking him to his core.

Then another shape moved forward, and he became a Wyandot boy running in blind fear from white soldiers who had just killed his parents. When the bullet tore through his back, Father Grady felt it, and then again when the soldiers guided their horses over the boy's body, trampling him to death. Father Grady experienced every shattered bone, every burst organ.

Then another shape moved forward.

And then another.

And another.

There were so many, an endless number, some hundreds of years old, some as fresh as last week. Some were distinct memories, some just raw emotions, nothing but fear and rage and hatred.

Before each spirit stepped forward, there was a pause, as it weighed its hunger versus what it had seen happen to the spirit before it. A few turned away.

During those times, Father Grady thought of Mary Rose and imagined the good dreams getting through, dreams of her growing up carefree and happy, with several siblings, in a home where there was always enough to eat and tragedy struck but rarely.

A home where there was a dreamcatcher above every child's bed.

In the midst of his pain, Father Grady smiled.

It was good. It was right. It was as it should be.

Onizhishin.

EL JEFE DE LA COMANCHERIA

Mario Acevedo

April 1886

As bounty hunters, Malachi Hunter and I live on a financial diet of feast or famine. Presently, we've got two nickels and a quarter between us, and it's only the middle of the month. Working as partners, I figured that him with his smarts and me with my vampire powers, we'd always be flush with cash, but that's seldom the case.

People tend to look askance at a human riding with one of me. And when I'm among my kind, they wonder why I bother palling around with a mortal. Truth is, Malachi and I were tight as brothers years before I was turned, and nothing about my undead existence could ever undo the confidence we have in one another.

Today we were riding our horses at a slow trot along the Rocky Ford–Pueblo Trail, musing where our next paycheck would come from. A crow circled overhead. Its stuttering movements told me this was no living bird, but a messenger. When it approached, Malachi and I tugged on our reins. The crow landed on the pommel of my saddle in a flutter of wings black as obsidian. Gears inside the crow's mechanical body clicked and purred, and when it opened its beak, out slid a rolled-up piece of paper.

The instant I took the paper, the crow catapulted into the sky in an explosion of artificial feathers, wings stutter-flapping once more until it soared out of sight.

I unfurled the note. The message was in loose script written with a dip pen: *Ambrosio Zamora. Lagrimas Mine, Huerfano County.*

Ambrosio was a con artist who had cheated and defrauded people from El Paso to Deadwood, Kansas City to San Francisco. Catching him was like catching smoke.

I read the note aloud, then turned it over. "Doesn't say who sent it."

"Obviously someone expects us to settle a score with Ambrosio," Malachi replied. "But that's all right with me since the marshal in Santa Fe is offering a five-hundred-dollar bounty on his head. Let's get to work, Felix."

We trained our horses toward Huerfano County.

Just as the note had promised, we cornered Ambrosio in the Lagrimas Mine. Thanks to another stroke of luck, we found his wife's horse tied up next to his in a nearby arroyo. Though Elsa wasn't on the arrest warrant, she'd been partner to plenty of his schemes, so I figured hauling her in meant an extra bump in the reward.

Malachi and I took cover behind boulders outside the mine entrance, and we pulled our revolvers. He shouted, "Ambrosio, we know you're in there. There's a warrant for your arrest and—"

"Like hell I'm going!" Ambrosio hollered, his voice echoing from inside the mine. He unleashed a barrage from his gun, its muzzle flashes bursting in the dark tunnel.

Bullets whistled past us. We fired back, aiming for the mine's ceiling since we wanted to take him and his wife alive. Our bullets cracked and whined as they ricocheted inside.

Ambrosio answered with another volley.

"I'll keep them occupied." Malachi fired another shot. "You flush them out."

We'd scoped out the mine beforehand and discovered a chimney vent about a hundred feet up the hill. The vent was just big enough to crawl through since it doubled as an escape in case the entrance collapsed.

Being a vampire and possessing superior night vision, I had the task of shimmying down the hole. After I reached the vent, I crouched over the opening, peered into the darkness, and saw nothing but chiseled rock all the way to the bottom. I let my *kundalini noir*—the supernatural force that animates us vampires—unwind so it could sense the air like an antenna.

Ambrosio's whisper rose from the tunnel below. "Elsa, they got us trapped."

Then silence.

"Elsa?"

More silence.

Feet scuffled across rocks but I couldn't tell if it was Ambrosio, or Elsa, or the two of them, or someone else.

Time to earn my share of the bounty. Sprouting my fangs as I climbed down the vent shaft, my *kundalini noir* buzzed with uncertainty. Stealthily as a spider, I made it to the tunnel's ceiling and paused. To my left, Ambrosio mumbled, "Elsa, goddammit, where did you go?"

I let myself drop as quietly as I could, the dirt floor muffling my boots. A shadow cut across the light spilling from the entrance. Drawing my Colt Navy, I tucked myself against the wall and sidestepped toward the shadow until I reached Ambrosio hiding behind a pile of crushed rock.

So where was Elsa? Scanning the tunnel, I caught no sign of her.

At least I had Ambrosio. I aimed my revolver over his head and fired, the report sounding loud as a cannon. He spun around, only to find himself face-to-face with the muzzle of my gun. But it was the sight of my fangs that made him wither in fear.

He crossed himself and slumped against the rocks. "*Vampiro sicario.*"

"Guilty as charged." I snatched the pocket revolver from his hand before I booted him to the entrance. I shouted, "Malachi, I've got Ambrosio."

"What about Elsa?" Malachi shouted back.

I poked Ambrosio in the back. "Where's your wife?"

"I dunno. Has to be down the mine. Where else?"

Malachi approached, his boots crunching over the tailings leading to the entrance. I tossed him Ambrosio's revolver and said, "I'm going to get Elsa."

Ambrosio and Elsa made for a fine pair of swindlers. He planned the scams while she lulled the victims into relaxing their guard. Besides her feminine wiles, Elsa had another ace up her sleeve—when cornered, she had a way of slipping out of the tightest noose. Had she done that now?

Not likely. Malachi and I confirmed the mine had only two exits. Out the front and up the vent, and she hadn't left either way. If she wasn't still inside, the only explanation had to be a secret escape route.

Regardless, I had no choice but to proceed deeper into the mine. My *kundalini noir* hitched in trepidation. As an undead bloodsucker, I didn't fear much, but the thought of being buried terrified me. Even if crushed by tons of rock, I'd still survive for months—years even legend has it—but in agony as a smear of goo until I eventually starved to dust.

Dank air pulsed from the depths as if the hill was alive and breathing. I caught the sooty odor of burnt lamp oil, indicating that Elsa had gone this way. The tunnel leveled off and forked. Fresh shoeprints—Elsa's I was sure—left a trail in the dust going left. In the distance, a lantern's glow fluttered across the rough rock walls, rounded a corner, and disappeared.

I shouted, "Elsa, give it up." I quickened my pace, remaining alert in case she was luring me into a trap.

Down and down we continued, ducking under timbers shoring up the ceiling, scrambling over rocks from cave-ins, as we descended into this gloomy labyrinth. Water dripped on me, and timbers whispered frightful groans like those of a tortured beast.

The corridor made a sharp right, and a faint green light spilled from around the next bend. My *kundalini noir* tripped an alarm; something unexpected and powerful waited ahead. Gun in hand, I hugged the corner.

The lantern stood on the floor of an empty cave. Her cape lay discarded in a puddle of water. Opposite from me, an oblong spot of lime-green light on the rock wall faded.

I didn't want to believe what I knew just happened. Elsa had walked into the wall and disappeared. I'd heard about similar magic—beings sucked through solid rock and getting whisked to someplace else. I kept my distance from the wall. If I got sucked in, who knew where I'd end up?

Just in case this was a trick, I studied the chamber for a hidden door, but finding none—and the way my *kundalini noir* kept insisting that I hurry out of there—confirmed that Elsa had used a supernatural getaway. This hocus-pocus did a lot to explain how she'd been giving her pursuers the slip all these years.

Retrieving her cape and lantern, I trudged back to the entrance.

When I emerged outside, Ambrosio was on his knees, hands tied behind his back, stripped of his boots and barefoot. Dirt stained his white shirt. Strands of sweaty hair hung over his handsome face. At the moment Ambrosio appeared thoroughly defeated, but he had a habit of turning a bad draw into a winning hand, so I stayed wary.

Malachi had retrieved Ambrosio's and Elsa's horses and searched their saddlebags. His eyes lifted in my direction. "Where's Elsa?"

"She escaped." I waved her damp cape at Ambrosio. "Anything you want to share?"

"I don't know," he yammered. "I swear. She's never told me how she does it."

"Does what?" Malachi asked.

"Disappears," I answered, then explained what I'd seen.

Whenever Malachi found himself confronting a mystery, he lit a cigar. A self-educated man, he was also deeply religious, ready to quote Scripture as quick as Shakespeare and Sir Isaac Newton. Despite what he believed of science and theology, he also sided with me, the embodiment of all that is supposedly impossible and evil. He was there years ago when I was turned. In fact, he carried me—mortally wounded—to a *chamán* who saved me from oblivion the only way he could, by making me into a vampire.

When I finished telling Malachi about Elsa's vanishing act, he tilted his head back and exhaled a hearty plume of smoke. "It's not up to us to make sense of this world." He took another puff and let it seep out from under his mustache. "That's up to the Almighty."

I stood over Ambrosio. "Where did Elsa go?"

"Probably to find the rat who told you I was here." He scowled. "So who was it?"

"Even if knew, I wouldn't tell you." Whoever had sent the crow had done so in secret and knowing their identity didn't matter. Someone wanted Ambrosio caught, and we'd caught him.

Malachi and I sorted through what we'd emptied from Ambrosio's pockets—coins, tokens, loose cartridges, assorted keys. From the horse saddlebags, forged promissory notes and phony letters of credit.

Ambrosio mumbled, "I have a stash of gold."

"The Deming-Cheyenne payroll, no doubt," Malachi replied. "Maybe that's where your loving wife went. To abscond with your loot."

"She has no idea where it is." Ambrosio chuckled. "I never told her. I love her, but not that much. She'll be back because without me, she has nothing."

I hoisted Ambrosio to his feet. "She can visit you in prison."

He kicked his legs and tried to wrestle free. "*Cabrónes! Cabrónes!* I'm not going."

A solid punch on the nose took the fight out of him. A few minutes later, we had him tied to his horse, lashed to the saddle and gagged with a stick of mesquite I'd cinched across his mouth. Blood dripped from his nostrils and past his lips.

I tethered Ambrosio's horse to Malachi's. Since we didn't need Elsa's horse, I removed its saddle and tack and gave it a swat on the rump to make it gallop away.

We then rode east toward the border between the West Kansas and New Mexico Territories. Ambrosio was a prize wanted by many, and we steered clear of any settlements to avoid getting our prisoner lynched.

My mind shifted between maintaining vigilance on our surroundings and wondering about Elsa. Would she return to rescue her husband, or had she fled from his side forever? What other magic tricks could she count on?

Our path wound over and around low hills dotted with sage and creosote. The ground rose gradually toward the distant mountains. We were climbing into the foothills when my *kundalini noir* buzzed like the rattle of a sidewinder.

Ahead and about three hundred yards distant, a string of men on horses held still on the slope's crest. I didn't know their business, but it wasn't coincidental that Malachi and I had captured Ambrosio right before these men showed up. I didn't know how they found out about our prisoner, but as the *viejos* say, the wind has ears.

Or was it they who had sent the mechanical crow?

"Trouble," I said.

Malachi replied, "I see 'em. Any ideas to keep the odds in our favor?"

"I'll hold back and outflank them," I said. "Come up from behind."

Malachi waved a gloved hand. We ambled on as if we hadn't noticed the men. When we dipped into an arroyo, I slowed my horse and at the next fork, turned right as Malachi and Ambrosio continued straight. Ducking flat against my horse's neck, I stayed low as I proceeded in a wide looping maneuver. When I'd gone about a quarter mile, I circled to the left along a dry creek bed.

The advantage I had on any guard watching their flank was that he had no idea I was coming his way. My *kundalini noir* shifted through the faint traces of my various senses to gauge what trouble might be lying ahead.

A trembling in the center of my chest told me to slow down.

From up the dry creek bed, a horse snorted faintly.

Stealthily, I slid off my horse and patted its hindquarters so he continued up the sandy wash. I scurried to the left, low to the ground like a ferret, sneaking from cover to cover. Upon reaching a narrow draw, I found the guard tucked against one side, his back to me, where he watched the creek bed. A tattered, misshapen sombrero draped a wide shadow over his frame. His serape was thrown back over his shoulders to allow quick access to his holstered guns. Glancing about, I made sure he was alone.

From the dry creek came the *crunch, crunch* of my horse's hooves in the sand. The guard perked up and readied a revolver.

The sight of the empty saddle on my horse made the guard tense with suspicion. He shied back into the draw and closer to me.

I extended my fangs to dispatch him because a gunshot would spook his companions. The closer I crept upon my mark, the more my *kundalini* buzzed. The slightest wrong move—my foot tripping a rock, a branch of creosote scraping my clothes, the sudden flight of a hidden bird—would spoil my attack.

My horse kept the guard distracted. I moved to his right, fangs out, fingers tense.

I grabbed his leg and yanked him off his saddle. As he fell toward me, I clamped my hand around his throat to keep him quiet. A tiny gurgle managed to escape his lips. With my vampire strength, I carefully lowered him to the ground and held him still. His eyes bored into mine, and they brimmed with terror.

I plunged my fangs into his neck. His blood—hot and delicious—spurted into my mouth. He squirmed for a moment until my undead juices flowed into him, and he lay quiet like he'd been given a dose of laudanum. Suspecting that I might not have a blood meal for at least a couple of days, I helped myself to several hearty mouthfuls—but not too much lest I become sluggish and lethargic.

His swarthy face paled to the color of sun-bleached bone. He might live or he might die; that wasn't my concern as long as he was out of my way. Wiping my mouth and savoring the lingering taste, I pushed up and dusted off my clothes, then climbed back on my horse.

I followed hoof prints up the draw, over a slight ridge from where I spotted the rest of his party skylined on the next ridge over. From their direction, the air carried the fragrance of incense. I stayed out of sight until I found where my horse and I could sneak through a stand of juniper. The men were so fixed on Malachi's approach that I emerged unnoticed right behind them and on their left flank. In case of trouble, my fangs wouldn't be enough, so I drew my revolver.

I counted five in the group, arranged around a stocky, leathery man whose pate of cropped gray hair reflected the afternoon light like a ball of cut wire. Cartridge belts kept his white cassock in place. Sunlight glinted off the silver crucifixes adorning his saddle and tack. A mother-of-pearl handled pistol and matching Bowie knife hung from his crimson waist sash.

The riders at his immediate left and right carried lantern torches, the glass panels illuminated with images of the Virgin of Guadalupe and of Saint Michael slaying a dragon, the panels lit by an oil lamp within. The incense fragrance I'd smelled earlier came from the scented smoke vented by the lanterns. The smoke swirled around the silver crosses fixed on top of each lantern, where the eyes of the crucified Jesus glowed red with judgment and vengeance. As a western vampire, I was immune to both crucifixes and sunlight. Otherwise, I would've perished long ago.

What all these religious trappings meant was that Malachi and I, unfortunately, had attracted the attention of the Brotherhood of Penitentes—vigilante enforcers of the Holy Roman Catholic Church of the Sangre de Cristo Mountains.

The other two men of the group rode as flankers and they spurred their horses to line up with their leader.

Malachi, with Ambrosio in tow, rode out of the arroyo and halted at the bottom of the slope in plain view. My hope was that Malachi and I could continue without bloodshed, but that was up to the Penitentes.

From his vantage on the slope, the leader's gaze settled on

Malachi. "I am," he lisped in Castilian, "Padre Bendito Matamoros, *el hermano supremo*."

"We know who you are." Malachi touched the brim of his hat. He panned the group and acted as if he hadn't noticed me. "We are honored by your presence."

"Where is the third rider?" Bendito asked.

Malachi turned in his saddle, surveyed the arroyo, then faced Bendito and shrugged. "He was never the reliable sort. I think you scared him off."

"You need to choose your companions with greater care," Bendito said. He nodded to the flanker on the left. He wore a beaded, canvas vest but no shirt. The flanker tossed a small leather pouch into the arroyo to land with a metallic thunk beside Malachi's horse.

"Five hundred pesetas in silver coin," Bendito announced. "One hundred of your Yankee dollars for Ambrosio."

"Sorry, padre, no can do," Malachi replied.

Bendito nodded once more to the flanker and another pouch landed in front of Malachi.

"One thousand pesetas," Bendito said, his voice sharp. "We demand justice for this *desgraciado*'s violations against the laws of both man and God."

I wanted to laugh. It was well known in these parts that one of Ambrosio's violations had been bedding the padre's favorite concubine and getting her pregnant.

Malachi began, "We have to deliver Ambrosio to—"

"Ambrosio belongs to us," the flanker shouted. He shrugged off his vest to reveal a torso corded with muscle and lacerated with gruesome scars. Penitentes showed their devotion to the brotherhood by flagellating themselves with iron-hooked cat-o'-nine-tails and branches of chollas. "We fear nothing as we have proven ourselves to our Lord, the Creator." He crossed himself and dropped his hand to an enormous dragoon revolver sheathed in a saddle holster.

I silently cocked back the hammer of my Colt.

Bendito raised his gloved hand to quell any forthcoming trouble. "Tell me Don Justos's bounty. I'll match it, plus you may keep the silver."

Don Justos was Justos Zamora, Ambrosio's father, but he was more than that. Much more. He was *El Jefe de la Comancheria*.

My *kundalini noir* tightened as I realized that the stakes to all of us had been raised a few notches. I wondered if Malachi picked up the gist of what Bendito revealed.

So Don Justos had a bounty on his own son? Perhaps he was behind the mysterious visit by the mechanical crow.

Malachi kept a poker face as he said, "Our task is to deliver Ambrosio to Don Justos."

Just like that, Malachi had switched our plans. We were no longer going to hand over Ambrosio to the marshal but to Don Justos. The strained look in our prisoner's eyes became heavy with certain doom.

Bendito said, "You're a long way from the Comancheria."

"It wouldn't be wise to get crossways with Don Justos," Malachi replied, "He won't take it kindly if you delay the reunion with his dear son."

Bendito knew that his cutthroat acolytes were no match for Justos's marauding comancheros: half-Comanche, half-Mexican roughnecks as fierce as desert wolves. After a moment, he inhaled deeply, then said, "You're not only a long way from the Comancheria, but also a long way from anyone who could help you."

"That's right, gringo!" the flanker exclaimed, his hand tightening on his dragoon. I raised my Colt Navy. He shouted, "It's just you and us."

Bendito and both of his flankers went for their guns. By the time they had cleared leather, my revolver roared once, fire and smoke bursting forward, the bullet striking the shirtless flanker square between the shoulder blades. He flung his arms up, the dragoon spinning away. As he toppled from his horse, I aimed at the lantern carrier closest to me and fired. My bullet caught him in the side and he toppled from his horse, dragging his lantern on top of himself. When he hit the ground, the glass bottle of lantern oil shattered, the volatile oil exploding, the blast of light and heat causing our horses to rear back. The lantern carrier rolled on the ground, on fire, screaming.

The other Penitentes whirled toward me. Malachi pulled his Schofield and fired, a tongue of flame and smoke lashing to the flanker on the right. He rocked back in his saddle, dropped his gun, and hugged his chest.

Bendito had his revolver drawn and his head whipped from me to Malachi, back to me, then to the lantern carrier rolling and kicking on the ground as he burned, his shrieks of pain tearing across the landscape.

Bendito lowered his revolver toward the man, aimed at his head, and muttered, "*Deus miserere animae meae.*" He fired once and the lantern carrier slumped against the ground, dead, flames flitting over his corpse like hungry rats. Smoke eddied around us.

The man Malachi had wounded wheezed and struggled to remain on his horse. The flanker I'd shot lay face down, twitching, blood seeping out the hole in his back while more blood pooled around his side. So much spilled blood. What a waste, especially for someone with my unholy appetite.

Malachi holstered his Schofield. "Padre, I'll pass on your offer, tempting as it is." He tapped the brim of his hat in salutation. "Perhaps next time our acquaintance will be more cordial. *Adios.*" Malachi snapped his reins and started toward the Arapaho Trail. His horse stepped around Bendito's bags of silver.

As I urged my horse down the slope, I kept Bendito and his forlorn crew covered with my gun as they whispered, "*Vampiro,* devil's spawn." Upon reaching Malachi, I put myself between Ambrosio and the Penitentes in case any of them decided to do something brash. Ambrosio wasn't worth a drop of my sweat, much less any of my blood, undead as it already was, but Malachi and I had a bounty to collect.

When the Penitentes were far behind us, I rode close to Malachi and kept my voice low so Ambrosio couldn't overhear. "What gives?"

"The padre tipped his hand," he said. "I've never known him to be a generous man so if he was offering us two hundred dollars, I figure Don Justos's bounty on Ambrosio is ten times that."

Two thousand dollars. "And the marshal?"

"I'm sure he knows all about the bounty. He pays us five hundred and keeps fifteen hundred. Seems that you and I were getting played for suckers."

I glanced back to Ambrosio and wondered how he'd wronged his father to deserve such a bounty.

The rolling hills flattened into high desert—the Comancheria—a landscape as inhospitable as the moon. Across the desolate wasteland, formations of jagged mountains arched through the desert floor like the spines of monstrous dinosaurs.

Twilight fell upon us, bringing a night as dark and cold as

the day had been bright and hot. Malachi and I could press on but our horses couldn't, so we made camp in a buffalo wallow.

I staked Ambrosio to the ground and removed his gag. "It'll behoove you to keep your mouth shut," I told him. "We're surrounded by Comanches, and they've got a score to settle with you as well."

Ambrosio rubbed grime from his face and stretched out on the dirt. In the dim light of a crescent moon, the bottoms of his bare feet glowed white as fish bellies. Even if he got loose, he wouldn't walk far, not across this treacherous expanse of cactus, sharp rock, and venomous critters.

All around us, coyotes yelped back and forth, singing their mournful songs. But I was certain Comanche scouts accounted for a good amount of the yowling as they kept tabs on us. The next morning, after a cup of freshly brewed but bitter coffee, we were on the trail again.

Every mile closer to our destination, Ambrosio seemed to shrink, like a slice of bacon shriveling on a hot skillet. I couldn't blame him. Who knew what fiendish punishments waited at the hands at his father?

We followed the trail down a slope that emptied onto a wide flat valley, crisscrossed with dry streambeds like so many of life's empty promises. Horned toads scurried from shadow to shadow beneath the prickly pears. Gradually the valley narrowed into a canyon that squeezed against us like the jaws of a vice.

My *kundalini noir* buzzed again. Dust devils swirled around us—atop the canyon walls and along the canyon floor—and as they vanished, comancheros appeared in their stead.

I counted seven above us on the left, six on the right. Turning around, I spied another seven behind us.

From up ahead, a second group of riders rode closer. Six women on horseback. I realized all the riders surrounding us were women. *Female comancheros.* Black lace wafted from their rangy frames as if the garments were made of smoke. Each of the women bore aspects inked and painted to resemble *Dia de los Muertos* skulls. They weren't only comancheros, but Justos's elite bodyguards, escaped slaves of the various Plains Indians and who had reclaimed their scarred lives by becoming *las brujas malditas*—the Damned Witches. Had one of them dispatched the telltale mechanical crow?

Ambrosio tensed like his blood had turned into bile.

One *bruja* rode ahead of her compatriots. From behind a diaphanous veil, green eyes glowered within black swirls. Silver conches embossed with skull and crossbones decorated her saddle, tack, the gutta-percha grips of her holstered revolvers, and the small top hat pinned to her veil. Her cropped red hair shot out in all directions like the quills of a porcupine.

She nodded and wheeled her horse back down the canyon. Malachi and I, with Ambrosio, followed her lead, her comrades flanking us.

Our horses crunched over the occasional scattering of bones. We turned an abrupt corner and a hundred yards distant, a tall wooden palisade crossed from one side of the canyon to the other.

We passed through an open gate into an enclosed yard. What dominated the space was a towering statue of an Aztec god carved from sandstone. I wasn't familiar enough with them to tell which one. The figure held a rattlesnake and squatted on a plinth of human skulls. Deep-set eyes glowered from a face carved into a perpetual scowl as if this effigy saw nothing worthy of salvation.

To the left and right, various structures—sheds, houses, stables—had been hewn into the canyon walls. Directly ahead sprawled Justos's home. Balconies circumscribed its two stories, and pennants hung limp from the peaks of its gabled roof. Though not palatial by big-city standards, out here the house was a bastion of luxury.

The *brujas* formed a U and herded us to the house. Once there, Malachi and I swung off our horses and hauled Ambrosio to the ground.

The green-eyed *bruja* spoke, in Spanish accented with Kiowa Apache. "*Sueltenle la mordaza.*"

I cut loose Ambrosio's gag, which he spit out. He gazed defiantly at the *brujas*. "All you bitches can go to hell."

A *bruja* with feathers braided into her hair leapt from her pony and landed in front of Ambrosio. She whipped him with a riding crop. With his hands tied behind his back, he was helpless to defend himself. Grabbing his shirt, she stared into his eyes. Then she opened her mouth wide and gasped like a serpent, showing him the mutilated stub of her tongue.

Ambrosio recoiled and dry heaved. Can't say I was pleased by the sight either.

"Hell? We've been there, *perdido*," the green-eyed *bruja* said, then warned, "Behave yourself, for there's more of you to chop off than your tongue."

I kept my hand loose, ready to draw my revolver in case she wasn't just talking to Ambrosio.

The feathered *bruja* climbed back onto her pony. She prodded it toward our horses, took their reins, and led them to a water trough at one side of the porch.

"*Adentro,*" Green-Eyed *Bruja* ordered. "*Todos.*"

So it wasn't enough that we delivered Ambrosio, Malachi and I had to wade deeper into this pit of perdition. I nudged Ambrosio forward and Malachi stepped alongside. Climbing the short flight onto the porch, we moved slowly and deliberately while Green-Eyed *Bruja* and another of her witches dismounted and trailed behind us.

The front door swung open, and in the darkened foyer appeared a pale, ghostly figure. She wore a crisply ironed white shift over a white ankle-length skirt, white oxfords, and a light-blue cape. Her blonde hair was pulled back and tucked under a white cap imprinted with a small crest. Eyes the deep blue of a mountain lake sparkled from a soft face with rosy cheeks. Compared to the hard-bitten *brujas*, she appeared as menacing as a stick of butter.

Cool, humid air spilled over her shoulders. From behind her and deep inside the house, some kind of gigantic machinery rumbled.

"Welcome gentlemen." She curtsied and spoke English with a German accent. "I am Helmina Kolmar, Don Justos's principal medical attendant."

She winced as our gazes met, and that mountain-lake look in her eyes clouded over. She touched the silver crucifix on her necklace. "I hadn't expected one of *your* kind."

"I hear that a lot."

She blinked as if to make sense of what I was doing here, then gestured down the hall. "This way, if you please." Green-Eyed *Bruja* and her lieutenant fell in behind us.

As we proceeded inside, the air now smelled tangy and metallic. The rumble took on a cadence and became louder. Cool droplets spit upon us from rows of ceiling vents. The pulsating noise and the moist breeze brought to mind the same uneasy thought I'd had when following Elsa into the mine, that I was descending into the bowels of a gargantuan beast.

My *kundalini noir* hummed like a taut string, plucked hard.

Helmina led us down a corridor to a set of double doors, which I expected her to open in a theatric flourish—*Behold, Don Justos!* Instead she cracked open the one on the right and let us slip through.

At the back of the room, a battery of glass cylinders filled with amber liquid reached from the floor to the ceiling. Bubbles in the liquid churned in rhythm to the syncopated tempo trembling the air. Glass and polished-metal tubes twisted spaghetti-like from bronze manifolds along the top of the cylinders. These tubes led to a shallow bassinet-like metal contraption set against a bureau and a long black curtain. Cradled within the bassinet rested an old man in a baggy gown.

"Don Justos," Helmina announced. "Your son is here."

At the mention of his name, Justos perked up, and his dull, rheumy eyes became clear and piercing.

So this was Don Justos Zamora, the feared *El Jefe de la Comancheria*. I'd never seen him before, but considering his reputation I expected a giant of man—a Mexican Thor reposed on a throne of iron and thunderbolts.

What greeted us though, was half a human, meaning exactly that—Justos from the waist up! I don't know had happened to the rest of him, but there couldn't have been much left since the bassinet was maybe a foot deep. Waxy, jaundiced flesh sagged from his face as if he was dissolving. His body emerged from layers of fleecy blankets bundled around him.

Justos reached for the sides of the bassinet to sit up straight. His movements were at first palsied and hesitant, which only added to his crippled presence. But when he brought his gaze upon Ambrosio, it was like a fire had ignited inside the old man's emaciated torso.

Ambrosio didn't avert his eyes, and he squared his shoulders as if ready to face an execution squad.

"Bring him closer," Justos ordered in a gruff mumble.

"In time," I said. "There's the matter of the bounty."

"As you said," Justos replied, "in time. First, allow me to speak with my son."

Malachi nudged Ambrosio to take a step, but Ambrosio remained rooted in place. I elbowed him hard, and he staggered forward.

"*Mijo*," Justos said, "when you were younger, when I looked into your face, I saw my own. Now what do I see? A thief. A swindler. An embezzler."

Ambrosio's lips pruned in disgust. "What bothers you the most, *viejo gastado*, is not that I stole, but that I also stole from you."

"Indeed. You stole much. You squandered your birthright. You've forced my hand, Ambrosio." The old man's voice softened to a regretful whisper. "If I'm to retain the respect of my hacienda, of my neighbors, and most importantly, of my enemies, I have to make an example of you."

"As you did to Mother?" Ambrosio cut his gaze to a polished human skull on the nearby bureau. "This is family love among us Zamoras." He spit a gob to the floor.

Green-Eyed *Bruja* kicked the back of his knees, and he crumpled sideways, then collapsed onto his back.

Malachi and I jerked away, startled, ready to shoot our way out of here.

In a tired voice, Justos said, *"Alimentalo a los zopilotes."* Feed him to the buzzards.

When Ambrosio opened his mouth—to curse, to scream, I don't know—the green-eyed *bruja* yanked a leather belt around his neck and choked him to silence. The two *brujas* lifted him by the armpits and were about to haul him out when Justos announced, "Wait. He needs to see one more thing."

He beckoned Malachi and me. "You two *pistoleros*, our business is not yet completed."

What did he mean? My *kundalini noir* reared back, ready to strike. I sensed Malachi also putting himself on a hair trigger.

Justos turned to his nurse. "Helmina, the bounty, *por favor*."

She pivoted toward the bureau and unlocked a drawer, withdrawing a small strongbox, which she brought to Justos, who then balanced it on the edge of his bassinet. From inside his gown, he fished out a cord and key, and with trembling fingers, opened the strongbox's padlock.

"Every day I sit in this tub is torture," he said. "But to endure, suffering must have meaning. And the meaning for me is to have my enemies brought here, one by one, and let them taste Comancheria justice."

He reached into the lockbox and retrieved a pair of cloth bags each the size and shape of a large sausage. They sagged heavily in his hands. *"La recompensa, señores.* Two thousand dollars."

Malachi's guess about the bounty had been correct.

Justos tossed the bag to me, and I caught it with my left hand, my right remaining close over my revolver. Malachi kept watch as I opened the bag. Fifty-dollar gold coins clinked into my palm.

Malachi took the money and counted. "This is only half."

"What's going on?" I asked. "You said the bounty was two thousand dollars."

"So it is," Justos replied. "Two thousand dollars paid upon the delivery of my son Ambrosio to those who brought him in."

He tossed the second bag toward the curtain on the other side of his bed. It thumped on the wooden floor. "Half to you both." Justos pointed to Malachi and me. "Half to her." He pointed to the curtain.

Her, who?

Someone moved behind the curtain. My *kundalini noir* tensed, coiling. The curtain parted and out stepped a woman wearing a riding skirt, waistcoat, and boots spattered with mud. She picked up the bag of coins. A frizz of russet-brown hair framed a complexion bronzed by long days in the sun. She wasn't exactly pretty, but she had dark, enchanting eyes that could make a man—or woman, depending—do plenty of immoral things. But the most remarkable feature about her was the mechanical crow perched on her shoulder.

Details clicked into place. The crow. The note. Ambrosio. Elsa's disappearing act. The bounty. The crow again. The woman. *Elsa.*

She grinned at me. I grinned back. I had to acknowledge that she had been one step ahead of everyone else, even if by using supernatural means.

Ambrosio thrashed against the floor. The *brujas* loosened the belt around his neck enough for him to give a ragged whisper, "Elsa. You!" His voice sounded like gravel. "It was *you* who gave me up."

When Elsa turned to Ambrosio, her grin heated into a glare. "When I asked you where you hid your treasure, you wouldn't tell me. After all that we've done together, all those swindles and scams, all those times we looked away from each other's infidelities as we drew our victims into folly, and you still didn't trust me? If I couldn't earn your trust, then I had to do something worthy of your mistrust." She bounced the bag of coins in her hands.

His face reddened and contorted. "Traitor! Traitor!"

The *brujas* tightened the belt until Ambrosio's eyes bulged and all that came out of his mouth was a spray of froth. As they dragged him out the door, he beat his naked heels against the floor until they bled.

Justos sighed. "Our business is done, *señores*. Close the door on your way out."

Malachi tugged at my coat sleeve. We turned about and started the long trek home.

THE PETRIFIED MAN

Betsy Dornbusch

Creede, Colorado
April 13, 1892

I never thought I'd see Jefferson "Soapy" Smith again once Denver instituted its new regulations against gambling, but I'd just finished a case when his telegraph came from Creede—a telegraph concluding with, "Something strange is going on." Soapy knew how to pique my curiosity even if I only half believed him.

A bunko man, gambler, and possible murderer was an unlikely friend for a lawman like me, the founder of the Rocky Mountain Detective Association. Not that he fought crime for the sake of any societal goodness. Soapy Smith solved crimes when it was good for Soapy Smith. Nobody cuts into a criminal's business like another criminal. But Soapy and me, we'd seen some odd goings-on in our years hunting criminals. Ghosts, spells, and monsters were at the root of enough crimes we solved to always consider the supernatural a suspect . . . until our last case when he'd lied to me about a witch's curse to direct suspicion at his competition.

Fresh-cut lumber hotels, shops, and saloons in Creede faced each other across a dirt road. Ladies-of-the-evening and miners mingled together in the early evening. The excited din of men just coming off their shifts in the mines and women just coming on their shifts in miner's beds seemed to echo off the mountains that crowded the town. Overhead, the butcher and a restaurant had strung banners across the road. Constant hammering on new buildings created the cacophony of a town on the rise. Off in the distance, explosives went off, and closer in town, a pistol shot. No one batted an eye.

A certain tension tinged the hum of conversation, though, tension I had come to recognize. The name Maggie rested on several lips as I strode toward the Orleans Club, Soapy's new saloon and gambling hall. An American flag flapped from a pole atop it as if put there to help me find my way.

The last of the daylight seeped through the dusty windows and red glass shades filtered lamplight. A few women in ruffled dresses leaned on the bar and over the shoulders of intent gamblers, but the pleasant early evening had kept people outdoors for a while yet. The men who weren't on the street were still out at the mines, scraping the rock for silver without pause in underground hells fueled by steam power and prayers.

I asked for Jeff Smith at the bar, and the barman gestured with his towel. I needn't have bothered, though. Soapy was striding across the room toward me by the time I turned around, clean and trim as ever. Must've bathed for the occasion.

"General David Cook," he said.

I gave him a nod and offered a hand to shake, studying him closer. He had a fresh bruise on his cheek. "Somebody finally get a swing at the famous Soapy Smith?"

He scowled at me.

I grinned. "Who's Maggie Maslow? I keep hearing her name."

"Ever the detective."

"She's dead, isn't she? Murdered?"

"She's got nothing to do with my problem."

"She's all the conversation out on the street," I said. "You know her?"

"Everybody knows everybody in a place like this."

People looking for fortune had flooded the valley since Alpha Mine started producing great amounts of silver in 1889, but not too many to ignore an important event like someone dying.

Soapy rubbed the back of his neck. "You sure can sniff 'em out. All right, she got herself murdered. Beat to death by a miner, most likely."

"Is the law on it?"

"I am the law in Creede." He shrugged. "Cap's my deputy." William Light, his brother-in-law. I'd heard Soapy had declared himself camp boss within weeks of his arrival.

"Heaven help Creede, then," I said.

Soapy snorted and gestured me to a back room, an office that had two straight-back chairs, a table, a safe, and a long pine box. "Maggie isn't my problem. That is." He pointed to the coffin.

"Usually your problems are with your safe." I raised my brows and went around the table to open the casket.

"It's empty, so don't bother yourself. McGinty is supposed to be in there. My petrified man." Soapy shoved a newspaper across the table.

The Creede Candle
April 10, 1892

Now Announcing!

THE PETRIFIED MAN is available for viewing at the ORLEANS CLUB. Ten cents to see the amazing REAL petrified corpse of a dead man with perfectly preserved muscles and hair, even eyelashes! Skeptics especially welcome. Games of chance for your further entertainment and the finest selection of four whiskeys available West of the Divide.

I tossed it down. "Someone stole your latest hoax? This why you called me up here, Jeff?"

"It's not a hoax. It's a real dead man. Petrified. Perfect. Only cost a dime to see him—"

"Ten cents," I said dryly. "What a bargain."

"Got to give them incentive to try to win it back so we can fleece them in the real games." He never pretended he wasn't on the con, not with me. "That's beside the point. I spent three thousand dollars on McGinty, and I want him back."

I wasn't easily caught off guard by the stupid amounts of money people spent, but that was an enormous sum, even for Soapy. "Sounds like you're the one who got fleeced. Three thousand dollars for a statue?"

A muscle twitched in his bruised cheek. "I'm telling you, McGinty is a real man, and he's gone, and I want him back."

Soapy had a temper, but I saw something else in him. Desperation, maybe a bit of fear. It couldn't be just the money. Soapy had just sold his saloon down in Denver for a pretty penny, and he managed his finances well enough to be a generous man to good causes...and bad. "When did he disappear?"

"Yesterday morning. Before dawn."

The corpse was probably halfway to Denver by now. "Any idea who took him? Or why?"

"None, damn it. Why do you think I called you up here?"

"And what about the strange part?"

"He comes to life in the night."

I got to my feet and put on my hat. "Goodbye, Smith."

"He does! And he's violent." He gestured to his own bruise.

"Like that witch's curse made Tom Horn kill that gang cutting into your business? And nearly got me killed in the process, I'll add."

Soapy stared at me, nostrils flared.

"I'm not going to help you unless you're straight with me."

Soapy lowered his gaze, his jaw set. "All right. I knew you'd come if I said something strange was happening."

"Hmph. I ought to get back on the train and go home."

"You won't, though."

"Damn you, Jeff Smith." But my words didn't have much bite. Lack of strangeness aside, a murdered dance-hall girl and a missing corpse were right up my alley. Everyone deserved justice in death, even if they hadn't quite deserved it in life.

No one wanted to discuss the missing McGinty. All the talk was about Maggie Maslow being found beaten to death behind the Orleans Club—a fact Soapy had failed to mention. I picked up the evening copy of *The Creede Candle* and nursed a drink while I read about the robbery of McGinty. It was all speculation, but interesting nonetheless.

A deep voice interrupted me. "Hello, General."

The man who had approached me was tall and broad and wore a good-natured grin under his curling mustache.

"You have me at a disadvantage," I answered, folding up the paper.

"Pete Burns." We shook, his big hand swallowing mine. I knew the name. One of Soapy's gang.

"Welcome to Creede," he said. The words held a question.

I sat up straighter to look him in the eye. "It's not for pleasure. I'm investigating the disappearance of Mr. Smith's petrified man."

"Strange thing, that."

"The man or the disappearance?" I asked.

Grin. "Both."

"You wouldn't know anything about it, would you?"

"I sleep here in the club with the rest of the gang. Heard some banging down here about the time McGinty disappeared."

"Did you check the time?" I asked.

"No, too busy coming downstairs to see if some drunk was trying to break into the place, but the club was dark and empty. Checked the safe to be sure and found the back door to the office was open. So was the coffin."

"And the safe?"

"Sealed up tight. No sign of messing with it neither."

"Did you check the street or alley?"

"Sure did," Pete Burns said amiably. "And there she was."

"Maggie Maslow," I said.

Pete Burns clucked sympathetically. "Knew she was dead soon as I saw her. I reckon she ran across the thieves. Probably coming to find Soapy, but he wasn't here anyhow."

"Anybody with you?"

He snorted. "All still sleepin' their whiskey off like babes in a manger."

"You don't drink?"

He shrugged. "I can hold my liquor."

By the size of him, I didn't doubt it. "I'd like to see her body."

"Whoever done it left her a right mess."

"Even so." It wouldn't be the worst I'd seen. The only thing more shocking than spending three thousand dollars on a dead man was the way people made each other dead in the first place. I wanted to see her room, too, if it wasn't already occupied by another dance-hall girl.

Pete Burns pointed. "The man you want to see is Clyde Lewis, over there. Self-appointed Creede mortician. He's taking care of her."

"He get a lot of work?"

"Where there's minin' there's dyin'," said Pete Burns. A philosopher and pugilist. "Come on, I'll introduce ya."

Clyde Lewis was wiry and held himself like he was old and lame, leaning an elbow on the table and holding the other arm close to himself. After an exchange of pleasantries, the conversation turned to Maggie Maslow.

"I'd like to see the body," I told him.

"She's nailed up inside her coffin, and I already got Reverend Fraser to say a few words tomorrow morning between shifts. I'm burying her after."

I reckoned mortician work was a way to tide himself over until he struck silver. "I'll come early then."

"Got to check with Soapy first," Clyde Lewis said.

"Can't imagine he'd care. Besides, he's the one who asked me up here from Denver."

"I'm still gonna ask. Heard tell he was half in love with her. Even paid to bury her."

"I told you Maggie Maslow has nothing to do with McGinty," Soapy said again. "Leave the poor woman in peace."

"Right. Except she was beat to death right along the time Big Pete says McGinty disappeared, and right along the path the thieves took to escape. You have enemies, Jeff. Who hates you enough to come up here, steal your sideshow, and murder your lover?"

"She wasn't my lov—"

"You paid for her casket and funeral. Don't tell me she meant nothing to you."

Soapy reached for his drink. "I saw her sometimes. Not that night."

"Often enough to pay for her funeral," I said. "Where were you that night?"

"Not with her," Soapy growled. "If I had been, she'd still be alive."

He wasn't boasting. Soapy was good with his fists and pistol. "Who was the lady with, then? Were you jealous?"

"She was no lady, and I'm no cold-blooded murderer. You know that, David."

I didn't actually, but the men he killed had it coming and I'd never heard otherwise. "What about this?" I tossed the latest edition of *The Creede Candle* down. "Seven disgruntled men trying to steal McGinty?"

Soapy glanced at it, then turned it around to study the story I had it folded to.

"It's all trumped-up bullshit to sell papers."

"They report there was a witness."

"There are no seven men. It's fake news."

"If I know you, there are seven-*score* men who'd like back at you one way or another."

Soapy's lips thinned. "None of this is finding McGinty."

I took off my spectacles and rubbed them free of the dust with my handkerchief. "Oh I have a hunch on that."

Soapy groaned. "You and your hunches."

"I have a hunch," I repeated, "that if we find Maggie Maslow's murderer we find McGinty's thief."

Soapy scowled, but he just drank down a glass of one of the four kinds of fine whiskey behind the bar and ordered another.

The next morning I stepped out of the Creede Hotel to a bright, busy day. Some ten thousand souls called Creede home, and it felt as if most of them were out on the street. Throngs of men walked to a shift at the Alpha Mine while others trudged to their beds. Denver rarely felt as crowded.

Miners are a tough, dirty lot who don't show their hurts. These men were no different...all but one. He staggered along like a drunk about to topple, gaze skittering across people in his path, one hand pressed to his head, the other arm wrapped around his middle. People walked around him, intent on their own destinations, but gave him the occasional suspicious look.

I strode out to him and caught his arm. "Here, now. Step over this way."

He looked at me, mouth open. Curious I didn't smell spirits on his breath. But he was bleeding under the hand pressed to the side of his hatless head. "What happened to you, fella?"

"Some...thing...beat me up."

He must not be quite right since he took a knock to the head. I gentled my tone. "What's your name?"

"Robert Ford. Who're you?" he mumbled through swollen, bruised lips.

The name sounded familiar but I couldn't place it. "General David Cook."

"I need the law."

"I am the law." I led him into the hotel, shouldering open the door, and deposited him on a sofa.

Mr. Zang, the hotelier, started forward. "Now, General, don't you be bringing that sort in here."

"We need a bowl of water and a towel, please. The man has been attacked."

Zang scowled his disapproval, but he scuttled off.

I turned back to Ford. "Mr. Ford, what can you remember?"

His eyes took a bit to settle on me. "One of those dead things come at me in the dark."

I exchanged glances with Mr. Zang, who'd returned with the items. He shrugged.

"Dead thing?" I asked.

"Gotta nail the coffins shut or they'll get out."

"Did this happen outside?" I asked him. Fires lit up the streets for building at night.

"Behind my dance hall. I tried to fight back but it felt like hitting a brick wall." His knuckles were bruised and bleeding, but that could happen over a man's face, all right.

"Ford's Exchange, General," Mr. Zang said shortly. For all his irritability, he'd brought salve and a bandage too.

Years in the army, doing law work, and dealing with dangerous people had given me some skill at patching up a man. I got to work. "Mr. Ford, anyone got it in for you?"

Ford's lips went thin and white. "General. I remember now. You're friends with Soapy Smith."

And after that he wouldn't say another word but a gruff thanks when I was done bandaging his wound. He took a drink at the hotel bar and staggered off back the way he'd come. I thanked Mr. Zang, who shot me another ill-tempered glare in response, and I followed Ford. But he just shut himself inside a little house at the end of town. Hopefully he'd sleep off the damage done. So I headed off to my date with Miss Maggie Maslow.

Clyde Lewis shook his head. "Soapy said no."

"No? Why?"

"Not mine to question."

I could go hassle Soapy about it or I could handle this here and now. "I don't give a damn what Soapy Smith says. I'm going to see this body." I gave him a speculative look and raised a fist. "If you're worried about trouble from him, he might believe I overcame you in a fistfight if there's evidence of one. A good crack to the jaw ought to convince him."

Clyde Lewis glared at me and stepped back, still holding his crowbar. "Don't you hit me or..."

"Or what?" I held his skittish gaze. "Give me that before you hurt yourself with it."

He scowled and slapped it onto my palm. I used it to pry up the pine coffin lid, and the smell was about rank as you'd expect. Soapy had wasted no money trying to make her pretty again. Her bloodied face had swollen over broken, misshapen bones. Blood from her shattered nose and teeth stained the lace of her dress and her hair, including two crooked blue ribbons. Her hands rested at her sides rather than crossed over her chest, but she was a gruesome sight. I expect Clyde Lewis had wanted to touch her as little as possible.

I reached in to lift up her skirts.

"Hey now—"

"She's dead. She doesn't care anymore. And Soapy doesn't have to know." But there was no bruising on her thighs that I could see. Maybe she'd been punched in the stomach, but her corset kept me from doing a more thorough search. I reckoned it no longer mattered and smoothed the skirts back down over her puffy, pale legs. A necklace around her neck glittered in the low light. I reached in and pulled the pendant around to her front. It was a locket with a picture of an older lady in it. I laid it gently on her breast and reached for the lid to close it over her again.

Scratches marred the soft pine. I looked at Clyde.

He shrugged. "I use scraps from the buildings. I sanded the top though," he added defensively.

Indeed he had. I tried to pick up one of Maggie's cold, swollen hands.

She was hard as stone and it wouldn't move, her fingers curled into fists.

"She's still in rigor. That puts her less than eighteen hours dead." I looked at the scratched inner lid again. Damn it.

Clyde Lewis tsked. "She was well past dead yesterday morning when I put her in here. I checked her myself."

Despite his reassurances, I placed my fingers on her throat and fell still. No pulse. Then I held the back of my pocket watch to her nostrils. No condensation marred the shiny silver surface. I was inclined to believe him. Dead bodies did strange things, and spring nights were cold in the Rockies. Maybe she was a bit frozen. Clyde put the lid down and hammered her back inside.

"Do you nail all the coffins shut?" I asked.

"Sure."

"Seems like extra work for a body going in the ground."

"Soapy ordered it done."

"Indeed?"

"He's camp boss."

I decided Lewis was the sort not to question his betters, especially those who paid well, and dropped the issue. "It is fine work on the box," I lied, by way of making amends for threatening him.

He shrugged. "I'm getting good at it, unfortunately. Second one I've built inside a week. What'd you learn from her, General?"

I sighed. "Precious little. I want to see her rooms."

"She had a tent out back of Zang's," he said.

But it had already been taken over by someone else, so that was a useless endeavor. None of the soiled doves nearby knew who Maggie Maslow had been with on her last night or who might have attacked her.

I didn't much feel like drinking, but I needed to visit Ford's Exchange. I wanted to take a look around the saloon and see if I could find a witness to either beating. The place was empty but for one man guarding the liquor, chair tipped back with his boots on another, hat tilted down over his eyes. He didn't appear to be the most alert guard, but he shoved his hat back and peered up at me when I entered.

"Not open yet," he growled.

I introduced myself, but he didn't return the courtesy. "Your boss got attacked this morning," I said to him. "Early, still dark. See anything?"

He shook his head and spat some chew. "Who done it?"

"He says he doesn't know. You have any ideas?"

He shrugged. "Plenty of people'd like to see him dead."

"Why is that? Does he water down his alcohol?"

"Nah. Ford killed Jesse James."

I stared at him. "I'll be damned." I knew I'd recognized the name.

"I heard you're here for Soapy anyways." His lip curled.

"We go back a ways, yes," I said cautiously. "Someone stole his petrified man."

"Why don't you ask him, then?"

My brows raised. "I can't, seeing how McGinty is dead."

He ignored my lame attempt at humor. "Ask Soapy who beat up Ford. Rumor has it Soapy Smith is trying to get someone to do him in."

"I know you admired Jesse James. You got a beef with Ford over killing him, Jeff? Enough to pound on him a bit?"

Soapy shrugged and got up to put a stack of bills in his safe. "He's a murderer. But like I said before, I didn't try to kill him or hurt him, and I didn't kill Maggie." He gave me a dark look. "I know you went to look at her corpse."

"Don't blame Lewis. He threatened me with a crowbar." Remembering that made me think of something. "Why'd you order the coffin nailed shut?"

"Seemed the thing to do. She's being buried in a gold locket from her mama. I don't want anyone to steal it."

"Lewis says you ordered all the coffins nailed shut. All the corpses got gold lockets from their mamas?"

"It's just the men talking. Don't know a damned bear when they hear one." Soapy slammed his safe door shut and spun the dial with an irritable twist of his fingers.

"What are you talking about?"

"They walk by the cemetery at night after shift and think they hear something. They can't see straight after being underground, so they think they see things. It's bears or some other animal. Or nothing at all. But Coltrain nearly got himself killed when he started shooting in the dark, so I told them we'd start nailing the coffins shut."

"So the corpses couldn't escape?" I raised my brows.

"To pacify a bunch of drunk miners, yeah."

"Is that what you meant by something going on in this town, Jeff? That the dead come to life? So you have to nail them into their pine boxes?" The coffin caught my eye like a bad omen, even if I'm not a superstitious man. "Except for this one. You didn't nail this one."

No lock on the box, just a row of cabin hooks. Soapy hadn't cared to protect his investment that much. Why didn't the thieves take McGinty in the coffin? Surely it'd be a safer way to transport a petrified body, which I imagined was rigid and brittle, prone to damage. And surely carrying a box would draw less notice than the stiff, dead body of a man.

I lifted the lid.

And stared.

The inside of the lid was scratched all to hell. Just like Maggie Maslow's had been. I examined the sides. They were scratched too. But the outside was well sanded.

I sat back on my heels, my pulse kicking up until I could feel it in my throat. "Maybe you have a good explanation for this, Jeff."

Hell, in that moment, I'd even have been square with learning Soapy Smith stuck an enemy in that coffin. Maybe just to scare him. Soapy was wild and rough and criminal.

But he wasn't sadistic.

Soapy gritted his teeth. Paced a few steps and spun on me. "I tried to tell you when you got here. You wouldn't listen."

"Can you blame me after you concocted that fool story about the witches?"

"You were supposed to believe me after what we've been through together."

"That lie nearly got me killed." I ran my fingers along the scratches. "We have to catch him. Destroy him."

"How? I don't think an axe would even go through him. He's hard as stone."

Like hitting a brick wall, Ford had said. "We burn him to ash, then."

"We can't. It's too dangerous. We could set the whole valley on fire."

That was true enough. Fire was too big a risk. "Then we catch him and nail him into this pine box and bury him with the rest of Creede's dead, where he can't hurt anybody else." I gave him a look. "Like Maggie."

Soapy cursed low but his shoulders fell. "Right. What do we do?"

The cemetery was quiet as we approached it in the dark. I stopped the horses several times because I kept thinking I heard rustling amid the trees, boulders, and dried grasses on either side of the narrow dirt switchbacks. Soapy, for his part, kept watch, even though he was irritable about being here, irritable about capturing McGinty, and really irritable about locking him up for good. I didn't have to urge him at the end of my revolver, but I was ready to if it came to it.

We set up near a low crypt that was already looking the worse for wear from the Colorado winters, got some tools and weapons out of my pack, and scouted out the cemetery. There was no sign of McGinty, giving us time to make our preparations. I watched the shadows of neighboring woods and the rise of the hills.

"What if he went back down to town? He could be anywhere."

"We'll go along back down if we don't see him here," I said.

"Why would he hang out here anyway? This is a fool plan."

"Because the dead know they belong in graveyards." I lifted my hand to shush him. It sounded like someone might be riding up to the cemetery, or several people, like the tattoo of hooves against the hard dirt. But it didn't change in volume, like it would if horses were approaching.

Our horses shifted and lifted their heads from nosing around for grass. One tossed his head and stamped. "Do you feel that?"

Soapy shook his head. "Feel what?"

I got to my feet and walked a bit, avoiding graves but the noise kept on. The sounds were muffled, dull, and a coldness seeped into me that had nothing to do with the drop in temperature as night fell in the mountains. I stepped onto a grave, knelt, and put my hand on the dirt. Random vibrations seemed to seep up through the ground into my hand. "My god. It's true."

Soapy snorted and started to say something when the mare I'd been riding whinnied in fear. The other pinned his ears and tugged against his lead, which I'd secured to an iron railing, hindquarters shifting. Soapy hurried over to him. "Whoa, boy." He patted the gelding's neck and checked the tie. It wouldn't do to have the horse slip loose or break its lead—

The gelding reared, shoving Soapy back. Both horses struggled against their ropes. The fence started to bend and rock with every tug. Soapy cursed and let the horses run free. They galloped away toward town. He cursed again and looked at me. "What spooked—look out!"

The rumbling thuds from underground increased in tempo. I spun and even without having seen McGinty or a photograph, I knew he was the ghoul lurching toward me in the dark. A gaunt brown face with empty eye sockets and a gaping mouth came into sharp relief. I had no air to scream, not that I'm given to it anyway. But if something would make me scream like a terrified little girl, that visage would be it.

I snatched at my revolver, but he reached me first and swung at me. His fist caught me across the temple. The world went wobbly and dark, but I instinctively struck out. My fist met a stomach like boiled leather, thick with no give. Like a wall. Pain shot up my hand and arm. Soapy shouted from behind me. I stumbled back, nearly falling over a rock. McGinty followed, hands outstretched. McGinty cinched his fingers around my throat, doing his damnedest to crush my windpipe. I tried to rip free, but his grip only tightened. I tore at the man's arm. I might as well have been trying to break a thick tree branch.

Soapy tackled both of us, and even though I felt something snap in my middle, it served to knock his hands loose. I rolled free, consumed with gasping air. It felt like minutes but maybe was only seconds before I heard Soapy shouting and grunting again. I shoved my resistant body up. Soapy rolled on the ground with McGinty, trying to beat him into submission and not succeeding. "Goddammit, Cook, get over here and help me!"

I had no way to get a clear shot at McGinty, and how do you kill a dead man anyway?

I stepped forward, stripping off my coat. "Hold him."

"If I could, damn it—oof!" McGinty headbutted him.

I grabbed one of McGinty's legs, tough as a tree root, and wrenched it with sheer strength toward the other. He got free and kicked me in the jaw. I doggedly shoved back up and came at him again. McGinty struggled and Soapy was barely able to hold him, but I managed to tie his ankles together with my coat sleeves. McGinty never made a sound and his expression didn't change, just his body moving herky-jerky like someone twitching on his strings. Then I stripped my belt, took the holster off, and together we wrangled it around his arms and body. McGinty convulsed on the ground trying to get free, but to no avail. We panted and wiped the blood off our faces with our sleeves.

"That's my best coat," I said. "My wife is going to tan my hide."

"*That's* your best coat?"

I punched his shoulder, hard. "This is all your fault. You strung me along knowing McGinty escaped himself."

"You wouldn't believe me. I tried to tell you, like I said."

"You should have made me believe. Maybe I at least could have spared Robert Ford a beating."

"Yeah, shame McGinty didn't manage to do him in." Soapy

took on a musing expression. "I could build a cage. I reckon people'd pay *fifty* cents to see a dead man come to life."

I lost my temper. "Blast it, you don't even care about Maggie Maslow! You only care about the money you can make off this damned monster."

"I never said I did care for her. Besides, I made it right, didn't I?"

Made her death right by paying for her funeral? That was a messed up brand of logic right there. "He's an abomination, not a sideshow. Besides, all these corpses are alive in their coffins. Won't take long for someone else to figure it out. And it won't take long after that for one of them to get dug up and kill someone else. No, we burn him up."

"We agreed we'd bury him," Soapy said.

"That was before I saw him."

"We can't. The whole valley'd go up. Remember the Middle Park fire?"

Tens of thousands of acres had burned some years back, bad enough to still remember. I nodded with a sigh. "Then we bury him with the rest of Creede's dead, even though they all ought to burn."

Graveyards in the high country often keep open graves for anyone who might pass away when the ground is frozen. This one was no different. Soapy grabbed McGinty's shoulders, and I tucked my pistol into my dragging waistband and grabbed McGinty's feet. We dropped him once as he convulsed, trying to get free, but finally we rustled him into the grave with the open coffin at the bottom. Soapy slammed the lid down and jumped down into hole, his boots thudding on the coffin. I handed over the hammer and nails, glad I'd taken the pack off the horses before they'd bolted. Then we went at the ground with shovels, dumping dirt onto the rattling pine box. Behind us, Maggie Maslow and the other corpses struggled in their coffins, keeping us eerie company.

Daylight stretched over the peaks by the time we finished, and the dead quieted in their graves. It was a bit of a walk home. We ate breakfast at Zang's silently and I headed back on the train that afternoon, glad to put my back to McGinty, Creede, and Jeff "Soapy" Smith.

But it was not to be. Weeks after I solved the mystery of the

Petrified Man, a fire took all of Creede, including the Orleans Club. It didn't take Soapy long to come back to Denver and get back to his old tricks in town. I never could figure why the dead took their nightly sojourns in Creede, but Soapy told me the fire stopped all that anyway. We even solved another crime together . . . monsterless thankfully, before he headed further west and eventually settled in the Alaskan frontier.

I never heard much word about Soapy until his death, and even that not until months after. But when a fellow lawman visited from Washington Territory, he told me a story over whiskey about a series of severe beatings and murders that had taken place in late 1895 by an obviously deranged man. Then, suddenly, they just stopped.

"You ever catch who did it?" I asked.

"Nah. Damnedest thing. People thought this sideshow statue did it."

I sat up straight. "A statue. What kind of statue?"

"I never saw it. People said it was a mummified man or something."

"Mummified?" My eyes narrowed. "Or petrified?"

The lawman snorted. "Neither. Those traveling sideshows are full of tricks and lies. Anything in the name of the almighty dollar."

Right. Anything for a dollar. I growled under my breath and ordered a double. *Damn you, Soapy Smith.*

STANDS TWICE AND THE MAGPIE MAN

Stephen Graham Jones

This was after the massacre Stands Twice had woken to, which was after the summer the white scabs burned through his tribe, which had been two years after the winter most of them starved, which was right after the treaty at the white tents that was supposed to have stopped the massacres from happening.

Stands Twice hadn't run from the soldiers that morning, didn't want to let them see him running from them like that, so their bullets threw him back into the lodge. He crawled out from those ashes hours later, touching his own chest and stomach, not sure where the holes were, not sure why he wasn't in the sandhills with the rest of the dead. It was the same as when he'd tended his wife through her sickness, when she was dying: The scabs never boiled up from his armpits or the tops of his feet like they had at first with her. They never came at all. And, though he'd stumbled out of that starvation winter weighing what felt like half as much as he had in the fall, still, he'd been walking. Unlike so many.

What he came to figure, it wasn't that he couldn't be killed, it was that he was being punished—that the pale road that led to the ghost camp wasn't for him. But there had to be a way to get there.

He stripped down to nothing, walked into the sacred hills without nodding to the four directions, and with no bite of fresh liver to leave on a smooth rock in offering.

If the soldiers and the cold and the starving couldn't grant him passage, maybe poor behavior could. Maybe his death already

233

lumbered through the dark trees, its breath steaming down in twin plumes against the pine needles.

What he got instead was a magpie.

It hopped in front of him, daring him, so he skipped a rock at it. The magpie lifted up on its wings, floated back down, chattered at him like a squirrel.

"Go away," he called ahead to it. "I'm looking for my death."

The magpie laughed at him so he rushed forward, dove into the sky after it, only to come down into a creek that folded his ankle over with a crack. He limped up from the water, his hands balled into fists, and walked and walked and made himself walk, trying not to look at his swelling ankle.

That night he dropped a chunk of flint into his fire until it was hot enough, then used a stick to roll it downhill to another creek. The flint shattered in the cold water. With one of the sharp flakes, he split the purple skin of his ankle.

The swelling went down with the fire, and then was back again when he woke, and the ankle still didn't work.

"Where are you!" he called up the mountain.

He was talking to his death.

Only the magpie answered, its chatter a laugh that didn't echo.

Two days later, walking with the help of a thick branch, he made it to the center of the holy place. There was an old rifle there, the wood rotted off, the metal flaky and brown. There was a tall, round rock that had a story that went with it. There were braids of hair tied to the branches of the tree, the hair unbraiding year by year, becoming bird nests.

He rolled the rock away, he beat the rifle against a tree until it crumbled into nothing. He reached up to pull the hair down, but it felt like it was still attached to people somehow, so he left it there with the prayers it was tying down.

When he walked away the next morning, there were bear prints in the frost, but the bear had just walked past, hadn't even cared about him. Probably because, in the fall like this, bears need fat for the winter, not stringy Indians who haven't eaten for four days.

He followed the bear anyway.

It led him to a giant rotting log. The bear had dug into the soft wood for . . . something. Bugs? Rabbits? Snake eggs?

That night he slept in what was left of that log, waiting for the next bear, but it never came. The next morning, ravenous, he went down to the grass and dug some turnips, ate them without boiling them, and was sick the rest of the day.

The magpie watched him, but didn't say anything.

Either the next day or the one after, he looked up into some birch he was trudging through and saw a young owl sleeping. He brought it down with a rock, chased it through the trees, and made himself build a fire to cook it instead of just chewing in. He threw the feathers back up in the sky, watched them drift away.

The magpie flitted at the edge of his vision. It didn't care if he killed all the owls and ate them.

Instead of scaring the magpie into the sky this time, he followed it.

It swooped and glided ahead, led him down and down through the flat grasslands to what turned out to be a covered wagon just sitting there. He watched it for the rest of that day—nothing—and, nodding off with sleep, was pretty sure there wasn't a fire that night either. At sunrise he was standing next to it.

Inside were four dead women, their wrists in chains, their hair long and black. Not Indian, but not white either.

From their dirty clothes he fashioned something to wear, and, removing their clothes like that, he found one of them had a knife wrapped around her thigh with wire. He took that too, left them in the wagon and, a half day later, he found the team that had been pulling the wagon, along with two men. They were all dead, but no arrows, no bullet holes. Stands Twice looked back in the direction of the wagon, tried to imagine the story that got them from there to here, but there were too many ways it could have happened.

He started to take one of the men's boots because it had silver conches on the side, but when he pulled it off the dead foot, it was full of fluid and decay.

The magpie called, and he followed.

He wore one of the women's bonnets now.

He walked into a prairie dog town, plugged up enough holes that he could dig down into one for some meat, down in the cool darkness.

He cut the prairie dog's haunches thin with the knife, dried the strips on a rack of willow branches, a fire smoking beneath it. He carried the meat in the bonnet now.

"I'm trying to die," he said to himself through the days.

The magpie laughed at him.

"What do you know?" he said to it.

It floated ahead, ahead.

Two weeks later, it led him to one of the square lodges the farmers liked to live in. In the gentle hill behind it was a dugout with wood framing the door to keep it up. He watched the family move from the stalls to the cabin to the dugout, and then nodded when the magpie landed on the top rail by one of the horses.

"This will do it," he said.

When the chimney was just breathing smoke and the one window wasn't yellow anymore, he crept down to the stall, rolled under the lowest rail, and cupped his hands around the horse's nose and mouth to keep it quiet, whispering to it the whole time.

He was just feeling around the horse's neck for a hank of mane to pull himself up with when twin hammers cocked behind him.

The farmer told him something in his white tongue. Stands Twice smiled into the horse's neck—this was it, it had to be—and turned, the knife already in his hand.

The farmer stepped back, stumbled, fell, discharged both barrels of his shotgun into the sky. The flash left Stands Twice blind for a moment, the sound left him deaf, but, furious at the farmer for stumbling, for not finishing this as he was supposed to, for not playing his role, he rushed ahead, held the man's chin up so the knife, dull now, could open his throat.

The man burbled and died, the horse snorting and stamping from the smell of blood.

Stands Twice looked to the door of the square lodge, to the woman standing there, holding her two children behind her, and he stood, was on them before she could even scream.

They were the ones who had brought the scabs, they were the ones who were supposed to have sent meat that winter, they were the ones behind the guns that morning of the massacre.

He lined the four bodies up in front of the house, heads north, faces up, and he regarded them. Instead of eating their food, he burned their square lodge and pulled down the wood frame of their dugout door. Instead of stealing the horse—it was for the plow, not for running—he chased it away to die somewhere else.

The magpie landed on the face of the woman, pulled at her lower lip.

"So you just wanted to eat?" Stands Twice said to it. "That's why you brought me here?"

The magpie pulled, having to flap its wings to be strong enough to get any meat.

That night the coyotes came in to feast as well, their eyes flashing in the moonlight, their tails bushy to show how big they were, how scary they were.

Stands Twice opened his arms over the farmer and his family, said to take what they wanted. When he woke the next morning, sleeping on the other side of the stall he'd used for firewood, the girl was standing there staring at him.

He started back.

Her head was still crushed in on one side from where he'd hit her against the frame of the door over and over, and the coyotes had pulled a lot of her meat off, but she didn't care.

"You too?" Stands Twice said to her.

He threw rocks at her until she fell down and couldn't get up, and then he stomped on her and hit her with a board from the stall, and then he pulled her apart, piled her with some wood, burned her.

She didn't rise from the flames.

Standing beside him now, though, was the farmer, his head lolling from how deep the cut on his throat was.

"What does it take to kill white people?" Stands Twice said.

The farmer didn't answer.

"What does it take to kill me?" Stands Twice asked himself.

He thought of his wife and he watched the dead farmer who wouldn't die, wondered if he thought about his dead wife.

He tied the farmer to a smooth post, waited for the wife and son to rise, but they never did. What he figured was that there was one spirit, and it had been in the girl, but when she died it had gone to the farmer. If he died, it would go across to the wife or the son. But if he just stayed tied up, the spirit would stay there with him.

The days passed, and the sun cooked the farmer's skin into leather, and the wife and the son dried up. Not even the birds were coming in for them anymore.

Far in the distance, a line of covered wagons passed like white tents being carried, to make some treaties somewhere.

Stands Twice ate turnips and boiled them in a pot he salvaged from the ashes, and he watched the tied-up farmer, and then he watched the magpie land on the rounded top of the smooth post the farmer was tied to.

Without waiting even a moment, the magpie jumped forward, onto the farmer's shoulder, and then forced its head into the farmer's mouth and clawed onto his lips with its feet, forced itself into the farmer's mouth.

It lumped down the farmer's throat, into his chest.

Stands Twice took two steps back, didn't look away.

The farmer fell down in a pile and that night Stands Twice slept a walk away, in the trees. When he woke, the farmer was squatting across from him, his face still leathery with death but the cut on his throat covered now with a knotted sash. The farmer spoke with a magpie's harsh voice at first, then settled down into a man's voice.

"I should go to town," it said.

"Why?" Stands Twice asked.

"Why," the magpie man said back.

"They'll shoot you," Stands Twice said.

Magpie Man looked down at his caved-in leathery chest, touched it with his fingertips.

"I can still have children," it said.

"You want to?" Stands Twice said.

Magpie Man stood, looked to the right, the west, like looking into the future, and said, "They'll grow up to...well. They'll be like me, I guess."

"Dead?"

"Fun," Magpie Man said, bringing his eyes back to Stands Twice.

"Like a magpie," Stands Twice said.

Magpie Man smiled, his dry lips cracking from it, and then he turned all at once: a covered wagon behind the rest of them was limping into camp.

"Hide," Magpie Man said to Stands Twice.

Stands Twice did, but he watched, too.

Magpie Man worked on one of the hind wheels of the wagon with the two men, and then they built a fire from the pulled-down stall, and Magpie Man told them the story of marauding Indians killing his family, burning his cabin. He could speak their language, too. Because magpies are always listening.

Then they all slept curled close to the fire, and when Stands Twice shook awake, it was dark and the fire was embers. Magpie Man moved from sleeper to sleeper, holding his hands over their nose and mouth until they stopped kicking. Until the last one. This last one, the last of the two children, he would suffocate him nearly all the way, then shake him awake, hug him close, then do it again. This went on until one time, it went too far, and the boy couldn't be shaken awake.

"You can come in now," Magpie Man said.

Stands Twice edged in, watching Magpie Man, and he could see it, now: this dead man with a bird for a heart doing versions of this in every town, and having children too, leaving them behind, those children growing up to chew through the town the same way, but not before having children themselves, so that one birdheart would leave a flock of killers for the next generation, and an even bigger flock for the next, and on down through the years.

That morning, when Stands Twice had woken to the soldier's spinning guns, he'd known immediately, without even having to think it, that there was nothing Indians could do against that kind of firepower. Not when they were starving. Not when so many were already dead from the white scabs.

This, though, this was better than any gun, wasn't it?

A warm flush spread up Stands Twice.

"This is why," he said to Magpie Man, "this is why I had to live this long, through the scabs and the bullets and the hunger and the treaties. To do this."

Magpie Man smiled his bird smile, his eyes not blinking even once.

"But they'll shoot you," Stands Twice said. "They'll shoot you before you can even have any children."

Magpie Man just stared at him.

Stands Twice looked at him and then past him, far back, to the first white men any of them had even seen. These white men had shot an antelope out in the grasslands, and then thrown it across the back of their horse. Stands Twice and the other children had stalked beside the horsemen in a creek bed until the men came to a tree. What the white men did then was cut the antelope here and there on its back legs and tail, and then tied loops of rope through that loose skin, and tied the other ends of the rope to the trunk of the tree. Then, with even more rope, they reached into the antelope from the back, tied into some bone and looped the other end of that rope to a saddle, backed that horse away until the skin peeled off the antelope all at once, stripping it down to the muscle.

Then they cut the meat they wanted off, rode away.

Stands Twice and the other children crept in, studied the naked antelope. The skin they took back to camp, to show the holes, act out what had been done. The old men laughed at this, gave the hide over to be tanned and then stretched it into a drum, because that had been a special antelope, they said. That antelope had played a trick on the white men—it had convinced them that its skin didn't matter, that it was trash that could be left behind. But now the skin would last down through the years, provide the heartbeat for many ceremonies.

The skin would last.

Stands Twice smiled a slow smile.

"They'll shoot you," he said again to Magpie Man, "but it won't matter, will it?"

He sharped the knife from the dead woman against a stone all day, then, when it was dark, he cut a long section of skin up from the inside of his forearm and draped it over the willow rack he'd tied together with grass.

Next was the back of his calves, then the top of his thighs.

It burned and made him bite down hard enough his mouth bled, but he kept cutting and pulling.

His chest, in as big of sections as he could, and his hip on the right side.

"I'm kind of bulletproof, see," he explained to Magpie Man.

Magpie Man just watched, and waited, his eyes hungry, the stiff fingers of his right hand opening and closing.

When the skin was dry enough on the rack, Stands Twice carved off his braids, fashioned an awl from the smallest of the boy's fingerbones, and used his hair to sew the patches of his skin into a shirt.

It wasn't pretty, and there was no beadwork, and the skin hadn't really been tanned, but it was the best he could do, especially with the flies crawling all over his exposed muscle.

He draped it over Magpie Man's head, forced it down over his face and ears. It hung there stiff and uneven.

Magpie Man looked down to it.

"They'll shoot me?" he said.

"It won't matter," Stands Twice said, patting him on the chest.

It made the medicine shirt stick to Magpie Man, so Stands Twice patted all over. The shirt formed to Magpie Man, became his own skin almost.

He nodded, looked up with a smile.

"How can I repay you?" he said.

"You're going to town?" Stands Twice said.

Magpie Man nodded.

"You're going to have lots of children, and they'll all be like you, and they can have their own children?"

Magpie Man nodded.

"And they'll all be...mischievous?"

Magpie Man smiled his smile.

"You don't owe me anything," Stands Twice said, and then pointed the direction Magpie Man should go.

After he was gone, Stands Twice stood and stood, unable to sit down anymore because all the missing skin hurt. The scabs forming were stiff, and cracked and bled every time he moved.

"I'm ready," he said to the four directions, but got no response.

Far off through the grass, a pair of coyote eyes watched him, because of the blood scent he leaked into the air, but the coyote turned away after a moment, padded off.

"Well then," Stands Twice said, and then, working calmly, he piled the four new bodies and the two older ones into the wagon and set it on fire, careful to stomp out any embers that drifted too far. Magpie Man walking into town against a backdrop of flames would give away what he was, wouldn't it?

The next day when the sun was high he kicked through the ashes, found they felt good on his raw places, so he packed ash against all the places he was bleeding. He wondered if now, without his skin, he could get shot and die, or if he would just get shot and have to live with that bullet burrowing through him. He looked to the four directions, decided on one, and stepped that way once, twice, all year, for enough winters that he quit trying to count them, and sometimes if you're still at night, after the fire's died out, if you wait and only look beside where he's crouched out there in the darkness, you might see the shape of him moving back there.

He's drawn in because he misses people, because he misses hearing words, because he misses hearing these stories. That's why we speak them loud like this, so if he's around he can hear. Maybe you'll see him, maybe you won't, but who you definitely will see, who you can't help seeing, are the children of the children of the children of that one magpie, spreading down like a fan through the years. They're the ones pulling people into dark alleys, to chew the face meat away. They're the ones holding their hands over the noses and mouths of the cities, choking them down breath by breath. They're the ones whose eyes flash with humor when someone falls down, and can't get back up. They're the ones who walk into crowded places and get a glint in their eye when they realize there's only one exit.

We couldn't massacre the soldiers back like they massacred us, no, but we learned something from the white scabs. We learned that you just have to send one bad magpie into town. Sometimes one is enough, and if you wait long enough and if you're hungry enough—that's one thing the treaties did to us that can't be taken away: they left us hungry, they taught us to creep up close, to part the tall grass and look through it, and to wait.

BLOOD LUST AND GOLD DUST

Travis Heermann

They call me Colorado Charlie Utter, but I mostly just go by Charlie, or Mr. Utter, if we ain't pards. I'm gonna tell you this story, *niños*, because I was there, but it ain't about me.

And it ain't about the time Wyatt Earp came to Deadwood. But he did, for a spell.

And it ain't about my friend Wild Bill's murder, but maybe it kinda is.

And it ain't about the smallpox epidemic, or the trouble with the Indians, or the blizzard that nearly suffocated us all under six feet of snow.

But maybe those things helped bring *it* down on us. I can't rightly say, though, as I'm just a wagon driver and a bullwhacker.

It started the day I heard some hang-about blathering on about how Wyatt Earp, the Kansas lawman the papers loved to carry on about, had showed up in Deadwood and was dealing faro at the Bella Union, where "mirth is high and jokes are low." By the time I got there, the crowd of 'neckers had already spilled out into the street. I pushed through them far enough to get a glimpse of Earp, coolly dealing cards to a handful of wide-eyed miners. He looked just like his picture in the papers, with a sweeping mustache and flinty eyes.

The howl of a coyote-that-wasn't announced the arrival of Calamity Jane. She sauntered in, hooked me by the arm, and dragged me up to the bar. "Buy me a drink, you fuckin' dandy. I'm a bit embarrassed today."

She called me that on account of my hand-tailored, fringed buckskins, silver belt buckle, and my "bizarre habit" of bathing and shaving daily. I couldn't abide filth, was all. First I laid eyes on her was in a saloon in Fort Laramie, about the roughest looking human being I ever seen. Most days, she was blind as a bat from looking through the bottom of a glass. Tall, built like a busted bale of hay, and as obnoxious as a badger, but after all the caring for the sick she done when the smallpox hit, everybody knew Jane's heart was purer gold than anything they could pan out of Deadwood Creek.

Today, she was only mildly squiffed, her hair slightly less unruly than a patch of tumbleweeds.

She told the bartender, "Shot of booze and slop it over the rim."

"Make that two." I slapped a dollar onto the bar.

She grinned at me as she tossed it back. "Potent enough to kill an ordinary alderman."

"I'd be better off with lead in my gut." I tossed it back anyway and let it burn.

"One more," she said, this time with a catch in her voice, and I knew what was coming.

"You're damn right one more."

With two glasses full again, we looked at each other.

"To Bill," she said.

"To Bill."

We drank, and the tears were in her eyes, just like always.

She looked deep into her empty glass. "There has never been anything fuckin' finer in the way of physical perfection than Wild Bill Hickok. Prettiest corpse I ever seen." She wiped a trickle of snot.

Wild Bill Hickok had been gone three months now, but the wound still bled—for both of us. When the maudlin hit Jane, most often I had to carry her back to whatever dark corner she was using to bed down. The rest of the times, she ended up in an alley riding bareback with the first half-blind soul to cross her path.

Some half-soaked yayhoo, howling at the ceiling like a poor-tuned fiddle, slewed up to the bar. "I'm a wolf, and it's my turn to howl!"

Jane squared on him. "It's your turn to shut the fuck up."

The poor, ignorant soul howled again.

Against his ear, Jane's Colt said, *click*.

His howl trailed off.

Jane's grin lacked humor. "Once more and it'll be your last this side of hell. Now, apologize."

"Wh-whut?"

"I said, apologize. You see, friend, I'm a howling coyote from Bitter Creek. The further up you go, the bitterer it gets, and I'm from the head end." She aimed her six-gun at his feet. "I run the howling business around here. Now apologize before I shoot your fuckin' toes off."

His tail went so far between his legs he could almost suck on it.

We might have been launched into another of Jane's legendary hootenannies had not one already started outside.

The hullabaloo drew everyone into the street, where we became witness to a spectacle unprecedented even for Deadwood—two women engaged in the screamingest, scratchingest, hair-pullingest dustup I had seen in many a moon. They spilled out of the Gem Saloon across the street with their crowd of cheering onlookers, betting in progress. Between the two of them, they weren't wearing enough clothing to wad a shotgun. One was barefoot all the way to her ears, and the other wore about as much as if she was dressed in a pair of suspenders.

When I brought the wagon train from Cheyenne back in July of '76, along with my pard Wild Bill Hickok, Calamity Jane, and a dozen dainty daughters of sin—all of them ahorseback with a foot in each stirrup—the fanfare at the sight of them twelve women set a thousand lonely miners and layabouts a-whoopin'.

On this day, though, a cold, pissing rain had turned the habitually muddy street into the vilest, reeking cesspool of rottenness anybody ever whiffed. A river of rubbish, slops, and emptied chamber pots, tromped into an impassable quagmire by horses, mules, and oxen like the world ain't never seen. You could lose a wagon in it.

From the balcony, the proprietor of the Gem, Al Swearengen, a notorious blackguard bereft of human decency, a lanky hunk of leather with slick, black hair and mustache, watched the affair with a greedy smirk. Beside him, Swearengen's wife wore a shady eye herself, like most days. Swearengen's girls, mixed in the crowd, were a motley crew of ungainly features and uncertain ages. If dark eyes made women beautiful, Deadwood's were top-shelf, as long as you didn't object to one eye being darker than the other.

The two combatants were covered in what we'll call mud, but that didn't seem to dampen their temper. Blood flowed from lips and scratches.

That's when Seth Bullock showed up, true to his duty as acting sheriff. Tall and erect with steel-gray eyes, eyebrows like a razorback's mane, a face full of angles, nose, and chin, he pulled his pistol and fired it in the air.

The noise brought the affair to a sudden cessation. The larger girl, Emmaline, halted in midpunch.

But then the smaller one, Cassie was her name, jumped into that pause and latched onto Emmaline's ear with her teeth. Emmaline screamed. Swearengen's sapheads, Dan and Johnny, yanked the girls apart by the hair. As Emmaline clutched her ear, blood flowed between her fingers and down her neck.

Bullock shot another hole in the sky. "What the hell is going on?"

His shot distracted everyone but me. I saw something made my skin crawl and my throat cinch tight. Cassie had bitten off a chunk of Emmaline's ear, but didn't spit it out. She was chewing with satisfaction, quiet and sly in Johnny's grip.

From the balcony came Swearengen's gravelly voice. "Just a little entertainment, Bullock. Fifty dollars to the winner. Betting is free." He flicked cigar ashes onto the crowd.

Bullock's bushy mustache twitched. "This is a goddamn disgrace, Swearengen, even for you."

"Beg to differ, *Sheriff*. Been advertising this little soiree for a week."

Bullock shook his head and addressed the crowd. "How about you all take it inside before I start arresting people for disturbing the peace and public drunkenness?" He pointed at Swearengen. "Starting with you."

Swearengen scoffed and chuckled. "Pull the other leg."

"How about a sconce full of lumps?" Bullock said, pistol still in the air.

The moment hung there. Then Swearengen said, "Is that the inestimable Wyatt Earp I see before me?"

Earp stood at the edge of the crowd. "Who's asking?"

"Al Swearengen, proprietor of the Gem, finest saloon, theater, and entertainment house this side of the Missouri. The best whiskey, the friendliest girls, and drinks on the house for the next fifteen minutes."

"Huzzah!" yelled the crowd.

Earp flashed a look at Bullock.

Darkness like the shadow of a grizzly crept into Swearengen's voice. "What are you doing here, lawman?"

Earp said, "I'm not here as a lawman. But I hear there's opportunity aplenty for them that can grab onto it."

Swearengen said, "If you've a strong grip, Mr. Earp, you come to the right place. Now, everyone, we don't want our fine patrons to run afoul of our august constabulary..."

The crowd filtered back into the Gem. The two women glared at each other with a hatred that made me glad neither had a knife.

Bullock approached Earp. "Seth Bullock, acting sheriff of this camp."

We weren't even a proper town, on account of this was Sioux land, and sacred to them to boot. Eight months prior, Deadwood Gulch had been wilderness. Now it boasted six or ten thousand souls, counting prospectors and all the painted ladies, gamblers, saloon barons, and thieves lined up to fleece them.

Earp said, "Wyatt Earp. Pleased to make your acquaintance, Sheriff."

Their gazes met like two axe-heads striking edge-to-edge. Bullock could outstare a riled-up rattler and a charging buffalo at the same time, but Earp held steady, with a dangerous glint in his eye, like waiting for the spark to catch on an old flintlock. He had more guts than a smokehouse.

Deadwood was in clamoring need of law. Two days before, I'd seen a bill posted outside the Gem Saloon, where the Board of Health met—Deadwood's only governing body, of which Bullock was one. The bill read thusly:

No person shall discharge any cannon or gun, fowling piece, pistol, or firearm of any description, or fire, explode, or set off any squib, cracker, or other thing containing powder or other explosive material without permission of Mayor E. B. Farnum.

I envisioned some doughty desperado dragging a twelve-pounder about the streets, flaunting the mayor's express permission to give it go as the occasion might require. Of course, a man could *carry* whatever hand howitzer he wanted.

Now that Bullock and Earp had the measure of each other, I could breathe again. Jane had been standing next to me throughout the proceedings. We traded glances. This could get interesting.

With Swearengen and the crowd filtering back inside the Gem, Earp muttered, "The love of decency does not abide in this place."

Bullock, Earp, Jane, and myself bellied up to the Gem's bar, a couple of rough-cut planks stretched across barrelheads. Swearengen poured us drinks, and Bullock chewed on his mustache. The love lost between them wouldn't fill a thimble, I reckon because Bullock had a soul.

After a dousing with water to clear the mud, the two shivering women balled up their fists to recommence hostilities on the theater stage. Cassie still had Emmaline's blood on her lips and hunger in her eye.

Just then a scream rose from the back, and bloodcurdling don't cover it.

The Gem was a wide-open space, thirty feet across and hundred feet deep, with rooms above and in back for the girls to ply their trade.

Johnny Burns, Swearengen's box herder, ran for the noise, Bullock and Earp hot on his heels. Jane ran back, too, lips tight and one eye twitching. She had a soft spot for the "upstairs girls," made friends with some of them, and didn't take kindly when they came to harm—an occurrence all too regular.

The screamer slumped against the wall, across from an open door.

Bullock took one look inside and, backing away, almost stumbled over her. "Jesus Christ!"

Earp stood there looking like he'd taken a ball peen hammer 'twixt the eyes.

Over Earp's shoulder, in the shadows of the room, Shorty Muldoon knelt, with his face dark and wet from the nose down, grinning at us like he'd just eaten a piece of berry pie. He was naked, and so was Lucinda Mae, sprawled across the bed, but she was dead as a can of corned beef, opened up. I reeled away from what I saw in there, the parts of her were missing—the softest parts.

"Hey, Bullock, want to try a piece?" Shorty said, like he was inviting us to supper.

"Jesus Christ!" Bullock said again. The 'neckers crowded in

for a peep. "Everybody, get the hell back!" He pulled his smoke wagon and let one fly.

Shorty turned back to his repast, but just then Jane shouldered up through the crowd, took one look, and with a cannonade of profanities, pulled her guns and let fly. Through the smoke, he spun away, faster than I'd ever seen anybody move, 'cept maybe Wild Bill. Then there was nothing but his bare ass diving through a window. Jane sent another round after him to unknown effect.

Earp and Bullock pushed past everyone and charged out the back door in pursuit. I shoulda followed, but my legs wouldn't pony up.

Swearengen parted the crowd using profanity like a plow. "Shorty fucking Muldoon. There goes the fucking night." He turned on the crowd. "Everybody, come back in an hour. We'll have this sorted out and be back open for business."

The girl who'd screamed, Kansas City Katie, still rocked against the wall, tears streaming.

The men shuffled off to the Bella Union or Nuttall and Mann's No. 10, muttering amongst themselves. I heard exclamations from the far entrance of "Goddamn, it got cold out!"

In the lantern light of the Gem's back-room-turned-slaughter-house, bone-chilling winter poured through the shattered window, wetness splattered the floor and one wall. I covered my mouth and nose with a handkerchief, but it couldn't hold back the eerie odor of death and the grave. The air in that room was so cold it hurt to breathe.

I pointed to dark splatters on the wall. "That look like blood to you?" It looked more like coal oil or runny tar, but threads of ice spread from it across the bare wood. It stood out against all of poor Lucinda Mae's blood. Stranger still, a patch of her flesh was frosted over, a hand-shaped patch on her thigh.

"I know I hit him," Jane said, voice trembling. She staggered back into the now empty main room, clamping a bear trap on her sobs. Lucinda Mae was one of them she called friend. I tried to offer Jane comfort, but she threw my arm off. "Get the fuck offa me! What is wrong with this place?"

I couldn't answer.

Jane went on. "Shit ain't been right since Bill died. First that, then the raid on the Sioux—which the poor redskins didn't fuckin' deserve—then the smallpox, then that deranged girl wandering in the woods for four days eating bugs. Feels like a fuckin' pile o' evil just stinking to high heaven."

"A big ol' pile of shit," I echoed. A couple weeks before, one of the girls from the Bella Union disappeared. Then turned up again four days later, walking along the trail, got picked up by a couple of gamblers riding into town. She said she'd been living on bugs. Wouldn't say what she was doing out there. Trouble was, she wouldn't take normal food no more after that. Only bugs. Except for the business end of a shotgun she ate a week after that.

Jane had walked her own share on the trail of madness. How many nights had she wandered Deadwood Gulch, blind drunk, howling her grief, like a coyote calling out in desperation? Sometimes that howl would raise the gooseflesh all the way to my nuts. Sometimes I could swear something *answered*.

At the bar, she clamped her head in both hands. "And, that prissy fuckin' General Crook buying up all the groceries, there ain't flour to make a fuckin' biscuit don't cost two dollars."

When General Crook brought his command through Deadwood, half of 'em afoot for eating their horses, they'd bought up all the flour, bacon, coffee, everything they could find. Eggs were a dollar apiece now, flour ten dollars a pound. No game within ten miles. Them with the poorest claims would soon be eating boot leather.

Two pistol shots echoed outside through the rising wind.

Jane kept talking. "But things come to live in a pile of shit. Maggots and bugs and such. What if... what if evil is like that? What if it draws things..."

Deadwood Gulch had drawn Wyatt Earp here, just like it had drawn Wild Bill. Hell, it had drawn me. People didn't come here because they favored the company of civilized folk. What else had it drawn here?

A thought glimmered through Jane's inebriation. "Fuck!"

"What you talking about?"

"Don't crowd me, I'm trying to remember..." She rubbed her temples to massage something loose.

I happened to glance at the two women on the stage. One of the other girls tended to Emmaline's mangled ear, while prim, proper little Cassie sat a chair, arm thrown casually over the back, still barefoot up to her ears, foot bobbing absently, her gaze plastered all over poor Emmaline like she was a Christmas goose, just waiting for a chance to dig in to a nice roasted breast.

Something cold settled into my belly, a foreboding.

Just then, Bullock and Earp burst through the back door, snow swirling around them amid a blast of frigid air. They shook their heads.

Bullock's eyes glinted like they had fire behind them. "Son of a bitch got away, but he won't get far. Stupid bastard left his boots and britches."

The temperature had dropped twenty degrees in the last ten minutes. The wind outside howled like it was living.

Bullock said, "Hey, Charlie. Doesn't Shorty Muldoon got digs in Whoop Up?"

I couldn't get Shorty's eyes out of my mind, just before he went for the window. They were *wrong. Black.* Like it wasn't Shorty looking out from inside...

"Charlie!" Bullock snapped.

I stumbled back out of that nightmare and nodded.

Deadwood was, as had been said, "three miles long and fifty feet wide," a strung-out collection of camps along the creek, not a town. The Badlands, where we stood, looked like a pile of fruit crates dumped in a yard, some of them propped up on broomsticks. Buildings clung to the ridges with their forepaws. Whoop Up lay a few hundred yards from where we stood, the place Shorty Muldoon and his pards all scratched away at a claim that left them poor as hind-tit calves.

Swearengen looked at Bullock with an expression as black and deadly as I'd ever seen. "You find that stumpy shit stain. We'll stretch his skin on the fucking wall. Then we'll use his nut sack for gold dust."

Bullock clomped toward the back door, mad as a peeled rattler.

"Wait," Earp said. "I reckon you'll need a hand."

"I can handle Shorty Muldoon," Bullock said.

"You sure about that? A man with at least two bullet holes in him who can still run like a jackrabbit?"

"A jackrabbit who don't bleed blood," I said, cold beetles crawling up my back.

Bullock chewed on his mustache. "Let's go, then."

Looking outside, we couldn't see across the street for the snow. A moaning wind drove snowflakes into my cheeks like needles. I never seen weather change with such speed.

Earp said, "People will be piling on the firewood tonight."

Bullock said, "When it's over, we'll have to bury them that couldn't."

Jane seized Bullock's sleeve, eyes gleaming. "Listen! I got it!"

Bullock scoffed. "Got what?"

"When I was scoutin' for the Army, I heard stories. There was this Ojibwe tracker, Jim Charging-Hawk, told me about this thing, like an evil spirit, comes to camps where people are starving, where there's famine, suffering, and it makes 'em..."

"Makes 'em what?" Earp said.

"Makes 'em want to fuckin' eat each other. It comes in the winter, mostly. They's stories of whole camps disappearing, where all they found in the spring was bones."

"Bullshit," Earp and Bullock said.

Jane sniffed and spat a wad of chaw. "You fuckers don't have to listen to me. Let's find Shorty 'fore he hurts anybody else."

Heading for Whoop Up through a thickening whiteout, the four of us clung to the boardwalk, but it was drowning in mud. The wind's razor teeth nipped at my fingers and ears.

The saloons and brothels we passed hooted and hollered, as if the Mother of all Blizzards was not chomping at every scrap of shelter right that second.

In such a storm, a fella's mind can wander off. I took enjoyment in my share of booze and sporting ladies as much as the next fella, but a queer realization swept over me that that's all Deadwood was. A frenzy of taking, a plague of locusts descending, eating everything, shitting the place up, and then moving on. Here we were, eating the guts out of the Black Hills, a land sacred to the Sioux, and when the gold was gone, what next?

By the time we reached Whoop Up, eight inches of snow numbed my feet, and we'd only gotten lost once. Amidst the collection of tents, shanties, and sluice boxes, a bonfire blazed high.

As I checked my Colt, my skin stuck to the steel. I couldn't remember the last time I fired it, and I'd never drawn down on a man. But it was a shiny new Peacemaker cartridge model, so I wasn't worried about fouled powder.

Eight or nine men huddled so close around the bonfire, they were lucky to keep their beards.

"Shorty Muldoon!" Bullock called.

Nobody moved.

Jane wore an expression like a meat axe. "Speak up, you sons-a-bitches!"

They turned around, and my nuts cinched up and disappeared.

Earp pulled his long-barreled .45, his hand rock steady.

The miners' faces were gaunt, gray, eyes full of dark intention.

The day Wild Bill Hickok and I came to Deadwood, Bill told me—it was such a strange thing—he told me, "Charlie, I don't think I'm going to leave this camp. I'm gonna die here." Three weeks later, the greatest gunfighter who ever lived was shot in the back of the head playing cards. That same feeling swept over me, that I was going to die here, but I'd be damned if I let some evil spirit cash in my chips.

Shorty Muldoon stepped out of the white, a naked, bony ghost of his bow-legged former self, caked with blood and ice. His ribs, joints, cheekbones, even his hands looked swole up, blackened like from frostbite. "Look, boys! More meat on the hoof!"

They loosed a hungry growl, like a table full of vittles just sprang on 'em.

Then they rushed us.

I got no recollection of who shot what. All I knew was Swill Barrel Johnny and Texas Ford came at me. I must have fired at least once, but then they seized my arms. A powerful chill crept through me at their touch, like dunking my arms in icy slush. I managed to kick free of one, but not before the second bit down on these here two fingers. Ain't nothing like feeling your own bones crunch. I got 'em loose before he chomped 'em off.

Swill Barrel Johnny said in his Cornish burr, "What do ye say, Charlie? Give us a bit of haunch, won't ye?"

Jane spewed profanity and bullets. That black, ichorous stuff sprayed from each hole. Only with a skull full of lead did they drop for good.

Fortunately, the dog-bit fingers were not my shooting hand. I emptied my pistol into Swill Barrel Johnny's skull, then pulled my Bowie knife and stabbed it through Texas Ford's ear.

Bullock went down with two of the cannibals on him. Earp charged in, kicking and blasting, until Bullock got to his feet, bleeding from a nasty bite on his forearm.

That's when more of them came out of the tents, charging toward us through the icy slop. These had been busy eating some of their own. They came at us with their gory faces and slaughterhouse stench, but we beat them back. Without time to reload, all we could do was hammer them with our pistol grips. The blizzard became a storm of black blood and screaming that wasn't just the wind. My fingers and toes went numb. My face froze into a mask of hollering as skulls cracked under the butt of my pistol.

Then it was over. I was still hollering, I think. How many of them ran off into the swirling veils of white, I got no recollection.

Snow gathered on our shoulders as we stood knee deep in carnage. Somehow, the warmth of the bonfire only a few feet away wouldn't reach me. In the slicing wind, we reloaded. Its howling threatened to toss our words out into nothing.

"You all ever seen anything like this?" Earp said.

"I never even heard of anything like this!" Bullock said.

"I have!" Jane said. "But you wouldn't fuckin' listen!"

"All right then, Jane," Bullock said. "What do we do?"

"How should I know?" Jane spat. "I ain't no fuckin' medicine man."

"We got to find them all," Bullock said. "They're going to raise the kind of hell we can't even imagine. On a night like this, people will be helpless."

"Seth," I said, "what if they's connected—the snow and the eating. This thing Jane spoke of."

"The wendigo," Jane said.

I went on, because I'd had time to ponder on this. "That thing. What if it's kinda like the stories where the Devil comes and takes over some poor soul's body?"

"You're talking a lot of horseshit," Earp said.

"You're talking about possession," Bullock said. "There's stories in the Bible. You think Shorty is possessed by this wendigo?"

"Like I said...horseshit," Earp said. "Heathen superstition."

"What explanation do *you* got?" I said, yanking out my handkerchief and wrapping it around my bitten fingers. The bleeding had mostly stopped, on account of the cold. "This ain't natural. Can't you feel it? There's a presence. Something bigger than these miners, like something came down out of nowhere, out of the Canadian tundra, all the way from the moon for all I know. A thing made of hunger and sadness and fear and greed all coming together and squirming like a nest of rattlers. It didn't come here by accident. Somebody called it. *We* called it. Souls cry out in this valley every day. Beaten, fallen women. Brokeback miners. Them poor fuckers that die in alleys with their throats cut for a poke full of gold dust."

Earp said, "How about we continue this indoors?"

Screams filtered through the dark and howling wind.

Jane looked into the swirling white, stricken, a wounded coyote howling for something to come and take its life. "Goddammit," she muttered. Then she cocked both pistols. "God *damn* it!"

"We got to finish this," Bullock said.

"What if," I said, haltingly, trying to cipher it all, "what if, you know how one person can bring smallpox into a camp, and pretty soon..."

"It spreads," Jane said.

"If we take out Shorty—" Bullock said.

"Goddammit, I liked Shorty," I said. "Up until he ate a woman right in front of me anyhow. Little sumbitch could play a hell of a mouth harp."

"Which way did he go?" Earp said.

Jane pointed at a set of bare footprints filling with snow. "That way. Towards the Number 10."

Heading back down the gulch, we faced a gale wind. My mustache and eyelashes froze stiff as porcupine quills. Tears froze to my cheeks.

By the time we saw the lights of the Saloon No. 10, knee-deep snow masked the street mud. Every step was a frigid, exhausting slog. I couldn't feel my face, my ears, my whole body shivering like a lizard looking for a hot rock.

We walked into the No. 10 like four frozen specters, shivering too bad to hold our guns. The place was full of patrons but quiet as a sick cow in a snowbank.

"Shorty Muldoon," Bullock said. "Seen him?"

Billy Nuttall, standing behind the bar with a haunted look, gestured toward the poker table in the back.

Sitting at the table with his back to the door, in the chair where Wild Bill Hickok had been shot in the back of the head, his flesh as gray as a month-old snowbank, his hair a frozen bramble, was Shorty Muldoon.

Nuttall leaned over the bar. "We didn't know what to do

with him. He just walked in, naked as the day he was born, and sat down."

The three other former poker players stood away from the table, their hands shaking, but not like they were doing the shaking, more like they were being shook, too fast to see, like a guitar string. Their faces lost their edges, like my eyes were blurred, but only just their faces. People edged away from them. Then the moment passed, and for a moment they seemed normal again. Up until they walked up to three other patrons, seized them by the shoulders with irresistible strength, and tore out their throats with their teeth.

Pandemonium erupted. Guns waved, bullets flew, knives flashed, boots pelted for the door.

In the back, laughter as deep as thunder.

Earp and Bullock tried to shove through the crowd, hollering for order, but they were fighting upstream.

Gunshots erupted as them that still had some shreds of courage cut down on the attackers. All I can remember of that knock-down-drag-out is bloody flesh hanging from teeth, terrified eyes like a herd of stampeding critters, fists flying, chairs crashing, glass shattering amidst the smells of blood, smoke, and cheap whiskey, and a trainload of cursing. Worst part was, several people found themselves with lead poisoning didn't deserve it. It was a godawful mess.

Jane jumped up on a table, howling her grief and rage. She leaped like an antelope from one table to the next, scattering glasses and cards, as the tumult raged.

I could see where she was headed. "Jane, no!"

She jumped down behind the thing that wore Shorty's skin.

There was nothing human in that face anymore. Those coal-black eyes, that amused grin, that hunger, all lodged in my bones like an arrowhead. That moment still haunts me some nights, as I lay in the dark wondering when I might see that face again, looking out from somebody else's eyes.

Jane leveled her pistols, but before she could fire, its black hands seized her wrists. Her pistols hung limp as it squeezed, but she kept hold of them. Obscenities gurgled out of her as it stretched her arms wide, fixing to tear them off like chicken wings. Its arms were too long to be human now.

Earp had one of the attackers in a headlock, hammering the man's skull with his pistol butt.

Bullock ducked a flying chair, only to be flattened by a panicked miner clambering for the door.

Jane was a goner.

With a trembling hand, I leveled my pistol at Shorty. I might have hit Jane, but if I didn't shoot right goddamn then, she was dead anyhow. So I let fly.

The bullet plowed a narrow trench across the top of its skull and ricocheted into a lantern, casting deeper darkness into the back. My shot must have staggered it, as Jane struggled with it in some sort of hurdy-gurdy dance.

Oil from the shattered lantern spattered the pot-bellied stove and caught fire.

In the rising firelight, I saw Jane wrestle one of her arms free. She leveled her Colt and blasted a hole through one of its eyes. It released her other arm and seized her around the throat. Hands free, she brought both hoglegs to bear. More obscenities strangled out of her as she emptied both her pistols into its face, spraying cold black ichor all over the same wall that once wore Bill's blood, as well.

It let her go, stumbling backward.

Bullock had regained his feet. Nuttall tossed him a shotgun, and he charged toward the back.

With two perfect shots, Wyatt Earp cleared Bullock's way.

"Jane, get back!" Bullock roared, leveling the scattergun at Shorty. Jane ducked away, and Bullock blasted both barrels. What was left of Shorty Muldoon dropped like a poleaxed mule.

The booming laughter faded into the blizzard like a receding locomotive.

When I finally reached Shorty's body, it had shriveled up like a black, leathery raisin. Goddamn if the face didn't look, just for a moment—just for the shortest moment, so quick I couldn't be sure—just like Wild Bill's face on the day we put him in the ground. Then the whole body collapsed like melting pork fat, bones and all.

By midnight, the temperature had dropped to five degrees, and the storm lasted for three days.

Cassie, the little lady who'd decided Emmaline's ear looked like bacon, claimed she couldn't recall the fight at all. That didn't stop Emmaline from cutting off Cassie's ear one night about a week later. What happened to them both after that, I could never get Swearengen to say.

Then six feet of snow melted, the mud thawed and deepened. The stories percolated, festered, and faded into the fabric of daily iniquities. We drank instead of ate.

What became clear to me, watching Earp and Bullock in the time after, something had broken in these two lawmen who used to look at the world in a certain way.

Seth Bullock lost the election for sheriff a year later and went back to the hardware business with his friend, Sol Star. Later, he and Teddy Roosevelt got thicker'n feathers in a pillow.

Wyatt Earp spent the winter selling firewood at a hundred dollars a wagonload, said he'd never get warm again. When he left Deadwood in the spring, riding shotgun on a wagon full of gold headed for Cheyenne, they say he had five thousand dollars in his pocket.

Jane stopped howling for Bill, but she remained calamitous until the end of her days. She hid the finger-shaped frostbite scars on her neck with a bandanna. She ran with Buffalo Bill Cody's Wild West Show for a while, but hated it. Ten thousand people came to her funeral in Deadwood.

History don't remember the likes of Colorado Charlie Utter or other decent folk that came through Deadwood, or those that got swallowed up by it. History cloaks the respectable and venerates the Wild Bills and Calamity Janes. Deadwood likes its people with the hair on. All I know is that the four of us—Jane, Earp, Bullock and me—we done for that thing that came to Deadwood that winter, call it whatever you want.

I'm reminded of another story some fifteen years after the aforetold, about a town called White Pine. They say something awful came down on that town and the nearby reservation—but old Charlie's getting tired. Bring me another iguana for supper tomorrow, and I'll tell you that story.

You *niños* run along, now.

ABOUT THE CONTRIBUTORS

About the Editor

David Boop is a Denver-based speculative fiction author and editor. He's also an award-winning essayist and screenwriter. Before turning to fiction, David worked as a DJ, film critic, journalist, and actor. As editor-in-chief at *IntraDenver.net*, David's team was on the ground at Columbine making them the first internet-only newspaper to cover such an event. That year, they won an award for excellence from the Colorado Press Association for their design and coverage.

David's debut novel, the sci-fi/noir *She Murdered Me with Science*, is back in print from WordFire Press. David went on to edit the bestselling weird western anthology, *Straight Outta Tombstone*, for Baen. Dave is prolific in short fiction with many short stories and two short films to his credit. He's published across several genres including media tie-ins for *Predator* (nominated for the 2018 Scribe Award), *The Green Hornet*, *The Black Bat* and *Veronica Mars*.

He's a single dad, Summa Cum Laude creative-writing graduate, part-time temp worker and believer. His hobbies include film noir, anime, the Blues and Mayan History. You can find out more at Davidboop.com, Facebook.com/dboop.updates or Twitter @david_boop.

About the Authors

Shane Lacy Hensley lives in sunny Arizona where he runs Pinnacle Entertainment Group. He's best known for creating the world of Deadlands and the Savage Worlds role-playing game. He's been an executive producer on numerous video games, written a passel of novels and short stories, and loves to run and play games with fans all over the world.

~

Charlaine Harris is a true daughter of the South. She was born in Mississippi and has lived in Tennessee, South Carolina, Arkansas, and Texas. After years of dabbling with poetry and plays and essays, her career as a novelist began when her husband invited her to write full time. Her first book, *Sweet and Deadly*, appeared in 1981. When Charlaine's career as a mystery writer began to falter, she decided to write a cross-genre book that would appeal to fans of mystery, science fiction, romance, and suspense. She could not have anticipated the huge surge of reader interest in the adventures of a barmaid in Louisiana, or the fact that Alan Ball would come knocking at her door. Since then, Charlaine's novels have been adapted for two other television series. Charlaine is a voracious reader. She has one husband, three children, two grandchildren, and two rescue dogs. She leads a busy life.

~

D.J. (Dave) Butler has been a lawyer, a consultant, an editor, and a corporate trainer. His novels include *Witchy Eye* and sequels from Baen Books, *The Kidnap Plot* and sequels from Knopf, and *City of the Saints,* from WordFire Press. He plays guitar and banjo whenever he can, and likes to hang out in Utah with his children.

~

Mike Resnick is, according to Locus, the all-time leading award winner, living or dead, for short science fiction. The author of seventy-eight novels, ten books of nonfiction, and 286 short stories, Mike is the winner of five Hugos (from a record thirty-seven nominations), plus a Nebula and other major awards in the USA, France, Croatia, Poland, Catalonia, Spain, Japan, and China, and has been shortlisted for awards in England, Italy and Australia. Mike was the Guest of Honor at the 2012 Worldcon.

~

When she was growing up, **Jane Lindskold** read Louis L'Amour novels and daydreamed about what it might be like to live in the Wild West. She's lived in Albuquerque, New Mexico, since 1995, so she guesses that dreams do come true.

Jane Lindskold also dreamed about someday being a published author. With over twenty-five published novels, seventy-some short stories, and numerous works of nonfiction to her credit, she's achieved that, too. Her novels include the Firekeeper Saga, the Breaking the Wall series, the Artemis Awakening series, the Athanor novels, and a number of standalone works. She's also written in collaboration with David Weber, Roger Zelazny, and Fred Saberhagen.

When she's not writing, Jane Lindskold rides herd on a passel of cats and guinea pigs. You can find out more about her and her publications at www.janelindskold.com.

~

Jeffrey J. Mariotte is the award-winning author of more than seventy novels, including thrillers *Empty Rooms* and *The Devil's Bait*, supernatural thrillers *Season of the Wolf, Missing White Girl, River Runs Red*, and *Cold Black Hearts*, horror epic *The Slab*, the *Dark Vengeance* teen horror quartet, and others, including works set in the worlds of Narcos, Deadlands, Buffy and Angel, Supernatural, Superman, Spider-Man, 30 Days of Night, The Shield, CSI, NCIS, and more. With partner and wife Marsheila Rockwell, he wrote the science fiction/horror/thriller *7 SYKOS* and the video game tie-in *Mafia III: Plain of Jars*, and has published numerous short stories. He also writes comics, including the long-running horror/Western series *Desperadoes* and original graphic novels *Zombie Cop* and *Fade to Black*. He was VP of Marketing for Image Comics/WildStorm, Senior Editor for DC Comics/ WildStorm, and the first editor-in-chief for IDW Publishing. Find him online at www.jeffmariotte.com.

~

Frog and Esther Jones are a husband-and-wife writing duo from the Olympic Rain Forest. Their work can be found in a number of anthologies. The descendants of both the Lorents and Neilson families are still summoners, and appear in the Gift of Grace series of urban fantasy novels.

~

Brooklyn born and raised, **Derrick Ferguson** is the author of several novels, short stories and comics. He says he's been writing as long as he can remember, inspired from classic pulps like Robert E. Howard to *Mad Magazine*'s *Spy vs Spy*. When Derrick was finally able to retire, he focused on full-time writing. He's written new pulp, westerns, and more, including characters like Dillon, a soldier-for-hire, Hollis P.I., Fortune McCall, and Sinbad the Sailor. "I like telling stories," he said. "It is no deeper than that." Derrick is also renowned as a movie reviewer. Read his reviews on his blog, "The Ferguson Theater." He can be found at dlferguson-bloodandink.blogspot.com and www.facebook.com/derrick.ferguson.566.

~

Cliff Winnig's fiction appears in the Escape Pod podcast, as well as the anthologies *That Ain't Right: Historical Accounts of the Miskatonic Valley, Gears and Levers 3, When the Hero Comes Home: 2, Footprints,* and elsewhere. Cliff is a graduate of the Clarion Science Fiction and Fantasy Writers' Workshop and a three-time finalist in the Writers of the Future contest.

When not writing, Cliff plays sitar, studies tai chi and aikido, and does choral singing and social dance, including ballroom, swing, salsa, and Argentine tango. He lives with his family in Silicon Valley, which constantly inspires him to think about the future. He can be found online at cliffwinnig.com.

~

Jennifer Campbell-Hicks' stories have appeared in *Clarkesworld*, *Galaxy's Edge*, *Fireside Magazine*, *Daily Science Fiction* and many other magazines and anthologies. She lives in Colorado with her husband and children, a dog and a guinea pig. You can find links to her stories and more on what's coming next at jennifercampbellhicks.blogspot.com.

~

Alex Acks is an award-winning writer, Book Riot contributor, geologist, and sharp-dressed sir. Angry Robot Books has published their novels *Hunger Makes the Wolf* (winner of the 2017 Kitschies Golden Tentacle award) and *Blood Binds the Pack* under the pen name Alex Wells. A collection of their steampunk novellas, *Murder on the Titania and Other Steam-Powered Adventures*, is available from Queen of Swords Press. They've had short fiction in Tor.com, *Strange Horizons*, *GigaNotoSaurus*, *Daily Science Fiction*, *Lightspeed*, and more, and written movie reviews for *Strange Horizons* and *Mothership Zeta*.

They've also written several episodes of Six to Start's Superhero Workout game and races for their RaceLink project. Alex lives in Denver (where they bicycle, drink tea, and twirl their ever-so-dapper mustache) with their two furry little bastards. For more information, see www.alexacks.com.

~

Steve Rasnic Tem is a past winner of the Bram Stoker, World Fantasy, and British Fantasy Awards. His novels include the Stoker-winning *Blood Kin*, *UBO*, *Deadfall Hotel*, *The Book of Days*, and with his late wife Melanie, *Daughters* and *The Man on the Ceiling*. A writing handbook, *Yours To Tell: Dialogues on the Art & Practice of Writing*, also written with Melanie, appeared in 2017 from Apex. His young adult Halloween novel *The Mask Shop of Doctor Blaack* appeared in October 2018 from HEX publishers. His YA collection *Everything is Fine Now* recently appeared from Omnium Gatherum. He has published over 430 short stories. The best of these are in *Figures Unseen: Selected Stories*, from Valancourt Books.

~

Multiple Scribe and Rhysling Award nominee **Marsheila (Marcy) Rockwell** is the author of twelve books to date. Her work includes *Mafia III: Plain of Jars*, co-written with writing partner/husband Jeff Mariotte and based on the hit video game; *7 SYKOS*, a near future SF/H thriller (also with Mariotte); *The Shard Axe* series, the only official novels that tie into the popular fantasy MMORPG, Dungeons & Dragons Online; an urban fantasy trilogy based on *Neil Gaiman's Lady Justice* comic books; a trilogy based on the TV series *Xena: Warrior Princess* (co-written with Mariotte); dozens of short stories and poems; multiple articles on writing and the writing process; and a handful of comic book scripts. She resides in the Valley of the Sun, where she writes dark fiction and poetry in a home she and her family have dubbed "Redwall." Find out more here: www.marsheilarockwell.com.

~

Mario Acevedo is the author of the national bestselling Felix Gomez detective-vampire series, and the YA humor thriller, *University of Doom*. His short fiction has appeared in numerous anthologies. His work has won an International Latino Book Award and a Colorado Book Award. Mario serves on the writing faculty of the Regis University Mile-High MFA program and Lighthouse Writers Workshops. He is the editor of the anthology *Blood and Gasoline*, from Hex Publishers. Mario lives and writes in Denver, Colorado.

~

Betsy Dornbusch is the author of several fantasy short stories, novellas, and five novels, including the *Book of the Seven Eyes* trilogy and *The Silver Scar*. She likes writing, reading, snowboarding, punk rock, and the Denver Broncos. Betsy and her family split their time between Boulder and Grand Lake, Colorado.

~

Stephen Graham Jones is the author of sixteen novels, six story collections, and, so far, one comic book. Stephen's been an NEA recipient and has won the Texas Institute of Letters Award for Fiction, the Independent Publishers Award for Multicultural Fiction, a Bram Stoker Award, and four This is Horror Awards. He's been a finalist for the Shirley Jackson Award a few times, and he's currently a finalist for a World Fantasy Award. He's also made Bloody Disgusting's Top Ten Horror Novels. Stephen lives in Boulder, Colorado.

~

Freelance writer, novelist, award-winning screenwriter, editor, poker player, poet, biker, roustabout, **Travis Heermann** is a graduate of the Odyssey Writing Workshop and the author of *The Ronin Trilogy, Rogues of the Black Fury,* and co-author of *Death Wind,* a horror-western novel and screenplay set in the same universe as "Blood Lust and Gold Dust."

His short fiction pieces appears in anthologies and magazines such as *Apex Magazine, Alembical 4,* the *Fiction River* anthology series, and Cemetery Dance's *Shivers VII.* As a freelance writer, he has produced a metric ton of role-playing game work both in print and online, including the Firefly Role-Playing Game, Battletech, Legend of Five Rings, and the MMORPG, EVE Online.

He enjoys cycling, martial arts, torturing young minds with otherworldly ideas, and monsters of every flavor, especially those with a soft, creamy center. He has three long-cherished dreams: a produced screenplay, a *New York Times* best seller, and a seat in the World Series of Poker.